"The boiling-hot duo of Max Savoie and Charlotte Caissie returns, and the thrill-ride just keeps getting better. . . . This series is a mu—"

—*Bitten by Books*

"A para[...] with intriguing characters and [...] . . Gideon masters the tension require[...]p her complex and engaging story moving."

—*Publishers Weekly* (starred review)

"Sizzling . . . dark and compelling!"

—Susan Sizemore, *New York Times* bestselling author

"Vivid, dark, and memorable. . . . I couldn't put it down."

—Janet Chapman, *New York Times* bestselling author

"Brilliantly spellbinding with fascinating supernatural aspects, heated passions, and unanticipated dangers."

—*Single Titles*

"An exceptional read. It will have the reader laughing one minute, crying the next. It's a compelling story and a tremendous first book in Gideon's new series."

—*Reader to Reader*, NewandUsedBooks.com

Seeker of Shadows

NANCY GIDEON

Pocket Books

New York   London   Toronto   Sydney   New Delhi

Pocket Books
A Division of Simon & Schuster, Inc.
1230 Avenue of the Americas
New York, NY 10020

This book is a work of fiction. Names, characters, places, and incidents either are products of the author's imagination or are used fictitiously. Any resemblance to actual events or locales or persons, living or dead, is entirely coincidental.

Copyright © 2012 by Nancy Gideon

All rights reserved, including the right to reproduce this book or portions thereof in any form whatsoever. For information, address Pocket Books Subsidiary Rights Department, 1230 Avenue of the Americas, New York, NY 10020.

First Pocket Books paperback edition June 2012

POCKET and colophon are registered trademarks of Simon & Schuster, Inc.

For information about special discounts for bulk purchases, please contact Simon & Schuster Special Sales at 1-866-506-1949 or business@simonandschuster.com.

The Simon & Schuster Speakers Bureau can bring authors to your live event. For more information or to book an event, contact the Simon & Schuster Speakers Bureau at 1-866-248-3049 or visit our website at www.simonspeakers.com.

Manufactured in the United States of America

10 9 8 7 6 5 4 3 2 1

ISBN 978-1-4391-9951-0
ISBN 978-1-4391-9954-1 (ebook)

*For all my friends in the blogosphere
—thanks for getting me out there!*

Seeker of Shadows

Prologue

He checked his watch, concerned though not yet worried. She could have been late for any number of reasons.

He risked another impatient look down the sterile hallway. Meeting in such a public place was dangerous, but neither of them could wait another three days for her schedule to open up. Anticipation growled through him. Hell, he couldn't wait another three minutes.

He paced the storage room, hating circumstances that forced them to steal time together in closets, into hiding what neither of them was ashamed of. It wouldn't always be this way, not if he could help it. She deserved better. She was worth more than a rushed tangle of heavy breathing on a hard tiled floor.

The door slipped open and she was in his arms, her soft scent masking the antiseptic odor of their surroundings.

At the first touch of her lips, he forgot everything beyond the sweet satisfaction of holding her tight. For a moment, consumed by the sensual feast, desire overcame the fear of discovery.

She trembled in his embrace—with eagerness he thought, until tasting the salt of her tears.

"What's wrong?" he whispered, trying to draw her closer to the dim light so he could see her face.

She ducked her head, refusing to answer as her shaking intensified. Her breath came in quick snatches as her hands anxiously kneaded his forearms.

A cold thread of alarm began to uncoil in his gut. Then the door flew open, flooding the small room with glaring light. His first move was to thrust her behind him, shielding her from view. But she wouldn't release him. Her hands clutched his arms, slowing his reactions for the second it took to lose whatever little advantage he might have had.

Pain, sudden and swift, dropped him to his knees. Burning, then numbness raced down his extremities until his arms and legs grew useless.

He heard her cry out in shrill distress.

"No! Don't hurt him! Please! You promised!"

The raw emotion in her tone, the scent of her fear, tore a roar of near madness from his throat. He tried to stand, fought to get one foot under him. The effort was excruciating, yet still he struggled.

Something struck him in the temple, sending him crashing to the floor, where his arms were secured behind him in cuffs of silver that ate like acid into his wrists. He pulled against them, trying to get free. To get to her.

The sound of her weeping was more caustic than the silver as his ankles were also bound, leaving him trussed and helpless.

What was happening? He couldn't let them take her!

He tried to shout her name as a muzzling mask wrapped about his face, sealing out light, sealing in his furious snarls.

Then her hands covered his, squeezing frantically as she sobbed. "Don't fight. Please. Just let them take you. I'm sorry. I'm sorry."

What was she saying? Sorry?

Then realization hit hard.

No!

With the sudden sharp stick of a needle, anguish gave way to a slow roll into unconsciousness. Her voice was the last thing he clung to as awareness slipped from him.

"It has to be this way. I love you. I will always love you. Remember that. Remember how much I love you."

Then, nothing.

One

So this was how a lamb felt at the slaughter.

Nothing in Susanna Duchamps's isolated world prepared her for the barrage of sensations within the dark walls of the Shifter club. Sound battered her ears. Music pounded in a visceral pulse. Brutish figures hunched over tables, their voices loud and rough, their laughter carnal. Even the scent burning her nostrils was frighteningly feral, urging her to step back before she was noticed. Before she became a tender meal.

The moment she'd crossed the threshold of *Cheveux du Chien*, the safe separation between their species was gone and she became the unprotected prey.

And at *their* mercy, instead of the other way around.

Too frightened to move, Susanna feared she wouldn't survive this huge mistake.

"You made it."

Recognizing the direct voice of Nica Fraser, she turned, hoping her smile wasn't wobbly with relief.

For an instant, the sight of the deadly mercenary-for-hire in her guise of waitress confused her. The last time she'd seen the tall, willowy assassin, she'd been in a stylish cashmere sweater dress and tall boots, looking more like a society fund-raiser than a black-denim-jeans-and-skinny-tank-topped barmaid. But in the cool, measuring stare, she saw the dangerous chameleon who'd risked her life to restore the one thing that made Susanna's worth living. That's why she'd answered Nica's surprise call to come quickly and secretively to New Orleans.

"You said you needed my help, so here I am. It's the least I could do to repay you."

Nica waved off her gratitude. "Believe me, I was paid plenty."

"Not by me," came Susanna's somber response. She glanced around, aware that their meeting was drawing attention she couldn't afford. "Is there someplace we can talk privately?"

Noting the carry-on bag with its Chicago–New Orleans tag still attached, Nica asked, "Don't you want to get settled in and freshen up first?"

"No offense, but I don't want to settle in here. I'd rather get right to business."

Nica's quick smile softened her rather hawkish features. "Now I remember why I liked you. Follow me. We can use my boss's office while he's in the stockroom checking in a new shipment."

They threaded a gauntlet of crowded tables. Hard rock rained down from an extensive sound system tucked in between ductwork and industrial lighting that dangled by chains and pulleys from the refurbished warehouse's soaring flat, black ceiling. The beat was as primal as the clientele. Up close, the brute power of the rugged males was as raw as the harsh liquor in their glasses. Gleaming stares fixed upon her, some just curious, some vaguely menacing. She clutched her bag tighter and stuck close to her companion.

"Your boss?" she called over the noise. "You work here?"

Nica chuckled without looking back. "Quite a drop in pay grade, but my man's a stickler for legality. Honest work for honest pay and all that self-righteous nonsense. Good thing he's more relaxed in other areas or I'd never put up with him."

Startled by the comment, Susanna glanced at her shoulder. Faint scarring showed beneath the thin straps of her tank top. "You're bonded."

"Amazing, huh? Good thing *he* admires *my* other qualities or he'd never put up with my lack thereof on the domestic front. They say opposites attract."

Susanna said nothing as they climbed a short flight of wide steps to a room off a dark hall that had probably once belonged to the plant supervisor, who could keep an eye on his laborers through a broad expanse of glass. Those windows now gleamed with a reflective opaque of privacy.

Given the rough element in the bar area, the office of *Cheveux du Chien* was surprisingly professional, from its red, black, and chrome décor to the surveillance equipment and high-end computer. Closing the door sealed out the raucous sounds from the floor.

"How was your trip?" Nica asked as she waved her guest to one of the black leather couches.

"Long. I'm not particularly fond of train travel."

She sighed as she sank into comfortable cushions and let her heavy bag drop along with her anxiousness.

"But it's expedient and difficult to trace," Nica justified. "You didn't have any trouble with the tickets I sent, did you?"

"No. I didn't expect to. I know you're very good at your job. I wouldn't have come here, otherwise. I'm sure you appreciate the danger this puts me and my family in, just talking to you."

"I do. But I also know you're not as delicate as your expensive pastel suit would suggest. I wouldn't have asked *you* here, otherwise. We're professional females, you and I, and there's little we won't do in the name of business or family."

"Why am I here, Nica? Business or family?"

"A bit of both, and I think you'll find it very worth your trouble."

A pique of interest pushed away her travel fatigue. "Go on. What kind of family business requires an obgyn?"

Nica hesitated for just an instant, then amended, "That's not all you are. You're a geneticist in a very specialized field." Catching the jump of alarm in Susanna's eyes, she added, "I had to know who you were, and what you were involved in, when you hired me. That information goes no farther than the two of us if you decide you can't help me."

Susanna relaxed, forcing her mood to become equally receptive. She trusted the other woman. Nica understood the importance of secrecy and security when survival was in the balance. It was how both of them lived their very different lives.

"So," she ventured carefully, "exactly how much do you know about what I do?"

"Everything. I know your practice within the human world is a cover so you can access their databases. I know your private interest is in combining Shifter and Chosen DNA, and that even though the Purist Movement has offered to fund your research, you've refused their aid because of their reputation for, shall we say, meddling."

"They don't care about honest research. They're only interested in furthering their propaganda of separate being better, and separate and *not* equal, better still."

Nica grinned. "Bet it feels good to say that out loud."

Susanna returned a wry smile. "One watches one's words when political ears are everywhere."

"And long, unforgiving memories. It must get tricky hiding your true focus from them."

Again, Susanna had no comment. The shadow of her enemies reached too far for her to feel comfortable speaking her opinion. There was too much in the balance. Instead, she asked more pointedly, "What part of my research concerns you?"

"Shifter regeneration properties."

Her reply was cautious. "Personal or military application?"

Nica laughed. "I'm no friend of the military, or anything governmental, for that matter. I'm enjoying my

newfound freedom a little too much to place it anywhere near their opportunistic hands."

"Personal then."

"Yes. Not me, personally, but a friend. I owe a debt,
and in settling mine, you can satisfy yours to me. You
aren't obligated in any way. You're free to say no and
get back on the first train north with no hard feelings.
Your work is valuable. I wouldn't want to compromise
it in any way."

Compromise. That was the last thing she expected
to hear from the razor-edged warrior. Susanna didn't
know much about Nica Fraser except that she'd suc-
ceeded when no other could with an unmatched deadly
skill and cunning. But this softer side was a new facet
to her, one that perhaps came with settling down with
a mate. A wistful pang twisted through her, but it was
pushed away as she turned back to business.

"Why does your friend need a geneticist?"

Nica's shrewd gaze assessed her for a long moment.
"Whatever I tell *you* goes no farther."

"Of course."

"My friend is close to a human who was critically
injured and has no chance of recovery. This friend of
mine is bonded to a Shifter male and through that bond-
ing process, her own life was saved because of the regen-
erating qualities passed to her during the mating ritual."

"Your friend is human?" Surprise gave way to fas-
cination.

"It's complicated. Let's just say she and her mate
both bring interesting DNA to the table, and because

of that, she thinks these properties could be used to heal her friend. Given all the research you've done, do you think that's even remotely possible?"

Susanna blinked. What Nica suggested was a shocking bit of science fiction with huge moral consequences. It was one thing to tamper with genetic traits within their own species, but to dare cross those lines artificially . . .

"I would need samples from her and her mate, and the human."

Nica brightened. "You think it can be done?"

"In a lab, maybe. In actuality, I don't know. I'm not sure it should even be tried. There are implications far beyond what any of you have considered."

"But you're willing to find out?"

Susanna drew in a shaky breath. Her thoughts swelled with intriguing possibilities, expanding until her mind could barely contain them. Could she?

Should she?

"No promises. I'd like to sleep on it first."

The door to the office burst open. A huge figure filled the frame, backed by the blaring pulse of a heavy metal mix.

"Nica, I need you on the floor. How much longer are you gonna be?"

Even before Susanna looked around, even before she heard his booming voice, she recognized the unmistakable scent that scrambled all her senses. She sat paralyzed with shock as the large male's gaze touched upon her and held. For an agonizing moment, she feared he knew her, but then she realized he somehow recognized her not for who she was, but rather what. What she was, was not one of them.

"I'll be just a minute, Jacques," Nica assured him, her intuitive gaze snapping back and forth between them.

"Who's your friend?" It was more demand than request as displeasure furrowed his brow.

Susanna stood, locking her knees to keep them from shaking. Her smile was as cool and impersonal as her tone. "I'm Susanna Duchamps. Nica and I have known each other for years. She was kind enough to help me find a place to stay when she heard I was visiting New Orleans."

At the sound of her accent, his posture tensed. "And where are you visiting from, Ms. Duchamps?"

"It's Doctor. Illinois." She met his stare unblinkingly, challenging him to make more of it.

"Suze, this is Jacques LaRoche, my usually well-mannered employer." When her curt tone failed to shame him, Nica sighed. "I was just giving her directions to Silas's old place. She's going to crash there for a couple of nights."

Unable to read anything in his employee's stoic glare, Jacques turned back to Susanna with a thin smile. "Enjoy your stay in the Big Easy, Dr. Duchamps." Without taking his eyes off her, he backed from the room and let the door close behind him.

Jacques LaRoche may not have remembered her face, but he recognized her kind. He'd been in the North and he knew she was of the Chosen.

And that could make Susanna's stay all kinds of difficult.

From his place behind the bar, Jacques's narrowed stare followed the petite female as she skirted the busy tables, keeping her eyes cast low and her bag clutched close. It was impossible to ignore her.

Outside on the city streets, she wouldn't be a novelty with her tiny stature and delicate features. The designer clothes would allow her to blend in with the tourists flooding the Quarter now that the weather was turning cool in the North. She could pass for human, but not so easily as a Shifter. Their females were sturdy, curvy, athletically rather than intellectually inclined. They didn't look as though a harsh glance could break them in half.

What are you doing in my city, Dr. Duchamps?

And why had his best waitress invited her amongst them?

"She won't cause any trouble."

Jacques didn't take his gaze from the female in question as he growled, "Says you. What do you know about her?"

"I know she came down here at great risk to herself because I asked her to do a favor for me."

"That makes her your responsibility. I don't want her kind in here. I don't take in strays."

Nica laughed and reached across the bar to lightly pat his rough cheek. "Yes, you do. We're all strays here, and you're just the big softy who scoops us all up."

Jacques was smiling ruefully at that title when the deep brown eyes of the woman across the room lifted to connect with his stare. And he felt again the same jolting shock he'd gotten when he first saw her, as if cardiac paddles had jump-started his heart.

Reason enough, even without knowing where she'd come from, to make him wary.

As she slipped out of sight, he turned to Nica, his features grim. "Don't bring her here again. Consider that a favor to me." He nodded behind her. "Table six is waving for you."

Nica studied him for a silent moment before she picked up her tray and got back to work.

His place, his rules. Not too much to ask of the strays he'd taken under his wing.

Jacques went back to polishing his bar top until the wood gleamed like satin. His place. Pride in that accomplishment filled him, nudging out the uneasy feelings the Chosen female had stirred up. Nica was right. They were all strays here in New Orleans, the place where misfits were swept to be out of sight, out of mind, and kept out of trouble. And they'd been complaisant, scared, and isolated for far too long. But perhaps not for much longer.

Or at least that had been his hope until the fire.

It had been almost three months, and the insurance company and arson investigators still hadn't cleared the way to reopening the Trinity Towers. The urban reclamation project that was to have been their sanctuary had almost become their funeral pyre. It stood unoccupied, another of Max Savoie's promises gone up in flames, this time literally. Jacques had had two whole days living within those walls, pretending his life had gotten miraculously better before reality singed those dreams. And where was Savoie now? Not here, seeing to the interests of his clan. He was too busy settling his own affairs.

Jacques threw the bar rag into the sink behind him. Those dreams were like the lovely Dr. Duchamps, tempting but out of reach for someone like him.

He'd been happy with what he'd worked to carve out for himself until Savoie showed up with his glorious promises. He'd managed to remake his life upon the uncertain shadows of his past. A good life. His own business. A decent day job. Respect. Security. What more did a man need? Even a man who wasn't by definition a man at all?

Then Savoie got him wanting more.

"Hey, Jackie. Busy night."

Jacques poured a beer for Philo Tibideaux as his friend settled onto one of the bar stools. "Not complaining. How's yours been?"

"Quiet," Philo grumbled as if wishing it were otherwise.

Philo was one of those people who had changed drastically when Savoie stepped in with his big talk and bigger trouble. The carefree amusement of the lanky redhead's world had been torn away in an instant when his brother was murdered. There was no more laughter in his eyes, just anger and a cold ash of emptiness. Even his appearance had evolved from shaggy disregard to a close-cut, hard edge of nerves and fury that made Jacques tense just being around him.

"Seen Savoie tonight?" Jacques asked.

At the mention of Max's name, Philo's lips curled. "Not around here. Him and his new boy have moved on to greener pastures. Could have told you that was coming."

Jacques shrugged, but he feared Philo was right. Maybe Savoie's attentions *had* turned to a new focus, one that didn't include an interest in his adopted clan. Or in Jacques's concerns over the appearance of a Chosen emissary from Illinois.

In the not so recent past, Jacques could have discussed his misgivings with Philo, who had formed a security group to deal with the threat of outsiders. But Philo's Patrol had taken on a certain paramilitary tone that made Jacques uneasy with his confidence. It was something he should have discussed with Max, but Max wasn't here, and his promises had become as mercurial as his legend.

So Jacques poured himself a glass, clinking its rim against Philo's in a companionable gesture as he glanced toward the conspicuously empty table at the back of his club. Screw Savoie. He didn't need dreams. He already had everything he wanted.

Except a way to soothe the ache resurrected by the mysterious female from the North.

That longing for things he couldn't recall.

Two

Susanna? I've been out of my mind with worry. Are you all right?"

Guilt assailed her at the unexpected shake of panic in Damien Frost's voice. "I explained everything to you in my note."

"You explained nothing. 'I'll be out of town for a few days. I'll call you'? All I could think was that it was happening again, the same as with Pearl."

"Oh, Damien, no, I'm so sorry. I never considered . . ." Her heart twisted as she considered it now, her partner going through the same agony she'd endured when Pearl had been taken from her. During that awful time, Damien had remained beside her to keep her focused and sane. "I'm fine. I'm truly fine. You don't need to worry."

"Of course I'm worried," his gentle tone broke. "What possessed you to just run off without a word to me? This isn't like you, Susanna. Not at all."

Again, all she could do was apologize, feeling worse as she listened to his ragged breathing. "I'm sorry, but I had to make this trip and I knew if we spoke, you'd talk me out of it."

"Out of what? What are you involved in?"

"I can't tell you, Damien. Nothing dangerous." A necessary lie. "Nothing that will compromise us." Another lie, greater than the first.

"Where are you? Can you at least tell me that much if I promise not to interfere?"

"I can't."

"Is it something I've done?"

The distress in his question tormented her as she assured him, "It's not you. You know better. You're my one true constant. You've made everything in my life possible."

"Then why are you treating me this way? As if I can't be trusted?"

Susanna drew back behind her caution. "It's to protect you and Pearl. For no other reason." That had been true at first, but now other issues had come into play. Other more personal, even selfish reasons. "I'll be gone just a couple of days. It's for a research opportunity, one that may never come again. I'm safe. I'm sorry, that's all I can say."

"What am I supposed to tell Pearl when she asks for her mother?"

Susanna's will almost broke, but she held firm. "Tell her I love her and am thinking of her always."

"And if something should happen, if she should take a bad turn, how can I get ahold of you? Your number is blocked."

She shivered at the thought of her greatest fear. "I'll check in frequently. If there's an emergency, I can be home in a matter of hours. That's the best I can do."

He sighed in frustration. "And hopefully that will be good enough. What am *I* supposed to do, Susanna? Wish you well on this mysterious journey?"

"Yes. Could you do that?"

His tone evened into its practical cadence. "All right. I wish you well and a speedy return home."

"Thank you. I knew you'd understand."

"I don't. I think this is reckless and unwise of you, but it's done and what I think obviously didn't enter into your planning."

She cringed beneath his cool censure. He'd done so much for her. This act of secrecy was an unworthy response to the freedoms she'd been given. "Of course you matter," she said quietly. "I'm doing this for us. I'll be able to explain better when I get home."

"Make it soon. You have obligations here, where you belong."

Obligations. He couldn't have chosen a less persuasive word. "I'm well aware of them. I won't disappoint you. Good night, Damien. Give Pearl a kiss for me."

The call disconnected abruptly on his end.

She closed her phone and sat unhappily in her borrowed room. She'd brought fear and anguish and upset to her companion. She'd provoked him to emotions he rarely displayed: anger, irritation, even possessiveness, a shameful betrayal on her part.

She'd lied to him. And to herself.

She'd come to New Orleans not just to settle a debt of conscience, but to escape the smothering press of her life in the North. The favor asked was an excuse to slip out from under those oppressive obligations so she could have the chance to breathe. The chance to feel. Things forbidden in her stringent world. To be what was born within her seven years ago when she'd allowed herself to taste freedom, never guessing how she'd hunger for it every day and night since then until she was emotionally starved.

But control that appetite she would. She had to, because these delicious sensations were only temporary.

Her life was in Chicago.

But, she'd just discovered unexpectedly, her heart was still where it had always been.

Here in New Orleans, with the man now called Jacques LaRoche.

She paced the small apartment, exhausted yet too keyed up to rest.

When she'd first stared at those tickets to Louisiana, she should have experienced fear, not excitement. She should have given the danger to her family, to her position, to her safety precedent over any obligation she might have felt to a mercenary who'd just been doing her job. She should have thought of the delay in her own work while traipsing off on some ill-conceived adventure. Being adventuresome was not a desirable trait in a Chosen citizen.

But to see and experience what life could be if she dared embrace it . . . A life denied her in the rigid North. A life of emotion.

Those feelings ran rampant now, thrilling and terrifying her.

New Orleans was everything her life in Chicago was not. It exploded with sensory temptations. Standing at the open window, she let the sensations drift over her like the caress of a lover's hands.

The warmth of the evening air seeped in to stimulate her soul. The city's heart beat with energy, with its sultry mélange of cultures and music. Its aroma enticed her. There was nothing to smell in her clinical confines in the North. Here, every inhalation was a potent potpourri of flavors, laced with a tang of salt and an earthy sense of history. Rich, deep, beckoning odors, not all of which were pleasant. The intensity overwhelmed her as she breathed in and savored the olfactory sensation.

Only once before had she felt so alive, so eager to embrace a new awareness with all five senses as they stirred restlessly within her. She'd been young then, too naïve to know caution, to understand the power of such emotions while caught up in her desperate wonder. She hadn't thought of consequence then. Now, she couldn't afford not to.

She stepped away from the window, but left it open to invite in the tease of nightfall. She used the Spartan bathroom to shower away the stale drag of travel, then returned to the bedroom, determined to unwind. But how could she close her eyes and deny herself the joys that seduced her?

The circling of the ceiling fan moved the silk of her

pajamas against her skin in an unbearable ripple, creating shivers of memory.

Making Susanna think of his hands upon her.

Jacques LaRoche.

She hadn't expected to see him here. She hadn't wanted to know where he'd gone, fearing she couldn't resist the need to follow. Seeing him in that doorway had shocked her system almost beyond recovery. But over these past years, she'd learned to rebound quickly without betraying any personal impact. She'd had to in order to protect those things that mattered most.

Jacques LaRoche. That wasn't who he'd been when she'd known him.

Stretching out on the big yielding bed beneath the cool, rhythmic pulse of the fan, Susanna shut her eyes and allowed herself to picture him at the Shifter club. Big, bold, dangerously magnetic. She struggled against that fateful pull of attraction, but finally gave in, at least for this private moment. Her sigh trembled with complex longing as she superimposed the image she'd carried in her heart of the first time she'd seen him.

He was the first shape-shifter Susanna had ever met up close, and despite her outcries for equality between Chosen and Shifter kind, he'd scared her to death with his rough intensity. Chosen males were refined and gracefully made. Her Shifter bodyguard was built like a fortress instead of a cathedral, all blunt, sturdy fortifications of muscle upon a massive utilitarian frame.

The fit of his black one-piece uniform had done little to disguise his blatant power as fabric strained to contain broad chest and wide shoulders. Even his features seemed hewn from granite by fierce, chopping blows instead of artful strokes, each line strong and squared from jaw to heavy brow. Upon that brutal facade, his full lips seemed overtly sensual even when unsmiling.

But his eyes had held her captive. From his position of servitude, they should have been kept submissively downcast. To look boldly upon her could have meant his death. But as she listened to her guardian explain how to use the remote controller as a safety measure to keep her new servant in check, he'd slipped a rebellious glance up at her. She hadn't expected eyes so startlingly blue beneath the slash of dark brows. Or a stare so penetrating. Instead of alarm, she'd experienced a sudden tremor as forbidden as it was unwise.

Her first thrill of sexual awakening.

He'd changed little since that day. The same long legs and barrel chest, brawny arms and menacing scowl. But the thick hair she'd loved to feel between her fingers had been shaved to a dark, downy shadow like the whisker stubble that gave him such rugged ferocity. His skin was darkly tanned, even the expanse of his chest displayed by the deep veed opening of his underbuttoned shirt. Her gaze could have lingered there all night, and loitered now in her recollections.

She still found him breathtaking. That hadn't changed.

He hadn't recognized her, which was both relief and curse. The confident way he carried himself said he was no longer anyone's slave, but his own master, and she couldn't have been more proud of him. He'd done well on his own. Better than he could have managed had he remained at her side.

That was some consolation on this lonely night, one of thousands since they'd parted.

It was foolish to indulge in such thoughts, to invite the warm curl of memories to heat her blood and stir long dormant passions. Foolish *and* dangerous, that temptation to play the *What if?* game.

What if she'd made a different choice?

Three

Now we're of one mind, one heart, one soul. Nothing will ever separate us again. There's still doubt in your eyes. Let me prove you wrong."

Her mouth took his with a convincing fervor, tongue teasing, then plunging deep. She tasted of desire and dreams. Her hand closed possessively about him, warm, soft, determined, arousing beyond his wildest imaginings with her unskilled strokes.

As his breaths quickened, he began to believe the words she said were true.

Let them be true!

Jacques had jerked from sleep to find himself alone in the hot, sweaty tin can of his trailer, his breathing ragged, and so painfully hard it took some urgent pounding in the shower to beat out the tension. But when he stopped at the club to do some paperwork before his shift at the docks, that restlessness returned. Because the scent of the Chosen female lingered.

Jacques leaned back in his office chair and rubbed at his eyes. He hadn't woken from one of those agitating dreams in a long while and he knew it was the outsider's presence that brought them back to torment him.

Dreams or memories, he was never sure, but their power to disturb him lasted for hours, sometimes days. No amount of work or alcohol or companionable sex could fill the emptiness, yet he couldn't convince himself he was free to commit to another.

Because he knew his mated female yet lived. Somewhere. He just didn't know how to find her.

That was the hell of it. As long as that frustrating bond existed, he was stuck in an emotional limbo, unable to move on. Like being mired in the bayou up the heart with no way to pull himself out, yet unable to sink into a peaceful oblivion. Sometimes he got so weary of the struggle, he longed for that permanent surrender. Anything was better than the loneliness that constantly cut away pieces of any hope he held for happiness.

Movement caught his eye out on the floor. The exterior doors were still locked so he knew it had to be one of the staff coming in early. He smiled as he recognized Nica's bold stride. He liked the tough female for her cleverness and swagger, and had briefly entertained the idea that maybe he and she . . . But then she'd gotten a look at Silas MacCreedy, and never glanced away again. It had been the same with Savoie and his feisty human girlfriend.

Had it been like that for him and his mate? Wondering made him scowl. It did no good to look back when he knew there was nothing for him to find. All such things, all the personal and emotional details that shaped who and what he was had been torn from his mind at the ruthless hands of their enemies in the North, leaving only questions. Had he left family behind? Was he a good man? What had he done to deserve exile from his own past, his own memories? An endless, agonizing swirl of unknowns.

Seeing the Chosen intruder in Nica's shadow didn't improve Jacques's mood.

The dainty female, Susanna, waited rather nervously out amongst the lower tier of tables while Nica strode up to the office. He met her in the hall with a growl of, "Something wrong with your hearing, Fraser?"

"Forget how to be an obliging host, LaRoche?"

He could count the number of people on one hand he'd let get away with speaking to him with such boldness. Nica was lucky to be one of them. He trusted her, considered her a friend as well as an employee, who would never do anything to harm him or his. So why was she pushing on this particular hot spot? She knew the reasons for his wary prejudices, yet still she pressed. Which made him all the surlier.

"I told you not to bring her back in here."

"Relax, boss. It's not like I'm going to leave her unchaperoned. We need to use your computer for a minute, then we'll be out of your hair."

Jacques rubbed his palm over his shorn head with a grumbled, "Very funny."

Nica touched his forearm. "It's important. Please."

The unexpected humility took him off guard, making him waiver, big softy that he was. They both knew

he was going to give in, but he made a masterful effort
to appear undecided as he studied the interloper.

This morning, she wore a pair of beige tailored
trousers with sensible heels and a silky cream-colored
blouse. Her jewelry was simple and gold, her makeup
meticulous, accentuating elfin features and big, doe-
like eyes. Fine, straight hair of rich caramel was tucked
behind her ears, barely grazing a fragile jawline. She'd
have been a perfect fit in the posh spires of City Central
but her appearance was totally inappropriate for this
end of the Quarter. An outsider who didn't know how
to blend. Trouble he didn't need.

Trouble that had his palms sweaty as he caught
himself imagining how soft and sleek her perfect skin
would feel beneath them. And that suddenly had him
recalling the erotic nature of his dream with an intensity that startled, alarmed, and dismayed him all at
once.

"Make it quick. Lock up behind you."

Something about the female had gotten tangled up
in the threads of his fantasies, tying them together in
a manner too intimate for close quarters. So he would
back away, making her Nica's problem until he could
get a better handle on his unsettled feelings.

He wasn't leaving Nica in charge because he trusted
her. He didn't trust himself to remain.

Susanna watched them talk, noting Jacques's obvious
displeasure. He knew she was Chosen, maybe from
instinct rather than recognition, and he clearly wanted

no part of her. That was good, she thought, ignoring the tiny pang of anguish as he looked away from her dismissingly, as if she were nothing more than an annoyance. She didn't react to the longing that swelled inside, an achy desire to see something else in his eyes. Better to not tempt fate, she told herself as her gaze followed his exit down the hall and out the rear door. He still moved like a brawler wading through a crowd.

And it still excited her heart into hurried palpitations.

"C'mon, Suze," Nica called to her. "We don't have much time before the first shift comes on."

As Susanna stepped into the office, she paused to take in the music piped over the interior sound system.

"That's Yo-Yo Ma's Bach in G Major," she murmured in surprise.

"If you say so." Nica didn't glance up from the computer keyboard. "The boss calls that highbrow stuff his thinking tunes. I had him pegged for a death metal man. Who would have thought, huh?"

Susanna thought it made perfect, if unnerving, sense.

Then she pushed thoughts of Jacques away.

Questions, probabilities, consequences, and potential all jockeyed for her attention, drawing her deeper into this opportunity to explore not only the scientific avenues, but the sociological as well. This was a culture openly scorned and despised by her own kind as ruthless and barbaric. Perhaps it was. Yet perhaps there were other things within it that her people feared.

Those things they'd separated themselves from with their lofty intentions and cold ambitions. Things she could examine and, if she was brave enough, enjoy so she could form her own conclusions, that until now had been a safe hypothesis within the isolated walls of her lab.

Nica brought up the files she'd gotten from NOLA chief medical examiner Dev Dovion. Samples from two individuals showing startling properties. She dropped into the desk chair, unable to take her eyes off the screen.

"I've never seen patterns like this. Who do these belong to?"

"Sorry," Nica told her. "That's confidential until you commit. How did you sleep last night?"

"Tossed and turned," Susanna admitted as her gaze darted about the screen in amazement. "And I probably won't sleep tonight after seeing this. Have you any idea—?"

"Yeah, I do. I wouldn't have sent for you otherwise." She leaned her forearms on the back of the chair and regarded the screen without comprehension. "What do you think?"

Susanna pointed out several groupings. "That's Shifter." She gestured to the other graphic. "That's human." Then she identified similar clusters in both. "But what's this? It's not Chosen. Is it some kind of mutation? Some anomaly?" Excitement trembled in her voice.

"Have you ever heard of the Ancients?"

Susanna twisted to look up at her. "The origin of our species? Is that what this is? Has the strain survived? How? In who?"

"I can't just give you this information without some kind of assurance." Nica straightened, her expression cautious, her eyes cool. "How's your little girl?"

The unexpected turn of conversation struck the air out of Susanna's lungs. Had she been foolish to consider Nica an ally? "Are you threatening my daughter?" she managed to gasp.

Not a muscle moved in Nica's stoic face. "Chosen don't honor family. They don't hold to any kind of sentimental familial unit or emotional tie. I thought I was like that until I came here, until I met these people. They believe in that bond and hold it sacred above their own lives. I've come to feel the same way. I need to know if you can understand that concept so you'll know to what lengths I'll go to protect them.

"I thought I saw panic and terror in your eyes when you believed your child was lost to you. When I put her back into your arms, I thought I recognized love in those tears on your face. Was I wrong, Susanna?"

"No," Susanna replied softly, forcing her response past the huge knot in her throat. "I understand love and sacrifice and loss. And I won't betray those you hold dear. I swear it on my own child."

A narrow smile creased Nica's hard surface. "Okay then." She nodded at the screen. "Can that do what my friend needs it to do?"

Susanna looked back at the diagrams, her heart

pounding. "It can do a lot more than just that." She took a big, shaky breath and jumped in. "I am not exaggerating when I tell you the potential here is both miraculous and catastrophic, and that our very lives will be in the balance if even a hint of what we've got leaks out. Do you understand?"

"Yes. Are you in?"

"All the way." Her fingertips touched the monitor. "How could I not be?" She shook off her reverie, her tone now clipped and efficient. "I'm going to need a secure place to work and access to a lab. We'll have to have absolute secrecy, only Need to Know involved. I'll want to take fresh samples and interview the subjects. When can I start?"

Nica grinned. "How about now?"

Jacques lingered in the weak morning sunshine, drawing in deep breaths, hoping to clear the confusion from his brain before heading for his Caddy and the stack of invoices waiting for him in his dockside office. No such luck. The Chosen doctor's scent muddled his mind like a hefty hangover, leaving him unsettled and annoyed.

What was it about her that had him so agitated? It went beyond the threat she brought with her. It was something visceral, instinctive, disturbing. Something that pried at the dark area of his brain where his memories had once resided. Had he known her, seen her before? Unlikely, since she'd betrayed no spark of recognition. Perhaps she merely represented something that had been stripped forcefully from his mind by her coldly vicious kind, leaving behind a mysterious blank.

The sound of crunching gravel beneath the wheels of a fast-approaching car caught his attention. He identified Philo's Charger by the smell of burning oil. The rumbling car, still in dull gray primer, stopped just shy of running over his steel-toed boots.

Philo climbed out of the driver's side, eyes concealed by dark glasses and the downward tip of a Saints ball cap. He came around to yank open the squawking passenger door to help one of his Patrol members get out. The fellow's face looked like a pulpy tomato. He swayed on his feet as Philo tipped up the seat to drag another figure from the back.

Philo threw the stranger down on the stones, placing his boot on the back of his neck and the barrel of a gun to his head while another of his men wiggled out of the close confines of the backseat.

"What's going on, Tib?" Jacques asked, looking from the bullet hole in the prone man's arm to his friend's taut features.

"There were two of them," Philo told him tersely. "Managed to keep this one alive. Need a place to have a conversation."

"Who is he?"

"That's what we want to find out. Caught him and his pal sneaking around, asking questions. No ID, no nothing." He nodded to his companions. "Take him inside."

Not sure if his female guests were still there, Jacques

growled, "I'm not gonna have him bleeding all over my office. Take him down by the bar. Looks like you fellas could use something cold as a bracer 'fore you get to work."

"Thanks, Jackie. We'll try not to make a mess." Philo stepped back to let the others drag the wounded male to his feet, then they all moved inside.

The office door was closed. No way to tell if Nica and her Chosen friend were still within. Jacques had never asked about Nica's former employment, but he knew she was smart enough not to stick her nose into dangerous things that didn't concern her. He hoped she'd be able to get the two of them out the back without being seen once matters intensified on the main floor.

Jacques went behind the bar while Philo and his friends secured their prisoner to a chair, binding his hands behind the back and his legs to those of the chair. He was bleeding badly from his wound and from a gash in his forehead but showed no emotion of any kind. Jacques didn't need ID to know what this man was. The stoic, nondescript features, dark, made-to-blend-in suit that screamed G-man, eyes glittering with unholy fierceness. He'd been face-to-face with two of his brethren, and he and Savoie's cop girlfriend had barely escaped alive. The man was an elite killer bloodhound sent down from Susanna Duchamps's kind in the North for purposes that could be no good for his New Orleans clan.

After nodding his gratitude and taking a long pull

at his beer, Philo asked easily, "Let me have that Louisville Slugger you're so fond of so we can get down to business."

Jacques wasn't opposed to violence when necessary and had dealt out all types for varied reasons. He enjoyed a good knuckle-bruising fight and would never run from one, but killing never sat well with him, even when unavoidable. He'd never experienced the bloodthirsty fury he could see boiling in his friend's gaze when he passed Philo the baseball bat, and he wasn't looking forward to what was to come.

Weighing the bat thoughtfully, Philo approached the bound man. His tone was pleasant.

"You're gonna tell me what you and your buddy were doing here in New Orleans or I'm gonna break every bone in your body. Then, after you heal 'em, I'm gonna do it all over again. I'm betting you're gonna get tired of it 'fore I do. Let's find out." And he swung.

Jacques winced at the sound of the humerus splintering, but he didn't look away. Tito Tibideaux, Philo's younger brother, had been a damned good friend of his and the way he'd died had been brutal and undeserved. This silent assassin knew what to expect and was trained to receive it. They'd never get a sound from him, let alone a confession, but the process might allow Philo to work off his grief. For that reason, Jacques wouldn't interfere. Paybacks were never pretty.

Philo was zealous in his interrogation and true to his word to exact as much damage and pain as possible, but his prisoner was a professional, refusing to allow him the satisfaction of a response. And that provoked the redhead from diligent purpose to frustration-fueled rage. His actions turned dark, from retribution to frenzy.

And while all focus was on his punishing intensity, Nica attempted to slip Susanna out the back.

Jacques saw the two of them start down the hall.

So did the prisoner. His bloody face grew suddenly attentive, causing Philo and the others to follow his gaze.

And that gave the Tracker the distraction he'd been waiting for.

Without a sound of warning, he exploded out of the chair, tearing through his bindings as if they were sewing thread. He snatched the bat from Philo, knocking him to the floor with a hard swing to his head. As the other two gaped at him in surprise, he ripped through them with razor-sharp claws.

Jacques knew Trackers could move fast. He'd seen them before, but was still amazed at how quickly their captive leapt, with Philo's gun in hand, from main floor to hallway. He caught Nica by the hair and pitched her down the stairs. Then, with his massive paw curled about Susanna's throat and the gun muzzle to her temple, he turned to use her as a shield as he backed down the dim hall toward freedom.

Jacques's gaze went to the hostage to assess her state of mind. She was terrified and trembling, a split second from instant death, but her dark eyes met his with an eerie calm, as if she knew rescue was coming. As if she had absolutely no doubts.

Without thought or hesitation, Jacques pulled the pistol he kept beneath the cash drawer in case of emergency and strode purposefully from behind the bar. In one smooth move, he leveled the barrel and fired a single shot into the shadows, punching a neat hole through the Tracker's forehead that blew out the back of his head.

With a quick glance to see that Philo was moving, Jacques strode across the club, lifting Nica by the forearm to settle her into a chair before bounding up the steps to where Susanna stood.

She'd staggered free as the dead man fell. Her pulse, so steady and calm while caught in the grip of danger, began a rapid pounding, sending a dizzying rush of blood to her head. Her entire focus haloed about the grimly set features of her rescuer.

"Nice shot," was her breathy comment.

"Are you all right?"

She frowned slightly at his concerned tone, then followed his gaze down to the front of her blouse where her assailant's bloodied sleeve had left damp smears of crimson all over the front of it.

As her head lifted, her eyes gave a brief flutter and she dropped dead away into Jacques's arms.

"You're safe now. I have you."

The rumble of his words caressed her cheek, followed by the soft graze of his lips. Never in her life had she felt such a sense of security as within the strong wrap of his embrace. His chest provided unconditional sanctuary, his arms curls of unbreakable steel. The fierce hammering of his heart spoke a vow of perpetual devotion, each beat comforting because of the next that was sure to follow.

So this was love, this huge engulfing blanket of tenderness tucked about her with a promise of forever.

This was love.

She opened her eyes to gaze into those clear pools of blue, drowning in the emotions she saw there. Need, desire, worry, loyalty, each sensation taking root in her own soul as it was recognized.

She whispered his name like a prayer of thanksgiving.

And he bent to kiss her, slowly, searingly, endlessly.

"It's all right. You're safe."

Susanna gazed up into the blue of his eyes and for a moment all was confused. She lifted her hand to his face, almost surprised to feel the very real warmth of stubbled skin beneath her fingertips.

"You saved me," came her dreamy sigh.

Her touch grew more bold as she lost herself in the familiar textures, stroking along the broad plane of his cheek, her thumb riding the swell of his lower lip. She watched his brow pucker and his eyes go a shade darker until finally his large hand covered hers, holding it gently, drawing it away from him to settle it on her middle, atop the other.

"Do you know where you are? Do you remember what happened?" he asked with somber concern.

Susanna blinked once, twice, scattering the overlap of time and place to ground her in the moment. She wasn't in a stairwell in Chicago. She was in New Orleans, stretched out on a leather couch with Jacques LaRoche hunkered down beside her. "Yes, of course," she told him, managing to sound lucid. "Is everyone all right?"

"Nica's at the bar putting ice on my foolish friend's head. His two men were injured, but nothing fatal. You fainted."

"I—I did? How unlike me."

He smiled faintly at her embarrassment. "You've had a lot of guns pointed at your head by stone killers, have you, to just shrug it off as an everyday occurrence?"

Her own lips curved ruefully. "Not every day, but this wasn't my first go-round, Mr. LaRoche. I apologize for inconveniencing you."

He straightened, rising to his feet to tower over her. "Apology accepted."

Her hands stirred, moving over unfamiliar cotton fabric. Glancing down, she found she was wearing a man's white shirt.

Seeing her question before she spoke it, Jacques explained, "You had blood all over your blouse. It's soaking so the stains won't set."

Her eyes widened. "You—you took off my clothes?" The idea of his hands on her, undressing her, made her pulse quiver.

He mistook the reason for her alarm, saying quietly, "Nica did. I only supplied the shirt. No need to worry that I soiled you with my touch."

"That's not— I'm sorry. I didn't mean to offend you."

"You didn't, Dr. Duchamps."

Her chuckle mocked his brittle reply. She put out her hand to him. "Could you help me up or are *you* afraid of getting dirtied?"

His hand engulfed hers, tugging slightly so she could sit up, fighting waves of threatening nausea as she did so. He released her immediately, unconsciously wiping his palm on his jeans. She marked the movement with another wry smile.

"Considering how much you dislike me, Mr. LaRoche, I'm surprised you would risk such a bold shot to save my life."

"I wasn't the one who had something to lose if I missed."

She didn't react to that sharp bite except to say, "I'm sorry my presence here upsets you."

"Your existence upsets me."

She despised the prejudice he barely bothered to conceal. They were joined by the same ancestors. Distant relatives, but family nonetheless.

Family wasn't a concept the Chosen believed in. Selective breeding was. She couldn't fault them for the narrow logic of their opinions. They didn't know any better. They were emotionally bankrupt. But Jacques LaRoche didn't have that excuse.

"How can you say that? You don't even know me."

"I know what you are, what you believe, how you treat my kind like filthy animals incapable of intelligent thought."

Her gaze grew as narrow as his mind-set. "It's *that* type of statement that leads to *those* kinds of assumptions. You do not know me. You don't know what I believe, what I like, or what my favorite color is."

"Red."

"What?"

"It's red," he said again, this time disturbed by that certainty.

She stood, teetering unsteadily both in body and emotion. Jacques started to reach out to her, but arrested the gesture. They stared at each other, at an impasse.

Finally, Susanna said, "I'd better go before you start to wonder if you shot the wrong individual." As she turned toward the door, his direct question made her pause.

"Did they come here because of you?"

She didn't favor him with a look as she firmly said, "No," and left the room, closing the door quietly behind her.

Jacques moved to the one-way glass overlooking his club, his gaze following her down the stairs on her way to join Nica and a groggy Philo. His shirt swam on her like a choir robe, emphasizing how small and fragile she was.

He was sorry for his gruff words, knowing that

they'd hurt her, but he'd reacted out of primal self-defense. When she'd opened her eyes to stare up at him with such obvious longing, when she'd touched his face as if he were the love of her life, he'd tried to take a breath and found himself unable to consume air.

Because it was that look, that touch that haunted him behind the veil of his forgotten past, that same intense spark of emotional connection so agonizingly missing from his life. Something about her hurried his heartbeats until his chest ached to contain them.

He'd been shocked by his willingness to allow her, no, to encourage her with his silence, a stranger, an enemy, to stay just so he could drink in these unexpected sensations until that long emptied well was full again.

She was confusing him, stealing in to lay claim to tiny bits of a life he didn't remember. That's what they did. Lied. Manipulated. That's what they were good at. That much he knew with a bitter certainty.

Red. Why had he said that as if he knew it was true?

And where had he learned to handle a gun?

He'd taken the piece off a rowdy customer and tucked it away without even checking to see if it was loaded. It fit his hand like an extension of his arm. He'd fired with unerring instinct and cold purpose, letting himself in on another unpleasant secret.

Some time ago, in that past hidden from him, he'd been a stone-cold killer, too.

Four

Charlotte Caissie was not what Susanna expected.

Nica said she was a police detective and the mate of Max Savoie, the leader of the New Orleans clan who also headed an extensive criminal empire. But other intriguing properties had her studying the female with interest as Charlotte entered the club and crossed to the bar as if she had part ownership in the place.

The tall woman with exotic looks and quick eyes, who garbed her curvaceous form in what Susanna could only describe as Goth dominatrix style, leaned across the bar to squeeze Jacques in a reciprocated hug, then turned her attention to Philo, fussing and scolding as she gestured to the evidence on the floor behind her. Both men regarded her with a respectful affection that Susanna envied. Then, suddenly all business, the detective bent over the still figure of the Tracker, flipping back the shrouding drop cloth so she could get a look at his face. She restored the cover and shook her head, obviously not recognizing him. From her crouched position over the body, her attention cut to Susanna and held for a long, contemplative minute.

This human hybrid was the key to Susanna's research, the way to resolve her own frustrations and fears.

All she had to do was overcome the tremendous chill of suspicion present in that stare as Charlotte approached and put out her hand.

"Dr. Duchamps, thank you for coming down to see me. Sorry to greet you with such drama."

Susanna shook hands, refusing to flinch from the double-barreled stare. "Detective. As a scientist, I couldn't resist the invitation."

Charlotte settled into a chair between her and Nica, pleasantries at an end. "Nica tells me I can trust you, but I'll make up my own mind about that."

Susanna smiled. "Likewise, detective."

That bit of boldness earned a return smile. "So you think what I propose is possible?"

"From what little I know, I can't make guarantees, but I'm optimistic. And I have a few conditions of my own."

Again, that cautious glint. "Name them."

"Privacy, secrecy, safety. I don't want anyone to know who I am, why I'm here, or what I'm doing."

"I agree completely."

"And freedom to work not only on your agenda, but on my own."

Now that steely reserve flattened her tone. "I guess that depends on the nature of your agenda, doctor."

"I'm a scientist, yes, but also a physician. I've devoted my area of study to genetics on the reproductive level. And I believe that might be of interest to you, due to your circumstances."

"What do you mean?" she all but growled with a protectiveness that confirmed what Susanna already knew.

"When is your child due?"

"What?" Nica exclaimed in surprise. "You and Max?"

Ignoring that outburst, Charlotte conceded, "In early spring. And I'd appreciate you keeping it quiet, since I haven't discussed it with the other party involved."

Nica leaned across the table with a salacious, "Max doesn't know?"

"He's got a lot on his mind and I didn't want to say anything until I was sure . . . until I knew everything was all right. I heard there could be problems."

Susanna didn't make light of her fears. "It depends on the type of conception, but yes, the danger is very real to both you and the child. That's my condition. I want to follow the progress of your pregnancy. Because of your unusual situation, the information is invaluable."

Charlotte reared back, eyes flinty. "You won't make my baby into an experiment."

Susanna caught her hand, pressing warmly. "No, that's not what I intend at all. We're each in a position to be of tremendous benefit to the other, personally, not just professionally. I understand your reluctance. I'm a mother, too, and the last thing I'd ever allow was my child to become the subject of clinical study. I can help you. I can monitor the development to make sure there are no problems. If there are, I'm your best chance of finding a positive solution. I've made this area my life's work. You couldn't be in better hands if something goes wrong."

Susanna knew she was playing upon the other woman's fears and emotions and did so with only the slightest regret. The opportunity was too important to let slip away. Not just for this growing hybrid child, but for her own.

"I'll have to consider it," Charlotte said carefully.

With a final squeeze of her hand, Susanna released her. "Of course you do."

The detective took a deep breath, reluctant yet obviously desperate for the chance she was being handed. Her tone was clipped and concise as she returned to her original agenda.

"First things first. An answer to your conditions."

At Susanna's questioning look, she lifted her hand and motioned to the big bartender.

"Who's the little dish?" Philo asked, following Jacques's covert stare to the trio in the shadows. He was slumped over the bar, head resting on his arms, holding a cold bottled beer against his brow.

"Friend of Nica's. A doctor of some sort." An extremely vague summation, but Jacques wasn't ready to throw gasoline on the fire of his friend's temper so soon after dousing it with ice and pain meds.

"Maybe I should have her look at my head."

"I don't think she's *that* kind of doctor."

Philo smiled. "I dunno. Might be kinda fun looking at ink blots with her on a couch somewhere."

Jacques was used to his friend's randy attitude when it came to females and usually thought nothing of it, but his comment stirred an unexpected desire to bash in whatever remaining brains Philo had left.

A sudden bite of pain had him forcefully relaxing his hands, where he was surprised to find lengthening nails had punctured his palms. He had no reason to feel protective of the bothersome female. But it was hard to ignore the aggressive prickling that had him rubbing at the back of his neck.

"What does Savoie think about all this?" Philo asked, glancing grimly at the bloodstained floor where his companions had almost died. They'd been claimed by family members, leaving only the cleanup. Once Philo's group had picked up the first Tracker he'd slain, they'd be by for this one; then it would be a quick trip to the swamps for an unceremonious burial.

"Hard to tell when he doesn't return my calls," Jacques grumbled. "He's in some kind of meeting with his attorney. It's not like we don't know how to tidy up after ourselves without his say-so."

He found Philo staring at him.

"What?"

"That was one hell of a shot."

"Just luck."

"Didn't look like luck to me."

"This from the fella who left the better part of his mental faculties over there on my floor?"

Jacques could joke about it, but in truth, it spooked him plenty. He didn't know where the skill had come from, who had taught him, or for what purpose.

What had he done for the Chosen during his years in the North?

He scowled over at the table of females, wondering what they were up to. No good, from the way Charlotte was casting glances his way. When she beckoned him over, a mood of wariness came over him as he approached, as if an attractively baited trap was about to spring on him.

He paused behind the empty chair, asking politely, because Nica had called him on his rudeness, "Something I can do for you ladies?"

Charlotte smiled up at him and he felt the sharp snap of the trap's teeth.

"Now that you mention it, yes, there is."

She'd made it sound so simple. Practical and precautionary was hard to argue with, even when it meant an invasion of his privacy.

The disgusting truth was, he *was* a softy, just as Nica said. He might growl and posture but there was nothing Jacques wouldn't do for those he cared about. And he considered Charlotte and Nica part of that makeshift circle.

Setting aside his initial alarm and reluctance, he

could see the logic of the request. That didn't mean he had to like it.

Susanna Duchamps needed a quiet, safe place to do some computer work and his office fit the bill. Never mind that he'd be majorly inconvenienced. Never mind that the thought of the dainty little doctor in such close proximity made his palms sweat. Charlotte had looked up at him, dark eyes filled with an urgent pleading, and he'd gone to grits.

She wouldn't tell him what they were up to, only that it was something intensely personal and that he couldn't tell anyone about it, especially Max. As annoyed as he was with Charlotte's oh so self-important mate, that tipped things in her favor.

Charlotte hugged him fiercely. Nica smushed a kiss to his cheek. And Susanna Duchamps regarded him somberly, vowing to stay out of his way. He wouldn't even know she was there.

Yeah, right.

His reply to her was as courteous as he could make it.

"You bring trouble into my place, you'll wish you'd never set foot in it."

From the look in her eyes, she was regretting it already.

The plan was for her to arrive at the rear door just after closing, around three in the morning. She had no problem with the time, saying she often worked odd shifts when caught up in a project. Then she'd set up at his desk and use those hours when the club was quiet to do whatever hoodoo that Charlotte felt she'd do so well.

What could go wrong?

Jacques was asking himself that very thing as he hurriedly entered in the previous day's receipts so he'd have no excuse to linger.

What could happen while he harbored a Chosen scientist with an unspoken agenda in his, so far, under-the-radar club for Shifters only?

Disaster. The good doctor was just the sort of infiltrator Philo and his Patrol were out prowling the streets to protect against, and here he'd invited her in, offering a soul-sucking vampire the opportunity to drain away the lifeblood of their freedom. The more he thought about it, the more troubled he became. He knew her for what she was. He couldn't plead any kind of ignorance. He knew all too well what her kind was capable of and that they weren't to be trusted. His mind was funny that way. He just knew things without any memory being attached to them.

And he was going to leave her alone, here at the heart of the life he'd built for himself out of nothing, trusting her not to act against them in favor of her own self-interest.

What had he been thinking?

Susanna Duchamps was right in her assumptions. Cleverness wasn't in the genetic makeup of his kind. He was a big, linear-minded beast bred to follow the dictates of others. Creative thinking wasn't in his résumé, action was. Quick, impulsive action with brutal consequences, as proven earlier that day.

And that's where things got sticky. Part of him wanted to toss her nice little fanny all the way back to Illinois. But another urged him to keep her close, to guard her carefully. That same fierce instinct that prompted his quick-draw response to her life in danger.

Jacques didn't like outside influences directing his actions. And Susanna Duchamps had been plucking at them since her arrival.

Unconsciously, he rubbed at the back of his neck, fingertips inches shy of the raised scar just beyond his reach, where Philo had cut out an implanted device just after he'd awakened in his new home, to his new life. A pain stimulator used by the Chosen to keep their subjects under control. He was under no one's thumb now, and that's the way he planned to keep it.

He turned the movement into a stretch and glanced out the window into the body of his club. Business was good tonight, as it was most every night. He provided a service unequalled in the Quarter, a place for his kind to be what they were inside without any interference or repercussions.

Was he jeopardizing that comfortable haven by inviting an outsider in?

Max Savoie was seated at his regular table. The welcome surprise at seeing him was blunted by the fact that his friend hadn't come straight back to the office to see him. A small thing, but it aggravated him like a sliver under the skin as he shut down the program he was working on and stepped from the calm silence of the office to the wrenching pulse of an R&B tune wailing beneath the din of voices.

Max turned, instantly sensing his approach.

Savoie wasn't like him. He was a Shifter, but he was more. There'd never been a question about that. Sleek, impossibly quick in body and mind, he had a deadly edge to him that commanded attention and respect. No longer content to hide with them in shadows, he moved boldly through the Upright world and fearlessly within their own.

At first, Jacques had been cautious but Max had won him over with his bright vision for the clan, making him want to believe, fueling his confidence, daring him to reach for a future he'd only imagined.

Then Savoie's entanglement in the human realm brought devastation into theirs, not just with the destruction of the Towers but of their hope that they'd have that *more* Savoie promised. More of the same was all Jacques was seeing now. And that sorely shook his desire to have faith.

"Where you been hiding yourself, Savoie?"

A noncommital smile. "In plain sight. I got your message. What's going on?"

No invitation to join him at the table. He shouldn't have needed one, but tonight Jacques wanted one. He needed to feel like a valued friend instead of a hired crew chief delivering a report on the status quo. And to add to the perceived insult, Max's attention wasn't on him, it was a room away on the tall figure making a direct approach toward the table.

Silas MacCreedy was a puzzling enigma, crossing the lines between human and Shifter in his role as NOPD detective and Max's emissary to the outside clans. His intelligence, business acumen, and cool ability to make things happen earned him the suddenly vacant spot at Max's side. Francis Petitjohn, Max's human nemesis, had disappeared from that position at Legere Enterprises International, the extensive and legally ambiguous conglomerate Max had inherited from his former mentor/employer, and word was, he wouldn't be returning.

Jacques liked MacCreedy well enough and found him to be a reliable straight shooter who happened to be bonded to his best waitress, but that didn't keep him from feeling resentful of his sudden rise in importance within their tight community.

"Max, I've got those papers you wanted to look over." MacCreedy dropped into a chair and glanced up to favor Jacques with an acknowledging nod that was stiffly returned.

Max took the folder Silas pushed toward him with an undisguised eagerness to get into it. He tore his focus from whatever intrigues it held to look back up at Jacques with only the tiniest edge of impatience, just enough to put up a wall between them.

"Sorry. You were saying?"

He was saying nothing Savoie wanted to hear.

Jacques gave a dismissing wave. "Nothing. It's been taken care of. You don't need to worry about it."

Max's brow furrowed. "You sure?"

Something as small as an invitation to join them would have scattered all hard feelings. But the two of them with their folder full of LEI business just looked up at him through tolerant expressions, waiting for him to speak his business and leave so they could return to theirs.

Jacques smiled. "Yeah, I'm sure." And with a nod, he turned and walked away.

Susanna set her bag down next to the computer. She'd let herself in the back door using the numeric code she'd been given and had slipped into the empty office without turning on the overhead lights. With the sound system turned off and the door left ajar, she could hear the echoing voices from the remaining staff on the floor below. Two of the waitresses were cashing out their drawers and she could see Jacques behind the bar polishing the taps as he polished off the rest of his bottled beer.

"All balanced, boss," the brunette with the gravity-defying chest called. "Busy night. I've got enough tip money here to retire . . . until my shift starts tomorrow."

A big, booming laugh sounded as Jacques turned off the lights and came out on the floor to join them. "I'll walk you ladies out," he offered, draping his beefy arms about their shoulders to steer them toward the steps.

Even knowing they couldn't see her, Susanna took a cautious step back from the window.

She could hear them right outside the door. The buxom one blurted, "I forgot my keys," and darted back down to the servers' galley. That's when her blonde counterpart made her move.

"The night's still young, boss. I've a case of cold ones in the fridge and clean sheets on the bed just in case I get lucky. Wanna see if some of that luck will rub off?"

"I thought your roommate was back on days? Wouldn't want to wake her up."

"Oh, trust me. She wouldn't mind at all. Three's a partaay."

A playful chuckle. "I'm too old for that shit, Jen."

"What? Since when? Last weekend? I didn't hear you complaining then."

"Good night, Jennifer."

A loud, juicy-sounding kiss. "If you change your mind . . ."

A tolerant chuckle this time. "Be careful out there."

"Where's the fun in that? Night, Amber."

"Night, Jen."

The outside door opened and closed.

After a long silence, she heard Amber ask, "You okay?"

"Sure. Why wouldn't I be?"

"I don't know. Looks like you got a case of the blues. That why you turned down the case of cold ones?"

Jacques laughed. "That's not what Jen had a case of, darlin'."

An amused chuckle was followed by Amber's own more subtle overture. "Why don't you stop over on your way home and I'll fix you up a bowl of gumbo, and if you feel like talking, I'll listen."

"Thanks, but I'm not much in the talking mood."

"You can just sit and not say anything. That'd be fine, too."

"I'm fine with my own company tonight. Another time."

"You need someone to take care of you, Jacques."

"You volunteering to be my mama, *chere*? Git on outta here so I can lock up."

A laugh followed by a contented sigh. "A girl could do worse, you know."

"And a hell of a lot better. G'night. Give your little *bebe* a kiss for me."

"So you can break her heart, too? See you tomorrow night. Don't stay too late."

"Yes, Mama."

Susanna was quick to turn her back to the door but she could still see his reflection in the glass. He filled the door frame, head lowered, broad shoulders slumped, then moved by a tremendous breath. He looked up, studying her for a long minute, features in shadow.

Did he hate so much that she was there?

When she turned to regard him, his blatant masculinity hit her like an El train. In Chicago, he'd been a sanitized version of this hulking, primal male. He'd added mass to his upper body, showcasing that new dimension with his sleeves rolled up and his white shirt only partially buttoned to display a gleaming acre of muscle. There was a different attitude, as well: tough, cocky, a bit reckless, yet still with that cautious caginess. She envied the females who'd felt free to put their hands on him, hoping that pang wasn't evident when she said, "You have a very attentive staff."

"They're nice girls. We all take care of each other here. Something I don't expect you to understand. Your kind frowns on the baser needs like companionship or affection."

Oh, she understood just fine, aching for a little of either from him at that moment. But of course she'd made that impossible. No use crying about it now. Her words came out purposefully tart. "I'm almost set up here. You don't need to stay any longer. Your gumbo is getting cold."

He chuckled and stepped into the room. "If you were an ordinary female, I'd say I heard a bite of bitchiness in that remark. But you don't stoop to spite, do you?"

Her heart clenched in a sad little spasm at his hard summation. "No. Of course not."

Instead of leaving, Jacques crossed over to one of the couches, dropping onto it with a groan, pushing his long legs out in front of him and arms overhead in a leisurely, devastatingly sensual stretch.

"No, really," she emphasized. "You don't have to stay."

"I think maybe I do."

"Afraid I'll crack your security and steal your famous bar mix recipe?"

He showed his teeth in a strong flash of white, then grew sober. "Afraid my overzealous friend might stop in, find you here alone, and put a no-questions-asked end to you."

"We wouldn't want *that* on your conscience," she drawled.

"*That* wouldn't be," he brutally clarified. "I made a promise to keep you safe and I will. Failing to keep my word to a friend *would* bother me."

"Thank you for your honesty."

"No problem." He bent to unlace his chunky work boots. For a moment, she was fascinated by the play of muscles across his back and shoulders as he said, "You won't even know I'm here."

Susanna turned back to her computer screen, her insides tightening at the sound of creaking leather as he lay down on the cushions.

Yeah, right.

Five

Despite his intention to remain alert, Jacques slept like the dead, waking to the heavy lethargy of undisturbed rest.

"What time's it?"

Susanna still sat at the computer, her back to him as she wiped at her eyes and answered in a gruff voice, "Eight fifteen."

Jacques sat up, brows lowering as he looked from the light blanket draped over him to the woman making an effort to hide her face. "What's wrong?"

Her shoulders stiffened. "Nothing. Just tired." She pulled in a shaky breath. "Eye strain from the smoke."

Knowing his office had excellent filtration, Jacques kept his doubts to himself. She'd been crying. If she wanted to hide that fact from him, he wouldn't call her on it. He'd signed on to provide safety and shelter, not an empathetic shoulder.

Still, a female's tears always made him anxious and guilty, as if he'd somehow failed to protect her from her distress. He didn't know what she had to cry about any more than he knew why she'd dropped that blanket over him, and considering either thing too deeply could only lead to problems. So he said nothing as he reached for his boots.

"I've got to get to work. You're staying at Mac-Creedy's place, right? I'll drop you off."

Her gaze jumped to him. *Eye strain, my ass*. There was no way to disguise the swollen redness of weeping eyes.

"You don't need to do that. I've got more to finish up here."

"Shut it down, doc. Time to go."

He couldn't miss her scowl of displeasure. Probably wasn't used to an inferior species telling her what to do. Well, this inferior needed to get to work and wasn't about to let her wander through the Quarter lugging her heavy bag of scientific tricks. Not on his watch.

Jacques gave a limbering stretch, pausing when he heard her sharp inhalation. He chuckled to himself. She wasn't intimidated by him, but she wasn't as indifferent to him as she pretended.

To provoke her genteel sensibilities, he stripped off his rumpled shirt and crossed, bare-chested, to his credenza, pulling open the drawer where he kept a stack of clean T-shirts. He tugged one over his head, then turned, thinking to catch her leering.

She was busy moving data to her flash drive, a high flush of color in her cheeks.

So, the sterile Chosen scientist got all flustered ogling him. Shame on her. The notion made him smile.

Susanna stood and turned toward him, her lowered eyes directed at his feet. Slowly, that gaze lifted, pausing at his thighs, at his inseam, making a leisurely slide up his torso to linger on his mouth. And surprisingly, his internal temperature rose along with that appraisal.

When her gaze finally connected with his own, what he saw burning in the dark intensity of her stare wasn't lust or curiosity or distaste. It was something else, something so fierce and possessing, he took an awkward step back, nerves rattling like window blinds in a sudden gust of wind.

Then, in a blink, the clinical coolness returned and she reached down for the bag on the floor by her chair.

"I'll get that for you," he quickly offered.

He moved closer, bending to pick up the bulky shoulder bag. She froze as he straightened, his arm grazing hers, his nose brushing past her hair for a deep inhalation.

Jacques's senses swam with the perfume of her scent. Its seductive familiarity knotted him up into a hard ache of longing and desire he couldn't begin to understand. But he knew it. He'd felt the strange, torturous pleasure, the hot, mindless euphoria years ago, back before his memories began. Again, his instinct remembered what his mind could not.

Want. Need. Craving so sharp it razored through his gut, then his groin, in swift, brutal strokes.

For this woman? This *Chosen* female? He reared back in denial. No, never. He knew their kind; he despised her type. Cruel, cold, and condescending. Users, takers, never givers.

But he knew that was wrong. One of them hadn't been that way. The one he'd loved. The one who'd accepted what he was enough to let him claim her. The one he'd lost.

He turned away, agitated by the feelings this foreign female stirred inside him, and growled, "Let's go."

She followed without a word. He would have believed she hadn't noticed his reaction to her if she didn't go out of her way to stay an arm's length from him. He smiled ruefully.

Well, at least she wasn't crying.

Jacques slid a glance at his passenger as he negotiated the narrow streets of the Quarter.

He'd expected her to peer down her dainty nose at the condition of his ride but she'd smiled at the sight of his slightly listing old Cadillac, raising her brows at the big dents on the roof and hood where metal had buckled under the impact of weights dropped from high above, his own being one of them. Even now, as she sat beside him, her fingertips caressed the leather dash and sent the chunky green, purple, and gold Mardi Gras beads hanging from his crooked rearview mirror swinging so that they glinted in the early morning sunlight. He tensed as if feeling that touch personally.

As he accelerated from a stop, the huge boat of a vehicle shuddered and coughed. "C'mon, Louise," he muttered. "Don't get temperamental just 'cuz we've got company."

"Louise?"

He glanced at Susanna, then patted the steering wheel affectionately. "We've been together for over five years. My longest relationship with a female. Probably 'cuz she's older, more reliable, and appreciates my attention."

"Not like the younger, faster models who are all show and no go."

He grinned. "Something like that."

She flipped through the stack of cassette tapes strewn on the seat between them. "Hmmm. Muddy Waters, Metallica, and Mozart. An interesting cross section."

"And those are just the *M*'s."

Jacques was still smiling slightly as he rounded the next corner and cozied up to the curb in front of Mac-Creedy's building. He cut the engine and hopped out, trotting around the back of the vehicle to open the passenger door. She gazed up at him, vaguely surprised by the gesture.

"What? I have manners. Just choosy about when I use them." He put down his hand and after a slight pause, she slipped hers into it, letting him lift her out of the low seat. When he opened his fingers to release her, hers traced over his palm and thumb.

"You have nice hands," she mused in a tone as soothing as her touch. "Strong, warm, gentle."

He jerked away, making a fist. "Don't forget rough and thick-skinned." Angry over how easily she unsettled him, Jacques reached through the open rear window to haul out her massive leather bag that doubled as purse and briefcase. "I think you can manage this from here." He let it drop to the sidewalk, then was quick to put the width of the Caddy between them. He'd opened the door when she called his name.

"Jacques?"

He cast a fierce look her way, then found his gaze caught by hers. Such soft, melting eyes.

"Thank you."

Simple words, sincerely offered, shuddered through him like the delight of her pleasing scent.

He got in the car without registering a response, slamming the door with unnecessary force, before tromping on Louise's accelerator, leaving Susanna at the curb with her polite intentions wreathed in a sputter of exhaust fumes.

Susanna had managed a full six hours of deep, dreamless sleep when an insistent knocking woke her. After peering through the peephole, she opened the door to let Nica breeze in.

"I'm here to take you shopping."

Susanna just stared after her blankly as she disappeared into the kitchen.

"I'll make you coffee while you get dressed."

"Shopping? For what?"

But Nica, who was rattling around in the cupboards, didn't answer.

With a weary and perplexed sigh, Susanna shuffled back into the borrowed bedroom where she was still living out of her open suitcase. She hadn't gotten enough rest, and fatigue hung as heavily upon her shoulders as her guilt. It had taken only a few brief minutes talking to her daughter that morning to shake all her best intentions.

She missed the little girl with an intensity none of her own kind would understand. She yearned for the morning routine they shared; brushing teeth, getting dressed, talking about the day to come. She longed for the soft scent of her child's hair, for the delicate feel of her in her arms, for the unconditional love found in her hugs and kisses. They'd never been apart except for that terrifying week of forced separation, until Nica had returned her. After that, it was a daily agony to let her out of her sight even to attend her classes.

She didn't doubt that Damien was taking dutiful care of her. He would see to all the necessities, perhaps even fill in for her during their nightly reading from *The Lion, the Witch and the Wardrobe*. And perhaps that time alone, just the two of them, would foster a bond like the one he could never quite understand that existed between mother and daughter. That bond her own kind saw as unnatural.

Moody and a bit melancholy, she followed the corrosive scent of scorched caffeine into the living room where Nica was waiting with her cup and a raised brow. Her gaze ran from neck to toe as she shook her head.

"That's why we're shopping."

At the cryptic reply, Susanna glanced down at the beige silk blouse and matching tailored slacks she was wearing. "I don't understand. What's wrong with what I'm wearing?"

"Nothing if you live in that world of expensive bland up north. Jacques spotted you right away and the others will, too. You need to look a little less Lake Shore Drive and a little more N'awlins, if you know what I mean."

She did, and was angry at herself for not seeing it sooner. Her world was one of neutral shades all blending together into pale sameness. Everything in her wardrobe was built from that same palette of white, cream, and beige without the slightest shock of color, as if the life had been bled out of it. Of course she would stand out against the gaudy backdrop of the Crescent City, as glaringly as cultured pearls next to colorful shiny beads.

"I'm sorry. I didn't think."

"Don't feel bad," Nica soothed. "I made my living learning how to become invisible. You want to look like you fit in, like you belong, not like you're the cream rising to the top. I suppose that's your favorite color."

Susanna took the mug she was offered and took a sip without making a face before she swallowed. "No. Actually it's red."

"Then let's go paint the town red."

Susanna had never shopped. All her purchases were done electronically. She'd never experienced the sensory overload of styles and color and texture, the feel of different fabrics brushing against her skin, the adventure of seeing herself portrayed in an entirely new light. It was like being reborn.

Nica dragged her into large chain stores in the Canal Street mall for the basics, then through dozens of small boutiques on Chartres and Royal for just the right finishing touches.

At first, Susanna balked at the startling suggestions but once she'd timidly tried them on and had gotten over the shock of viewing her transformation in progress, she plunged into the idea of making over Dr. Duchamps, Chosen scientist, into Susanna, a sensuous female stretching like a rainbow above the Quarter.

The colors dazzled her. Peacock blue, emerald green, electric teal, hot fuchsia, a sunrise of orange and yellow. And reds, from daring scarlet to rich claret. Warm, bright, vibrant hues, making her feel alive—and free. Free to express all the emotions bursting inside her.

And Nica was far too astute not to notice.

They sat at a café table on high stools at Antoine's Hermes Bar, surrounded by piles of packages, dining on Kobe beef po'boys and airy potato puffs. Susanna's attention was pulled between watching those who strolled by the open doors, and watching her own reflection in the massive ornate mirror behind the bar. She looked like one of them, seated in her skinny jeans and strappy shoes, wearing a snug bloodred T-shirt with a spangly scarf draped about her neck to fill the plunging V of her neckline. In a quick dash through a hair salon, her severe cut had been softened by layers, shot through with highlights, and given a dash of attitude with spiky bangs. Instead of her usually perfect finish, her makeup was more natural, with a dusting of color across her cheeks, accented by liner and shadow that played up her eyes to almost anime proportions. She looked relaxed . . . alive. And she felt wonderful.

"He won't be able to ignore you now."

Nica's comment came out of the blue.

"Who?"

Her companion chuckled. "Who, indeed. Who have

you been fixated on since you got here? You're stripping him with your eyes every time he's in the same room."

Susanna's jaw dropped.

Nica simply laughed at her expression as she chased the ice about her glass with her straw. "I certainly don't blame you. He's an eyeful. If you're considering a walk on the wild side, he's the path I'd recommend."

"I'm not—he's not—I never—" Susanna grabbed for her glass and took several quick gulps to cool the fire of embarrassment and sudden panicked arousal.

"If you never, maybe you should," was Nica's calm advice.

Susanna gripped her glass with both hands to keep them from shaking as she said, "I have a mate already," as if that would put an end to Nica's scandalous suggestion.

Nica made a rude sound. "Mate. Pffft. You mean companion. Someone a computer picked for you for the purpose of breeding and compatibility. I've met him, remember. I can't exactly picture him ripping off your beige separates to throw you down on the rug for some good, sweaty, screaming sex."

Susanna went as red as her new shirt, then pale. "He's very good to me and to my daughter."

"My man is good to me, too. He makes coffee in the morning, picks up his towels in the bathroom, doesn't drink out of the milk carton. He makes the perfect roommate, but that's not what makes him the perfect mate. He wants me. All the time, anytime."

Susanna swallowed hard, thinking she should pro-

test the intimacy of the conversation, but too fascinated to stop it.

"I'll come home from a hard day and he'll have a
glass of wine ready and massage my feet. He's got the
most unbelievable hands. We'll be arguing over some
little thing like folding my shirts with the design on
the inside and the next thing you know, we'll be naked
on the floor panting like animals. Just thinking about
him makes me so hot I can barely sit still. All the time,
anytime. We touch, we snuggle, we have sex, we make
love, we fuck each other's brains out. Is that what you
do with your mate?"

Susanna's silence was her answer.

"Yeah, that's what I figured. Nothing says inani-
mate like a Chosen male. You might as well live with a
very nice looking piece of furniture that's not really all
that comfortable."

"I didn't come to New Orleans to have sex with
someone other than the one I share my life with."

"Is that what you're sharing with him? I rather
doubt that. Don't sit there looking all nervous and
tell me that since you walked into *Cheveux du Chien*
your blood hasn't been boiling over imagining what
it would be like to get naked with Jacques LaRoche."

Susanna couldn't deny it. And she didn't have to
imagine what it would be like.

She knew. That was the problem.

But the fact was obvious. "He despises me."

"What you are, definitely, but not who you are.
He's got eyes and they're all over you."

"They're all over every female, from what I've observed," was Susanna's dry comment.

"He's a very healthy male animal without any ties. The perfect physical partner."

"Why not?" Susanna ventured carefully.

"Why not what?"

"Why no commitment to any of them?"

"He's not just a casual player, if that's what you're asking. There was someone in his past from what Amber told me."

Amber, the busty brunette with the foreplay gumbo. A reliable source.

Nica frowned slightly. "He doesn't talk about her, or about his past, but from what I hear, he was mated to some female up north and never got over her."

"What happened to her?"

"I don't know, but she sure ruined him for anyone else. The heartless bitch. If I ever find her, I'll make sure she regrets tossing him away."

That bit of savagery made Susanna shiver. A threat Nica had already made good on without even knowing it.

Then the former assassin smiled. "You could be just what he needs."

A cynical smile in return. "Another female from up north to use him and dump him? That's not what this doctor would order."

"He's a guy. He'd enjoy the using as long as it's mutual. And he'd enjoy the company of someone with an IQ in the triple digits. You'd both know it was a temporary thing so there'd be no expectations, no hurt feelings. It's not like you'd be falling in love."

No, of course not. An exquisite pain shot through Susanna's heart. She'd already taken that dangerous tumble.

"So, your recommendation is that I just walk up to him and say, 'Let's do it'?"

Nica laughed and finished her drink. "I think you should put yourself in front of him and let nature take its course."

Put yourself in front of him.

Not a good idea. Not at all a good idea.

Susanna sat at the keyboard in the empty club office, the data on the screen not as compelling as the muscular male behind the bar below. She watched him grin and laugh as he interacted with his customers and staff. He didn't seem particularly heartbroken.

She knew part of the problem was in her own nature. As a scientist, she weighed everything out to the microscopic detail and consequence until the question became clinical study. But in this case, she found it difficult to separate her feelings from the equation.

What were the pros and cons of an uncomplicated fling with Jacques LaRoche?

Sex would relieve the tension between them, but it was far from uncomplicated. She'd longed for the pleasure of his touch, had dreamed of feeling those sensations, those rewards again, but would rekindling that passion invite dangers that rendered the risk unwise?

Would their union awaken memories buried in Jacques's subconscious?

And after experiencing the thrill, could she find the strength to leave him once again?

Though Nica was right on target in her assessment of Damien, it didn't lessen Susanna's obligation to be loyal. He'd singled her out for his personal attention, to mentor her studies and groom a quick path for her career. He'd protected her interests and her reputation. He'd stood by her without judgment, without demands, when any other male of their species would have condemned her. She was treated with respect and kindness and given latitude in her pursuits. After all he'd done for her, could she betray him with the reckless release of emotions he feared and despised?

Yet how could she be so near her every desire, her every dream, and not risk all for just a taste, just a reminder to last the rest of her lifetime? Could she ever forgive herself if she let that moment pass?

Damien Frost held her allegiance but Jacques LaRoche owned her heart and soul. She'd given both to him, freely, gladly, without reservation or regret when young and foolish. But even now, when older and hopefully wiser, she couldn't take them back. He would hold them forever.

So which would rule her, conscience or emotion?

"How are things going?"

Charlotte's intruding question had her nearly jumping out of her new shoes. Covering up her guilt with a smile of greeting, she turned to the detective who'd entered the room without her noticing.

"I've gotten a lot of information from the new samples but that's as far as I can go without an actual lab."

"Field trip time. Grab your stuff."

Medical examiner Devlin Dovion saw nothing strange in receiving company at two A.M. in the bowels of the hospital. A big man with a mass of curly hair that had begun to slide from the top of his head to gather at his ears and shoulders, he greeted the police detective fondly and her with a shrewd interest.

"Busy night, Dev?"

"What can I tell you, Lottie? You're sending too much work my way." He peeled the glove from his right hand to extend it to Susanna. "I'm Dev Dovion. To what do I owe the pleasure?"

"Susanna is my OB. She has some experience in the, um, particulars of my situation."

Dovion's brows lifted as he studied her. "Interesting. A friend of Max's?"

"Not exactly. Let's say the other side of that same coin."

From the cryptic dialogue, Susanna learned two things. Dev Dovion was to be trusted, and he knew about the Shifter presence in New Orleans along with something of their politics.

"She needs access to a lab and I told her you might be able to help."

"I see." His sudden caution said he did, indeed. "And what type of materials would you need processed, doctor?"

"Genetic, mainly."

His brows hiked even higher at her reply.

"I'm having Mary Kate moved back here from California, Dev, and placed in a private care facility," Charlotte abruptly told him. "Susanna's going to begin an experimental line of treatment she believes can reverse some of the physical and mental damage."

Dovion was quick. "The way Max brought you back." When he noticed Susanna's puzzlement, he explained, "Our fearless detective here tangled with some of your kind and ended up in the ICU with her bones and internal organs mashed like Sunday's sweet potatoes. We were getting ready to administer last rites and pull the plug when she made a miraculous recovery. An inexplicable recovery. Is that what you have in mind with Mary Kate?"

Neither woman answered.

To Susanna, he said, "You know she's human, don't you? A nun. That she was burned over eighty percent of her body and still has a bullet lodged in her brain?"

No, not precisely those details, but she did now.

To Charlotte, he added, "And you have her permission to conduct these *treatments* that she might consider out of the moral ballpark?"

"She's my best friend, Dev," Charlotte answered mulishly. "She's there in that damned storage facility because of me. Because of me and Max. What am I supposed to do? Just let her die? You think it's a better moral choice to let her go to hell? Because that's what she believes. Dying by your own hand is suicide. I'm willing to risk her annoyance rather than her soul."

But maybe he wasn't. That was what Susanna read in the impasse that followed.

Just because you can doesn't mean you should. A doctor's constant dilemma.

"And what does Max think about all this?" Dovion challenged.

Charlotte's eyes narrowed. "He'll agree with me . . . when I tell him."

"Will he?" Dev challenged.

Charlotte's jaw squared and rose with an arrogant tilt. "Yes."

She was good, Susanna mused, using fierceness to conceal her uncertainty.

Under other circumstances, that might have been her cue to take a cautious step back. In her tenuous position as an outsider, the last thing she needed was to run afoul of the leader of the New Orleans Shifter clan in a spat with his not-quite-human mate. But Charlotte's covert agenda, as intriguing as it might be, wasn't the one compelling her to set aside her reservations.

She needed this opportunity for study. Desperately. And so, she remained silent, suppressing her misgivings regarding what they were about to do.

Dovion finally broke the silence, heaving a big sigh and throwing his hands wide. "All right, Charlotte. You know there's little I can refuse you. Let's give your friend a tour and lay down a few ground rules. Rules not even you will be allowed to break."

"Whatever you say, Dev."

———

Susanna keyed in the entry code on the rear door of the club, her mind still racing with probabilities and pathways for her research.

Though far from the sophistication she was used to, Dovion's lab facilities were adequate, and what he didn't have on site, he had access to. Reluctantly, he'd helped Charlotte create an identity for her, linking Susanna to an ongoing case so she'd have full run of the technology and testing she required, putting his own career on the line in doing so. If she had someone with his loyalty and dedication at her facility up north, how much smoother her studies would go.

Here, with free rein, she'd have the opportunity, if not the time, to explore her hypotheses, and perhaps discover the breakthrough she knew in her heart was there just beyond the reach of her next idea.

She couldn't wait to get started.

The club's interior was pitch-black and quiet as she hurried down the hall toward the open office door. A faint light shown within from the recessed fixtures she'd left dialed low. It was five A.M. She'd have only a few hours to set up the appropriate protocols and was anxious to boot up and begin. As she crossed to the big desk, the overhead fluorescents flashed on, momentarily blinding her like a lightning strike, as a startling thunder boomed behind her.

"Where the hell have you been?"

Six

The sight of Jacques LaRoche blown up into a temper rooted Susanna to the spot.

He was magnificent in his fury, brows lowered storm clouds over the now iridescent blue of his eyes, nostrils flaring like something wild and dangerous scenting a fight . . . or a female. His posture was all aggressive male, leaning in to intimidate, squared up to accentuate his impressive dimensions. In a moment, he'd be beating his chest and letting out a conquering roar.

And Susanna had had enough.

She'd been bullied and threatened and submissive for the last time. Fisted hands on her hips, she drew herself up with the added inches of her new shoes to a puny five foot four, placing her level with his sternum.

"Who do you think you are, taking that tone with me?" she snapped with the fierceness of a terrier attacking a Rottweiler.

If anything, her retaliation only fueled his anger. "I'll take any tone I please. This is *my* place and you are a less than invited guest here. Where have you been?"

It registered in the back of her mind that he'd been worried by her absence, but she couldn't get past the arrogance of that snarling masculine entitlement.

"I don't have to check my schedule with you," she countered. "I'm using your computer. That doesn't make you my babysitter or master."

"When you're supposed to be here and you decide to be elsewhere, you *will* check with me. You're my responsibility," he growled, "whether I want it or not."

And he didn't want it, or her. That truth was a hurtful jab but still her pride rallied. "You don't owe me anything. I don't want your sense of obligation hanging on me like chains. I've had all of that I can tolerate. Now let me do the work I came here to do." In her frustration, she put her hands flat on his chest and shoved. Set like a mountain, he didn't budge.

Huge hands curled about her wrists, startling a jump in her pulse. Suddenly, his hot gaze dropped, sweeping her from top to toe like the spotlight on a police cruiser. His deep voice became a gruff rumble. "What have you done to yourself?"

Uncertain whether his tone implied approval or disgust, Susanna rebelled against it. "Nothing for the likes of you."

His features flushed with angry insult and a more uncontrollable emotion she feared and conversely hoped was desire. The sudden darkening of his eyes warned he'd been pushed beyond his limit, too, as he yanked her up against the unyielding wall of his body.

The contact shocked both of them into a moment's pause. With the breath panting from them, their gazes held and searched in a confusion of helpless attraction and dismay. And then Jacques bent inexorably down to her in a measured move that she could have avoided if she chose to. She didn't choose to. She waited, her heart sighing urgently, *Oh, yes. At last.*

His kiss was a pure glimpse of heaven, forceful at first because she'd stirred his passions into a frenzy, yet quickly softening to a yearning so sweet she ached to the soul in response. The familiar cushion of his full lips intensified by the prickly outline of facial stubble had her lost in a delirious haze. Nothing had ever felt so strong, so right as the emotions crowding up inside her.

Before she could wake herself to take action, to touch him, hold him, to respond to the hunger surging through him into her, Jacques abruptly jumped away to regard her through wide, stricken eyes.

Susanna lifted a shaking hand to her mouth, not to scrub away the taste of him but to marvel at the delicious bruising of her lips. She couldn't catch her breath. How had she existed for so long without this crazy zing of feelings, her skin tingling, her blood hot and heavy, need pooling damply at the apex of her thighs? Her body cried out for more, but one look at his frozen features told her nothing else would be forthcoming, except what she didn't want to hear.

"I'm sorry," he whispered, apparently devastated by his lack of control as she stared blankly up at him, trembling in what he had to assume was a trauma of shock. "I never . . . I would never . . . I don't know what happened."

She made her words necessarily cold and concise. "You overstepped yourself, Mr. LaRoche, and it *will* not happen again." Her conscience writhed as she watched him assemble his scattered thoughts behind a self-preserving wall.

"Don't worry, Dr. Duchamps. I'm not the kind of guy who has to force himself on females."

"I'm sure you're not. You have them trailing behind you throwing beer and gumbo in your path." He almost started to smile but she couldn't allow him even that little bit of relief. "I am not one of those females. I have a mate and a child waiting for me at my home in Chicago. I have no interest in the kind of dalliance you might offer."

Finally, umbrage overtook all other emotions as he told her with a prideful stiffening, "You have no idea what I might have to offer and I'm not about to enlighten you." Then he surprised her again with his sudden gruff admission. "I would never do anything to disrespect you or your family. Again, I apologize."

Her mood and tone thawed despite her intention of keeping him at arm's length. "Accepted. I'm here to work and I appreciate the offer of your facilities. In return, I'll do you the courtesy of letting you know when I'll be here and when I won't be so you won't feel obligated to worry."

He gave a brief nod and after a few awkward steps

back, turned to escape his office without further comment, shutting the door behind him.

Jacques threw open the hinged pass-through at the end of the bar, gratified by the sudden startling noise it made as it slammed against the counter. The jarring sound echoed through the empty cathedral of his new life and through his equally shadowy soul.

What the hell is wrong with me?

He stopped before the small sink and twisted the cold tap, filling unsteady hands and splashing his face with the bracing chill. It failed to cool an overheated body or his wildly inappropriate thoughts.

He refused to glance up toward the dark blank of his office window where she was probably still shivering in dread and disgust. Because he was exactly what she feared.

A rude brute. An unmannered beast. An untamed animal. Growling, grabbing at what wasn't his to take or desire. A primal, inferior species unable to harness his carnal needs.

Jacques started to reach for one of the jewel-like bottles stacked in tempting rows, but let his hand drop away. He stared at the face in the mirror behind them that had been that of a stranger when he'd first seen it seven years ago. He'd had no idea who those features belonged to before that moment. He could have been anything, anyone. What he'd become had been born in that instant of nonrecognition.

What he did know was that he'd belonged to them,

to those pitiless users in the North, who'd obviously trained him to serve their capricious whims. The scar between his shoulder blades told him that much. Had he pleasured their females? Had he hunted and killed his own kind the way the Tracker who'd died in the hallway had? Had he been a mindless drone who went about their business with a blind obedience? Was he so conditioned to their commands that he had no self-control even now?

Had the riotous emotions spiraling through him been programmed to be there to protect their kind from his natural impulses?

Resentment simmered as he paced, movements dangerously predatory even as his thoughts panted in raw confusion.

Why can't I get a grip? This isn't me. This isn't what I've made of myself. Why am I letting her get to me? She's one of theirs, not one of mine. She belongs to one of them, not to me. Not to me.

So why was every primal pulse of his blood denying that fact?

There was no explanation for the way his heart had stumbled when he'd looked into his office and discovered her gone. Instantly his mind had blanked with alarm and self-blame, thinking some harm had come to her. That crippling wave of fear had almost taken him to his knees. The response came from no place he recognized, but he'd been there before. When he'd seen that Tracker place a gun to her head.

He would never stand for injury to come to any

female, to anyone weaker or defenseless. Not in his place, not on his job site, not in his presence. He just wouldn't tolerate it. But these instincts, so overprotective and nearly pathological where Susanna Duchamps was concerned, defied logic or understanding.

So he stalked behind the bar, circling from one end to the other and back again, like a wild thing in a cage, trying to outdistance the emotions churning through him. He was still shaking inside, all his senses in a heightened state pumping raw adrenaline like a crude oil leak. The need for violent action spiked, fever hot, because sex was out of the question.

Sex was what he wanted. Sex with that maddeningly irresistible female cowering in his office. The taste of her burned through his blood like grain alcohol, frying his thought process, enflaming his lust. He'd felt her heartbeat leap beneath the press of his fingertips, and for a moment had believed it was spurred by an answering passion.

He would have taken her right there on the floor with the slightest encouragement, without a thought to who she was, what she was, or who she belonged to, so lost to mating madness nothing mattered but finding a way inside her as quickly as possible.

Madness. No other way to describe it.

You'd think he was a rutting youth sniffing out his first female.

You'd think he'd discovered his one and only all over again.

But the fragile Chosen doctor was not his chosen mate despite what his pounding desires told him. He'd lost that treasured female when his memories were torn from him, her fate unknown to him. He'd lost his right to be content. He'd failed her and he couldn't go forward because there was no going back to right whatever terrible mistake he'd made that had erased her from his future. There was only here and now and at the moment, he couldn't bear the bleakness of that knowledge.

Jacques pulled a bottle from the neat lineup, carrying it without the civility of a glass to a table where he could drink without being seen through the one-way office window. The first long swallow was as harsh as his mood, burning his throat, wetting his eyes. After that, like his situation, it lost the power to hurt him.

Susanna gave up on trying to work. Her thoughts were fragmented; her emotions, rarely tested or tried, were in a knot. Fatigue and sorrow twisted about the sense of blame that refused to let her alone.

She'd done the right thing. Seven years ago, she'd done the only thing she could to save them all. There'd been no other choice, no options, and if she hadn't let him go, instead of pacing the floor in an agony of frustration, he'd be dead. That simple.

But knowing that truth didn't lessen her pain.

She couldn't destroy him with the knowledge that had her heart breaking.

Damien Frost wasn't her bonded mate. He was.

Tears burned in her eyes as she watched his restless movements, knowing he struggled against feelings he couldn't understand. His desire for her wasn't natural, not like the earthy affection he had for his female staff, yet it couldn't be broken by distance or anger or the drink he finally reached for. Its power couldn't be explained, rejected, or denied. She knew. She felt it, too.

She could still taste him, feel him, smell him. Wanting him growled through her like a hungry beast, terrifying in its strength, devastating in its potential.

And it would only get more difficult.

She had family; he had a life here. Their politics, their pursuits, their physiology, none of them were compatible. There was no hope for a future, no solution now, any more than there had been then. She'd been wrong to think so once, but she'd been young and giddy with passion. Now, she had no excuse, only a sad sense of culpability as she watched him find solace in alcohol-drenched dreams.

Resigned, she shut down the computer, unable to endure another minute of the self-destructive torture. But she did leave a note, printing neatly on a cocktail napkin, "Have gone home. S," tucking it gingerly beneath the motionless stretch of his fingers. So he wouldn't worry. It took every ounce of her willpower not to touch that still hand or stubbled cheek.

The misty new dawn air felt good against her skin as she walked the quiet streets. The exercise freed her from the tension twining through her. She'd ask Nica to return the foolish purchases she'd made and to find her another place to work, one without dangers or distractions. She'd concentrate on her research and let Jacques LaRoche get back to his gumbo. She couldn't afford to put herself in his way again lest both their wills give way.

She hadn't come to New Orleans to relive an ill-fated past. She'd come to guarantee a future for the child she loved more than herself.

As she moved along the uneven sidewalks, Susanna's focus returned with a renewed purpose. Her thoughts stepped free of miring emotions in pursuit of scientific avenues. As she climbed the stairs to her borrowed apartment, she was busy formulating the direction of her next twofold study to restore life in one and protect life in another. First she'd attend to her body's need for sleep, then she'd be ready to attack her work with new vigor.

Using the key Nica had given her, she unlocked the door and stepped into the dark living area. Just enough light filtered through from the large windows on either end of the narrow shotgun apartment for her to find her way over to the café-sized table to place her satchel on the floor. She gave a slow stretch to release the tension in her shoulders.

That's when her weary gaze caught on the glitter of broken glass on the floor beneath the windowsill.

Something moved behind her, a shift of shadows without sound.

Before Susanna could turn, a rough hand clamped over her mouth, effectively stifling her scream.

The scent of coffee cut through the heavy fog of Jacques's dreams. Probably the same way it would eat through the table if spilled.

Nica couldn't have made worse coffee if she used kerosene instead of water.

He slit open his eyes to see the sturdy ceramic cup next to his nose resting at an odd angle, then realized his head was lying on the tabletop. Beyond the mug, he could see the fuzzy outline of a nearly empty bottle of bourbon. If he poured the remainder into the cup, would it improve the taste?

He tried to sit up. Bad idea. With an anguished moan, he gave up on the attempt.

A light kiss brushed his throbbing temple, followed by the plop of a cold bar rag.

"Morning, boss."

"Don't yell," he groaned.

Nica's chuckle danced behind his closed eyes like shards of chipped ice.

"Want me to see if I can find a bendy straw so you can sip your coffee without moving your head?"

"That would be nice. Thank you." He let himself drift in that dark, quiet world on the inside of his eyelids for a moment, then muttered, "Do I care what time it is?"

"Time for all good boys to be out earning a living. Don't worry. I called you in sick."

"Did I ever tell you hiring you was the smartest move I ever made?"

"No, but it's nice to hear." She rubbed his shoulder affectionately. "You'd better drink up. You've got company."

Something in her tone alerted him enough to risk opening one eye all the way.

Max sat across from him, wearing one of his expensive suits and an inscrutable expression. "We need to talk," was all he said.

Jacques dragged himself upright in the chair, brushing at his rumpled shirt and reaching for the coffee cup with a less than steady hand. After the second swallow, the taste and the caffeine struck a jarring two-fisted blow, allowing him to focus in surly humor.

"You got nothing to say to me for months and all of a sudden you want to talk," he growled. "So talk. What's on your mind, Savoie?"

If his tone hit a nerve, the suave clan leader never betrayed it. "Charlotte flew to California this morning. She's bringing her friend Mary Kate Malone back with her. She seems to think the woman you've been harboring here can somehow repair her injuries. Where would she have gotten that idea?"

Affecting a casual shrug was worth the pain it caused him. "Not from me. I don't go around pretending to be more than what I am."

Max never blinked. "Who is she?"

"A doctor, that's all I know."

"And you didn't notice anything different about her?"

"She's a nice dresser and has good manners," Jacques offered, being deliberately obtuse in hopes of provoking a response. But Max sat calm and closed off from whatever was going on behind his cool green eyes. Eyes that lifted from him to glance across the room.

Ah, the other side of the coin. Jacques scowled as MacCreedy strode toward them. He was also dressed for work: a cheap navy blue suit coat to cover his police-issue sidearm, plain tie knotted about a white collared shirt and jeans. Nica met him at the table, scooping her arms about his middle as she tipped her face up to receive his quick kiss. Hard to miss the way his steely stare warmed when it touched on her and harder not to like him for it.

"Anything?" she asked.

"Made a mess of things. Probably cost me my damage deposit."

Jacques suddenly sobered. They were talking about MacCreedy's apartment.

Susanna.

His focus honed in on a damp paper square left for him on the table. A sharp punch of alarm had him staggering to his feet. "What's going on? What are you talking about?"

Nica's words stabbed to the heart of him. "There were a couple of guys going through Silas's apartment when Susanna got there." Seeing the emotion jump in his gaze, she quickly reassured him. "She's okay. She called me and I brought her back here."

"When was this?"

"About a half hour ago."

Jacques pulled his cell phone from his back pocket and there it was. Missed call at 6:45 A.M. She'd been in danger. She'd called him and he hadn't answered.

Max directed his question to MacCreedy. "Were they there for you or her?"

Silas's hand stroked soothingly over Nica's hair as her arms tightened about him, his attention on Savoie. "I don't know, but I don't think it would be a good idea for either of us to go back there."

Jacques turned toward the blank office window as a terrible guilt twisted about the residuals of his fear. Again, his emotions careened wildly, way outside the normal spectrum of concern that he should have felt for a near stranger.

Forgetting the small gathering at his table, he started to move away, unable to satisfy his anxiety until he saw for himself that she was unharmed.

Max's hand caught about his wrist.

"She's a danger to us," he summed up with that cold, conclusive way he had. "She needs to go."

"You don't get to make that decision. She's under my protection."

Max's unblinking stare called him on that. *And look what a good job you've been doing with that so far.* Aloud, he said, "What do you know about her? Do you know why she's here, who she works for? She could be an infiltrator. We need to get rid of her now."

The back of Jacques's neck prickled and his canine teeth lengthened as he drawled, "I didn't know anything about your agenda when I took you in. Look how well that turned out for me, for all of us. You don't get to choose when it's convenient to care about what goes on here, and you don't get to play leader of the pack only when it suits you. Susanna Duchamps is with me now, and only I get to say when she comes and goes. Worry about your own female's agenda and leave mine to me."

He could have been mistaken but it looked as though Nica did a quick fist pump.

"Jacques," Max began, but LaRoche cut him off angrily.

"Maybe you should keep to your own place to do your business and leave us here to take care of our own. Seems like one has nothing to do with the other anymore."

He pulled his arm back, knowing he couldn't break Savoie's grip unless he chose to let him go. The tight band of fingers loosened, allowing Jacques to jerk free and continue without a backward glance toward his office and the female waiting there.

The female he'd just publicly declared was his responsibility.

One he'd failed miserably.

Seven

There were no lights on in the room. Susanna sat on one of the couches, her slight figure steeped in shadows. Her head lifted when she heard him come in, giving him a brief glimpse of her pale features before it lowered again, masking her face behind the curtain of her mussed hair.

"I should have listened to you." Her words were quiet and inflectionless. "I didn't and I'm sorry."

She was sorry. It took Jacques a moment to process that. She thought *she* was to blame.

When he was able to speak, his voice growled like thunder. "Get your things. You're coming home with me."

No argument. No hesitation. That in itself alarmed him as she shouldered the straps to her bulky purse and gathered the bags from her earlier shopping spree. She wouldn't meet his gaze as she approached in silence, and that uncharacteristic humility added weight to his guilt. She stopped when his hand touched her shoulder but didn't wince beneath the slight press of his fingers.

"Do you trust me, Susanna?"

She glanced up then, surprised because he hadn't

used her first name before this. Still, no expression registered as she told him, "Not at first, but I do now."

Something about that small admission wedged up in his throat, forcing him to clear it before he could ask, "Do you need to get anything from the apartment?"

Her shudder was slight but unmistakable. "No. I don't want to go back there."

"I have a toothbrush you can use."

A very faint smile. "Then I have everything I need."

If she'd been his as he'd boldly snarled below, Jacques would have snatched her up close and simply held her. But she wasn't, so he didn't. Instead, he stepped back, letting her precede him to the car parked in the rear alley. He never spared the small group down by the bar a glance or another thought.

Susanna sat still and silent while Jacques drove. Her only sign of agitation was in the quick, shaky pulls of breath that seemed unusually loud over the banging in his head. Her hands rested in a relaxed pose on her knees. He frowned at the sight of blood on one of them.

"Are you hurt?"

She blinked up at him in confusion.

"Did they hurt you?"

She shook her head, then followed his nod to her stained fingertips. Her gaze fixed there for a long moment. "I scratched one of them on the neck."

"Did you see their faces?" He was careful to keep his tone level as fury began to boil up inside him.

"No, not really. It was dark and they surprised me. I'm afraid I'm not a very good witness."

His jaw clenched tight as he kept his eyes on the road. "I'm sorry," he said at last, unprepared for her startled look.

"About what? None of this was your fault. I was careless. You have every right to be angry."

She was taking the blame for his own mistakes. She'd been sitting there expecting him to chew into her for her disobedience while he was close to drowning in shame.

"I'm not angry with you," he gritted out. He drew a savage breath. "I didn't answer your call."

Again, the guileless blink of her eyes. "There was nothing you could have done even if you had." After that cool logic, she turned away to stare out the side window, dismissing any further apology or explanation.

His guilt boiled and thickened over a flame of impotent anger.

The impact of his decision to take her home with him didn't sink in until Jacques brought the Caddy to a stop outside his current residence. When he stared at the shabby construction trailer, his humiliation twisted into an unbearable knot.

What was he thinking bringing her here?

Susanna was a classy female, obviously from wealth and privilege. He imagined her horror at being cloistered in his dingy bachelor accommodations and almost put the car into reverse. But where would he take her? To his apartment in the Towers where most of his stuff lay under a tarp of ash soaked in smoke? To a hotel room he couldn't afford? To Savoie's big mobster mansion out on River Road? That last pushed his embarrassment out of the way of his pride. He didn't need Savoie's charity, nor did he think it would be cheerfully given to a woman he considered a danger.

Susanna was his responsibility. She would have to make do.

But that didn't stop him from cringing when he opened the door and a potpourri of burnt coffee and overdue laundry rolled out to greet them. He decided grimly that it probably didn't smell any worse than he did.

"Welcome to my very humble abode," he drawled, adding ruefully, "emphasis on *humble*."

She stepped around him and paused in the center of the main room to look around. His gut tightened as if for a blow but there was no sign of disgust on her dainty features, just curiosity.

"You work here, too?" she asked, touching the stack of invoices he'd left on the stained Formica-topped table.

"Yeah, it's convenient. I like to be on-site so I can keep an eye on things." He made a sweep of the office, loading his arms with beer bottles and coffee cups, carrying them to the tiny kitchen area where he survived out of the microwave, coffeepot and ancient, rattling, and meagerly stocked refrigerator. He thought about offering her breakfast but all he had were frozen bean burritos. Breakfast of champions and bachelors. There was a half inch of furry sludge in the coffeepot. He quickly dumped it into the dish-crowded sink before she noticed he was growing cultures of his own.

But Susanna wasn't watching him. She'd set down her things and was moving about his living/working space as if it was some sort of museum of the single male animal. She picked up and examined the magazines scattered across his couch: *Entrepreneur*, *Time*, *Bloomberg Business Week*. Thankfully, Philo had five-fingered his latest pictorial issue to admire the tri-fold airbrushing. She studied the front of one of the magazines and with a lift of her brows, showed it to him. *Chicago Magazine*. He pressed his lips together, offering no explanation. He kept hoping something familiar within those pages would spark a memory. How pathetic would that make him sound?

"You have interesting taste," she commented, setting the periodical down.

"My *Metropolitan Home* and *Food and Wine* come next week."

She smiled and glanced at the books he'd stacked on the floor. Titles on small business operation, time management, and a couple of embarrassing volumes on developing personal power.

"When do you find time to read, working two demanding jobs?"

"While I'm not sleeping."

There was no hint of mockery in the look she gave him. He wanted to think he saw admiration there. However unlikely, he still felt uncomfortable with it. He gestured down the narrow hall.

"The bathroom and bedroom are down there." As he said it, Jacques tried to remember when he'd last changed the sheets, hoping it was after the last time he'd shared them.

"A shower sounds wonderful." She glanced at her bloodstained hand and couldn't quite catch the shiver that shook her.

"It's nothing fancy," he told her, thinking of his generic toiletries and worn towels. He rubbed a palm over his shaved head. "Sorry, no hair dryer."

The sudden flash of her grin staggered him. Her eyes warmed with amused gratitude.

"It's fine. It'll be fine, thanks." Then, more earnestly, "Thank you, Jacques."

He swallowed hard, then muttered gruffly, "I'll get you some towels and that toothbrush."

He rummaged through the tiny linen closet looking for the least threadbare offerings, then turned into the bathroom, staring in dismay at the uninviting fixtures. He usually showered at the club, using this cramped turnaround only to wake himself up after a night like the last one or when he was under the spray with a guest who wasn't as interested in his cleanliness as she was in a form considered close to godliness.

Which would be the better part of valor, letting her

use the space as it was, asking her to wait while he did some furious scrubbing?

He glanced over his shoulder to see her moving past the door. She looked ready to drop from fatigue. With a regretful sigh, he set the towels on the closed toilet lid and searched through the medicine cabinet for a toothbrush, finding a lone red one still in the package behind his shaving gear. He placed it on the freestanding sink and quickly tossed the used pink one it replaced into the wastebasket. He was careful not to meet his own reflection in the mirror as he dry swallowed four pain relievers, thinking a pistol would have been quicker and more merciful.

Susanna was seated on the edge of his bed. The sight of her there gave him a hard jolt, until he noticed she had one shoe on and one off and was clutching her cell phone in shaking hands.

"Susanna?"

She looked up through eyes swimming with distress. "I was going to call my daughter and I couldn't get any words to come out."

He dropped down onto one knee so they were eye-to-eye and rubbed his palms soothingly over the tops of her thighs. It was easier to touch her in these casual clothes, without the barrier of status between them. He made his tone low and quieting.

"It's all right."

Her eyes glistened, finally releasing tears to stream down her porcelain cheeks. Her words mystified him.

"I hate being afraid all the time."

That awful clench of blame had him by the throat again. He managed to whisper, "I'm sorry," before she cut him off with her stunning claim.

"You make me feel so safe when I'm with you."

She leaned forward, her arms slipping about his waist, her head nestling beneath his chin as if his chest made the perfect pillow. Her scent overpowered him with a force the bourbon couldn't match. Heat and urgency and a strange contentment flooded his system as Jacques encircled her with his embrace, careful not to crush her close the way instinct demanded. He brushed his lips across her tumbled hair, then let his cheek rest there with a familiarity that had him shaking almost as nervelessly as she was.

To distract them both, he asked, "What's your daughter's name?"

"Pearl."

"Pearl," he repeated softly. "Unusual. Like the little girl in *The Scarlet Letter*."

She went very still for a moment, then asked, "Did you see the movie?"

"I read the book. A great cure for insomnia, but it did have some interesting moral dilemmas. No one can make *sex* a dirty word like a Puritan."

He smiled when he felt a chuckle vibrate through her. Then his expression tightened as her fingers loosened their grip on his shirt and her hands began to make slow circles upon his lower back. He couldn't mistake the way she nuzzled his throat as her head came up to rest on his shoulder. Her breath blew across his skin in a warm sigh.

"You continually surprise me," she murmured.

"Why? Because I know what a moral is? Or because I have them?"

He felt her smile against his neck. She freed one arm so her hand could cup the cap of his other shoulder. Instead of answering, she said, "You're a good man, Jacques LaRoche."

A fierce bolt of desire shot straight to his loins. Not so good, apparently. He eased back out of the sweet entanglement of her arms. "You'll feel better after a shower. Then call her."

Susanna rubbed her palms over her face and tired eyes. "She'll be in school by then. I think I'll just catch up on my sleep."

"I might have that copy of *The Scarlet Letter* around here if you need some help nodding off."

Her laugh did all sorts of crazy things to his insides.

"I don't think I'll have any trouble." She put her phone on his nightstand and levered out of her other shoe. Then she surprised him completely by pressing those soft palms to either side of his face, fixing him in place as she slid a light kiss across his lips, breathing a gentle, "Thank you," over them before she stood.

As the shower started running, Jacques turned to drop onto his backside, letting his hands lace over the top of his head as he slumped against the side of the bed. He closed his eyes but could still envision her naked body beneath that tepid spray, could feel the smooth, slick heat of her flesh against his. His hands following those intriguing curves. Her lips burning against his chest. And lower. His fingers clenching in her hair as his breath shuddered from him.

The sound of his ragged inhalation had him blinking his eyes open, disoriented and dismayed, from the all-too-real fantasy.

What the hell had he gotten himself into?

It was more than the heat of the water that made Susanna's tension swirl down the drain.

She shouldn't have hugged him. Kissing him had been madness. But the feel of him, the taste of him, revitalized all her senses.

She'd never been so alive as when in his company. Surly or sweet, it didn't matter. Even if she wasn't still crazy in love with him, which she was, she would be falling for him all over again.

As she toweled her hair dry, she eyed the grim surroundings, comparing them to the sleekly professional gleam of his nightclub office. Both were parts of him, the rough and reckless and the neatly organized. The first was inherent within him and the second had been a gift from her. Just as her sudden courage and embrace of emotions were hers from him.

Only Jacques didn't understand his preoccupation with learning and culture that had survived the purging of his earlier life, just as his territorial attraction to her had endured.

There were so many things she could have told him

about his taste in music, his interest in books, his drive for self-improvement. She could have, but wouldn't. Because in knowing those things, he might remember who had stripped them away from him.

And then, even though he would never let her go, he would never forgive her, either.

So she lusted in silence as she watched him move about the microscopic kitchen, just she'd ached at the sign of another woman's toothbrush in his trash, where hers would soon be keeping it company.

He'd changed his clothes after apparently washing up in the sink. The collar of his T-shirt was still damp against the back of his neck. She longed to sample him there, to suck at that wet skin, to cup his denim-clad butt in both hands and squeeze. Delicious, decadent thoughts circled like that water swirling down the shower.

But as much as she loved him and yearned to be with him, there was one thing more important, the one thing created between them and holding them apart.

The life of the child they'd made together.

So Susanna backed down the hallway as quietly as she could and shut the door to the bedroom behind her. She shed her new clothes in favor of one of Jacques's engulfing T-shirts and slipped beneath his covers.

There she hugged one of his surprisingly comfortable down pillows, burying her face in the softness to breathe him in. Other scents entwined with his—musky female smells. Susanna blocked them out, refusing to blame him for seeking companionship where he could, envying those brief escapes of passion. He hadn't chosen to leave her, to forget all they'd shared and dreamed together. That was her doing, her choice. She'd forced him into this new life and couldn't begrudge him anything he did with it. Or who he did it with.

"Susanna?" A light tap on the door. "I've got to get to work. You'll be safe here."

"Okay." Her answer was muffled by the emotions crowding about her heart.

"Be back around six. I'll be close by. Stay here. Find something to read."

She could picture his smile, and her own trembled about her lips as she suppressed an impossible wish.

That he was coming home to her.

Eight

Jacques strode down the dock, eyes aching behind his dark glasses, mood sharp as jagged concrete. His purpose narrowed like a bullet trail when he saw Philo Tibideaux.

"Hey, Jackie," was all the redhead could manage before Jacques grabbed a handful of his jacket and dragged him behind a stack of shipping containers. "What the hell's with you?" he yelped in annoyed surprise as he was shoved against one of the metal walls.

Instead of answering, Jacques reached for the collar of his shirt, pulling it to either side, checking for scratches. Finding none, he wheeled away in a tight circle, struggling to control his anger.

"What were you looking for?" came his low, threatening snarl.

Philo regarded him in confusion. "I don't know what you're talking about. Looking where?"

"Were you there or did you just send a couple of your Hitler youths to scare the shit out of her?" He came up close, his stare burning fiercely down into his friend's eyes, looking for a sliver of guilt or defiance but seeing only uncertainty.

"Her, who? You mean that sweet little doctor you

been sniffing after?" No sooner had he said those words than he was yanked up onto his toes, nearly strangling in his collar.

"If you bother her, if you even *think* about bothering her, I'll be on you thick as spit on a sidewalk."

Temper flaring as well, Philo gave Jacques a hard push, growling, "I got no interest in your pretty piece, so back the hell off 'fore I start thinking there's some reason I *should* be givin' her a closer look."

Jacques let him go, caution overcoming aggression. Philo had become someone of influence, not on Savoie's level, but a reckoning force within the clan nonetheless. He was not someone to provoke unnecessarily. And he was a friend. Jacques blew out a breath and placed his hands on Philo's tense shoulders.

"I'm sorry, Tib. I didn't mean to go all crazy on you. She's got my eyes crossed and my head about to explode. I don't know what I'm thinking half the time."

A true ladies' man, Philo was instantly sympathetic. "I doan think it's your head that's about to blow. What's this about? Somebody spook your lady friend?"

"Broke into MacCreedy's place, where she's staying. She stumbled in on 'em. Says she didn't get a look at 'em but scratched one of them on the neck."

"What were they after? Did they take anything?"

Jacques shrugged. "She doesn't have anything but that chip on her shoulder. Maybe it had something to do with MacCreedy. He rubbed some pretty bad characters the wrong way before settling here."

"Could ask around if you like," Philo offered, relaxing his stance. "Maybe one of the boys knows something or heard something."

"'Preciate it, Tib. This one's special. Don't know why, but she is."

"You got her stashed away someplace for safekeeping?"

"She's staying with me."

Philo nearly choked on that. "At the trailer. Lordy, lord, I wouldn't take no lady to a place like that."

Jacques winced. "Didn't have a choice. 'Sides, I mean to keep her close. That'll make anyone out for mischief think twice." He caught Philo's right hand and lifted it into the light. "What's that?"

Grinning fiercely, Philo pushed up his sleeve to reveal a new tattoo. "Me and the boys all got them." The bold red and black tribal graphic was of a snarling wolf's head on the swell of his forearm bleeding into flames that ran down over the back of his hand. "You'll be seeing a lot more of them soon."

"Subtle," Jacques remarked, not sure why the tat bothered him, but he couldn't shake his uneasiness. "How are Boyd and Nicky?" He felt bad for not following up on the two the Tracker had torn into at the club.

"Mending. Don't suppose your lady stumbled on more like that one, do you?"

If she had, she wouldn't be safely under his covers. MacCreedy would be washing her out of his carpet. Just the thought made Jacques queasy. "More I think on it, more it seems like just a break-in gone bad."

"Probably just what it was. I'll catch up with you later at the club."

"See ya, Tib."

Jacques watched his friend cross the wide dock area to where a cluster of his Patrol members were loitering. And he hated the suspicion hanging heavily on his heart.

Straightening his collar with a tug and a shrug, Philo Tibideaux was quickly surrounded by his followers like a leader circled by his pack. The gratifying feeling went a long way toward dulling the guilt he felt over lying to his friend. His shrewd gaze fixed on one of the others.

"Morris, you'd best be covering up them marks. LaRoche sees 'em, you won't have anything left above your shoulders."

The not-much-for-brains but obedient Morris put his hand over the gouges in his neck. "For a doctor, she sure were a feisty one. Nailed me before I could catch onto her."

"Well, 'less you want Jacques to be catching on to you being the one who roughed up his lady, you'd best stay out of his sight. What did you boys find?"

"Nothing, Tib," the other part of the duo, Anderson, spoke up. "Jus' a lotta fancy clothes and this here picture. We didn't get a chance to go through her purse with all the ruckus she was making."

Philo took the photograph and studied it for a long, sinking moment before tucking it into his shirt pocket.

He took a breath and toughened his attitude. "I want to know more about this Dr. Duchamps. She just happens to show up and we got Trackers drooling down our necks? I don't think it's a coincidence. See what you can find out, but don't let LaRoche know about it. What he doan know woan get us killed."

Wondering how he was ever going to drag himself through a night behind the bar, Jacques unlocked the door to the trailer and opened it wide. He stood on the threshold, too startled to enter. He took a deep breath, wondering at the unfamiliar smell.

Clean.

Someone had been busy.

The vacuum he'd forgotten he owned shut off and Susanna emerged from the bedroom. For a moment, he forgot how to blink.

She had one of his blue bandanas tied about her head to keep the hair out of her eyes. A fine glimmer of perspiration shone on her brow and neck and dappled the gentle curve of breasts barely covered by the oversized shirt she had knotted beneath them. A pair of eye-popping short shorts topped gloriously bared legs, and painted toes peeped out of jeweled flip-flops.

"I thought I heard the door," she said a bit breathlessly.

"Excuse me, ma'am. I think I must have walked into the wrong place. I'm looking for a Dr. Duchamps. Have you seen her?"

She laughed, fingertips toying with the cuffed hem

of her shorts, immediately drawing Jacques's attention to the minuscule inseam. "Nica picked them out for me. Not exactly my taste in clothing but just right for a little housecleaning." She blushed slightly. "I hope you don't mind. I couldn't find your copy of *The Scarlet Letter*. I started digging and one thing led to the other." When he didn't respond, she grew worried. "Please don't be mad that I moved your things around. I think better when I'm busy and you told me to stay inside."

"I'm not mad," he said at last. "I'm mind-boggled. I didn't know I had a rug."

She grinned and relaxed. "A nice one, too. I found a whole set of matching glasses under the couch. And some rather risqué reading material."

Now he blushed. "I don't know how those got there. They're not mine."

"Then the other Jacques LaRoche must be wondering what happened to his subscription."

As Susanna stood in the center of his alarmingly tidy room, all flushed and sexy and happy, Jacques's world took a sudden turn in a direction he never would have believed. Here was a female dangerously close to capturing his well-guarded heart. And the thought of that provoked an adverse reaction.

"I don't expect you to pay for your keep by being my maid. It's beneath you."

The wounded shock in her dark eyes was quickly masked as her chin tipped up defiantly. "There's no shame in hard work. I enjoyed it and I enjoy breathing in here a lot better now."

"I'm sorry my existence offends you."

"Your existence doesn't. Your attitude does." Her nose wrinkled. "Go take a shower before you spoil all my efforts."

"We can't have that, can we?"

"No," she said tartly, "we can't. You've got just enough time before dinner."

He stared at her. "You made dinner."

"Well, no, not exactly. I'm warming it up. Nica brought some sort of beans and rice dish over. She thought we might starve to death on what's in your refrigerator."

"Good old thoughtful Nica."

"Yes, isn't she. Hurry up. I've got to finish making the bed."

Now his jaw dropped. "You did my laundry?"

She shuddered delicately. "I'm not *that* grateful for a roof over my head. I bagged it up and Nica stuffed it in your trunk."

He chuckled and asked, "How am I supposed to repay you for all this hard work on my behalf?"

"Oh, believe me, it was for my benefit, too." She studied him for a moment through bold, bright eyes, and said, "But I'm sure I can think of some way."

Jacques couldn't get the water cold enough to curb the heat in that suggestion.

She'd done his dishes. She'd scrubbed his counter and tabletop. She'd tidied up the clutter and arranged his work space into a neat, efficient area. She'd rounded up his wayward socks and stray T-shirts and the sundry cocktail napkins and matchbooks with names and phone numbers scrawled on them and probably alphabetized them in case he wanted to refer to them again. He didn't and wouldn't. And she'd put fresh sheets on his bed after sleeping in it.

He'd rather she left the old ones on so her scent would still be there.

He'd feared they'd be bumping into each other in the small space but the opposite was true. There was too much distance between them and he'd change that if he could.

If she'd let him. If his conscience would allow it.

Then suddenly that gap between them was filled with absent others: with his forgotten mate and her faraway family. Ghosts he brought with him to the table.

"Smells good," he commented as he took a seat. He couldn't remember the last time he'd used the table for a meal. Usually it was takeout on the couch or on the run.

"So do you," she slipped in casually before adding, "Nica wanted me to tell you that Silas made it so you wouldn't worry about her having a hand in the cooking."

"Handy fellow, that Silas," he grumbled as he filled his plate.

"You don't like him much, do you?"

Jacques glanced up to find her intent gaze upon him. "Silas? He's okay. Smart guy, cool head, good to Nica."

"Then why do you see him as a threat?"

"I don't," he said too quickly. "He and I aren't in the same league, that's all. He's educated, has been places, done things."

"And you're what?"

Her insightfulness was getting under his skin. "Not like that. Him and Savoie, they're . . . they're more like you."

"Like me? Other than intelligent and attractive, I don't see any similarities."

He almost smiled at that unexpected bit of wit. He stared at her for a moment, searching for a hint of condescension but there wasn't any. And then that annoyed him, too. "That's enough, isn't it?"

Susanna's eyes narrowed but not before he saw a spark in them. Anger? What did she have to be pissed off about?

She took a dainty bite of her dinner, chewing thoughtfully before saying with deceptive mildness, "So, we're the elite and you're what? A big, burly beast? Is that how you see yourself?"

"That's how you see me, isn't it?"

She refused to be provoked. "Do you want to know what I see? I see an ambitious, too-attractive-for-my-own-good male, though I'd prefer a bit more hair on your head, who has two successful careers, is respected by his peers, and is determined to improve not only his situation but that of those around him. That's what I see. But if you'd prefer the role of dumb, downtrodden brute, there's nothing *wrong* with that. The expectations wouldn't be as challenging. I would have thought you enjoyed a challenge. All these books and magazines would suggest that. I could be mistaken, but since I'm so terribly clever, I think not."

He met her cool stare for a long beat, then let out a booming laugh. He was still smiling as he started to fork up his meal with renewed gusto. "Got me all figured out, do you? You being so smart and all."

She cocked her head to one side, her lips pursing. "Oh, no. You're not that simple, Jacques LaRoche. There are some very deep pockets I find intriguingly dark."

"Too bad those deep pockets aren't filled with cash," he muttered.

"Cash is overrated."

"Easy to say if you have it."

A soft, sexy chuckle. "You've got something I value more. Honesty."

"Come from a long line of wealthy liars up north, do you?"

Some of the lightness went out of her expression. "Truth is flexible where I come from. We hide from it or hide behind it but never exactly stand up for it."

Jacques regarded her with interest. "Now who's pretending, doc? I take you for one of those straight-from-the-hip types who doesn't tolerate bullshit." He grinned. "Even when it's as attractively wrapped as mine is."

She didn't smile. The sudden sadness in her eyes

made him regret his teasing. "I live the same lies that we all have to. One does what one must to survive."

"Now you sound like MacCreedy." Then a shock of insight came to Jacques. "When you said earlier that you were afraid all the time, I thought you meant here. But you were talking about your life up north, weren't you?"

She stared at her mostly untouched plate, tension defining the line of her shoulders. "It's like balancing on a high wire, always careful, always mindful of the slightest shift in the breeze, the slightest sway of the tightrope. Because the fall is sudden, long, and fatal, and there's no net to catch you."

"I'd catch you."

She smiled then, a sorrowful curve. "If you tried, you'd fall, too."

"Then you wouldn't be alone, would you? Stay here."

That just blurted from him before he could think it over. *Here, with me.*

Susanna's dark eyes softened, then filled with anguish. She turned her head away, blinking quickly. "I love it here. It's so alive, so full of things to experience, to enjoy." She drew a deep breath and faced him somberly. "I'm not alone, Jacques, and I can't let Pearl take that fall with me. I won't."

Of course not. "And that's why you're not like the rest of them, isn't it? That's why you have to be so careful where you step, because you care about someone other than yourself while the rest of them are just self-centered hypocrites." His tone toughened. "What about this mate of yours? He'd just stand by and let you take a tumble?"

"No," she said with a conviction that pricked Jacques's heart. "Damien took a risk he didn't have to in order to protect me, to protect my daughter. He's an honorable man, a good man, but there's only so much he can do, that I'd allow him to do. You don't understand what it's like in our world. The dangers, the secrets, the plotting and politics. You say the wrong thing to the wrong person, you stand out when you should blend. You laugh too loud or smile too wide. It's a cold, airless prison, and I hate it."

He put his hand over hers. "I'll go get your daughter for you and bring her here."

Her fingers slipped between his, clutching tight. Her poignant gaze never left his. "Thank you, but it's impossible. I'll serve my time in that jail if it means her safety." She tried for a glib smile. "Besides, I didn't think you liked me."

"I called you cold and unfeeling once." Jacques's words were a low rumble. He brought her hand to him, brushing a kiss across her knuckles. "I was very wrong." He released her and stood. "Finish your dinner and I'll get you back to your research."

Susanna didn't think she could get a bite past the emotion welling up in her throat but she forced it down, the way she forced down her true emotions. From her prison of circumstance, she couldn't afford to express her feelings for this rough yet tender male.

Stay here. The temptation more than teased her. It was a physical pain tearing at her soul. She belonged here with him. That was the truth of it. She belonged to him and him to her. When she'd broken that trust, that vow, she'd made her own cage about her heart. It would never beat for another, yet she'd never be free to know happiness, not really. She'd experienced joy being here with him, sharing a meal, a conversation, a smile . . . a touch. She'd taken a prideful pleasure in righting his household, even though she could never claim it as her own.

He'd offered to go north, into the land of his enemy, against odds he couldn't possibly overcome, to bring her child to her. There was no bravado in his words, no shallow claim for effect or appeasement. At one nod from her, he was ready to risk everything he had, everything he was. For her.

Truth hit hard, lodging like that last swallow until she could barely breathe around it. She would gladly escape the wealth and privilege of her life up north to live here with him in his lowly trailer subsisting on rice and beans and his rare, dazzling smile. If only she could.

But fate had stolen that future from her just as cruelly as she'd erased his past. Leaving them separate paths to follow toward a loneliness they'd shoulder alone.

That was their future. They couldn't change it.

But neither could she deny these moments left to them while they were together.

Nine

Nica had been shooting him sly looks all night and by eleven thirty, Jacques was heartily sick of them. When she stopped at the bar to unburden her tray of empties and glasses, he growled, "There something you want to ask me, Fraser?"

She met his glower with an innocent blink. "There something you want to tell me, LaRoche?"

"Nothing that would be any of your business."

She leaned in on her elbows. "Sooooo, there *is* something to tell. Spill it, boss. The looks you two give each other have more sizzle than the fryers at Daisy Dukes."

"It's just looking," he told her, "and a little kissing."

That Cheshire smile spread wide. "Kissing! That's good news. It must have been good to have you blushing all the way up to your fuzzy dome."

"I am not," he snarled, casting a quick glance over his shoulder at the mirror to make sure it wasn't true.

"It was the new clothes, wasn't it?" she urged with a conspiratorial wink. "That was my idea. Figured you might need a little nudge to make that first move."

"I do not need your help where my love life is concerned."

She snorted. "Love life? If you had any life at all, that would be amusing. The two of you are about the sorriest pair I've ever seen. What's it going to take for you to snatch her up for some gumbo, dodo, and gogo?"

"You think food, dancing, and sex is the answer to everything."

"Everything worth anything, duh!"

"It would be if we were free to do anything about it," he admitted at last.

Nica gripped both his big hands hard, her expression caring and concerned. "Jacques, the only thing holding you back is a ghost, a memory. The life you once had is dead and long gone. You can't bring it back. You can only move on. It's time to move on."

"Even if I agreed with you," he said glumly, "it wouldn't much matter, considering she got a flesh-and-blood family waiting on her."

"Flesh and blood," Nica scoffed with a dismissing wave of her hand. "Have you ever seen a Chosen male? Stone and ice is more like it."

Jacques pulled his hands free to rub them over the top of his head in frustration, then asked, because he had to know, "What's he like? Has she said anything about him?"

"She didn't have to. I've met him. He's like all of them. Pretty, petty, powerful. Having sex with him would be like artificial insemination . . . *if* he even sleeps with her. A lot of their males prefer surrogates or mental fantasies." She shuddered with distaste. "She's not like most of their females. She's got warmth and feelings and she wants to share them with someone who'll know how to reciprocate."

"She said he was good to her, that he protects her."

"Pfft. Why wouldn't he? Not out of the goodness of his heart, if he has one, which I doubt. Our little doctor friend is one hot commodity. And I don't mean under the covers."

Jacques frowned. "What do you mean?"

"Do you know how we met?" When he shook his head, she settled into her story with eyes flinty and tone cold. "Some crazies from their Purist Movement, those nutjobs who want complete separation of the species, kidnapped her little girl. What kind of cold-blooded monsters do that kind of stuff just to get her to agree to work on some project of theirs?"

Fury pulsed through him with a killing intensity. "And she hired you to bring her *bebe* back?"

"He did. Frost. An appropriate name. I found the fools and, as ordered, made an example of them." Enough said about that.

"So he does keep them safe," Jacques mused, both relieved and annoyed.

"Safe in a glass case like some trophy he's won. Since the kidnapping, he's gone to extremes to see that no one can get near them or her work. In her place, I'd rather take my chances on my own than be locked in his gilded cage."

"She's not you," was his flat conclusion.

Nica shrugged. "She's female, she's been neglected.

She's ripe for some hot, beefy stud to blow her socks off. What's your excuse, hot stuff?"

None came readily to mind. He gave her a smirky grin. "So you think I'm a stud?"

"*A* stud, not *my* stud." She patted his cheek and carried her tray back to her section.

Stud. He chuckled at that, then cast a contemplative glance toward his office. Was that how Susanna saw him? He knew she did. Her sultry eyes said yes. Her tentative touches said yes. Her soft lips said *hell* yes. The only one putting on the brakes was him.

If it had been any other female, he'd have made his move long ago. What was holding him back? Conscience or fear? He was uncomfortable with the fact that she had family. It wasn't his way to dally with mated females.

A ghost, Nica called the figure haunting him in dreams. Perhaps she was right. He would never find her, wouldn't even know where to start looking. If she was alive and had wanted him back, seven years was plenty of time to locate him. Maybe it was time to accept the fact that she was dead or, as Nica suggested, she'd moved on. And so should he. There was no blame to be had, no guilt to be shouldered. It just was what it was. Part of someone else's life.

From what Nica said, and what he'd heard from others as well, Chosen males and females didn't bond like those of Shifter kind. They didn't raise families together. They bred offspring who were packed off to schools and training facilities as soon as they were weaned, sometimes sooner. Ties weren't emotional. They were economical. So, bedding Damien Frost's mate would be more like stealing from his wallet than breaking his moral code. Jacques had pillaged a pocket or two during his first lean months in New Orleans, to survive, not to prosper.

The problem wasn't moral. It wasn't guilt. It arose from that gut-deep panic Susanna Duchamps stirred inside him. The intensity of his reactions to her spooked him: protective, possessive, aroused, a minefield of feelings he'd led Savoie through as his naïve friend had lusted ferociously after Charlotte Caissie. That's what these sensations reminded him of, that helpless, out-of-control state males of their species struggled through until they claimed their mate. It wasn't the kind of path a wise fellow started down unless he knew he could successfully reach the end.

There would be no happily-ever-after ending for him and the Chosen doctor. They both knew it.

So, would a wise fellow stay away from the flames or jump in to enjoy the fire until it burned him to ash?

No one had ever accused him of being particularly wise unless the word *ass* was tacked on to the end of it.

Jacques was shooting a bit of bull with Philo when he saw Charlotte enter the club. Though she gave him a quick wave, her destination was his office and Susanna. Curiosity chafed at him as long minutes passed. Finally, he couldn't stand it.

"Tib, you mind taking over for me for a minute?"

His friend shrugged. "Sure, if I can help myself."

"To anything but the cash drawer and my waitresses."

He took his time winding through the crowded tables, stopping to chat, patting a back here, pumping a hand there, as his books on good business practices advised him. He even lingered to hear an oft-repeated joke, while his attention drifted to the blank glaze of his office window. After laughing at the anticipated punch line, he made his excuses and a beeline for the stairs.

He didn't knock. It was his office, after all.

The two women looked up at him, expressions defensive and unwelcoming. If his ego hadn't been bolstered by the title of Hot Beefy Stud, he might have taken offense.

"Sorry. Am I interrupting something?"

Charlotte offered a tense smile. She looked as weary as he felt. "Hey, Jacques. No. I was just on my way out." To Susanna she said, "I'll see you at eight." As she walked past him, she gave his arm a fond squeeze. "I'll tell Max you said hey."

"Do that," he muttered noncommittally. When they were alone, he noticed that Susanna was shutting down her computer. "Finished already?"

"Charlotte's taking me to see Mary Kate in the morning. I need to get some sleep. I was going to stretch out on the couch until you close."

"I'll take you home so you can get some real rest."

"You don't have to—"

But he was already walking out the door.

Home. Susanna mulled the word over for a bittersweet moment. She'd told him her home was in the North, but in truth, those cold, white walls had never seemed like one. She had no attachment to the place or the people there. She had associates but had made no friends. Not like here. Nothing like here, where she could be herself, express herself without fear of reprisal. Even Damien, whom she respected and depended upon, never let her drop her careful guard without a disapproving frown. Even in private, there were no tender touches, no honest expressions from the heart. Those were things she could only share with Pearl.

She watched Jacques stride back to the bar, her gaze unashamedly caressing his massive shoulders, narrow hips, and long, denim-clad legs. Big, bold, earthy, he wouldn't fit into her sterile world. This was his place and these were his kind. He belonged. He'd made these rough, basic beings his family and they accepted him for who he was. She envied him that and wouldn't dream of taking him from it, even for her own personal benefit.

Being in the soundproof room was like living in her world, cut off from the things that celebrated life. No music to tempt the toes to tap, no laughter to coax a smile, no mélange of smells like yeasty hops, honest sweat, and warm body heat. Hers was a cold-blooded existence and as such, the heat in New Orleans drew her with a fatalistic charm.

How was she going to surrender herself back up to that ice-encased existence where she'd never be warm again?

Jacques leaned over the bar to exchange words with his friend Philo, who nodded and shrugged in an accommodating manner. But as soon as the brawny bartender started back her way, she saw something change in Philo Tibideaux's expression as his gaze lifted to where she stood. She knew he couldn't see her there but she felt the hostile chill of that stare nonetheless. Philo knew she didn't belong here in their world, where she presented a threat to their safety and his friend's well-being. He didn't trust her intentions or appreciate her interference. Again, there was that honesty she admired: raw, faintly menacing, but deadly honest. And he was right to fear her.

"Ready to go?"

She gave Jacques a tight smile and picked up her bag.

He hesitated in the doorway for a moment, studying his computer, then asked, "Is any of your work saved to my hard drive?"

"No," she answered carefully. "All my data is on my flash. I remote into the programs on my lab computer. Why do you ask?"

"Just being cautious." He turned off the lights behind her and, for the first time, locked his door.

His palm settled at the small of her back to steer her down the hall. It wasn't a big deal. She'd noticed that with his female staff and friends he was a hands-on male. But she wasn't used to being touched with that easy kind of familiarity and was startled.

"Forget something?" he asked, responding to her jerk of movement. His hand remained where it was, spread wide just above the curve of her bottom.

"No." She forced a nervous smile. "Just distracted." And she walked quickly toward the outer door, away from that innocent contact that had her senses jumping.

The interior of the mammoth Cadillac had suddenly compressed into that of a subcompact. Or so it seemed during their ride to the docks. A clammy drizzle fogged the windows and had Susanna shivering slightly in her seat. Or was that trembling due to the man beside her? A soft, bluesy Robert Cray tune was accompanied by the slap of wiper blades and the hurried rhythm of her heartbeats. "I was warned about her love," the song lamented all too insightfully.

Since there was nothing to see through the windows, Susanna focused her attention on the large hands guiding the wheel. Strong hands, browned by the sun, roughened by physical labor. She remembered the feel of them on her body, their impatience as they tore at her clothes, their slow, seductive magic as they stirred a fire of passion inside her, a heat she'd never felt before. Or since. She squirmed restlessly on the leather upholstery, drawing his quick glance. He frowned slightly.

"You okay?"

The rough purr of his voice was like the drag of his palms, unbearably sensual.

"Fine." She managed a smile.

His brows lowered slightly but he let it go, turning his attention back to the dangerously slick streets.

Susanna pressed her thighs together, dangerously damp herself.

The docks lay under a heavy mist. Lights glowed like eerie eyes at regular intervals but failed to illuminate through that wet gloom. When Jacques turned off the ignition and the headlights blinked out, the darkness in the vehicle was complete. His hand was on the door handle when Susanna's quiet voice stopped him.

"Jacques?"

He turned toward her, his eyes adjusting to the blackness so he could see her anxious expression. Before he could ask again what was wrong, she reached for him, her hands cupping the back of his head to draw him toward her. In his surprise, he was easily manipulated. Her smooth cheek brushed his. Her soft lips pressed to his skin.

"Thank you," she whispered.

Jacques didn't move, not even to take a breath. When she didn't sit back, he murmured, "You're welcome," thinking that would be the end of it.

She started to ease back but as soon as their gazes met, she hesitated. Her eyes fluttered and that luscious mouth touched his, shyly at first, then with a light stroke of her tongue.

He fought not to groan as his system slammed into overdrive.

With a Herculean effort, he pulled back very slowly and smiled. "You are very welcome." He read her confusion and embarrassment and, to calm both, stroked his knuckles lightly beneath her chin and said, "We'd better get inside before all hell breaks loose." And he didn't mean the weather.

He got out of the car, manner casual so she wouldn't think he was running from an unwanted overture. *Keep it cool*, he told himself as he circled behind the vehicle. *Keep it friendly. Don't get excited.* Hard advice to follow after scenting her increased arousal.

He opened the door for her, offering his hand to help her out. She took it with the slightest hesitation and released him immediately to reach for her bag.

Crisis averted.

He started to place his hand on her back, then stopped himself. No sense in fanning those flames again. Instead, he started for the metal steps, aware of her close behind him. He unlocked the door and stepped back so she could precede him inside. By the time he'd switched on the light, she'd disappeared down the hall into the bedroom.

Relieved, yet as uncomfortably revved as his mighty eight-cylinder with its pedal to the floor, Jacques shook the rain from his shirt, stirring up the trace of her fragrance that lingered there. Pretty danged sure he wasn't going to get any sleep, he went through the motions anyway. There was nothing to clear off the sofa, a pleasant first. In fact, his whole place seemed fresh and inviting. Nice to come home to, even though it wasn't much of a home.

He was getting a light cotton blanket out of the hall linen cupboard when Susanna came out of the bedroom. They did a side-to-side dance until he finally flattened against one wall so she could slide by him and shut herself into the bathroom. He took advantage of her absence to retrieve a clean T-shirt and his gym shorts from his thrift store dresser and left a second shirt on the bed for her, hoping she hadn't let Nica talk her into sexy lingerie to go along with her provocative new wardrobe. There was only so much a male animal could take.

He heard a flush and the rush of water in the sink, but before he could scoot to safety, Susanna exited the bathroom, trapping them in that treacherously narrow hall once again. This time, she moved to one side but he quickly discovered there wasn't quite enough room to walk past her. When he turned sideways to edge through, her arm straightened to block him.

Oh, hell.

Her body swayed into him, the barricading arm curling about his waist, the other draping across his shoulders. She fit beneath his chin with a custom-built ease. Cautiously, he placed his hands in the safest place he could think of, just beneath her shoulder blades, and he held her, not tight, but with a relaxed compliance.

There was nothing relaxed about him below the belt. Couldn't do anything to hide it from her the way she was pressed over him like a fitted sheet. She didn't seem alarmed so he didn't make a big deal out of it.

And then she took a shaky breath, her face lifting so that the light from the bedroom glittered in her eyes and made her parted lips shine with an inviting wetness.

This was that point on the path where a wise man would have slammed things into a smoking reverse.

Damn me to hell.

Jacques lowered to take that irresistible offering, slowly, thoroughly, until her fingers clenched in his T-shirt and her legs trembled against his. *Gently, gently*, his saner self cautioned. Such a delicate creature wasn't used to aggressive male desire, raised as she was amongst the passionless, thin-blooded Chosen. He reined back so as not to frighten her.

And that's when she lunged up on her toes, thrusting her tongue so deeply into his mouth she must have speared his brain, because all his reactions short-circuited. He pulled back so abruptly his head cracked against the wall, and stared at her, eyes wide, his breath panting.

Susanna went flat-footed in dismay. "I'm sorry," she stammered, arms dropping to her sides, face flushing hot. "I thought—" She swallowed awkwardly. "Don't you want me?"

Her lips quivered, then firmed into an angry line at his sudden, booming laugh. Before she could mistake his response, he gathered her to his chest in a close embrace that tightened when she tried to squirm away. The effort of restraint rumbled in his voice.

"That's a question that shouldn't be asked or answered tonight if we're both as smart as we say we are."

Susanna burrowed her face against his chest until the shame heating her cheeks began to cool. The way his hands rubbed over her body from shoulders to backside in a rather lusty grope bolstered her self-confidence.

Finally, he held her away, his gaze a smoldering contradiction to his claim of, "I'll take the couch."

Susanna stared at the ceiling, painfully awake in the big empty bed. She was cold and restless and unhappy with the stalemated situation. With her situation in general. So she reached for the phone to cool the dangerous direction of her thoughts.

"It's late. Is there a problem?"

The comfort she'd hoped to find was stripped away by Damien's terse tone.

"No, no problem. Just checking in. How's Pearl?"

He avoided her question. "Checking in? The way you would with a supervisor? I am more than your employer, Susanna, or have you forgotten that?"

Anger simmered beneath his civility. His sharp question got her wondering: Were they? Had they ever been more?

"No, I haven't forgotten. You don't need to remind me."

"Apparently, I do." Her quiet words did little to soothe his mood, for he continued fiercely. "Your career, your future, your *child* are all in my hands and this is how you thank me? With secrets, with defiance? Where are you, Susanna? I want you here where you belong."

Was he threatening her? Threatening Pearl? Surprise became alarm. Then, for the first time, fear. She'd left her daughter in this man's care. Was she safe?

Her silence changed Damien's manner to one of soothing care. Perhaps a little too late.

"Forgive me, my dear. I'm fatigued. I've had to put in an enormous amount of time and energy to cover for your unexplained absence."

Instead of grateful, she felt increasingly unsettled. He was trying to manipulate her already guilty conscience. "You didn't have to do that, Damien."

"Of course I did. I couldn't have your colleagues thinking—" He broke off, then quickly added, "I didn't want them to be concerned."

He didn't want them to think he wasn't in control of the situation. In control of her.

And then his testy mood made perfect sense. Because, for the first time, he wasn't.

"I'm sorry to have become such a burden. That wasn't my intention. Good night, Damien. Tell Pearl I called."

"Susanna—"

She cut the connection before he could continue, her nerves frayed, temper still high, and thoughts running in anxious circles. Should she give in and return? Could he be trusted with her daughter in his current frame of mind? This was Damien! Kind, giving, encouraging . . . And furious with her. Because she wouldn't obey him. Couldn't obey him, not this time.

A creak and a muttering groan sounded from the living room followed by several loud thumps and a weary sigh.

Her strained mood fractured.

"How am I ever going to get any rest with you out there thrashing around?" she shouted.

Silence.

The rasp of overtaxed springs and a gruff, "I'll sleep in the car."

She sighed, frustration and an underlying fright making her draw the very danger she was trying to avoid closer. "Jacques, come here."

Silence. Then the sound of his reluctant approach. Her intentions nearly faltered at the sight of him in the doorway looking appealingly rumpled and grouchy. He squinted at her suspiciously as she lifted the covers and patted the mattress.

"I'm tired and you're too big for that couch," she explained like a rational adult while trying not to ogle his bare legs. "Get in, get comfortable, and for heaven's sake, get some sleep."

He hesitated for a brief instant, then fatigue won out.

The mattress dipped, gravity urging her toward him. She braced to keep her distance as he bounced and fidgeted and finally settled in, tugging the covers up to his chin.

They lay like guests on Dovion's table, side by side, breathing shallowly.

After uncomfortable minutes crept by, Jacques finally snorted disgustedly and extended his arm so that it slid beneath her pillow. With a crook of his elbow, she was rolled up against him.

"Better?" he whispered.

She smiled and reluctantly snuggled in, rewarded by a much needed infusion of heat. "Ummm, much. Thank you." Without giving it a thought, she hooked her arm about his middle and let her knee nudge over the top of his, clinging subconsciously to that solid strength he'd always represented. Threats and fears fell away.

He went very still, then she felt his lips move against her hair.

"You're very welcome."

Her skin burned against his, silk and fire. Clothing dropped away, giving him access to those delicate curves and taunting hollows. He'd dreamed of this, of her, but the reality . . . so much sweeter. He hesitated, not sure where to begin, until her hand covered his, leading it to her soft breast. An exquisite handful. Her innocent moan of discovery checked the hungry passion growling through him.

Slow. Gentle. Be worthy of her trust.

She trembled beneath his exploring touch, but

didn't resist it. In fact, the timid parting of her thighs gave him more encouragement than he'd dared hope for.

Opening the way to where both of them knew they shouldn't go, yet couldn't quite resist . . .

Her palm lay warm and relaxed upon his neck. Slowly, her thumb, then her index finger, rubbed along the rough line of his jaw, over the part of his lips, lingering until his tongue was teased out to taste her. He sucked on that curious digit, hearing her gasp as he bit down gently.

Her petite figure fit against his side, warm, inviting, pressing tighter into him as he followed the curve her hip with his hand. The dip of her slender waist rising in a tempting flare. The graceful rounding of one buttock. So perfect, so tempting. So . . .

Real.

Not a dream!

Jacques froze, his eyes flashing open to fix upon the soft gleam of Susanna's gaze. Flickering shut again as she stretched up to kiss him with a smoldering intensity. He went with it, letting her coax him into releasing the desire he felt for her. Slow. Fierce. Powerful.

He didn't question. He refused to reason. She wanted him and, in the darkness, in the embrace of his bed, that was enough.

He rolled up on one hip to take her in his arms. She gave a tiny squeak as his insistent hard-on jabbed her in the ribs. All at once, that struck him as both funny and unbearably arousing.

"Sorry," he whispered over her lips. "Can't do anything about that."

He drew a quick breath as clever fingers brushed over the bulging front of his gym shorts.

"I can."

Her husky reply almost made him come on the spot.

The friction from her hand conspired with the silky shift of material until his muscles tensed and strained, until an unstoppable pressure built and throbbed for release.

And at that tenuous instant, she kissed him again, her tongue wetting his mouth before she gave his bottom lip a sudden, unexpectedly sharp nip.

Jacques lost himself in a great shuddering wave.

By the time his senses returned, Susanna lay relaxed beside him, her head on his shoulder, her thoughtful gaze upon his face.

"Thank you," she said softly.

Her contentment confused him almost as much as her words. The unexpected intimacy she'd initiated was over. He wasn't complaining, just wondering. He smiled, perplexed. "For what?" It wasn't like she'd given him the chance to follow through.

"For letting me be here with you."

He'd heard the phone conversation. Though he had questions, he didn't speak them, instead saying softly as his knuckle brushed her cheek, "Again, you're very welcome."

Ten

They'd been in the car for less than a minute.

"So," Charlotte began in a drawl, "you're staying with Jacques LaRoche."

"I am." No sense in pretending otherwise.

"I seem to recall his place only has one bedroom."

"It still does."

After that, the detective's tone got decided prickly. "He's one of the best friends I have, one of the best men I know."

Susanna said nothing, letting her driver get to the point, which she did with sniperlike directness.

"It'll piss me off if you hurt him."

No one seemed terribly concerned that she was the one whose heart might be broken. "There's no danger of that happening," she stated with her jaw clenched.

Charlotte cast a sidelong glance at her. Today Susanna wore a pair of black jeans—Nica's favorite— and a gauzy wrap shirt decorated with colorful bead-work that drew the eye to a rather plunging neckline. The detective smirked.

"You're attractive, intelligent, and gutsy. I'd say danger ahead."

"It's not like I'm bringing him beer and gumbo to seduce him," she argued. No, that wasn't what she was doing. Her color heightened.

"He's a man, and all males of any species like to be flattered and pampered. But that's not what he's looking for." Charlotte let the topic dangle enticingly.

Susanna couldn't resist snapping at the bait. "What's he looking for?"

"Someone who'll take him seriously."

The answer wasn't what she expected. But it absolutely made sense. Coming from his background in the North where he was viewed as an object, as a tool with no identity, he'd hunger to make a mark for himself, to garner respect and authority. His greatest fear was to be seen as insignificant.

Susanna took him seriously. She always had. She'd seen the man behind the beast and that's what forged their connection. Because he'd seen the woman behind the scientist. An exciting and unique first for her.

Because Charlotte's comment opened the way for more discussion in a direction she couldn't go, Susanna turned the topic to discover more about Max Savoie. "Is that what your mate was looking for?"

"That, among other things. We support each other."

Not nearly enough information. "So he's all right with what we're doing?"

The exotic-looking detective pursed her lips and admitted, "Not so much. But he'd be a lot more pissed if I hadn't had the good sense to tell him about it up front. He's not fond of surprises. That was a hard lesson to learn, but I finally caught on."

Susanna squirmed, considering the way she was keeping Damien in the dark . . . and was on the edge of betraying a lot more than his trust. "I have a mate and a daughter."

"Yes, you told me."

Maybe she needed to remind herself.

Mary Kate Malone was housed in a small care facility. The staff was efficient and motivated to mind their own business by a hefty charitable contribution from Legere Enterprises International, the organization now run by Max. The severely injured nun lingered in her induced coma in a pretty room she would never appreciate, kept alive by pumps and hoses and narcotics. A merciful limbo, Susanna wondered, or a cruel delay of the inevitable?

Charlotte hung back at the door, her features stoic, her dark eyes suspiciously glimmering, while Susanna checked vitals and drew samples.

It was impossible to look upon the pale, hideously disfigured form and not be moved by pity. Working in a lab without actual contact with her subjects had spared Susanna the unexpected sorrow twisting through her now as she saw a vital life wasted.

Could she help this unfortunate woman or would she be raising her level of awareness to one of unending suffering and mental torment? Those kinds of questions never occurred to those she worked with in the North. They only saw results, not consequences.

Susanna covered the motionless fingers resting on pristine sheets and gave them a slight squeeze.

I'll view you as a person, Mary Kate Malone. I promise. And I'll see to your interests.

Charlotte had left the room. Susanna found her in a cheerful courtyard filled with plant life and uplifting statuary. Tension fairly vibrated through her posture.

"What do you think?" she demanded without turning.

"I think it's time for me to get to work."

Susanna had Charlotte drop her off at the club while the detective took her samples to the lab for Dovion to run. The cavernous space was dark and quiet, but the lingering whisper of Jacques's scent distracted her from what she needed to be doing. To avoid thinking about what she'd done last night, she considered this morning.

He'd made her breakfast.

The tantalizing smell of vegetables and spicy sausage sizzling had drawn her out of bed where she'd been both disappointed and relieved to find herself alone. She'd dressed quickly, then had stood in the hall for long minutes watching him tend the skillet steaming on a single hot plate.

Hunger growled through her, but that appetite wasn't for food alone.

Jacques filled the tiny domestic space, all brawny

shoulders, tight butt, and bare feet in his half-tucked-in T-shirt and snug jeans. Delicious. Without turning, he'd asked, "How hot do you like it, *chere*?"

"I'll take it any way you want to serve it up," she'd replied, setting a simmering mood at the table they shared.

Even though he didn't bring up the matter, it was only a matter of time before they sampled more of the temptation between them.

Shaken by that certainty, she forced herself to call Chicago to calm more pressing fears.

"Hello, Damien." Could he hear the desperation in her voice?

"Susanna, thank goodness."

The agitation in his tone brought a jump of alarm into her throat. "What's happened?"

"It's Pearl."

A great swooning blackness threatened her senses, but Susanna hung on determinedly. "What's wrong?"

"Her fever's back. She's weak and disoriented and has been asking for you. Susanna, you need to come home."

Before Pearl, she would never have understood how those few words could turn all her priorities upside down. Her first thought was to wonder how quickly she could arrange for a flight. Her baby needed her. Panic and a deep, cold terror clawed at her, shredding logic.

But only for a moment.

Her baby needed her to be strong.

"I can't," she pushed the words out. "I can't leave just yet."

Silence, then an aghast, "I can't believe you're saying that. Your daughter *needs* you."

"My daughter needs rest and fluids and her injections, starting immediately, three times a day. You know how to administer them, and if you can't be there, arrange for it to be done. She should stabilize within twenty-four hours." Then Susanna drew a breath and played a card she never thought she'd have to throw down to gain her partner's compliance. She was of the Chosen. "Damien, my work comes before any attachments. How could you believe otherwise?"

Again, the long pause, but she knew he couldn't argue against the tenets of their entire belief system. For the many, not the few. The wants of the individual never weighed above the benefits to the all. Never. In theory.

So she concealed her anxiety and personal fears behind that cool, clinical mien of their race, presenting her reasoning the way she would any logical conclusion.

"The research I'm doing is revolutionary. Its benefits far surpass my own selfish wishes. You'll understand when I'm able to explain the importance to our people." Then she added, to seal his cooperation, "The importance to *our* future."

The silence that followed was calculating, and in that moment, Damien Frost's integrity took a terrible plunge in her estimation, making her wonder if the reason for his concern was her daughter's health or her continued defiance. "I look forward to discussing it with you," he said at last. "By all means, continue."

Susanna closed her eyes, heart clutching. Damien would care for her child. That was all that mattered for the moment. "I'll check in every few hours. I should have plenty of time to return if her condition worsens. May I speak to her? It'll calm her to hear my voice."

A pause, then a faint little sigh of relief. "Mommy, when are you coming back?"

"Soon, sweetheart. Soon. Damien tells me you aren't feeling well."

"I'm fine now. I got sick at school and they sent me home. I was making you a picture and I didn't get to finish it. Damien says I have to stay in bed."

"You do as he says so you'll get stronger. You can make me another picture, baby."

"Can you take it to work with you?"

"We'll see," she lied. Personal items weren't allowed in her facility. No one would think to challenge that rule. They wouldn't attach any sentiment to a child's crude scribbling.

Susanna wasn't like them. And neither was Pearl.

They spoke for a minute longer, Susanna trying to keep the sound of her tears out of her comforting words. Finally, when the child's voice grew weak and a bit whiny, she wasn't above a maternal bribe.

"What would you like me to bring home for you that would make you happy?"

"My daddy."

Susanna had expected her to name some simple childish favorite like picture postcards or colorful bracelets. The shock of her daughter's request left her speechless.

"Damien's there with you, Pearl."

"But he's not my daddy." That was confided in a careful whisper.

A chill shook through her. "Why would you say that, baby?"

"Damien said so. He was cross with me because I got some of my numbers wrong. He said if I didn't work harder I'd be a dummy just like my daddy."

That chill became a sheet of ice. She struggled to keep her tone buoyant. "Oh, I'm sure you misunderstood, Pearl. We'll talk about it when I get home, all right?"

Silence, then a quiet admission that fractured her world.

"Damien doesn't like me."

"That's not true, sweetie. He's been very good to us. And he's very proud of you."

Pearl didn't answer, seeing through Susanna's false gaiety the same way she'd apparently looked into Damien's heart and read his distaste. And now, so did Susanna.

Why had she never noticed that her partner despised the child fathered by another male? A Shifter male.

She'd have a talk with Damien, too, when she got home.

"I love you, Pearl. You know that, don't you?"

"I love you, too, Mommy."

Susanna wiped her eyes and felt her determination firm. She'd done everything she could to protect Pearl, to make her world safe and uncomplicated, even if it meant withholding the truth of her parentage, at least until the girl was old enough to understand the choices she'd made. Now, with careless, spiteful words Damien had shaken that sense of autonomy. And Susanna wasn't sure she could forgive him that thoughtless cruelty.

She couldn't think about him now. She couldn't let emotion interfere with purpose. Pearl's life depended upon her ability to use the information she was gathering to battle the genetic confusion that was tearing her little body apart.

And then, perhaps, she could make other choices.

It was difficult to concentrate on her promise to Charlotte when her thoughts were pulled in a more personal direction. Finally, Susanna could go no further in her study of the Chosen/Shifter DNA blend: She needed specific material from the hybrid child the detective carried. Instead, she turned her attention to the information Dovion provided on Mary Kate. She was busy inputting the data. She didn't turn when she heard the office door open, believing it to be either Jacques or Nica since it wasn't even noon.

As she hit Enter, her program spun the projections she'd imported out into probabilities. Her attention spiked as the results rolled down the screen. Amazing results. She drew in an excited breath, then, as the scent filled her nose, she realized two Shifters had entered the room. And she knew them from their encounter at MacCreedy's apartment.

Susanna's quick glance over her shoulder confirmed what she feared. These were the two who'd torn through her belongings. She recognized the black and red flames tattooed on the backs of their hands, a detail she'd forgotten until this moment. To protect her work, she yanked out her thumb drive and tucked it out of sight behind the monitor; then, before she put the computer into hibernation mode, she tapped three quick words, then blanked the screen.

"Dr. Duchamps," one of them said flatly, "don't give us any trouble or we'll make plenty for you."

Susanna stood and turned to boldly face them.

And that was when she saw the handcuffs and rough sack in their hands.

Business was booming for LEI, which meant Jacques's day became a mad scramble to tend its interests. The unexpected absence of several of his crew forced him to fill in personally during the unloading of one of the freighters. He didn't mind. He enjoyed physical labor, and it kept his mind off other things. Like the female who'd spent the night sharing his sheets.

It wasn't like Susanna was the first to ever visit them. If he was without company, it was by his own choosing. His opportunities were plentiful and varied. But there was a difference between sleeping with a lady and spending the night with one. Perhaps that was why filling that space on a regular basis had never made him feel less lonely.

Until last night.

Having Susanna Duchamps beside him had been both comfortable and familiar, and not just because consummating sex was off the menu. With little or no persuasion, he could have pushed things beyond her surprising . . . and satisfying gesture and they both would have enjoyed it. But then she'd have become like the parade of female partners stretching before and after her: a moment's pleasure without a lasting peace. The frustration of restraint enhanced the fantasy—that a woman like her could belong to a man like him.

As tempting as that fantasy was, it wasn't enough. Because he already wanted more.

He was riding down on a cargo container when he spied a visitor on the docks.

Savoie, with his designer suit, quirky red sneakers, and imperious manner, stood out like filet mignon on an all-you-can-eat buffet. His presence signaled more problems Jacques didn't need.

"Where y'at, Savoie?" he shouted, making his employer and one-time friend shade his eyes to look up.

"Got a minute?"

"Be right down."

He jumped. A foolish thing. It wasn't the height. A one-story drop wasn't a big deal. It was the potential witnesses. To remain unnoticed in the Upright world, they were forced to act human. Displays of unnatural power were frowned upon as unnecessary risks to the illusion. But in a temperamental pissy fit, flexing of a bit of muscle felt good.

He landed easily, on toes and fingertips right at Savoie's feet. As he straightened, brushing off his hands, he met the narrowed gaze with his own belligerent stare, goading Max to make something of it. Max simply smiled, as if the nuances of the up-yours action were appreciated as they were intended.

"What brings you down here in your nice suit?"

"Wanted to let you know personally that the Towers are reopening on Monday, but you can move back in any time you're ready."

His surprise and gladness apparent, Jacques was still cautious. "It'll be a while before I can do that. My stuff's all damaged—"

"It's taken care of."

Jacques just stared at him, uncomprehendingly.

"I had my insurance people clean or replace everything. It might still smell a little smoky, but it's habitable. I apologize for the wait . . . and the inconvenience of the whole situation."

"You didn't have to do that," Jacques stammered. "It wasn't your fault, or your obligation."

"Yes. It was. Both things." Max gave a heavy sigh, his attitude of authority dropping away. "You're my most valued ally, Jacques, and my most trusted friend. None of what I've accomplished would have been possible without your help and your willingness to let me lead. I haven't done a very good job repaying you for those things. This is a small effort compared to what I owe you and yours."

Jacques cleared his throat of the sudden crowding emotion to growl, "You didn't have to come all the way down here just to tell me that."

"Yes. I did." He glanced away awkwardly.

It was the humility that drew Jacques to Savoie. Sometimes Max seemed to have no idea how powerful he was, how important he was as a rallying point for his clan. Genuinely mystified by their loyalty, he was reluctant to demand it, which placed him in his current precarious situation.

"You've stayed away too long," Jacques told him simply.

Savoie's gaze locked in, earnest and anxious. "Can the damage be undone?"

"It's not something your insurance people can handle for you."

"Is it something you can handle with me?"

That was the invitation Jacques had been waiting to hear.

Before he could reply, Max added, "If you still trust me."

Jacques had fought hard for his place within the clan. He was looked up to, respected, considered one of them, but, like Savoie, he'd been an outsider once. Philo Tibideaux and his brother Tito had vouched for him, easing his way in.

And Jacques had done the same for Savoie. Because he believed Max was the Promised, the one who would restore their honor and protect their interests. He still believed that right down to the marrow, even when the Towers debacle had many shying away to follow Philo's more aggressive lead.

Max was the one legend whispered about. The one who would bring the clans together and give them strength.

Personal slights fell away. They didn't matter. Max and what he offered were the only things that did.

The gesture wasn't difficult when motivated by belief. Jacques had made it only once before in front of all the powerful heads of Jimmy Legere's world of Upright criminals on behalf of his own kind: a show of fealty, of loyalty that could not be broken. A sense of purpose had been born in him at that moment, and was renewed now with the same intensity.

Jacques's head bowed. He leaned forward, butting against Max's shoulder in a pose of submission. Max's hand clasped firmly on the back of his neck, not to push him down but to lift him up so their eyes could meet as if they were equals.

"All I am is yours," Jacques told him, repeating the phrase Max had spoken to seal his allegiance.

Max smiled, still uneasy with the burden of unconditional trust. "Friends again?"

"I was never not your friend."

"But I wasn't being yours." His hand pressed Jacques's shoulder. "Forgive me for not seeing that. Charlotte had to point that out to me in her less than subtle way. Silas hasn't replaced you; he's joined us."

Now Jacques was the one uncomfortable with his own petty grievances. "MacCreedy's a powerful asset and a good man. He's got connections with the other clans and knows how they think, how they work. And he's got a weapon of mass destruction at his command."

Max raised a brow in question.

Jacques grinned. "Nica."

Max chuckled at that. Then he sobered. "You should take your lady to the Towers. She'll be safer there."

Now that they were being honest with each other, Jacques felt he owed his friend an explanation. "Max, she isn't—"

Max waved him off. "What she is or isn't is your business and I will mind mine. I won't tell you I'm happy to have her here. I don't trust where she comes from, but I'll accept your judgment about her." He drew a fretful breath, then admitted, "This plan of Charlotte's is more dangerous than she knows, but she's been there for me so many times, I can't refuse to support her in it. The secrets she dabbles in could destroy us all if your doctor takes them back to the North with her. Make sure she understands that and that her conscience guides her regarding our safety. Does she have one, do you think?"

"I will and she does."

"That trouble at MacCreedy's apartment. He can't be sure who was targeted. Perhaps it was him, but just in case it wasn't, keep your girl close. Trackers aren't the only danger out there. It surrounds us, and that circle is tightening."

Jacques nodded, well aware of the threat.

Max surveyed the bustling dock. "Get bored with supervision, or are you shorthanded?"

A quick smile. "A bit of both."

Max's expensive jacket dropped to the oily concrete and he rolled up his sleeves. "Tell me where you want me."

Having Max's help was a two-pronged blessing. He was quick to take instructions and impossibly strong. And the sight of him toiling alongside the lesser of the clan would go far toward mending any hard feelings. News of the Towers' reopening buzzed through the day crew, fueling a positive atmosphere missing since the fire; an excitement Jacques shared.

He couldn't wait to take Susanna there, not just for the sake of protection, but to show off his accommodations. He wasn't just a laborer living out of a trailer who read books about being important. He wanted her to see him as someone of influence, of potential.

What he didn't ask himself was why her opinion mattered.

What he didn't question was his eagerness to shower, dress, and hurry to the club. He didn't dare look more deeply for those answers.

Nica gave a wave to Jacques from behind the bar. It was the first day of her promotion. The idea of having an assassin as his assistant manager was as amusing as it was practical, and she appreciated the irony. She was reliable and respected and could take out any trouble with the well-aimed flick of a plastic fruit pick.

Jen and Amber were already busy getting their cash drawers set up, so that left him with no worries. Until he opened the door to his office to find it empty.

Perhaps Susanna was still with Charlotte.

That became more unlikely as he noted the computer was still on with the program running. She wouldn't have left it like that.

The quick click of a key woke it from its slumber to display the message Susanna had left for him.

Flame hand tattoo

Philo's men had taken her.

Eleven

Though the coarse-weave bag over her head kept Susanna blinded, she reached out with her other senses to learn about her situation.

She was on the docks. The same sounds, the same smells were present as at the trailer. She was seated on a hard straight chair, her cuffed hands pulled uncomfortably together behind the back of it. The hot, airless room was small. She could tell by the echo of voices and by how long it took to cross from the door to where she sat by the far wall. They were less than five minutes from the club by car but perhaps a world away from rescue.

Only one of the men remained with her now. The other had left a few minutes earlier after their rough questioning yielded no answers. She licked at the blood on her lip and used her anger to keep fear at bay. Did they think a few ugly threats and open-handed slaps would have her spilling her life history to a couple of thugs in a locked room?

Jacques would come for her. She had no doubt about that. But until he did, she needed to keep her wits about her and try to better her circumstances.

"Can I have some water?" she asked in a hoarse whisper, making her voice sound weak and fragile.

"No. You jus' sit there quiet until—"

"Until what?" she demanded, jumping on his sudden silence.

"Never you mind. Jus' keep still."

Until who, not what. She picked that inference from his uncomplicated mind. He was waiting for someone to give him instructions. The two who'd attacked her at the apartment and now had kidnapped her from the Shifter club weren't the brain trust of the operation. Someone was behind their rather sloppy actions and she wanted to know who.

These men weren't like the frightening Tracker in the bar. They were dedicated but untrained, laborers, not killers. And that was to her advantage. They underestimated her. They saw a delicate female. They'd forgotten that she was also Chosen.

What they didn't know was that Shifter strength and courage also coursed through her.

Susanna hadn't done mental tricks for a long time. Once her early-childhood testing had targeted her aptitude for science, they'd stopped developing her telepathic abilities. She'd learned the basics of projection and manipulation, but the more complex lessons were saved for future Controllers. Because she despised the notion of prying into another's thoughts or directing their actions, she'd allowed her talents to lie dormant, but now she was motivated to wake those slumbering skills for her own rather desperate purpose.

"I'm having trouble breathing," she gasped while quieting her mind, letting it gather about one idea. Slowly, she began to push it upon her guard. *You can't breathe. Your lungs won't expand. Your throat is closing.*

She heard a gurgling sound and experienced only a tiny drop of guilt.

"Take this bag off my head. I could breathe if you took the bag off."

"I can't do that," her watchdog choked.

"But it's so hot. I can't catch my breath. Please. I can't breathe."

Heat. Sweat. A clawing sense of smothering claustrophobia. Airway squeezing, shutting off that sweet, saving breath.

She was in his mind. She could feel his panic and amplified it.

"Take off the bag. Then you can breathe. Take it off!"

Suddenly, light dazzled her eyes as the sack was torn away. She blinked at her red-faced guard as he gasped and staggered, briefly pitying him until she saw the nearly healed scratches on his neck. Then she closed her eyes to focus her efforts.

You're trapped. You're a prisoner. You have to get away before they come for you. Feel the shackles on your wrists. You have to get free. They're coming. Open the handcuffs. Do it now!

She heard him scrambling, panting wildly. And then his sweaty hands were on hers. She could hear the key scraping across the metal.

"What the hell are you doing?"

The sharp, intruding voice broke Susanna's hold. She looked up to see two men in the doorway. One was the second man from her abduction and the other, the man behind it.

She smiled calmly. "Mr. Tibideaux, does Jacques know you've kidnapped his guest?"

"What Jackie doan know won't hurt either of us. Morris, get up from there."

"I doan know what happened," Morris was babbling.

"You let her screw with your mind. Now she's seen all three of us and that makes things into a bit of a mess."

A chill of dread shivered through Susanna at what it might take to clean up that mess. Surely, he wouldn't risk killing her.

"Get out," Philo snapped at his flunkies. "Dr. Duchamps and me are gonna have ourselves a little talk."

When they'd hurried out and shut the door, Philo took one of the other chairs and turned it to face her. He sat down and, with hands braced on knees, regarded her somberly.

"What am I gonna to do with you, doctor?"

"I suggest you let me go before Jacques gets here."

"I can't do that until you fill me in on a few things."

She stared at him. "I'm a Libra. I enjoy sunsets, spicy breakfasts, and yoga. Red is my favorite color. Now fill me in on you."

He gave a wry smile. "I didn't know your kind had a sense of humor."

"And you've known a lot of my *kind*, have you, to form that hypothesis?" When he didn't answer, she sighed. "You're right. Most of us are deadly serious and we frown on kidnapping. As will your friend, Mr. LaRoche."

"What are you doing down here in N'awlins?"

"I was invited."

"What are you *doing* here?" he repeated with pointed emphasis.

"Helping a friend of a friend. If they want you to know, they'll tell you. I'm not going to. So if you feel it necessary to slap me around some more, you might as well go ahead. I'm not going to give you any information. Or do you only ask questions when you have a baseball bat?"

He flushed slightly at that, either embarrassed or annoyed, but his stare remained coolly dangerous. Wondering what stirred behind that narrowed glare whittled away at her courage.

"I'm a physician," she told him fiercely. "I don't hurt people. I heal them."

"Ahh, is that what you call screwing with folks' minds and stripping them of their memories? You think Jackie'd be so quick to save you if he knew the truth?"

Susanna's belly knotted, but her tone was strong. "What truth? He knows who and what I am."

Again, the warped smile. "Oh, I doan think he has a clue."

Philo reached into his shirt pocket to withdraw a small photograph. He studied it for a moment before showing it to Susanna. It was the one she carried with her at all times.

"She has her daddy's eyes."

Susanna looked up at him, hiding her fear behind a harsh coldness. "You can't tell him."

"What? That his lady love is really the bitch that ruined his life and sent him to be killed?"

"Killed?" Fear fell away. "What are you talking about?"

"Doan play your games with me. You're not gonna twist my mind up in knots. I know what I saw, what me and Tito saw that night they brung him here to N'awlins."

A terrible trembling took hold of her as she asked, "What did you see?"

"A big black van with Illinois plates creeping along the docks seven years ago. They dragged him outta the back, trussed like a carcass on the way to the slaughter. He weren't moving and didn't make no sound when they was kicking the shit outta him."

"And you didn't stop them?" she cried.

"Hell no. None a our business. We doan go messing with nobody from the North. But then they cut loose his ropes and put a gun to his head. That's when it got to be our business. They was meaning to shoot him and leave him there so we'd take the blame for ending him. We found that to be irksome and a right unneighborly way for visitors to be acting.

So we stopped 'em. The way their eyes bugged out, you'd think they'd never seen a Shifter in his natural state of orneriness. They went running like we was demons jumped up outta hell." Philo chuckled at the memory.

"Caught one of 'em. Got him to tell us the poor fella's name before the other ones come back for him with bigger guns. 'Bout then, me and Tito figured it was time to cut and run. We drug the fella, Jack Stone was his name, off with us and let them Northern boys get away. Bet they went home boasting how they'd done their job by killing him, but just the same, we gave him a new name when he came around since he couldn't come up with his own."

"Jacques LaRoche," she concluded for him. "You saved his life and helped him start a new one here." Her eyes welled as she told him, quietly, simply, "Thank you."

Philo scowled at her. "You didn't know that's what they were planning?"

She shook her head. And then she understood. All this, the searching of the apartment, her abduction, was about Jacques. "I'm not here to harm him. I had no idea where he'd been taken. Somewhere he'd be safe is what I was promised."

"Looks like you was lied to. What we stumbled on weren't no catch and release. Them boys had murder on their minds."

And what weighed on Susanna's now was devastating.

Despite his promise, Damien had sent the father of her child to be murdered.

A sudden loud commotion from outside the little room distracted both of them. Then, as a ferocious roar sounded, the door was ripped away from its hinges.

Jacques wasn't sure what to expect when he lunged into the room, but it wasn't the sight of Susanna bound in a chair with her lip swollen and his best friend staring at him in guilty dismay.

"Give me a reason not to think what I'm thinking," he snarled, seconds from reacting in a manner he'd regret.

"It's not what you think," Susanna spoke up. That surprised him enough to let his claws ease back in. Aside from the split lip that someone sure as hell would answer for, she didn't look abused. Once her relief in seeing him had eased, her expression was calm, betraying no sign of fear or distress.

"Then tell me what I'm supposed to believe."

"His men brought me here because they saw the calls to Chicago on my phone. They frightened me and I hurt myself struggling. Mr. Tibideaux was furious with them and he was just about to let me go." Her voice softened. "You got my message this time."

"I did. Sorry it took me so long." His stare cut to Philo. "Let her go."

Without hesitation, Philo retrieved the key from one of his cowering associates and went to kneel down behind the chair. As he unlocked the cuffs, he said to her, "You were going to tell me about the calls."

She winced as she brought her arms in front of her to rub at her wrists. Her gaze never left Jacques as she said, "I've been calling to check on my daughter. She's ill and I'm worried about her."

"Something serious?" Philo asked as he straightened, pressing his hand briefly over hers.

Jacques thought he saw his friend tuck a square of paper into her palm but couldn't be sure since Susanna didn't react to it. She was concentrating on him and the effect of those dark eyes distracted him as she gave her quiet answer.

"It could be fatal if I'm unable to finish my work here."

Philo glanced to Jacques, then told her, "I'll spread the word that concern was unwarranted. You woan be bothered again, doctor. I hope your little girl gets better real soon."

"Thank you."

Jacques looked curiously between them. Something had been exchanged within their words but he missed the meaning. The one thing he did discern was Susanna's lack of animosity toward his friend. The slightest show of resentment or fear could have caused the situation to turn out differently, and he was glad it didn't have to. Still, he caught Philo's forearm and warned, "Control your dogs. You come to me first. Understand?"

Philo's eyes narrowed slightly, but he nodded. Jacques wasn't sure if that meant he agreed or just that he acknowledged the request. He didn't have time to worry about it at the moment. He stretched his hand down to Susanna, relieved by the feel of her delicate fingers crossing his palm and the reality of clutching them tight. Philo passed her oversized bag to her, looking uneasy enough to convey that he'd already gone through every penny and piece of gum in it.

As Jacques led her from the room out into the large warehouse, one of the two thugs scuttled backward, a look of alarm and distress on his face. It wasn't fear of him, Jacques realized. He was afraid of Susanna.

And then Jacques got a look at his neck where Susanna had left scratches. Only the feel of her shivering slightly against him kept his temper from exploding.

He looked between the anxious Morris and his equally uneasy companion, Anderson. "The two a you don't bother coming in to do more than collect your last checks." His tone ground with fury. "I'm minding my manners here for the lady's sake but if I see either of you on the docks or in my place again, I'm gonna get unpleasant right quick."

As the two of them blanched, Jacques circled his arm about Susanna's waist and walked away before he thought better of that uncharacteristic mercy.

"Could I get some water?" she asked as they passed a vending machine near the door.

Jacques fished out change to feed in and passed her the cold bottle. Her hands were shaking. After her unsuccessful attempt to twist off the top, he took it from her and opened it, then watched her drink greedily.

His heart was still racing. For all her calm, his emotions were unstable. Finding her gone had struck a dark terror in him and he was eager to get her safely tucked away as quickly as possible.

She slid down into the Caddy's wide seat like a weary child, sending his protective instincts into overdrive.

"I need to get my things from the club," she murmured.

"I have them in the trunk."

She nodded and closed her eyes, willing to turn the situation over into his hands. Hands that were suddenly damp and unsteady as adrenaline eased down. It helped that she sat quietly, seeming to doze as he navigated the maze of the dock area. She didn't stir when he stopped at the trailer.

"Stay put. I'll be right back." After her slight nod, he locked the car doors and made a quick pass inside, stuffing necessities into a drawstring garbage bag that joined her belongings in the trunk. Anyone watching would think he was taking out the trash.

Susanna's lethargy worried him, making him wonder if she'd been injured more severely than she let on. He detoured into a drive-through to pick up spicy chicken pieces, a side salad, and several large drinks, thinking the hydration, protein, and sugar might perk her up.

As the car started forward, he felt her fingertips

graze his arm, sliding down to rest atop his thigh. A quick glance showed her eyes were still closed, her features relaxed. Carefully, he fit his hand over hers in a protective and possessive gesture. The corners of her mouth took a slight upward curve as she drifted, trusting herself into his care.

It wasn't desire or lust or obligation or anything else that welled up in his chest at that moment. Though he recognized it, Jacques refused to give it a name. If he named it, he would have to own it, and he couldn't, not yet.

But the feeling wouldn't subside, wouldn't relent, wouldn't relieve its pressure so he could take a decent breath.

Dammit to hell.

He loved her.

The huge parking structure was all but empty. Max hadn't publicly released the news that the Towers were open, so for the next few days Jacques would have the central spire pretty much to himself.

He parked the Caddy by the elevator and gave his slumbering passenger a long look. Exhaustion etched the delicate features. Her soft breaths gently moved her breasts. He studied that mesmerizing rhythm until he heard how raspy his own breathing had become.

Stop it! Don't be a fool!

Jacques got out of the car, resisting the urge to slam his door as arousal and frustration stampeded over him. And fear. That was the worst of it. He was afraid of the things the fragile Chosen female awakened in him. Afraid to believe in them.

Susanna was off-limits, out of bounds, out of reach, out of his whole realm of existence. A brief yet satisfying moment between his sheets didn't change a damned thing.

When he opened her door, her head lifted and her groggy eyes struggled to focus. She made an uncoordinated effort to move her legs, prompting him to simply scoop her up out of the seat.

"I don't need to be carried," she murmured as, contrarily, her arms went about him and her face burrowed against his neck.

Hoping she was too out of it to notice how fast his pulse was pounding, Jacques urged the door shut with his foot. He'd have to come back down for the rest of their things. What was important was getting her safely behind secure doors.

The elevator was for tenant use only. He angled in to swipe his key and pressed for the eleventh floor, trying to ignore the way her breath stroked warm and light against his throat.

She felt so small cradled to his chest, but he knew she wasn't as fragile as she seemed. There was starch in her backbone and fire in her eyes. He couldn't imagine the courage it had taken for her to leave the security of her world to step, unguarded and alone as an outsider, into his. She was smart and brave and beautiful, and when she looked at him he felt as if he was suddenly more. More what, he wasn't sure, but he liked the feeling. And he liked the way she felt in his arms. And in his bed.

And if he continued with this line of thinking he was going to get himself into serious trouble.

His apartment was near the elevator but not so close as to disturb him with the comings and goings of his soon-to-be neighbors. New carpet and paint made the hallway inviting. Even though flames had never reached his floor, smoke and water from the faulty sprinkler heads had caused considerable damage. He held his breath when he opened his door.

The interior gleamed, the walls a pristine white, the vertical blinds at his balcony partially turned to let in a spill of natural late afternoon light. He sniffed, able to detect only a faint acrid hint over the scent of Susanna's hair. The furniture was new and stylish, from the tan leather couch to the rust and navy blue tapestried chairs and counter bar stools. An entertainment center housed a flat-screen television at least ten inches larger than the one he'd owned. The local art he'd picked out for his walls had been reframed and his lampshades replaced. There were just enough of his own belongings for him to feel welcomed home.

He carried Susanna to the sofa instead of the bed, thinking that would probably be safer. Once he'd settled her there, he stroked his hand over her hair to make her eyes flicker open.

"I'll be right back."

She made an unbearably sexy noise and snuggled into the overstuffed navy blue pillows.

Jacques practically ran for the door and, with some careful maneuvering at the car, was able to tote everything up with him in one trip.

Then he simply stood in the center of his living room and let a sense of satisfaction fill him.

His place. His home. His things.

Unbidden, his glance cut toward the couch.

His female.

Instead of shaking off that last claim, he allowed it to linger with the others, to become part of the poignant feel of belonging, of accomplishment.

How far he'd come from sleeping in doorways along Decatur upon waking to his new life in New Orleans. He had no recall of his situation before then so he couldn't judge if he was better or worse off. But what he had now would more than do.

He checked the main bedroom, surprised to find that, instead of his cheap full-sized mattress with its free metal frame, a mammoth king sat on an impressive dark wood base with heavy masculine foot- and headboards that matched the large five-drawer dresser. His clothes hung in the double closet still in their dry-cleaning bags and next to them a black suit he was certain he'd never seen before. He crossed to the floor-to-ceiling window, pushing open the drapes to a breathtaking view of the river. As he stood there, he blinked away the burn in his eyes and chuckled softly. Probably a residual from the smoke.

Before returning to see to his guest, he pulled out his phone and speed-dialed.

"Hey. Thanks."

"For what?" Savoie sounded genuinely puzzled.

"The upgrade to my place."

"Oh. No big deal. I like to take care of those who take care of me. Your music got water-damaged. Charlotte replaced what she could."

"Thank her for me."

"Thank us by having us over after you get settled in. I've been listening to you brag about your bourbon short ribs for long enough. Time to put up or shut up."

"How'd I end up with a tux?"

A pause. He could hear the mysterious smile in Max's voice when he said, "You never know when you might be called upon to wear one."

Where would he have to wear a tux? Except maybe to a wedding. Jacques's grin broke wide. "You and your detective—"

"Are going to be late for our reservations. In case you didn't notice, the bar and fridge are stocked, too. Have a good night."

"You, too, Max."

He was still smiling when he entered the living room. Susanna was sitting up on the couch, blinking uncomprehendingly at her surroundings.

"How are you feeling? You were out of it for a while there."

She rubbed at her eyes and temples, then glanced up at him. "Where are we?"

"This is my place. I just moved back in."

A sense of pride swelled as she looked around with an admiring sense of surprise.

"You'll be safer here," he added, "and a lot more comfortable than before."

She met his gaze, hers steady and direct. "I wasn't complaining."

His heart gave a strange shudder. "I know. I appreciate that."

"You've taken very good care of me," she continued in that same quiet voice that brushed over his senses like velvet. "I'm grateful."

Her gratitude wasn't exactly what he was after. He broke the tender/tense mood between them by gesturing to the table. "I picked up something for us to eat. Hungry?"

"Starved. Do I have time for a quick shower first? I feel like I've spent an afternoon tied up in a storeroom."

"Sure. I put your things in the bedroom. It's right through there."

She got off the couch, wobbling slightly, but put a hand up to keep him from offering assistance. He let her make her way unsteadily into the other part of the apartment. Then he stood, trembling inside at the thought of her in his shower.

Sucking in a saving breath of reality, Jacques went to the kitchen to check out the bar.

Twelve

After the minuscule space at the trailer with its lukewarm trickle, the forceful burst of hot spray in the roomy walk-in shower was heaven. Susanna stood beneath it, letting the heat soak into her achy muscles and rinse away the sweat of fear.

The mental exercise had exhausted her. Her head pounded and her system shivered from the strain. She'd almost managed her own rescue. Almost. But there was no shame in allowing Jacques to whisk her away from danger. His sudden appearance, all fierce and powerful, infused her with a different kind of weakness, the kind that had her knees shaking and made her thoughts go all swoony.

It wasn't a sense of obligation that had him racing to her side, claws sharp and eyes blazing with red sparks of fury. He'd come for her, to save her for himself, not for any other reason. And that was as frightening as it was flattering.

Philo Tibideaux knew her secret. She wasn't worried because it was in his best interest to keep it. What she couldn't trust were her own motives.

Everything she believed in had been shaken to the core, and the only one she could trust was the man she'd betrayed. The only way she could have him was to tell him the truth, but that truth would destroy any chance of them being together.

An impossible conundrum no matter how she looked at it.

She reached for the shampoo, frowning slightly at the two bottles. One was the brand she remembered from the trailer. The other was a floral botanical she couldn't quite imagine the burly bartender using to condition his shaved head. Tempted beyond her sudden jealous pique, she massaged it into her scalp, letting the fragrance envelop and soothe her senses.

Jacques had left a bag on the floor at the foot of the bed. She opened it to find their clothes heaped together in a careless fashion. With just the towel wrapped about her, she sorted and separated the garments into neatly folded stacks on the smooth deep blue bedspread.

She slipped on clean underthings and a loose pair of cotton drawstring pants over which she draped one of Jacques's swimming T-shirts. Not sure where she should put the clothes, she left them on the bed and padded barefoot with hair still damp into the main room.

Jacques was behind the kitchen bar, a bottle of beer raised to his lips. He paused midswallow when he saw her, something dark and faintly predatory coming into his eyes. Then he finished his drink.

"Food's on the table. Help yourself."

The smells coming from the open bucket had her mouth watering. Settling into a chair, she dove in for a drumstick and started to feast on it even as she scooped some of the salad onto her plate. She glanced up to see him regarding her with a smile.

"I see you haven't lost your appetite," he commented as she broke off two of the yeasty rolls.

"It's always been surprisingly healthy," she answered.

She thought she heard him growl as he turned to pull another beer from the refrigerator.

He came to join her at the table, an appreciative eye roving over her choice of clothing. As he walked behind her chair, she could hear him inhale. Then she felt the brush of his face against her hair.

"You smell fantastic."

Pleasure collided with a prickly sense of jealousy. "Just like all your other lady friends."

He paused behind her so she couldn't see his expression.

"What?"

"I figured it must be your preference, or did one of your guests leave the bottle behind?"

"What bottle?"

"In the shower." Her tone had grown as cold as that first blast from the faucet.

He was silent for a moment, then said, "Since you're the only female who's ever been invited here, my guess is Charlotte left it for you. I'll be sure to tell her you liked it." He moved to his chair and settled there looking annoyingly smug. Her irritation with him faded as she happily accepted that explanation.

"I'll be sure to tell her myself."

Jacques didn't look up from the meat he was pulling off the bones on his plate. "I was thinking of putting a computer in the second bedroom so you don't have to go back into the club. It would be safer and you could get more done."

She wasn't quite sure why that idea upset her so, but her tone was brittle with it. "And so could you, with me safely locked in your glass tower where you don't have to keep an eye on me."

He blinked up at her. "That's not what I meant—"

"That would be fine," she concluded. "I'm sure babysitting has grown tiresome for you."

After considering his options carefully and apparently not liking any of them, he didn't answer. They ate in silence for several minutes.

"What's wrong with your daughter?"

The question came as an unpleasant shock. She stumbled over it. "I told you, she's ill."

"Then why are you here, doing favors for near strangers? Shouldn't you be with her?"

"Damien's there for her." Even as she said it, she wondered if that were really true. *Damien doesn't like me.* "The answers to her recovery are here. That's why this research means so much to me. Hopefully I can turn my data into a treatment, maybe even a cure."

"For what? What does she have?"

"A genetic condition," she told him, careful not to give away too much. "She's fairly stable most of the time but I'm afraid that could change drastically at any moment." She looked away, emotions quavering until she felt his hand press firm and warm over hers. Her panic instantly settled.

Susanna ventured a look at him. Seeing the care in his intensely blue eyes, she took a risk. "If you were her father, would you urge me to stay here, even while my daughter's asking for me, so I can search for data that would prove a financial windfall?"

"You mean would I rather you be a mother or a moneymaker? I'd have had you on a plane yesterday. Family is more important than fortune. But I don't really have any family that I know of, so I guess I'm not much of an expert there." He glanced back at his plate before he could see the emotions softening in her expression.

Here was the man who should have been with her child. Not Damien, who, beneath the false face he'd worn to win her over, apparently cared for no one but himself. She'd cheated Jacques out of the chance to be that man and her daughter of the chance to know him.

Pain and uncertainty drove her from the table to sit tensely on the couch where she rubbed at her eyes in an effort to stay her tears.

How had she been so easily fooled? She'd believed Damien cared for her, for Pearl. She'd believed he was acting in their best interests instead of his own. She'd thought he'd wanted a family unit, not simply a very valuable life partner whose accolades and research he could turn into his own successes.

She'd accepted his lies because she'd been willing

to believe them. She'd seen good in him because she'd needed it to be there.

The cushions gave as Jacques sat down beside her. His arm rested along the back of the couch, surrounding but not touching her. His voice was low and achingly gentle.

"Anna, what's wrong?"

Anna.

He'd always called her Anna when they were alone, never Susanna.

With a soft cry of anguish, she turned and was in his arms.

"I've made such terrible mistakes," she lamented. "I've been so naïve."

He held her easily, providing that sense of comfort lost to her for so long.

The truth was there desperate to be spoken, all those ugly secrets ready to spill over, cleansing her spirit at the cost of shattering his. To silence them, she lifted her shimmering eyes to meet his, her hands raising to catch his face between them. And with an insistent tug, brought his mouth down to hers.

Her urgency quickly overcame Jacques's surprise as her lips moved upon his, sweeping, searching, waking a rumbling groan in his chest. The taste of him fueled her desperate hunger for more of the feast, encouraging her tongue to slip over and around his until he was coaxed to reciprocate with deep, lolling thrusts.

His kisses had always had the power to reduce her to pure sensation. She burned for him, for his touch.

But just as she was ready to lose herself in him, Jacques eased back just far enough for their gazes to meet, his a hot laser blue, bright with passion, tempered with one unspoken question.

"Please," she whispered against his parted lips. "I need this."

"We both do," was his response as he leaned into her.

His mouth teased hers in a tender stroke, caressing lightly over the slight swelling that remained at one corner, touching to her flushed cheeks, her feverish brow, to the flutter of her eyelids before sinking down to sample the frantic tempo at her throat. Susanna closed her eyes and let her head roll back against his shoulder as she clutched at the back of his head, rubbing over the bristle of hair he'd been letting grow out. She freed one hand to grip his, guiding it beneath the edge of the baggy T-shirt she'd borrowed, her body shuddering at the first warm glide of his fingers over bare skin.

It had been so long.

He continued to kiss her as he traced the outline of her bra, as he explored one lacy cup to excite a hard new pattern to rise against his palm. Her soft moan encouraged him. Her heart knocked like the bad valves in his Caddy as she kneaded the hard line of his shoulders with helpless, hurrying motions as he toyed with the center clasp. A sigh whispered from her as it popped open and he brushed that first barrier away.

Anticipation trembled through her, spiking goose-flesh all across her body as his thumb buffeted a sensitive peak. She arched her back to encourage him but he didn't need any urging. His fingers hooked the bottom edge of the T-shirt, drawing it slowly up to her chin.

The room's cool air was no match for the scorch of his stare as she angled back to settle against the slanted arm of the couch, her legs slipping across his thighs. Her lips parted in sultry invitation, bringing him down to her for a slow, searing kiss.

When her calf rubbed against the hard bulge behind his zipper, Jacques caught her knee to still the movement.

"Not a good idea," he whispered upon her lips. "Yet." She could feel his smile and relaxed, going temptingly languid so he could take his time.

Once he'd kissed her nearly mindless, he shifted his attention lower. Her breath hitched into a jerky rhythm as the scrape of his chin was followed by the delicious contrast of soft mouth and damp, teasing tongue. Her breasts quivered beneath that sensual assault as his hand slid lower still, trailing over the curve of her hip, caressing along her thigh.

"Please. Touch me." She didn't recognize the raspy purr of her own voice.

His palm cupped between her legs, pressing, circling until the cotton crotch of her bottoms dampened. Without leaving his tender worship of her breasts, he tugged the drawstring at her waist, loosening it so he could tuck his hand between soft fabric and softer skin.

So close already, all it took was the purposeful dip of his long middle finger, parting the moist folds of her body to sink deep inside her. A swift jolt of sensation sent a rolling climax through her, shaking along muscle groups, sizzling across nerve endings in a powerful wave. He swallowed her loud gasp with a heady kiss that prolonged her ride over those continuing crests until she sank into a satisfaction so deep it was like a dream.

A dream interrupted by the sudden loud buzz of the intercom.

Unwilling to be pulled from the intense pleasure of the moment, Jacques ignored the summons. The soft, luscious female he'd just brought to the first of what he'd planned to be many suspenseful peaks over the course of the evening was wet and more than willing for that journey. The scent of her arousal, of her readiness, fogged his senses like a thick perfume. The lambent glow in her half-lidded gaze spoke of her desire for him. The slow undulation of her hips pressing her hot sex against his hand demanded his attention.

And then that damned buzzer called. Once, long and forceful. Again, in three short, urgent blasts.

Susanna was struggling to sit up, hands leaving their appreciation of his body to wrestle the T-shirt down. She twisted out from under the claim of his palm to settle her feet on the floor.

"You'd better get that," she said breathlessly and scooted from the couch to the sanctuary of the bedroom while he dropped back against the cushions with a groan.

Cursing with every awkward step around an erection that felt like he'd tucked his Louisville Slugger down the front of his pants, Jacques crossed to the door. He punched the intercom and Philo Tibideaux's face peered up at him from the small closed-circuit screen that Max had installed in his apartment.

"Yeah?" he growled with a menace that would have scared most away.

But Philo looked deadly serious as he urged, "Buzz me up, Jackie."

Muttering another dark oath, he did so. Glancing down the hall toward the bedroom. The night was still young and she hadn't closed the door to the room or on his intentions.

Jacques was taking a long swallow of his beer and extended an opened bottle to his friend as he slipped into the apartment. Something about Philo's tense mood overcame Jacques's irritation.

"What's going on, Tib?"

He took a deep pull at the bottle before answering. In that time, his gaze did a quick sweep, noting the half-eaten meal, his boss's rumpled appearance, and the distinct odor of female.

"Bad timing?"

"Coulda been a helluva lot worse," Jacques grumbled. He gestured to the bucket Philo was eyeballing. "Help yourself."

Philo tore into a piece of the now cold chicken and munched thoughtfully before gesturing to the hall with the stripped bone. "Is she here?"

"Yes."

"She make any calls?"

"Not that I know of. What's this about? More conspiracy theory bullshit?" When Tibideaux didn't answer, his tone grew more impatient. "She's not spying on us. She's a doctor, not Mata Hari."

"Who?"

Jacques grabbed the phone from Susanna's purse and cued up her call history, breath held until he verified that none had been made while he was getting their things out of the trailer. More confident with that information, he faced his friend to warn, "Leave her alone, Philo. I'm not going to let you make her part of your witch hunt."

Philo met his stare angrily. "I've had over a dozen reports from my Patrol since this afternoon of strangers asking questions and being real aggressive about it. That's not *my* imagination. That's *real* trouble here in our city. If they're hunting, and it's not her they're looking for, I'm pretty damned sure who they're after."

Max Savoie.

"What are we supposed to do, Jackie, wait until they come knocking closer to home? Wait until they get rough?"

"Like you did with Susanna?" He hadn't believed her tall tale about injuring herself by accident while in their company. One of Philo's goons had struck her purposefully and he was still mad as hell about it.

"She's one of them, Jacques. Morris told me she was in his head, messing with his mind, getting him to do stuff against his will. That's one of their favorite tricks. Is that the kind of hoodoo she's been working on you? Open your eyes. Just because you're bedding the bitch—"

Jacques fisted his shirtfront, yanking the lighter man up onto his toes so they were eye-to-eye as he snarled, "Watch your mouth."

Philo knocked his hand aside and jumped back. "Watch your step. You can't see over your dick. She's leading them right to us. You're gonna be serving them drinks while they're tearing the hearts outta every one a your friends. You gonna have Savoie bury all of us in his backyard? That's what it's gonna come down to if you doan listen to me. Listen to me!"

"All I'm hearing is crazy talk," Jacques argued, fighting against his own worry that perhaps his friend was right. "You're as bad as they are with your 'Kill 'em all and ask questions later' macho crap. Our enemy is right *here*. It's the fear you're shoveling with both hands. What are you protecting? Your right to feel important?"

He knew he'd gone too far when Philo went still and simply stared at him through agate-hard eyes. Jacques palmed the top of his head in agitation, breathing too fast for logic to take hold.

"You think that's what all this is about?" Tibideaux finally asked with a deadly quiet. "You think this is about me wanting to be a big man? About me being jealous of Savoie? Well, maybe that's part of it. But you're forgetting the bigger part. You're forgetting what they did to Tito.

"I wish that coulda all been in my imagination. They killed my brother, Jackie. They beat the shit outta him, blew his brain apart, and threw him in the river like garbage. What part of wanting to keep them from doing that to *you* is about my ego?"

Jacques pulled his friend into a fierce one-armed embrace, hugging hard. The two brothers had taken him in like family, given him a place to live, work to do, a way to rebuild from nothing. Everything he'd made of himself he owed to them and their unconditional friendship. Everything.

So when Philo pushed away and confronted him with a somber expression and an even darker question, he didn't flinch.

"Where are your loyalties, Jacques? With Savoie and his human intrigues that are about to expose us? With this Chosen sympathizer who's wound her way around your ability to think straight? Or with your own kind, who've stood behind you and up for you for no reason other than you're one of us?" He gestured about the elegant apartment. "Doan let all this dazzle you into forgetting who you are. Doan let her confuse you into forgetting *what* you are."

With that challenge, Philo struck at the root of all Jacques's troubles. He didn't know those things. Not who he'd been or what he'd done before opening his eyes to stare up at a drizzly Louisiana sky.

Philo placed his hand on Jacques's shoulder and pressed hard. "All we got is each other now. We gotta stand together. Doan let Savoie with all his cash and big promises change that, or that pretty little piece of tail in there convince you that she's not your enemy. It's up to us to protect what's ours. You know that, doan you? You know I'm right."

And while he couldn't agree completely, in all good conscience, Jacques couldn't tell him to go to hell.

Philo clasped the back of his neck to give him a firm shake and to caution once more, "Keep your eyes open and remember who your friends are."

He was remembering after Philo left him with a promise to keep him posted. Remembering who and what was important.

Savoie hadn't bought him with extravagant gifts. Philo was wrong about that. Max had won him over with hope, with promises of freedom and pride in himself and for his race.

Susanna hadn't seduced him with sex. His friend was wrong about that, too. She'd intrigued him with her courage and honor. Simple sex didn't come close to describing the sensual hold she had over him.

But she *was* Chosen. How could he feel that compelling urge to mate with one outside his own kind? Because it had happened once before with a female he couldn't remember, under circumstances he couldn't recall? Or because she was manipulating his thoughts to make it seem so?

He glanced at the door that was now closed between them. She'd heard their conversation. He didn't check the knob. It didn't have to be locked to keep him out. Not while doubts swirled about his head the way the scent of her still did, confusing him, misleading him.

He took another beer from the refrigerator and carried it out onto the balcony where the breeze blew cool and heavy off the river far below.

Was he wrong to want to follow dreams no matter how impossible they might seem? If he listened to Philo and struggled to hold on to the way things had always been, he'd never risk extending his hand in hopes of grasping something better.

"Do you believe him?"

He hadn't heard her come outside. Now, Jacques was aware of nothing else as Susanna leaned on the rail beside him. The fragrance of her caressed his senses, making him slow to answer, which in turn aggravated her into a premature conclusion.

"So you think I'm some sort of witch here to trick you into revealing your secrets?"

Very quietly, he asked, "Are you?"

Her tone snapped with annoyance. "What could you possibly have in your head that's worth stealing?"

Susanna regretted it the moment she said it. Jacques didn't move for a long, suspenseful moment, making her wonder if she'd unforgivably wounded him. Then she heard the warm rumble of his laugh as it worked its way up and out. He grinned wide out at the night, his broad shoulders relaxing as if shrugging free of some terrible weight.

"Not much," he admitted. "It's more like a comic book rack than the Library of Congress. Lots of pictures, few words."

She smiled up at him. "But some pictures tell a better story."

"My story starts in the middle. No 'Here's what you missed on last week's show' to bring you up to speed."

"Your friend Philo told me how they found you. You don't remember anything?"

"Maybe it's for the best. Kinda like getting a second chance. I'm guessing whatever I did for them up north wasn't anything I'd want to take up again. Can't imagine that I left anything to be proud of behind."

Susanna said nothing. Her silence pulled his attention back to her.

His big hand stroked over her hair, then settled on her shoulder, drawing her gently against his side as he murmured, "So, what's your story? I've told you mine, now you tell me yours."

"It's not very interesting. An academic text, actually. Once my talent for science was discovered, I was placed in that community where I lived and learned and barely had time to breathe until a use for me was found."

"A use? What do you mean by that?"

"A way to be productive. I was enrolled in a human university where I could infiltrate their genetics program—so I guess you *could* call me a spy—and, due to my superior grades, I was selected for several governmental projects."

She felt his caution in the tightening of his muscles. "Doing what?"

"Research. Theoretical studies on DNA splicing. Testing for genetic defects and repair."

"Why did the Chosen want that kind of information on humans?"

"My studies weren't just on humans. Under the umbrella of their funding, I used their security clearances and equipment to pursue our studies."

"What kind of studies?"

She could tell the topic was unsettling him but she didn't back away from the answers. "It depended on who paid the most. Purists wanted to know how to separate Shifter and Chosen DNA strands, making them resistant to one another. Naturalists wanted to find a way to successfully recombine them. They called it science. I saw it as politics."

"And you played both sides?"

"I did the research. The research is pure. It's in the application that things get complicated. That wasn't part of my job."

"Isn't that like saying I just make the bombs, I don't decide where to drop them?"

Her gaze grew cool as did her tone. "While I appreciate your indignation, let me remind you that in my world, we have no freedoms, no rights, no choices. We do as we're told and we ask no questions."

"Or else what?"

"We're retrained or relocated."

His fingertips stroked lightly along the line of her

throat as she swallowed with difficulty. "Why don't you call it what it is? Brainwashing or exile."

Her chin notched up so she could meet his stare. Her voice was brittle. "We're brainwashed or exiled, but either way, we fit into the mold or the mold breaks us. Which would you have suggested for me?"

His palm cupped her cheek, his touch as soothing as his tone. "I'm sorry. I have no right to judge you for doing what you had to do to survive with no one there to protect you." His brows lowered slightly. "What about your mate? You said he took care of you."

She looked out over the river, tracking the lights on the lumbering barges as they moved toward the Gulf. "Damien was my mentor. He was responsible for brokering the projects I worked on, getting them funded, negotiating the rights to the research. I was his prize student, his best investment."

"His meal ticket," Jacques added dryly.

"Yes. He'd decide what grants to pursue and which to pass on, who could best benefit from our work and who might abuse it. I thought him the most honorable and generous man alive."

He had no comment about that. "And these were joint decisions regarding your work?"

"No." Try as she might, she couldn't keep that new tang of bitterness out of her voice.

"And how did he get such power over you? Did you love him that much, or were you required to hand that authority over to him when you mated?"

"Again, it wasn't as much a personal choice as a

professional necessity. He saved me from disgrace. At the time, I thought he did it out of the goodness of his heart." She started to turn away, to return inside and away from his questions, but he caught her by the shoulder, making her stop.

"He forced you? How?" The low growl of his words both appeased and alarmed her.

"It doesn't matter now."

"Of course it matters. Anna, what did he do?"

Anna. Emotion rose to clog her throat, preventing any further explanation. What could she tell him without revealing all?

She took a quick step toward the door just as his fingers closed on the shoulder seam of the T-shirt, pulling it away from what she'd tried to conceal from him.

Susanna heard his harsh intake of breath and risked a glance up at his face. Even in the shadows, she could read his shock as he stared at the telling scars.

"As you can see," she told him in a tight little voice, "I didn't always do as I was told."

Thirteen

You were bonded to a Shifter male?"

Jacques sounded so surprised, as if he were asking if she'd once had a second head removed from that spot between her neck and the cap of her shoulder.

"I was young. He was my bodyguard. I thought it wildly romantic, until we were discovered."

He blinked and shut his mouth with a sharp click. The muscles worked about his jaw as she watched understanding shutter his eyes. "You sold yourself to Frost so he'd save your reputation."

Her mouth quirked at the ugliness of that claim. "Something like that."

"Something like that or exactly that?"

"What does it matter? He made an offer at a time I couldn't afford to refuse it. I thought it all out very logically. It's what we Chosen do best."

Heart falling, Susanna went inside. What else could he believe? That was the truth. It was what they were: cold, unfeeling creatures motivated by numbers and profit rather than the emotions they reviled. Look how those treasured feelings betrayed her now. She would have been wise to remember what she was, rather than what she wished she could be.

She stumbled when his hands curled about her upper arms, drawing her to a stop. He stood close behind her. Though their bodies weren't touching, his heat seared her.

"Maybe that's what they do," he told her, "but not you. Was it the bond that changed you or have you always cared for others above yourself?"

"Why would you think that's true?" Her words were strong even as her lips quivered. *Please believe it.*

"Because you're here to help a friend. You're risking everything for those logic says you should cast aside." His voice lowered to a husky vibration. "Because you're ruled by your heart instead of your head."

"My greatest failing, according to Damien. The reason I need him to make my choices for me."

Jacques snorted at that. His arms formed a supportive circle about her, tightening until she was pressed against him. His head lowered to rest on her shoulder, his cheek rubbing over that telltale mark.

"What happened to your Shifter mate?"

"They would have killed him. Damien promised to help him escape as long as I never had contact with him again."

"Another term of your bondage to him?"

She nodded.

"Did you love him, your Shifter?"

Her eyes closed as she whispered, "Yes." Then, and now. "He showed me a world I didn't dare believe existed, one of color and light and dreams."

"And what did you give him?"

"The only thing I could offer. Freedom." Or so she'd thought. Until Philo told her of Damien's true plans. She'd sent Jack Stone to his death and he'd awakened as Jacques LaRoche.

"What was he like, your Shifter lover?"

Susanna placed her palm upon his rough cheek, her emotions twisting as she said, "He was like you. Strong, noble, gentle, a good man. You're a good man, Jacques."

Jacques forced a smile when she turned to look up at him, her dark eyes overflowing.

He didn't move as she stroked his face, as she turned and lifted up on her toes to kiss him.

He was like you.

Jacques scooped behind her knees, lifting her up in his arms as she continued to kiss him. He strode into the bedroom with her, pausing briefly in the mating of their mouths to rip back the covers on the big bed, sending their clothing to the floor in a colorful scatter as he lowered her gently onto that sea of dark blue silk. She never once glanced away as he stripped out of his clothes to stand before her, naked and bold. Her sultry gaze devoured the sight without a hint of shyness.

Jacques had no sense of modesty when it came to his own nudity. He knew he looked fit and powerful and was proud of that fact. He was used to females being enraptured with his sculpted torso and bulging arms, eager to put their hands on those rock-hard swells and delineating ridges.

He'd felt no threat from the existence of a Chosen

male as her mate, knowing they were delicate creatures more proud of their brain than their brawn. But when Susanna surveyed him through heavily lidded eyes, displaying admiration but no awe or alarm at his obvious masculinity, he wondered uncomfortably if she was comparing him to her Shifter lover, and how he fared in that study. That uncommon stumble of confidence made him hesitate, his focus slipping away from all that she offered.

"Jacques?" When he didn't respond, she came up on her knees, drawing his stare to her lovely dark eyes, to the slight curve of humor on her lips as she asked, "Wondering if you left the iron on in the other room?"

"What?"

"Second thoughts?"

And third and fourth.

She could have charmed him from his distraction with a touch but she didn't. She watched his face, waiting for him to think it through without complicating things further.

Maybe he was overthinking the issue. She'd been with another. So had he. They'd both lost the ones they'd pledged their hearts to with their bond. The past was a shadow, the future a void. All they would ever have was this brief time to ease each other's loneliness. What was wrong with that?

Nothing. Absolutely nothing.

"No second thoughts," he told her. "Not about this. Not about you."

"I'm glad."

Susanna reached for his hands, holding them in hers for a moment while marveling at their size and strength, then placed them at the edge of the T-shirt she wore, curling his fingers beneath the hem. All the encouragement he needed to lift it up and off her. She unfastened her bra and let it drop off her shoulders, then brought his hands to cover what satin and lace had bared.

A soft, plump handful. No more, no less. Perfect for him.

She put her hands on him, too, letting her palms roam the slope of his shoulders, play upon the contours of arms and chest. It wasn't the tentative exploration of an inexperienced lover.

Jacques sucked in a breath as her hands trailed over granite abs on their way to his even harder sex. No hesitation as she stroked him and cupped him, finally gloving him in a supple rhythm that broke a sweat on his brow and showed no sign of slowing even as the centers of his eyes swelled and his breathing faltered.

Before she brought things to too quick a conclusion, Jacques caught her by the elbows and lifted her from her knees. As she balanced on the edge of the mattress, his mouth cruised the silky curve of her belly as he eased her bottoms over the slight fullness of her hips and down shapely legs.

He stared, lost in his heated study. She was beautifully made, petite, pale, yet firm in those graceful feminine lines.

Her palms fit to his stubbled jaw, tipped his head

up so she could fall deeply into his eyes, her whisper husky with desire.

"I've missed this. I've been waiting all this time. For you."

Need shot through him like wildfire, scorching his senses, enflaming his lust until it was all he could do not to throw her down on the bed to pound away inside her to a desperate release.

For you.

That claim swirled about his emotions, stirring his raging passion into a fierce need to please her.

With one hand on the sweet globe of her ass, he used the other to lift her knee, drawing her leg over his shoulder. She clasped his head for balance, then gasped as he pressed his mouth against the mound of her sex, thrusting between her slick folds to sample her arousal with his tongue. Her body bucked and trembled as he tasted her, devoured her, until her breath grew tattered and her soft moans broke into a keening cry.

Then carefully, gently, he eased her down onto sheets as dark and cool as the night, spreading her before him, his heavenly body.

Her fair skin was flushed from the sensual exertion. Her eyes drifted open to fix upon his with a drowsy satisfaction, flooding him with a prideful sense of accomplishment, making him achingly aware of his own unmet needs.

Slow, he reminded himself. *Be gentle. She's not used to such vigorous pursuits.*

Ignoring the raging petulance of his body, Jacques

stretched out beside her, head propped up on the heel of one hand, the fingertips of his other drawing light patterns on her slightly damp torso. He smiled and she responded with a lazy, cat-in-the-cream expression that twisted his balls in a knot. Her fingers threading contentedly between his.

"We can go as slow and easy as you like," he murmured heroically.

She stared at him for a long moment, then cast an assessing glance at his pulsing hard-on. Her lips pursed. "I don't think so. I think I've done all the waiting I care to do. I want you. Now. Unless *you* need a nap first."

He grinned. "Just trying to be polite."

"Less polite talk and more get-to-the-point action, please."

His grin lingered. She was delightful, so soft and smart and unexpectedly sassy. And, best of all, insatiable. Everything he wanted in a female. In *his* female.

He drew a breath and let that truth shiver through him. He didn't just want her now. He wanted her always.

He leaned down to plant a soul-sucking kiss on her lips. The sound she made was liquid pleasure as her fingers laced behind his neck, pulling him over her, into the open valley of her thighs.

"Now," she whispered. "Please."

The feel of her, so hot and eager, was almost his undoing as he gradually sank into her center. Her body arched and shook wildly, making him slow his advance.

She broke from his kiss, panting unevenly. Her gaze

sought and found his. Then she smiled again as her legs circled his hips and pulled him in tight, seating him all the way to her womb with one fierce move. She gasped, eyes squeezing shut, then she opened them on a sigh.

"Oh, my. That was worth the wait."

He flexed his hips in a slow draw and thrust. Her fingers bit into his shoulder blades as he murmured, "Hang on, sweetheart. We're just getting started."

Once he was assured he wasn't hurting her, Jacques proved himself to be the skilled lover his cadre of fawning females suggested he would be. The few times they'd been together in the North, he'd been young and fierce, rough in his urgency, yet so exciting he'd stolen her wits, her breath, her very heart. The edge of excitement was the same, but years and experience had improved his patience and technique as he kept Susanna panting at the cusp of completion. He refused to let her hurry him from his steady, tantalizing pace no matter how hard she clutched at him and cried out for release.

Finally, with all his glorious muscles slick and bulging with strain beneath her palms, with his heart hammering against her breast, he tensed and surrendered control, allowing pleasure to coil and consume her in glorious waves and shudders.

His weight smashed her into the mattress but it was a lovely pressure. She couldn't make herself release him, her hands rubbing over his back, the soles of her feet caressing his calves and thighs, her lips whispering over the massive square of his jaw to the corner of his mouth.

Her thoughts were dazed and careless with sensual delight as she breathed into his ear, "Can we do this every chance we get until I have to leave?"

Until I have to leave . . .

She felt him flinch and instantly regretted speaking words that spoiled the moment. She couldn't, no, wouldn't take them back with false reassurances. It was better to remind him now than to let him—to let either of them—think anything else was possible.

She had to leave and he had to stay.

But until then, she could no longer deny herself the intimate aspects of his company. They would be friends, lovers, confidants, everything she'd desired and been denied in her own glacial world. And when they weren't indulging in those carnal pleasures, she would work every second to find an answer to their child's suffering.

And if she could find that answer, if Pearl could be cured, then perhaps they could revisit possibilities.

Jacques slid off her to settle on his back. His eyes were closed as he lay beside her but from the tension in his neck and shoulders, Susanna knew he wasn't relaxed. Her fingertips teased over his pectorals.

"Are you okay with that?"

"With what?" he asked, not opening his eyes.

"Being together like this."

"You mean exclusively?"

A sharp jab of jealous doubt took her in the heart. Perhaps that wasn't much of a deal for him. She couldn't fault him for previous encounters, but the thought of being forced to witness his flirtations with another—

"I'm okay with it." He looked at her then, expression somber as he added, "Until you leave."

Susanna curled into the tempting heat of his body, drawing an indescribable comfort from that closeness, determined to enjoy being with him while she could.

"I'm sorry. I wish I could offer more."

She felt his hand in her hair, the brush of his lips on her brow. Then he told her, "It's not your fault. It is what it is."

Unfair was what it was. Unbearable was what it was going to be when she had to let him go again.

"I wish—" She broke off, startled to have spoken that out loud.

His voice was a soothing vibration beneath her cheek. "What do you wish?"

Careful what you wish for, she cautioned herself. She settled for saying, "That things could be different."

He held her in silence for long minutes, then quietly confessed, "Me, too."

"Anna!"

Jacques shot upright, disoriented in the darkened room. His breath panted from him, his skin ran with sweat. He blinked back into awareness, letting the remnants of the dream fall away into confusion.

"Jacques?"

He rolled out from under the covers, thinking his

taunting nightmare had suddenly come to life beside him. As he stared up at her from his defensive crouch at the bedside, taking in the huge dark eyes against her ghostly pallor, pain thundered through his head in great, dizzying waves. With palms pressed to the floor to steady himself, he rode out the nausea and chills that often accompanied the dream, breathing deep until his head cleared to register time and place.

"I'm all right. It's okay," he softly panted, certain he'd scared her to death.

But it wasn't fright. It was something closer to an agony of distress. She finally blinked those shock-widened eyes, sending a trail of tears to score her pallid cheeks.

Before he could offer any further assurances, she slid off the bed to kneel with him, her arms circling his shoulders, her face pressing against the hurried pulse of his throat.

Jacques clutched her close, letting her warmth thaw his inner chill, letting her familiar scent steady his senses as he tried to separate fractured memory from this tender reality. Tried but couldn't seem to pull the two entwined threads apart.

Susanna straightened, placing her palms to his face, leaning in to kiss him quickly, feverishly. He cupped the back of her head, holding her still so he could deepen that intimate tangle of breath and tongues into a slow burning fire of longing.

He lowered his lips to those scars torn into her pale skin, where she'd been savagely scored and claimed by another lover. Her breath tickled warm against his ear, teasing him with the poignant gust of her sigh.

I will always love you.

That tender vow, long broken, whispered through his memory.

Or had it just been spoken?

Jacques pulled back, studying her features with a fierce concentration.

And then his cell phone rang.

Susanna regarded him, cheeks still bearing the tracks of her tears. Her dark eyes, steeped in that inner misery he didn't understand.

He drew a shaky breath, not knowing what to say to her.

Finally, he gave up for the moment, and reluctantly left her on her knees to go into the living room for his phone.

"LaRoche."

"Jackie, you know those strangers I was telling you about, the ones asking questions?"

It was Philo and his tone was deadly serious.

"Yeah?"

"They're not just asking anymore. They've started killing."

Fourteen

Susanna caught a glimpse of Jacques's tense features as he returned to the bedroom. She didn't question him as he jerked up a pair of jeans, then padded bare-chested and barefoot back into the other room. Hurriedly, she began dressing.

Jacques sat on the sofa, lacing on his boots while he spoke tersely to Max on speakerphone.

"Four of his Patrol are dead. A half dozen more are missing."

"Have him tell his men not to engage them, to gather up everyone they can and get them to the Towers. Give him your code. Get them to safety. I'm on my way to the club. Meet me there."

"Maybe you and Charlotte should come here to the Towers, too."

"I don't hide from the likes of them," Savoie sneered with an arrogant fury. "If they're looking for a fight, they're going to damn well get one."

"Be there in five, see you in fifteen."

As he snapped his cell closed to end the call, Jacques saw her standing in the hall. For an instant, her ethereal beauty struck the breath from him. Then he was all business, surging off the couch, striding past her into the bedroom to snatch up a black Henley pullover.

"Lock up after me. You'll be safe here. Don't buzz anyone in. Call if you need me."

"I'm coming with you."

He whirled to face her, brows lowered like the storm clouds thickening over the river outside his windows. "No, you're not," he growled in a no-nonsense tone.

"I'm a doctor. I might be of help."

"I hope like hell that won't be necessary, but if it is, you can do whatever you can from here."

"That won't be good enough."

"We're not arguing about this."

"No," she told him firmly. "We're not. If they've come for Max, I'll stay out of the way. They have no reason to harm me. But if they've come for me, there's no way I'm going to allow them to harm anyone else." *To harm you*, was what her heart was beating out in a fearful tattoo.

He stared at her, eyes flat and black. "Not a chance." He pulled on the shirt and started to push by her. She caught his arm and held tight. When he glared down at her through those wildly angry eyes, she stated one simple fact.

"It's not your choice."

He drew a harsh breath, holding it against all the protests she could see building in his gaze. So she placed her hand upon his mouth, stroking gently as she said again, with a quiet finality, "It's not your choice."

His stare was filled with a tragic frustration of fear and powerless rage. The fear for her, not for himself, and the rage directed at the circumstances he couldn't control.

They rode down in the elevator together. Tension jumped in his jaw as he refused to look at her.

"You'll stay behind me," he ground out.

"Okay."

"You'll do exactly what I tell you."

"I will."

"If I say run, you'll run like hell."

"Will you be with me?"

"No."

"Then I won't be running."

He turned on her, gripping her upper arms to give her a shake, his voice coldly furious. "This isn't a game, Susanna. This isn't some clinical test run in your sterile little lab. These are lives I'm talking about, the lives of those I care for. I can't protect them and be worrying about you at the same time."

"Don't worry about me. I'm safer with you than anywhere else I could be. You do what you need to do. I'll be fine."

He pulled her hard against him with a growl of "I wish I could believe that."

She clutched at his shirt, her eyes squeezing shut. She wished she could believe it, too, but a terrible panic was banging inside her. A fearful certainty that whatever was waiting for them wasn't something they'd easily walk away from. At least, not together.

"This is madness, Anna, you putting yourself in this kind of danger."

She could hear the strain shake through his voice, but there was pride there, too. She clung to that as fear flushed through her, telling him, "I'm not giving up a single minute I could be spending with you."

Especially if it was to be their last.

The club was full, its patrons milling about uneasily, spreading half-whispered rumors about what was happening. Nica met them at the office door, frowning at the sight of Susanna. Jacques pushed the doctor toward her.

"Guard her with your life, Nica. Keep her where I can see her."

The dark assassin nodded. "I will, boss."

Jacques continued on down the steps. Nica's arm hitched about Susanna's waist when she tried to follow.

"Let him go do his guy stuff. He doesn't need you there."

Susanna's breath hitched painfully, her knees buckling. Nica's support was firm and bracing.

"Don't you let him see that you're afraid," Nica warned with a toughness that fueled her own inner strength. Susanna straightened, inhaling deeply until the dizziness released her. Then Nica gave her an approving pat and a warm, "Good girl."

"How bad are things going to get?" she asked when she had control of her voice.

"Depends on how many there are and what they want. I'll feel a lot better when—" She broke off that sentiment with a gust of relief, her gaze fixed upon the tall Shifter striding toward them. "Hello, hero," she purred and cast herself into Silas MacCreedy's arms. Their kiss was like a violent force of nature. Nica finally rocked down from her toes, her arms still about his neck. "You bring my stuff?"

Silas passed her the backpack he carried. "I wouldn't want to leave you naked."

She grinned. "Yeah, you say that now." She gave him a push. "Go be a tough guy, but if you make me sleep alone, I'll never forgive you."

"Thought you didn't like my snoring?"

"Well, there's enough other things you do that I like to make me overlook that. Watch your back, lover."

"Always." His fingertips stroked under her chin, then he nodded to Susanna and went to join Jacques at the bar, Nica's gaze fixed on him like a targeting laser.

"How can something make you so weak and so strong at the same time?" she wondered out loud.

"I don't know," Susanna answered.

Noting the way the doctor's stare adored the big bar owner, Nica chuckled. "'Bout time. Have you told him?"

Susanna looked to her in alarm. "Told him what?"

Nica smirked. "I didn't need to see how you look at him. I've seen your daughter. No time like the present to make a confession."

"Not yet. I can't yet." Then she made a meaningful connection between her friend and MacCreedy. "Some secrets are kept for a reason."

Nica raised a brow and said nothing more.

Jacques's booming voice filled the cavernous room. "Those of you with families, get them and meet Philo at the Towers. He'll see you safely inside. The rest of you, stay with me. Drinks are on the house."

Two-thirds of the customers slipped away, hurrying out into the night. The others crowded in close to the bar to accept a free beer and huddle packlike. Jacques gestured his two waitresses over, hugging them both in close before telling them to go and go quickly. Jen bolted, but Amber lingered, worried eyes lifting to his.

"Go on, Amber. We'll be fine on our own. We can serve ourselves for once. You've got that little girl to take care of. Go on. And don't come back in until I call you."

She surprised him by grabbing on tight and not letting go. He cupped the back of her head, emotions twisting up, then finally shook her loose.

"You keep up this insubordination and I'll be rethinking that raise."

"Raise?" she sniffled. "For what?"

"Cost of living, darlin'." He pressed a kiss to her brow. "Now go earn it."

She darted off, pausing long enough to share a hug with Nica and to give Susanna a puzzled glance before disappearing out the back door. Nica dropped the heavy security bar across it and shouted, "Hey, boss. How 'bout some rock 'n' roll?"

She ducked into the office and AC/DC's "If You Want Blood (You've Got It)" came blasting out of the sound system. Her head bobbed in time to the tempo as she grinned at Susanna. "Good beat for getting down to business."

Susanna was too terrified to breathe until Nica nodded down to the gathering at the bar. "Is there anything sexier than hot men gearing up for some serious partying?"

She stared at her, aghast, until she noticed the brilliance of Nica's dark sapphire eyes as they caressed over her mate. Then Susanna turned her attention to Jacques LaRoche as he took his pistol out from behind the bar, checked its clip, and tucked it into the waistband of his jeans with smooth, dangerous movements. Her pulse gave a sudden quiver.

"I can't think of anything at the moment," she whispered.

"When did you first know you were in love with him?" Nica asked to distract her from what was coming.

"I was working late in the lab, trying to finish up a project," Susanna began quietly, her gaze never leaving the burly figure behind the bar. "I didn't like having a watchdog hovering over me but there'd been some threats so I didn't have any choice. I sent him to find me some fresh coffee, not because I needed some, but because I just wanted to be able to breathe, you know." She glanced over to catch Nica's empathetic nod. "I don't know how they got in or where they came from. There were four of them, armed, masked, determined. They told me if I made a sound, they would kill me. I believed them."

Susanna drew a slow breath, tasting the bitter adrenaline of that moment when her hands were bound and she was dragged into the dim stairwell, sure if they got her out of the building that she was going to die.

"He came swinging down through the stairwell from I don't know how many floors above to put himself between me and them. I'd never seen a Shifter in his natural form before and I don't know which frightened me more, him or the men he was protecting me from. I ran as he charged them. I could hear their gunfire but I didn't look back, I just ran. One of them managed to get by him. I fell down the last few steps and remember watching from the floor as that gun pointed at my head, watching that finger tighten on the trigger, knowing my next breath was going to be my last. And then he was there to shield me, taking that bullet meant for me."

You're safe now. I have you.

"He was the most exciting thing I'd ever seen, all covered in blood and full of bullet holes. And I remember wondering how something so deadly could have hands so gentle." Her voice faded into a sigh. "I've been in love with him ever since that moment."

"Tell him, Suze. Life's too damned short and lonely to keep those kinds of secrets."

"When this is done. I'll tell him then." Once that was stated, Susanna was distracted from the current threat to wonder how Jacques would react to the news. To the knowledge of what she'd done.

A commotion from the main entrance pulled all attention toward the hall as Max staggered into sight, dragging Charlotte with him. Jacques and MacCreedy were instantly beside them, Silas taking over the burden of his NOPD partner and Jacques getting Max into the nearest chair.

"What happened?" Jacques demanded, crouching down beside his leader, searching for serious injuries beneath the liberal splashes of blood, not finding any of significance. Most of it came from the gore dripping off Savoie's hands.

"Got a jump on us," Max panted, his vocal pattern broken, his movement spasmodic. "Used some kind of Taser. Couldn't turn all the way. Charlotte?" He tried to rise out of the chair to go to her but his legs gave out, Jacques's grip the only thing holding him upright. "She went down. What did the bastards do to her?"

"I don't see any wounds," Silas announced as ran a visual search over the limp form collapsed in the opposite chair. "What the—?" He plucked a small dart from the back of her neck. "What the hell is this?"

"Tranquilizer," Susanna told him, kneeling down on the other side of the now faintly stirring detective. "I've seen them used before. They're very powerful."

Charlotte's eyes flickered open, unfocused at first, then fixing on Susanna in alarm. Her unsteady hand reached for the puncture wound but she was too weak to complete the move. "What—?"

"They used a sedative. That's why you feel numb and disoriented. The effects won't last long," Susanna assured her. But it wasn't her own health Charlotte was concerned with as she gripped the doctor's wrist.

"The baby? Will it harm the baby?"

Susanna glanced at Max, seeing the monumental shock hit him as she said, "Don't worry. The baby's fine." She hoped, but she couldn't be certain.

"They're coming in!"

The shout from the hall sent the cluster of anxious Shifters scattering for the dark corners of the club, leaving the six of them isolated and alone.

"How many?" Silas drew his ankle piece and the one Charlotte carried. Both were filled with silver loads.

"A lot." Max's words confirmed the worst.

Jacques stood, nodding to Nica and Susanna. "Get Charlotte behind the bar. Stay there." To the others, he shouted, "Stand with me."

Before any of them could move, an object came flying into their midst.

"Get down!"

Silas's warning was followed by a huge percussive blast and a blinding starburst of light. The seconds that followed were ones of chaos and confusion until the vibration eased.

Jacques found himself on the floor, head ringing, spots of black and red dancing across his vision. Max had fallen with him and was struggling to tip up a table to use as a shield.

"Flash-bang grenade," came Silas's terse call. "Get ready."

Jacques could just make out the sight of Nica and Susanna hauling Charlotte toward the bar. A thick layer of smoke poured like heavy white paint across the floor, then began to rise in an acrid mist, concealing both friend and foe. Protect their leader and their women. Those were his only thoughts. He refused to consider what he knew was the truth: that they had no possible chance of defeating this deadly and efficient enemy.

From out of the wispy fog came a cold ultimatum as a large figure all in black partially emerged, eyes glowing red.

"We're here for Max Savoie and Susanna Duchamps. Don't get in our way and you'll live beyond the next few minutes."

Max *and* Susanna. A fierce objecting growl ripped through Jacques. No way. He let the beast inside him go, feeling the aggression and ferocity flood his system, fueling his powerful muscles, sharpening his senses with a razorlike focus. His enemy had the advantage of strength but he was defending his home, his friends, his female, and that made him more dangerous than they expected. Surrender wasn't an option.

Silas answered with a cold finality, hurling a low and deadly "Not happening," along with a quick, tight pattern of shots that struck the challenger dead center, flinging him back out of sight.

And from around the spot where the one had fallen, at least a dozen leapt forward.

Jacques made his shots count, picking clear targets,

aiming for head not chest, to kill not just to stop. From beside him, he could hear the methodical blasts from Silas's pistols as he did the same.

But they were too fast and too many. Their meager defense was quickly breached as the savage creatures swarmed over the three of them.

Jacques never saw his attacker. A wrecking ball force struck him in the chest, caving in his rib cage, bowling him over onto his back. Choking on the thick smoke and his own blood, he managed to angle his pistol up to place a single bullet into the gaping jaws coming down for his throat. He struggled to push that sudden deadweight off him as he heard Susanna's shrill scream. He had to get to her. Nothing else mattered. Not the agony of each tattered breath, not the huge swelling dizziness threatening to pull him down.

He got his feet under him, vaguely aware of his surroundings. He saw Silas engaged in brutal hand-to-hand with one of them before they toppled back and were swallowed up in mist. Unable to make a complete shift into his deadly form, Max grappled with another. And Jacques could see, where they crouched low and hidden, the glowing eyes of those who were too afraid to come to their aid.

He tried to shout out a rallying cry to them but only managed a frothy gurgle. Then he was driven to his hands and knees with one of the Trackers on his back, claws tearing through the side of his face and neck, fangs ripping into his shoulder. His ears rang as MacCreedy fired point-blank into his assailant's temple before being taken down to the floor by the lunge of another.

Unable to draw a breath past the thick fluid filling his lungs, unable to see through the smoke and blood burning his eyes, Jacques edged toward the bar in an awkward crawl. *Anna.* Though he no longer heard her cries, he could scent her fear. Claws dug into the slick floorboards as his arms shook with the effort of dragging his shattered body just a few inches at a time. *Anna.*

Then light exploded through his head, followed by blessed darkness.

The three of them huddled behind the bar, helplessly listening to the sounds of their men locked in battle. Nica pulled the handle from her battered backpack. With a quick twist, she separated the hard plastic into two sections joined by a shiny length of cord.

Charlotte struggled to stand, desperate to go to the aid of her mate. Susanna held her down, terrified for the fate of her own. She shrieked in surprise as a huge figure suddenly appeared on the top of the bar, crouched low with feral eyes blazing and sharp teeth bared.

Nica swung with deadly accuracy, sending one of the handles circling about the Tracker's neck. With a vicious yank, she snapped thin razor wire tight, severing his head in a fountaining spray. Susanna scuttled back as it dropped nearly in her lap, swallowing down her sickness as another sleek beast appeared above her.

She grabbed the Louisville Slugger and swung with all her might, connecting with ravening jowls in a loud crunch of teeth and bone. Then, smashing one of the pitchers from under the bar, Charlotte drove the jagged edges into the creature's throat, ending his threat as he flailed for balance.

A figure loomed up in front of them, hand flashing out to catch Nica's wrist as she slashed with a wicked blade. Instant recognition and relief lit her eyes as MacCreedy released her and tucked in beside them.

"Where's Max?" Charlotte's voice cut like the blade in her friend's hand.

"He went down. I lost sight of him." His eyes shone with an eerie laserlike brilliance from out of his scratched and bloodied face. He was breathing hard, elbow tucked in tight against his side where his shirt hung in shreds. He did a quick check of his clip and the way his features grew grim told the bad news.

"And Jacques?"

Silas gave Susanna a long, unblinking look, then he shook his head.

The life went out of her in a sudden whoosh. Susanna couldn't believe it, wouldn't believe he was dead. Reeling and light-headed, she staggered to her feet, forgetting about all the surrounding dangers in her desperate need to see for herself.

The second she cleared the top of the bar, huge claw-tipped hands caught her by the elbows, dragging her off her feet and out of sight.

"Suze!" Nica started up and found herself looking into a pair of fiery red eyes.

Silas's arm snaked around her, whipping her bodily behind him as their enemies were abruptly on all sides. He snarled low and fierce, bracing for a fight he couldn't win.

"Stop!"

Max.

"Don't hurt them. I'll go with you."

"Max, no!" With an angry cry, Charlotte surged forward only to have Silas catch her about the waist, holding her back as she spat and writhed, growling, "You're not taking him anywhere, you sons of bitches. Max!"

Her wild gaze flew up to her partner's.

"Mac, we can take 'em. Dammit, we can take 'em."

When Nica saw the ferocious pride squaring up his stance and the way that perceived threat brought the half dozen Trackers to an immediate alert, she did what she had to do to save the situation.

"There's a time to fight and a time to be smart. Si, be smart. We can't win this one."

When he remained unbending, she reacted quickly, gripping his hand and pressing his palm to her flat belly. At his questioning look, she explained softly, "Charlotte isn't the only one expecting." She waited for understanding to seep in, then urged, "Protect us."

As she knew they would, his defenses broke before his love of family. Slowly, with an arm about each of them, Silas went to first one, then both knees, subduing a struggling Charlotte and hugging his mate close as he assumed the humbling position of surrender.

Out on the floor of the bar, Susanna saw Max Savoie take a similar posture, kneeling so his hands could be shackled behind him in cuffs of silver and a mask secured over his head with razor-sharp blades across the faceplate to keep him from shifting form.

Her gaze skipped over him to do a swift sweep of the smoke-wreathed floor and then her heart staggered.

His name tore from her throat, a wounded, bleating cry. With a quick wrench of her body, Susanna pulled away from the big Tracker who'd been holding her loosely, not expecting her to struggle. She ran, stumbling in shock, sliding in the blood, to fall to her knees beside the still form of Jacques LaRoche. He lay facedown in a pool of slowly spreading crimson, his life seeping out from a hideous gash at the base of skull.

All her sacrifices, all her suffering and sorrow had been for nothing. She hadn't been able to save him after all.

Whispering his name over and over in dazed disbelief, she touched a trembling hand to the side of his ravaged face.

And began to sob as his eyes flickered open.

Jacques was confused at first, hearing his name chanted by a younger version of Susanna Duchamps. Only the name she said was Jack, not Jacques. As tears fell from her luminous dark eyes, those features altered slightly, becoming the familiar visage he loved.

He was on the floor. A loud buzzing roar in his head distorted the sound of Charlotte's furious scream toward those who still huddled low and out of sight.

"You cowards! You fucking yellow bastards! After all he's done for you!"

Jacques didn't understand her rage but it hurt too much to wonder over it. Instead he concentrated on the lovely face hovering near his, on the gentle stroke of fingertips upon his torn features.

"I'm sorry. I'm so sorry," she said, weeping as if her world was ending.

He tried to say her name to comfort her and ease her sorrow but couldn't form the sounds.

He saw her look up suddenly, her surprise evident at seeing the handsome male who'd come up behind her. An elegant hand reached down to her. His voice was soft and calm.

"Come with me and I'll make sure they live."

Jacques's last conscious sight was of her hand reaching up to take the one offered.

Fifteen

The liar who'd ordered her lover killed regarded her with a benign smile.

"Have some more water, my dear. You need to hydrate."

Susanna glanced from the proffered bottle to the man sitting opposite her in the sleekly expensive private jet. She hadn't spoken since she'd been hurried aboard, struggling to suppress her shock and anguish behind an impassive front. Just as she'd been taught.

When she had control of her voice, Susanna asked, "What were you doing in New Orleans, Damien?"

He smiled again, a gesture she'd once believed sincere, but now knew better. "I came for you, of course."

She made no comment as he reached across the table that separated them to twist the top off her spring water. Obediently, she drank, clenching her stomach muscles to keep the liquid down.

It tasted like blood.

When she didn't ask, he chose to explain.

"I was approached by some security officers who said they'd been notified of your presence in New Orleans in the company of several suspected terrorists. Imagine my surprise."

She'd have to imagine, because there was no trace of any emotion on the perfectly composed mask he wore.

"I assured them that you had no part in anything of a sordid nature, that you were doing research on a classified government project. That was rather difficult to sell since they were from the government and knew nothing of any such project."

Susanna caught a slight flash of irritation in his mild gaze. He tried to hide it behind a flustered gesture. He'd not only been surprised, he'd been humiliated. And he was still furious.

"I was beside myself with worry for you."

She disguised her snort behind a cough and took another small sip. Hydration was a good idea. She was thinking more clearly about the dangers of her situation.

"I had no idea, Damien. I would never compromise our work. You know that."

A thin smile. "That's what I told these very stern gentlemen. And of course, I was terrified for your safety. I agreed to help them find this vicious criminal they were after but only on the condition that I could come along to assure that you weren't inadvertently harmed, you being an innocent pawn in whatever scheme they were plotting. I was only thinking of you and Pearl."

He was only thinking of the potential damage to his reputation. She understood perfectly.

"How did you find me?"

"I activated the GPS in your phone."

"I never thought of that," she mused. "How very clever of you."

"A desperate man employs any means."

She took a deep, composing breath and did what was necessary to salvage her position. "How can I thank you, Damien? Again, you've rescued me from my own impulsive nature."

Her apology seemed to appease him, but only for a moment.

"How long have you known he was there?"

His rapier-quick question slashed painfully in a surprise attack. She parried with an honest stammer. "I didn't know. I've never known. I never even tried to look. It would have been . . . foolish."

"And dangerous," he supplied, the threat not terribly subtle.

"There was no danger. He had no idea who I was."

Damien Frost studied her through those unblinking black eyes. The reptilian eyes of a cold-blooded creature. "And you made no effort to rekindle your relationship with him? Tell me the truth, Susanna. You know I'd forgive you anything."

"No, I did not," she said with just the right touch of indignation. "We had an agreement. You kept your end so, of course, I kept mine. I'm no longer a child. I am fully aware of my position and obligations. I would never do anything to jeopardize them. Or embarrass you. I owe you everything."

"Yes," he said with a cold pleasure. "You do. I'm satisfied with your honesty."

Susanna didn't relax at his assurance.

She would have to be very, very careful. She was returning to a world filled with enemies, with those who would rip her security from her and destroy the one thing she'd struggled so long and hard to protect: her daughter's survival.

So she sipped from the water to hydrate, then pretended to fall into a restorative sleep. Only behind her closed eyes did she dare revisit the horror of the past few hours, of the sight of Jacques LaRoche sprawled upon the floor in a pool of blood that still discolored the clothing she wore.

But he was alive.

That was all that mattered.

And he would continue to live as long as she remembered how to play by the rules. Rules that might someday be broken with the materials contained in the bag she'd tucked beneath her seat.

Until that time, she would play the game under the wary supervision of Damien Frost.

To protect her future with the man and child she loved.

Jacques might have had worse days, but he couldn't remember when.

The club was dark and silent, its doors closed for the first time since he'd opened them four years ago. Someone, probably Nica, had stopped the last of his blood from running out onto the floor, cleaned up his face, and bandaged his shoulder. He'd been dragged up into a chair, force-fed a lion's share of raw meat to encourage healing, and left alone at his request. As soon as he could manage small, shuffling steps, he'd retreated into his office like a bear into its cave, taking a bottle of single malt to hurry the journey, hoping when and if he emerged, his world would have righted itself.

The leader he believed in was gone, tearing the substance out of the future he depended upon. The woman he loved had also vanished, betraying not only his dreams, but memories she'd somehow become entangled in. His best friend and trusted lieutenant blamed him for endangering them all, first by embracing Savoie and all he represented, then for opening their secret existence up to one of their enemies. And the Upright female he admired and respected had damned them all as cowards. He had no reason at all to poke his head out of his comfortable lair until the harsh emotional weather changed.

"You can't make things better by hiding in here."

The sudden intrusion of Nica's voice was not welcomed.

Jacques opened a bleary eye to squint at her where she sat on the perpendicular couch. "Says who?" he grumbled, reaching down from where he lay sprawled upon the other part of the sofa for the bottle he couldn't remember emptying. He stared at it for a surprised instant, then let it drop back to the floor.

"Experience," was her pat answer.

"Well, my experience has been the harder you fight, the more you lose." He closed his eyes, hoping she'd just go away. Wishful thinking.

"So you're just going to sit this one out?"

"What difference does it make? Leave me alone, Nica."

"You're a whiny drunk, LaRoche."

He scowled. "And you're a pushy bitch, Fraser. Get outta my office."

"If I left, who'd you have to smack you back to your senses?"

"No one. That was kinda the idea. Where's your loverboy?" he asked, to turn their conversation in a less personal direction. "Why aren't you off bothering him?"

"He's at the Towers trying to get everyone calmed down and settled in."

Good ole MacCreedy. Stepping right up.

"Kinda like locking the chicken coop after the wolves finished their dinner, don't you think? They got what they wanted. They won't bother with us anymore."

"He could use your help."

Wincing at the sudden sharpness of her tone, Jacques hugged his arms about himself. "He doesn't need me. He's a smart boy. He's got everything under control. Just ask him."

"Want some cheese with that whine?" she drawled.

He hauled himself into a seated position, gritting his teeth against the pain stabbing through his slowly mending chest, to growl, "What do you want from me, Nica?"

"A little backup would be appreciated. I used to be able to count on you for that."

Flinching from an even sharper discomfort, Jacques muttered, "Sorry to disappoint you."

Her eyes grew flinty. "This isn't about me, Jacques. It's about them. They count on you to give them direction."

He snorted. "Yeah, some leader. Follow me, right into this dead end. They wouldn't follow me across a room when I was depending on them to have *my* back. Probably the smart choice, considering." He slumped back against the cushions, the fight and heart going out of him. "I don't care where they go. I just don't care."

He braced for more of her right-to-the-bone repartee, deserving of her scorn. But he wasn't prepared for her sympathy.

"She didn't bring them here, Jacques."

Everything inside him shuddered loose as she exposed that raw nerve he hadn't realized was at the root of all his misery. "And you know this how?"

"Because I know her."

"That simple?"

"Yeah, it is. So why are you making it so complicated?"

Before he was forced to come up with an answer, the lights went on in the body of the club. Jacques twisted around, groaning at the effort, surprised to see some of his crew righting furniture and sweeping up broken glass and bullet casings. Amber and Jen went to work on the bloodstains with buckets and brushes.

"What the hell are they doing here? I didn't ask—"

"Must be worried about their job security. Can't think of any other reason, can you?"

Jacques gave her a look. "I can think of one, sitting over there looking annoyingly smug."

"And I can think of an even bigger one, sitting over there looking irritatingly clueless." She sighed. "Life goes on, boss. Time to get back among the living." She turned just as MacCreedy entered the room. "Hey, lover. Great timing, as usual."

Jacques had no real reason to bristle up with resentment just because Nica's mate looked freshly showered and ultracompetent after the grueling twenty-four hours he'd just put in. Time Jacques had spent licking his own physical and emotional wounds instead of seeing selflessly to others.

When Nica stepped up to him, MacCreedy folded her easily into his arms and just for an instant, he leaned.

"Get everyone buttoned in tight?" she asked as her hands pushed inside his cheap sport coat to rub over his crisp white shirt.

"I think so. Philo's been a big help rounding them up. Think he needed something to keep him busy. He's pretty broken up about losing so many of his friends."

And MacCreedy was there for him. Where Jacques should have been.

"How's your partner holding up?" Though her tone was conversational, her touch soothed and comforted.

"Getting ready to go solo on the Rambo warpath." His cool glance went to Jacques, then quickly away. "Maybe you can talk some sense into her, Nica, before she does something ill-advised."

Nica snorted. "You think I could be talked down if they'd taken you?" She revolved in the curl of his arms to look at the figure still slumped on the couch. "Jacques, you talk to her. She listens to you."

"I don't think she has much use for any of our kind anymore." His voice lowered. "And I don't blame her."

"Then let's see if we can change that by getting Max back for her."

Jacques stared at her blankly. "You gonna just head north and start knocking on doors?"

Her expression grew cunning, making Jacques all kinds of uneasy. "No. That's not what I had in mind." Her smile made him even more nervous. "Go down and thank the troops, boss. I need to talk to my man for a minute."

Cautiously, Jacques hoisted himself off the couch, clutching his rib cage as if to hold himself together.

MacCreedy's brow puckered. "You all right?"

"Fine." He growled, knowing he didn't look it. The left side of his face and scalp was a latticework of faint scars. He still wore his bloodied clothing, mainly because he couldn't manage to lift his arms high enough to shed his shirt. His breaths were small and shallow lest they incur painful retribution from his mending ribs. In short, he was a mess inside and out and not pleased to have that pointed out. Even if Nica did it so much sweeter.

She stretched up to hug him about the neck, murmuring, "You look like hell, boss. Just go home. Shower. Eat something. I'll say your good-byes for you and take care of things here."

"No. I'll do it. You can lock up."

"Got it under control. See you in about an hour."

And he needed to do the same with himself, was her insinuation. If MacCreedy had made that suggestion, Jacques would have tried to prove him wrong with both fists. But it was hard to stay angry with Nica when she was kissing him softly.

"No tongue," MacCreedy growled dangerously enough to make Nica smile.

Jacques straightened, unwilling to provoke the man who'd saved his life. He gave MacCreedy a steady stare. "Thank you."

"For what?"

"Having my back."

"No problem . . . as long as you take a step back from my woman right now."

The quick grin hurt Jacques's face but was worth it. "She's all yours."

Nica waited until Jacques had left the room and was making his way gingerly down the stairs to the main floor before cocking an eyebrow at her mate. "Your *woman*? Could you be any more Neanderthal?"

"Yeah," MacCreedy drawled, hands fitting to her

waist and tugging her up against him. "You got a problem with that?"

"None whatsoever."

Their kiss was slow and searing. Finally, Mac-Creedy leaned back and placed his palm on her midriff.

"Why didn't you tell me?" His voice softened. "Worried about the timing?"

Her eyes filled up with emotion, glittered like sapphires. She shook her head. "You?"

"No." He grinned wide, and his hands cupped her face. "Our own family. I couldn't be happier." His tone deepened. "Why didn't you tell me?"

"I was worried about other things. That's one of the reasons I brought Susanna here."

Alarm tightened his features briefly. "You're afraid something might be wrong with the baby."

"Not afraid. Cautious. I'd feel a lot better if she was still here. I was thinking maybe we should bring her back along with Max."

He touched her hair in a soothing gesture. "Would she come willingly?" His somber gaze said he might consider the idea in either instance.

A secret smile. "Oh yeah. In a heartbeat."

He kissed her brow and murmured, "What's on your devious mind, woman?"

"To find out where Max is, I'm going to have to use you."

"How?"

"I need you to make a collect call."

———

Industry stopped the second Jacques's crew became aware of him. His chest clogged up with more than just pain as one by one they smiled determinedly.

"I want things ready for doors to open tomorrow night. You don't think I'm gonna pay you all out of my pocket change, do you?"

"We'll be ready," Amber assured him from where she knelt over the dried stain of his own blood.

Mood darkening, he gestured to the floor. "Leave that one. A reminder."

"Of what happened?" she asked in quiet empathy.

"No. Of what didn't happen that should have."

He wanted his patrons to remember every time they saw that discoloration that he'd lain unprotected and vulnerable at the mercy of their enemies while they'd done nothing.

The crackle of the sound system was followed by a bawdy blues tune. He smiled at Nica's choice as Big Al Carson wailed, "Time to take your drunken ass home."

Yes, it was.

And as he stood under the hot spray of his shower, he was grateful for that slight residual inebriation that dulled him to all the reminders Susanna had left behind.

His tangled sheets held the scent of their passion. Her new clothes were still strewn about the floor. The smell of floral shampoo filled his towels and twisted about his heart.

He'd grown so used to her company, to the sight, sound, and scent of her, her absence was achingly apparent. But once those reminders faded and were gone, he'd be alone again. Then what would he do with the emptiness?

He dressed in loose cargo pants and eased into a white button-up shirt, securing only the bottom few and leaving it untucked. Then he cleaned up the remains of his last meal with Susanna from what seemed like days ago, grateful to be interrupted by the arrival of his guests.

He buzzed them up.

Nica led the way inside. She took in his spacious apartment with an impressed nod. "Pretty upscale, LaRoche. I didn't get a good look around before."

She and MacCreedy had been too busy hurrying him out ahead of an arsonist's flames.

"It's big," he agreed, and suddenly that didn't seem like such a good thing. All that open, unoccupied space for him to ramble around in. Alone. His ratty old trailer on the docks, surrounded by activity, crowded by his work and his world, held more appeal. "Get you something to drink?" he asked automatically.

Instead of reminding him that he might have already had more than enough, Nica shook her head. "No, thanks. I'm abstaining for two."

"Yeah?" The news was just the shot of optimism he needed. "Good for you, for both of you."

"I'll take hers." MacCreedy's typical buttoned-up reserve gave a notch as he loosened his tie and stuffed it into his coat pocket. A restless energy crackled about him. Something to do with the purpose of their visit, Jacques was certain.

He fetched two beers, raising a brow as MacCreedy took his down in several long, determined gulps before also taking the second one that he'd brought for himself. He carried it over to the couch, setting it on the wood-and-glass coffee table.

"So," Jacques began warily, "what's on your mind, Nica?" *What's got your mate so jumpy?*

"Sit down." *You'll be glad you did* was implied.

He settled onto the yielding leather cushions with Nica at his side. MacCreedy paced over to the sliders to stare out into the night.

"We need to find out where they're holding Max," she began with a calm logic. "Until we know, we can't plan any kind of rescue."

"So, how are we going to find out?"

"We're going to have to tap a friend on the inside for that information."

An ugly suspicion stabbed through him. "No. You're not putting Susanna in that kind of position. I won't allow it, even if you did know how to get ahold of her. Phones are too dangerous. He's going to be watching her."

Nica smiled. "We're not going to use a phone. We're going to use a direct line. Mind-to-mind long-distance."

Sixteen

Jacques took it all in without a blink.

Apparently, Nica and Silas weren't what they seemed. Neither were Max and Charlotte. Their DNA was supercharged, granting them special abilities. Powers that included mind reading, astral projection, walking on water, and probably X-ray vision that would allow them to see he wasn't wearing any underwear.

Yeah, and space aliens were going to fly out of his ass riding on sugarplum fairies.

He regarded Nica with a bland expression, hiding a smirk that said, *Tell me another one. How stupid do I look?*

Nica smiled. "I don't know about stupid, but the rest of you looks just fine." And her gaze lowered to his crotch for an appreciative assessment.

No, she couldn't—

Slowly, he crossed his legs and scoffed, "You don't expect me to believe all this?"

She pursed her lips. "It's not like we're claiming to be space aliens who can tell if you're wearing boxers or briefs . . . or not."

He drew a breath and let it out slowly. Okay, he knew the Chosen could do limited thought manipulations. Shifters could, well, shift shape. But the rest . . . that was myth, legend, fairy-tale stuff.

"You're talking about the Ancients. Like I'm supposed to believe they're real. Like you can just jump out the window and fly away."

"Well, I can't do that," Nica drawled, glancing over at MacCreedy. "Can you?"

"I don't think so. I suppose I could try if it would hurry things along."

Jacques leaned back into the cushions, realization hitting home. "So that's why they want Max."

"All they have now is rumor," Silas told him, impatient with his reluctance to just accept everything that had been shoved down his own throat. "If they start cutting him apart, they'll have fact. And how long after that do you think it'll take them to have a weapon?"

"And Susanna's research?"

"Will get them to that point that much quicker."

Nica placed her hand on Jacques's knee, squeezing tight. "We need to get Max away from them. We have to convince Suze to help us. She trusts you. She'll listen to you. She'll come back here for you."

A dizzying sense of hope soared at that suggestion, but reality grounded him. "She won't leave her lab or her little girl."

"Then we'll have to move everything here, won't we?"

Could they do that?

"What do I have to do?"

"We need to contact Susanna without them knowing it." She motioned Silas to come over, noting the way Jacques's eyes narrowed warily. "He's going to channel your thoughts to hers."

"And he can do that?"

"Sure." She simplified, not sharing the fact that her mate would be using the strength of the bond forged between Jacques and his own chosen female as that joining link. That wasn't her secret to tell.

MacCreedy sat on the edge of the coffee table facing Jacques. They exchanged uncomfortable looks until Silas told him to close his eyes.

"Is that necessary?"

"No. But I'll be a lot less distracted without you staring at me like you're waiting for me to suck your brain out your nose."

When Jacques hesitated, Nica leaned close to whisper, "Relax. I can't really see through your pants. Dammit."

He chuckled and let the tension drain from his body and mind. And he shut his eyes. He gave a slight jump at the touch of MacCreedy's fingertips upon either temple. The points of contact seemed to warm, until the heat penetrated through flesh and bone.

"Think of her, think of Susanna," MacCreedy coaxed in a low monotone. "Focus on the way she looks, the way she smiles, the sound of her voice, her scent. Breathe her in and out. Feel her."

Abruptly, everything fell away, sight, sound, sense, even his awareness of where he was. And from somewhere in that darkness a tiny light began to widen, growing bright, expanding. Even as his mind strained to embrace it, his physical being held firm, beginning to pull back, resisting.

The pressure intensified in Jacques's head. He struggled against it, feeling as though MacCreedy was trying to pry him open like a nutshell to get to the meat inside.

"He's fighting me."

MacCreedy's voice was far away. Jacques panicked, trying to find his way back to it, to the safety of his apartment.

"Let me." Nica's palm slipped inside his shirt to soothe over his bare chest, the sensation of warmth calming, comforting. Her breath blew in a teasing whisper into his ear. "Relax and listen to my voice. There's nothing to worry about. I won't let any harm come to you. Go to her, Jacques. Think of her. Say her name."

"Anna."

Susanna straightened from the lens of her microscope and rubbed at the back of her neck in an effort to relieve her sudden headache. It was late and she was tired, but determination drove her to continue well beyond her normal workday.

In the quiet lab, once her other coworkers had gone home, she turned her attention to her true focus, to applying data she'd planned to use in her serum for Mary Kate to a sample from her daughter. Almost immediately the divergent strands aggressively attacked and destroyed one another. Hours ticked by as she tried variations with no success. The right combination had to be there in front of her but her eyes were too blurry to see it. Chosen, Shifter, Ancient. It was like trying to re-create a recipe where none of the ingredients listed the proper amounts used. A pinch of this, a dab of that, too bitter, too weak, too strong. Where was that proper balance? The balance that would allow them all to exist together?

Her child was going to die and there was nothing she could do to prevent it.

She rested her head in her hands, perilously close to defeat.

"Dr. Duchamps, Mr. Frost sent me to drive you home."

She glanced over at the harsh-featured automaton Damien had hired to shadow her every movement. He needn't have worried that she might be tempted to seduce and run off with this one. Besides, there was nowhere to run.

"I need to shut things down. I'll be just a minute." Her tone chilled. "Wait outside, please."

Without a flicker of expression, the burly body-guard stepped out into the hall. The lock engaged behind him. Damien was taking no chances.

Susanna quickly saved the core data on her thumb drive, then wiped the system's memory before shutting it down. Tucking the flash drive into her bra next to the underwire, she gathered her personal belongings and tapped on the door.

And so ended the first day of an endless number in captivity.

The home she and Pearl shared with Frost was in a gated community in a northern suburb of Chicago. Those who lived behind the high private walls were others like them, Chosen living amongst human. Scientists, scholars, politicians, all figures of influence and affluence, pretending to be what they were not, for the good of all and not the one.

The house itself was ultramodern, of cold glass and steel. Lit up from within against the night sky, it made her think of incubation containers where the carefully segregated organisms living inside could be observed from a clinical distance. The same way Damien was watching her.

He was waiting for her at the door, attired in a charcoal-colored sweater and matching slacks, his composed features almost beautiful with their delicate lines and pale perfection. There was no warmth in his greeting or in his eyes.

"I trust your day was prosperous."

"Yes, thank you." As she stepped inside that sea of blinding white, she glanced up the stairs. "Is Pearl still up?"

"I sent her to bed a few hours ago. She barely picked at her meal."

"I should go up—"

Damien's hand closed about her upper arm, surprising her with the strength of his grip. "There are things we need to discuss first. Come with me into the parlor."

Reluctantly, Susanna followed across the pale wood floors with their fleecy white rugs. The word *parlor* inspired notions of a cozy gathering place for friends to relax and converse. In truth, it was a frigidly arranged cluster of austere furnishings that had nothing to do with comfort, more aligned to interrogation than polite chatter.

"Sit." Damien gestured to one of the hard straightbacked chairs. She settled into it without a sound. He sat opposite and regarded her through cold, black eyes. "I've decided after those dangerous doings in Louisiana that some alterations need to be made in our living situation."

She remained motionless, waiting for him to continue.

"I've tried to allow you every freedom possible, Susanna. Now I realize that was a mistake. Those careless liberties have led to what could have been a disastrous event for both our careers."

"I've apologized for that, Damien. No harm was intended."

"I know it wasn't intended, but it happened nonetheless. You could have been injured, even killed, and where would that have left your child? Your work? Our future?"

She said nothing. He wasn't interested in her response.

"It's time you took your position more seriously. There will be fewer distractions from now on. You will concentrate on your work and on your public appearances. I will, of course, be closely involved in both things. We're a team after all, are we not?"

She didn't dare answer that. Her lack of expression had no effect upon him.

"For your own protection, all your communications will be monitored, from the house and from the lab. Your work will be confined to the lab. I'll be remoting your progress from here and we shall discuss your advances each evening. I'll retain copies of everything for the sake of security."

Her insides trembled. How could she continue her work with Damien looking over her shoulder, poking through her studies? He wasn't an expert, but he wasn't a fool, either. He'd know immediately when she strayed from the proper path.

Very softly, she said, "Whatever you think best, Damien."

Her agreement pleased him into a small smile. "You'll find things will go much smoother without the distractions. And that brings me to the final topic I wish to discuss."

The way he approached it had her tensing, preparing for the worst.

But she wasn't prepared for how bad it would be.

"Pearl will be moving into a dormitory at the Center. She can continue her studies there and her care can be regulated around the clock. Without the stressful stimulation of outside activities, I suspect she'll be stronger in no time."

"Outside activities? You mean like school, friends,

family, home? Are those the things you think harmful?"

"Don't you?" he countered mildly. "You know how fragile she is. She should thrive in a less-complex environment."

"Away from her mother, you mean."

"Susanna, that's not what I mean at all. Of course you'll be able to visit with her, as her schedule allows. You'll be kept abreast of her progress in weekly reports."

"Weekly?"

"I believe that's fairly standard. My dear, I know you find this distressful, even punishing, at the moment, but you'll thank me for it. Frankly, our associates have been asking why the child was still living with us, why she hadn't been sent to be tested and assigned to a field of developmental study. We can only give her health as a reason for so long before they begin to wonder about the type of malady from which she suffers."

"What have you told them? Damien, what have you said is wrong with her?"

He waved off her shrill demand. "I've said she has a bit of an immune disorder. Nothing exotic or alarming, but enough to explain her fevers. They'll keep her comfortable without being too invasive. At least, for now."

The threat hung over her like a heavy club.

"You don't need to do this, Damien."

Her quiet petition fell on deaf ears. "It's done.

With Pearl out of the house, we can begin to concentrate on other things. Like having a second child. That should fill you with an entirely new sense of purpose."

What it filled her with was dread.

Damien had never touched her beyond a chaste peck on the cheek. Since demonstrative affection was frowned upon, no one thought their relationship strangely devoid of physical interaction. Many Chosen saw intimacy as an obligation toward procreation. They would have been horrified if they knew how she and Jacques LaRoche approached it.

Then she realized this wasn't about personal appearances or safety or propriety. It was about her and her Shifter mate. Damien couldn't erase what had happened but he was determined to do whatever he could to crush out all reminders. By removing their child from her arms. By replacing Pearl with his own progeny. By controlling every aspect of her days and nights.

He was trapping her in a cold, soulless hell to serve his own selfish purpose.

And seeing the flicker of horror she couldn't quite hide, he smiled in satisfaction.

Susanna stood looking down upon her sleeping daughter as emotions chewed like acid. Afraid she'd wake the child as her breath began a noisy hitching in her chest, she went to her own room only to stand in the doorway in dismay.

All signs of color had been drained away like her lifeblood. The small blue bed pillows were gone. The plush red slippers she tucked her feet into during blustery winter evenings weren't lying by the night-stand. The glass bottles she collected for the rainbow-colored stoppers were missing from her dresser. A green accent scarf, pink gloves, a yellow pin, all the little things she kept around her to brighten her existence, gone. Nothing remained but an unbroken field of sterility.

She sat on the edge of her unyielding mattress, try-ing not to succumb to the anger and fear surging inside her, struggling to keep these oppressive gestures from beating all hope from her heart.

What was she going to do? She couldn't let him take Pearl away. He might as well take her life.

Had it come to that?

As if in answer, a great surge of dizziness over-came her. All at once hot and cold, she huddled on the bed, as the impossible overwhelmed her senses. The scent of her mate. The heat of his body burning against her. The low thrum of his voice close to her ear, so close she imagined his breath blowing upon her skin.

"Anna, call me. You need to call me on a secure phone. We need to talk. Please. We have to talk."

She heard the numbers and grabbed frantically for a lipstick, scrawling them on her arm in Barely There Beige.

Then his essence was gone. No lingering trace for her to cling to.

And her with no way to call him back.

The doors to *Cheveux du Chien* were open and customers came and went in a weak trickle. Many were just curious and most kept a wary or embarrassed distance from the big man behind the bar.

"Think you could manage to crack a smile in that granite face?"

Jacques glowered at Nica. "No."

"Has she called yet?"

"No."

"Then can I have the rest of the night off to go have an orgy of wild, kinky sex with my man?"

"No."

"Well, thanks for nothing, boss."

As she started away from the bar with her heavy tray, Jacques called out to her. When she turned back, he said simply, "Thank you."

"You're welcome. For what?"

He let out a harsh breath. "You have less at stake than any of them in here and yet you put it all on the line for us. I appreciate it."

"Enough to give me a raise?"

A slight smile. "No."

"Okay then." A wink. She rested the tray on the bar so she could cup his rough cheek with her palm. "I have everything at stake here and I'd have none of it if it weren't for you. Don't forget that. I never will. As for them," she glanced behind her and curled her lip, "they've got a long way to go to earn any favors from me. Just thought I'd let you know some drinks may be spilled tonight."

He fit his hand over hers for a gentle squeeze. "Thanks for the heads-up." Then, with more feeling, "MacCreedy's very lucky."

"So I keep telling him. Gotta get back to work, boss. Tips to earn, drinks to fumble."

Jacques grinned as he watched her sashay away from the bar, his tension easing a little.

Why hadn't Susanna called him?

Maybe MacCreedy's hoodoo hadn't worked. Maybe he'd only imagined her scent, the sound of her hurried breathing, the sweetness of her hair brushing against his lips because he'd wanted to believe she was there. The way he'd most likely imagined her feelings for him.

"Hey, how can I get a drink around this place?"

"Ask," he told Philo as he pushed a bottle across the counter. Then he grinned. "And pay."

"Ooh, that's cold." Philo laughed, taking a quick swallow before reaching for his wallet.

Jacques scowled at him. "You know better than that. Your money's no good in here."

"Thanks." He took another drink as he studied his friend's face, then gestured to his own cheek. "How's that doing?"

"Scars are fading. Doesn't hurt." Not like the other, deeper wounds.

"I shoulda been here."

Jacques shook his head. "Wouldn't have made any difference. 'Sides, you were where you needed to be."

Philo accepted that with a slight nod, but guilt still weighted his expression.

"How many of your men did you lose?" Jacques asked.

"Eight, last count, for burying. Six just disappeared." He quirked a smile. "Funny, now that we got nothing worth protecting, I got more new recruits than I know what to do with. Probably just wanting an excuse to get a tattoo." He mused for a moment. "Probably feeling bad about what happened to you."

"They should be, chickenshit bastards," Jacques grumbled, popping a top for himself.

"But not as bad as I'm feeling. I believed her, Jackie." He heaved a deprecating sigh. "I fell for it, same as you."

"What are you talking about, Tib?"

Philo took another drink and shook his head. "I believed her when she tole me she didn't know you was here. She played the both of us like a pair of tambourines just to get us to rattle."

Jacques snagged Philo's wrist as he was about to lift his bottle again. "Who? Susanna?"

"Course, Susanna. Clever little bitch."

The pressure in Jacques's hand increased until Philo frowned at it and him. "You'd best explain yourself right now. I'm in no mood for riddles."

"Well, riddle me this, Jackie. How come it is you

fell for her like she was the Second Coming? That didn't seem even a tad bit strange to you?"

"Dammit, Philo—"

"Was probably her behind kicking you down here to be killed in the first place. Then when we got something she wants, she's back to cozying up to you, knowing you'd throw everything away to keep her safe. Knowing you'd take her in without heeding any questions, even your own. Why else would your brain stop firing the second you laid eyes on her? She's your mate, whether you recognize her or not."

Jacques's fingers went as slack as his expression, allowing Philo to pull away and rub at his wrist as he murmured, "I don't believe you."

But he did. It made an awful sense. All of it.

Philo was quick to grab him by the elbows when he took a staggering step back, knees starting to buckle.

"Whoa, there." He shouted over his shoulder, "Nica, take over here for a second while me and Jackie take care of some business in back."

After the first few stumbling movements, Jacques made a purposeful rush to his office and was heaving over his toilet by the time Philo closed the door.

"You okay?"

He flushed, rinsed, and spat in the sink. Stomach trembling, mind whirling like the water in the bowl, he collapsed on the couch with his head between his knees and hands laced over it.

"You're sure?" His voice was raw and aching.

"She tole me herself."

"That she wanted me *dead*?" His tone cracked at that final word.

"She didn't exactly admit to that. She tole me not to tell you anything. Why would she do that 'less she didn't want you to find out what she was up to? Why do you think she was here? Outta the goodness of her heart? After what she done to you, how could you think that?"

He couldn't force a coherent thought past the emotional upheaval. His mate. His *mate*, who'd used and abandoned him not just once, but twice.

"You think she was after Max?" he asked aloud, but he was wondering other things. She was a Chosen physician. The research was what brought her to New Orleans. Research for what purpose?

"Guess we'll never know. It's not like we can ask her."

Jacques said nothing.

"I'm sorry, Jackie. I shoulda said something. I was—I was afraid if you knew, you'd go north with her. I couldn't let that happen. You're the only family I got left."

She'd called him Jack.

"Why do you call me Jackie?" he asked suddenly.

"It's your name. Jack Stone. Me and Tito thought it'd be a good idea to give you a new one so's they wouldn't know you was still alive."

The office door opened and he heard Nica's brusque voice.

"Philo, tend the bar."

He left without comment as she came to sit beside Jacques on the couch. Her hand eased across his shoulders.

"He told you." It wasn't a question.

But Jacques had one. He lifted his head and slowly turned to look at her.

"Why didn't you?"

Seventeen

Nica gave him a sad smile. "Because I knew this would happen and I didn't want to see your heart broken."

It wasn't an answer, but again, it was. He dropped his forehead into his palm, eyes squeezing shut against the pain burning behind them.

"How could she just throw me away and then come down here and pretend there'd never been anything between us?"

Nica's arms went about him, her head resting on his shoulder as she told him gently, "Sometimes to survive, we have to lie, first to others and then to ourselves. If we're lucky, we get to believing them just to get from one day to the next."

"So it was all lies?"

His soft lament had her embrace tightening. "I don't think any of it was lies. I think it was necessity. If she'd told you the truth, would you have let her go?"

He took a small, hurting breath. "No." Then more forcefully, "No. Never." His shoulders shook. "How could she do this to me if she cared anything about me? How could she let them bring me here to execute me?

Wasn't stealing my life enough for her? Did she have to try to end it, too?"

Nica was silent for a long moment. "I don't think she was the one behind it. In fact, I'm quite certain of that."

"So she and I are *both* victims? Is that what I'm supposed to believe?"

"What do you want to believe, Jacques?"

Before he could reply, his cell rang. A glance at the area code purged every quiver of emotion from him. "I have to take this."

Nica's tone was tough but her eyes were tender. "Stay strong."

"I will."

As she stood, her hand stroked his jaw. "You have friends here who would do absolutely anything for you."

"I know. I have to take this."

As she closed the door behind her, Jacques took a deep, bracing breath, lying to himself about his ability to handle what was to come. Trying to believe it.

He pressed Talk. "LaRoche. Or should I say Jack Stone?"

Silence. Then a quiet, "You know."

"About time, don't you think?"

"Is that why you wanted me to call?"

"No. This isn't about us." As a lie, it was a whopper.

"Oh." Her voice faltered, then firmed. "What then?"

"We need to know where they took Savoie."

"I don't know."

"But you can find out."

"I can't. It's too dangerous. If you knew the risk I took just to make this call." She waited for him to speak. Probably hoping he'd say something supportive and stupidly sentimental. When he didn't, her tone changed, becoming cool and clipped. "I'll see what I can do. It might take a few days."

"Do you think he has them to spare?"

A pause, then an honest, "No, I don't. I'll find out what I can." Another break, then a softly sincere, "Jacques, I'm so sorry I hurt—"

He ended the connection and put the phone away. Time to get back to work.

Time to start learning to lie to himself.

The last thing Jacques expected was Max's bodyguard filling the penthouse apartment doorway like a brick wall. They'd exchanged looks before, but never words. And their first were testy.

"Is Charlotte here?" Jacques demanded.

"Do you know what time it is?"

"It's either late or early, depending on your point of view. So I brought beer and breakfast."

"Let him in, Giles," came a shout from the interior. "I haven't had beer with breakfast since the academy. Sounds good."

The two big men each took a side of the hall so Jacques could sidle by, a low warning growl rumbling in his throat.

"I'm not going to have to put down newspapers for you, am I?" Giles drawled.

Jacques showed his teeth. "I'll be on my best behavior."

"I hope not," Charlotte interjected, coming into the hall looking pale and as if she hadn't closed her eyes. She greeted him with a fierce hug. "This place could use some bad behavior. Whatever you've got in there smells good. I hope it's greasy."

"I never disappoint a lady," he assured her, keeping his arm about her shoulders as he glanced back at Giles, his eyes flashing a quick glint of ruby red. Giles gave a snort, not impressed.

"As much as I love macho bullshit," Charlotte warned, "I'm not in the mood for it today, so keep a lid on it, boys."

"Whatever you say, darlin'."

Jacques stepped into the huge living area and stopped, stunned. "Wow. When are you gonna be on one of them fancy magazine covers?" He hadn't been in the apartment since it was studs and wallboard. The decorator's touch was awe-inspiring from the stone waterfall wall to the amazing floor-to-ceiling view of New Orleans. "You could get lost in this place."

His casual comment had her jaw trembling. "I am. I'm so glad you're here."

His arm tightened. "Hey now, if there's gonna be waterworks, my grease and brews are going back downstairs."

"No weeping. I promise to stay dry-eyed," she cast a glance up at him, "if you will."

"Deal. Which way to the dining room?"

"Too far to walk." She dropped down onto one of the opulent couches. As he set the takeout bags and beer on the glass-topped table, she startled him by collapsing upon his chest. He scooped her up, feeling fearful shudders race through her.

"What am I going to do without him, Jacques?" she moaned against his shoulder.

"Here now, *chere*, don't you worry. I'm working on that already. I'll get him back for you. You're making a mess of my shirt. You promised."

"I lied." She sniffled, sounding shaky and fragile, and alarming him into crushing her close.

"There's a lot of that going around." He tipped up her chin, frowning at the waxen quality of her skin and the fever brightness in her eyes. She looked beyond fatigued. "Want to see what's in the bag?" he coaxed.

She nodded and sat back without leaving the curl of his arm, smiling as he laid out a pair of sloppy breakfast burritos and a double rasher of hash browns with packets of hot sauce. She sighed. "Oh, baby. The way to a girl's heart."

"Enjoy." He offered one of the beers to her.

She shook her head. "I'll just have a sip or two of yours. I'm trying to behave myself."

His gaze dropped to her middle and he grinned, "You're gonna be one badass, sexy mama." Still smiling, he pitched the extra can at Giles, who caught it and popped the top in one easy move.

"Yes, I am," she agreed, snuggling into the crook of his arm to munch contentedly on her burrito and drip grease all over his lap. "And this baby is going to have one badass, sexy godfather." She glanced up at his stunned silence. "Hey, no crying."

"It's the hot sauce," he muttered.

"Yeah, right. Pass some of that excuse over here."

Susanna's heart jerked as the six-year-old looked up at her through her father's bright blue eyes.

"Hi, baby," she called softly. "What are you working on?"

"A picture for you. You can't put it on the wall where you work so I made it small. You can take it with you in your purse like a photograph."

She continued to stand by the door so Pearl couldn't see the distress working her features. "I need to tell you something, sweetheart. Now that you're a big girl, Damien and I are sending you to a new school."

"I like my old school. I want to stay there."

"In this new school, you'll have your own special teacher who'll spend all her time with just you. And if you don't feel well, she'll be there to take care of you and make you better."

"I have you to take care of me and make me better. I don't need anybody else."

Susanna took a slow breath so her voice wouldn't shake. "You'll be starting there next week. I think we should go out and buy you some special things to celebrate."

"It's not my birthday. I don't want to go to a new school. I like my teachers and my friends. Will I still see them and be able to play with them at this new school?"

"No, baby. They won't be there."

"Can they come over here to play after school?" She'd never been allowed company before so the request took Susanna by surprise, making her founder.

"This is a very special place," she continued, trying to sound cheerful when her heart was breaking, "just for you. You'll be living there, Pearl, all the time. You'll have your own room and your teacher will come there to meet with you."

"And will you come to see me there?"

"Every chance I get."

Pearl had no more questions. Her head was bent over her drawing, her hand moving quickly. She was just a child, but Susanna got the feeling that she knew exactly what was happening, that she was being sent away from home into exile.

Smiling weakly, Susanna went to stand over the little girl's shoulder to inspect the artwork. There were four figures depicted in surprising detail. One adult figure was her with her gigantic purse, beige dress, and red slippers and the smaller figure Pearl, wearing what looked like a bright pink ballerina tutu and a princess crown. The male figure was big and bald and definitely not Damien.

"Who's that, Pearl?"

"My daddy."

The casual remark hit like a surprise punch. Susanna took an uneven breath and asked, "What's that you're holding? A doll?" The child had no dolls. Damien thought they were frivolous bits of gender propaganda.

"That's my baby brother. And this is where we live."

There was no mistaking the wide river snaking behind them or the sprawling branches of the live oak reaching overhead. In the sky was a star with a crescent moon above it like the one of the NOPD doorway.

New Orleans.

"Where did you see these things, baby? On TV?"

"Damien doesn't let me watch TV shows, just my DVDs. I saw them in my head."

"Like in a dream?" she whispered, skin going cold and clammy.

"No. I was lonely while you were gone and this picture came to make me happy. Does it make you happy, too?" Pearl glanced up and her expression froze when she saw her mother's face. "Did I do a bad thing?"

She clutched the child close. "Oh, no, baby, no. It's not bad. It just surprised me. I didn't know you could . . . see pictures." She held the little girl back by her shoulders, smiling. "How long have you been seeing them?"

"Since I was four. I saw a dog, but it turned out to be a toy you got me for my birthday."

Careful not to convey her alarm, she asked, "Does Damien know you can see these pictures?"

Pearl made a stubborn face and went back to her coloring. "He thinks the things I say are silly so I don't tell him anything."

Relief shivered through Susanna. "Let's keep this just between the two of us for now."

"Okay, Mommy."

She sank down on the edge of the bed to watch the child's industrious movements. Her daughter had Sight. Of all the Chosen gifts, precognition was the most prized. If anyone knew of it, Pearl would be taken away so her talent could be developed. And if it proved to be inferior, she would be used for other, less pleasant study.

"There. All done."

The child held up the picture. A family portrait. Her, Jacques, and their two children living in New Orleans. Her daughter's glimpse of the future and her every dream.

Susanna made the call from the cafeteria at work. She'd stolen the cell phone from the tray next to hers while the technician was reaching for tuna on rye. Her audacity shocked her. Her calm alarmed her, especially with so much hanging in the balance.

She got voice mail and left a brief message.

"I've got the information you requested. I sent it overnight early A.M. delivery to the club. If you have any questions, they'll have to wait until you get here."

Hands shaking, she ended the call and deleted it from the history. As she passed the young man enjoying his sandwich, she placed it on his tray with a friendly, "I think you dropped this."

He looked up in surprise and even as he mumbled his thanks through a mouthful of tuna salad, Susanna was moving quickly away, head down to avoid the security cameras.

Now all she had to do was pretend nothing out of the ordinary was going on.

Pain consumed Max from inside out, scalding along his nervous system, twisting through his joints and muscles, hammering at his brain until he was helpless to move or even think. He couldn't trust the visions that darted before him, not knowing if they were real or the product of whatever they were beating into his head in great cramping pulses. He hung shaking and sweating in the circle of his restraints, saving all his strength, all his concentration for one purpose, keeping them blocked from his mind.

A losing battle, a fool's battle, but hell, he had nothing better to do. He was alone. No one was coming to rescue him. Escape was impossible, resistance less than futile. The best he could hope for was making them work for it, making them earn in frustrated efforts and aggravation the time it took to break him down into nothing. He took a grim, if fatalistic pleasure in it.

They were persistent bastards, sending their mental, chemical, and electrical probes sneaking about his gray matter, to poke and dig, seeking a way to infiltrate. If he'd learned nothing else from those childhood lessons in paranoia and fear it was how to erect an impenetrable barrier about his thoughts. They couldn't breach it so they were reduced to looking for a way to surprise or weaken him into dropping it. Good luck with that. His lips curved away from gritted teeth in a goading smile that said, *Do your worst, you monsters.*

Then, as abruptly as it had begun, the attack ended.

The urge to slump in relief shuddered through him but he fought to cling to a wary edge. What were they up to now? Some new, sinister type of torture?

He had no chance to prepare for the stroke of cool fingertips along a fevered cheek or the soft sound of a regretful female voice.

"Oh, Max. Look what they've done to you."

Afraid to hope, let alone believe, he pushed into that consoling palm to inhale her scent, touched a dry tongue to smooth skin for a shockingly familiar taste. And with a jerk, his system collapsed.

"Mama?"

He slit bleary eyes open, doubly stunned by the features that swam just out of focus. A trick. It had to be a trick. A cruel, cruel illusion.

Too late to grab on to the raspy plea that moaned from him in broken desperation. Crying out for what he knew, *he knew*, wasn't real.

"Mama. Mama, please don't leave me."

Too late to shore up the walls of strength that crumbled about that mournful cry. He was lost. And he didn't care.

"Shh. Hush now," she whispered, bending close,

brushing back the sticky hair that had matted to his brow. "I won't let them hurt you anymore. But you've got to do as I say. You've got to trust me, Max."

Hazel eyes, not green like his own. Like his mother's had been. He flung his head back, smacking the metal table hard enough to make the vision before him dance and his mind clear once more. His tone growled out, low and harsh. "Who are you?"

Her reply was absurd. "Family."

"I have no family. Get away from me, liar."

"We don't have time for this," she ground out impatiently. She lifted her hand to her mouth and bit down hard, until rivulets of blood trickled from the puncture of her tiny fangs. She pressed that hot liquid to Max's lips. "Deny what you see, what you smell, what you taste, but you can't deny what blood reveals. Marie was my sister. I'm here to make sure you live."

She was telling the truth. He was too weak to question how or why, almost too exhausted to hold back the sobs that threatened to spill out in a crazy jag of relief. But a whisper of caution called him back to sanity. He had no idea what this woman was, tormentor or savior.

"Let me go."

"I can't. It's not that easy. They would know it was me and there are greater things involved than just you." She cupped his chin. "You look like him, that charming bastard Rollo, but I see Marie in your eyes. He told me she'd died but wouldn't tell me where you were."

"Why would he keep that a secret?"

"To save his worthless hide, I assume."

"When did you see him? Where?"

"In Baton Rouge, in the spring."

He went to meet family? Not to betray him? Bile rose up to burn Max's throat but he pushed it down. He didn't know that yet. Being family was no guarantee against treachery.

Her fingertips rubbed against his temples, relaxing his defenses, and just like that, in an unguarded second, with a quick connecting shock, she was flipping through his memories as if paging through a microfiche at the local library. The information gushed from him like blood from a heart wound and he was helpless to staunch the draining flow.

Finally, she'd learned all she needed and gently eased back from his mind. He crumpled, too sick and shaky inside to even hate her for the intrusion.

Now she would kill him. And then she would use what she'd discovered to destroy everything he cared about.

She knew about Oscar. About the child Charlotte carried.

"Don't be alarmed," she crooned quietly. "Your secrets are safe. I just needed to be sure. Oh, Max. You are more than I ever expected."

Hardly comforted, he groaned, "What are you? You're not a Shifter. Are you one of them?"

A musical laugh. "Oh, no. I'm like you. Different."

"Do what you like with me but don't harm them."

"I'm not in the harming business, brave boy. But if you want to save them, you must trust me. These people—"

"They're not people!"

"These . . . creatures will break you. That's what they do. It's all they do. They're still toying with you now but when they discover you will never give them what they want, they'll smash open your skull like a lobster claw and take what they need, then throw the rest of you away. You will not survive that. Then what good will your sacrifice be to anyone? To her?"

Charlotte. His attention sharpened. "What are you proposing?"

"If there's nothing there for them to find, you'll be of no use to them. An accidental wiping of your memories. It happens sometimes. Once they realize you're just a blank slate, they'll leave you alone and let you be imprinted and set free to go about productive business for them."

Like Jacques.

"So I'll remember . . ."

"Nothing before you open your eyes to a new life. Then they'll be safe. Isn't that what you want?"

"Yes." More strongly. "Yes." He took a steadying breath. "Will you do it?"

"In just a moment." She pushed a button and the table rotated, tipping back and then settling flat until he was stretched out on his back, the discomfort and stress upon his body easing. "There'll be no pain, Max. You won't be conscious. You'll wake and you'll be someone new, someone with no past, no dangerous secrets."

"An infiltrator, like my father?"

"Perhaps. Does it matter as long as they're protected?"

"No." What happened to him wasn't important.

"When it's safe," she continued, beginning to make adjustments to the levels on the machine next to him, "I'll find you."

"Why? I won't know who you are."

"Because, brave boy, I can bring those memories back."

That promise lingered like sweet perfume as she made more of the necessary changes and hung a new bag of solution on the stand beside the table.

In mere moments all he knew and loved would be erased. In a way, she would be killing him. Everything that made him who he was would be no more. He'd lose the sound of Oscar's laughter, the lessons his mother and Jimmy had taught him, the scent of Charlotte's *Voodoo Love*, the heat of her kisses. He'd never see his child. How could he let those things go? Unless he believed she could help him recover them again.

And because he knew that even if that was a lie, by disappearing from their lives, he would no longer be a danger to those who gave his life meaning.

"Do it."

She smiled and said with a soft conviction, "You are the one who will save us all, Max. I have no doubts about that now. Ready?"

He took a gulping breath as objection leapt. *Charlotte!* He could see the flash of her dark eyes above the tempting part of her lips. *You make me hot, Savoie.* He squeezed his eyes tightly shut and let that breath out in a slow, steady stream. "Yes."

"It'll be like falling asleep," she told him. "You'll feel the drug in your system, cold at first, then hot. Don't be afraid. I'll be right here with you."

A tingling chill started inching up his arm from the IV needle. Panic quickened his heartbeats. His body tensed.

"You need to relax, Max. It's more comfortable that way."

The icy serum branched out, down into heart and lungs, up into his brain.

What if she was lying to him? He pulled against the restraints, beginning to resist. It was like drowning, like dying. His blood vessels began to burn.

"Easy. Not much longer. Be still."

He began to pant. "Tell me something about my mama," he insisted even though he soon wouldn't recall the story. "About when she was young."

The woman . . . he'd forgotten to ask her name . . . rumpled his hair while her eyes grew faraway. "Marie was special. Blessed."

Max, you are special. Blessed.

Max sighed. And surrendered.

Eighteen

They moved down the hallway in tandem, all in black, from caps pulled low, impenetrable dark glasses, and gloves to military-style boots. Whether it was the stun guns clipped to their belts or the grimness of their expressions, personnel scurried out of their way. They'd gotten all the way to the end of the hall before someone had the nerve to intercept them.

"Excuse me. This is a private area. You can't be here."

A brisk voice interceded. "They're with me, doctor. Here are my credentials."

The sweaty little man glanced at the government ID and took a quick step back. "I'm sorry to have detained you."

A chill smile. "Don't apologize for doing your job. We're looking for Section C-7."

"Right through those doors, Dr. Duchamps. At the end of the hall."

"Thank you for your cooperation."

Susanna pushed open the double doors, closely followed by the two security guards. They'd only gone a few yards before one of them spoke up.

"You showed up just in time."

"Don't speak. Everything here is monitored. Let me do the talking." Her curt tone didn't betray how the sound of Jacques's voice shattered through her like an earthquake.

She'd expected to see Nica with him. Charlotte was a surprise. Though her features were pale as ice, the detective's tight jaw said she was fully in control. She'd come for her man. Heaven help anyone who got in her way.

Susanna was determined that none would.

Section C was a closed-off portion of the clinic, kept strictly off-limits because it supposedly housed the dangerously unstable. Susanna knew better. It held political prisoners who were being interrogated or broken. Or both. No one in her area knew anything about what went on there because no one who went in ever came out.

Until now, if things went as planned.

They bluffed their way through another security checkpoint. When asked what their business was, Susanna told the man with an icy disdain that his clearance wasn't high enough to ask that question. They were allowed to pass.

"You make a convincing bitch," Jacques murmured.

"I thought you were already convinced of that."

He said nothing more.

C-7.

Susanna put her hand on Charlotte's arm, surprised to feel her trembling slightly. "Don't react to anything you see. He may not even know you."

Charlotte's expression never flickered. "We're wasting time."

The room was small, stark, and glaringly sterile. One wall was mirrored for observation. An attractive woman slipped from it without a glance or a word as they entered.

Max was stretched out on a tilted table. Heavy cuffs secured him at six-inch intervals. He wore loose hospital scrubs that were soaked through with sweat. Wires ran from electrodes stuck to his chest, temples, and various pulse points, feeding information into a monitoring system humming busily off to one side. IVs pierced the backs of his hands. Under the searing lights, his skin glistened. Even though he appeared calm and unaware, raw abrasions where he was restrained showed evidence of fierce struggles.

Susanna gripped Charlotte's wrist in a precautionary warning as she spoke to the mirrored surface.

"I need to speak to someone right now. Cameras and recordings off, please. Official business."

A pinched-faced tech bustled in looking flustered. "I wasn't told of an inspection."

"I wasn't aware," Susanna leaned in close to the nervous young man to study his badge, "Mr. Bryon, that I had to clear my visit through you."

"That's not what I meant, doctor. You have our complete cooperation. If we'd known—"

"We like surprises," Jacques growled, making the poor fellow tremble. "We wouldn't catch anyone in any monkeyshines if we gave out a warning, would we?"

"I can assure you, sir, there are no . . . monkeyshines going on here."

"Then perhaps you can tell us exactly what the hell *is* going on here." The cold fury vibrating through Charlotte's voice drained him of all color.

"We're just measuring brain waves, sir, ma'am, and his vitals. Don't get too close, ma'am."

Charlotte turned that black-lensed stare upon him. "If all you're doing is taking his temperature, why should I be worried? What are you pumping into him?"

"Fluids to keep him hydrated."

"And?" she prompted menacingly.

"Something to keep him manageable."

"Get out," Susanna snapped. "I need a gurney with a portable IV hookup. And I want copies of all your readouts."

"I can't do that, doctor."

"Can you look for another job in the morning?" She reached into her huge bag and produced an official-looking document. "This says I can."

"Yes, ma'am. Right away."

After the tech bolted, Charlotte moved to Max's side, curling her fingers about his to squeeze firmly, whispering, "I'm here for you, baby."

His hand suddenly clenched tight and his eyes opened. "Charlotte?" A hoarse moan.

Before Susanna could warn her not to, she had her arms about him, her damp cheek pressed to his rough one as she told him, "We're here to take you home."

She leaned back just far enough to devour the sight of him.

"Charlotte . . ." He swallowed hard, with obvious difficulty. She bent close so that his lips moved against her ear. So she could barely hear him whisper, softly, firmly, "Don't trust me."

"What?" She leaned back, touching his face gently, confused by his words. But his eyes had rolled back and slid shut.

The tech reentered the room. Susanna snatched the charts from him as he mused, "I've never seen anyone pull out of it before. Once they go under—"

"There's nothing on this chart about a second IV. What's in that bag?" Susanna demanded.

"I—I don't know. Another doctor was just in here. She must have hung it."

"Take it out."

"I can't do that without—"

Susanna reached past him to ease the needle free. As she kept pressure on the vein, she leaned over to check the label on the medication and the amount dripping through. Her features tensed.

"Unhook him. All of it. Charges of misconduct are going to be made. If you don't want to be included, do as you're told."

"Yes, ma'am."

As soon as all the wires and restraints were removed, Susanna snapped, "Get that gurney in here now. If we're lucky this man won't be a complete vegetable."

"What do you mean?" Charlotte hissed at her when they were alone. "What were they doing?"

"Something I'm sure they weren't supposed to do. They started the imprinting process. I don't know how far it's gone."

"Imprinting?" Charlotte shook her head, losing even more color.

"Memory erase and reprogramming," Jacques told her, then his hard stare went to Susanna. "Is that what they were doing?"

"But I don't know why. I'd think they'd be after what he had inside his head, not in a hurry to empty it. It doesn't make sense."

The tech returned with a gurney and helped Jacques shift Max onto it. He stepped out of the way so they could get through the door. And then they were moving swiftly down the hall.

"I'll go with you as far as the elevators," Susanna was saying, walking purposefully ahead of Jacques so she wouldn't have to look at him. "Then you're on your own. I have to get back before I'm missed."

"Hey!" The tech shouted after them, but they didn't pause. "Hey, stop. There's something wrong here. Your clearance didn't go through. Wait!"

Jacques turned and fired a quick blast from the stun gun, dropping the tech into a twitching heap. "Enough small talk. Let's get the hell out of here."

But as they cleared the double doors leaving the unit, it was apparent leaving wasn't going to be a simple matter.

The security guards weren't at their posts. They were tucked out of sight at the doors, waiting to spring upon their unidentified visitors. Jacques zapped one of them and Charlotte took the other out with a brutal chop to the throat. They started trotting toward the elevator, but more security guards began to arrive, this time armed and ready.

Jacques's move took Susanna by surprise. He hooked one arm about her chest to hold her and pressed the stun gun to her carotid artery.

"Stand down," he bellowed at the uniformed guards. "At this range and velocity, a jolt will kill her."

The officers exchanged uncertain looks, not sure if they were dealing with a ruse or a hostage situation.

Jacques plucked the identification badge from her jacket and threw it toward the desk. "Her name is Dr. Susanna Duchamps. She's not acting of her own free will. She'll be released unharmed once we're clear of the building. Her partner, Damien Frost, is on the board of this facility. You don't want to screw this up."

The name was well-known and their aggressive stance eased.

As they raced for the elevator, Charlotte grabbed one of the guards to relieve him of his sidearm, trotting backward to cover their retreat.

The elevator doors parted and they rolled the gurney in. Jacques pushed for the garage level and the doors closed.

Susanna collapsed back against the hard wall of Jacques's chest. He caught her arm to support her.

"You did a real good job of acting scared," he told her gruffly, his breath warm and vital in her ear.

"I wasn't acting. You have to let me go, Jacques. You can't take me with you."

On the other side of the gurney, Charlotte wobbled, grabbing the rail for balance. Now she didn't look pale. She was a sickly green.

"Charlotte? Are you okay?"

She waved off Jacques's concern and tried to straighten. "Just a little woozy."

"Since when?" he demanded.

"Yesterday," she admitted. "Must have been the breakfast burrito."

Susanna pushed free of him to circle around to her side. She had her wrist, tapping into her pulse. "Light-headed? Sick to your stomach? Weak?"

"All of the above," she confessed, then drew an anxious breath. "The baby—"

"Just relax and breathe."

"What's wrong?" Jacques demanded, concern roughening his voice. "Is it the baby? Dammit, do something!"

Susanna ignored him. "Trouble keeping food down? No? It could be something as simple as low blood sugar. I don't have anything with me." She had her arm about Charlotte's waist, supporting her as she took slow, calming breaths.

"I'm better now," Charlotte murmured. Then she glanced at Susanna for confirmation. "Right?"

The doctor smiled. "I'm sure you'll be fine. Just too

much stress and too little of everything else you need. And breakfast burritos should probably be off the menu for a while."

The doors opened and Charlotte pushed away from her, gun in hand to assume an aggressive pose. "Next you'll be telling me to give up coffee."

The garage level was empty. Jacques ran to the nearest panel van and used his elbow to break the glass in the driver's door. Popping the locks, he loaded an unresponsive Max onto the rear seat and helped Charlotte climb in after him.

When he pulled Susanna toward the passenger door, she dug in her heels.

"Please, let me go. I can't go with you."

"I can't let you go until we're safe, until I'm sure they're safe. Sorry. I know the last place you want to be is with me." He yanked open the passenger door and shoved her in, aware that the rough move would look good on security video.

As he walked around the back of the vehicle, bullets thunked into the rear doors. Calmly, he turned and aimed the pistol he'd taken from Charlotte, putting rounds in the gun arms of both guards to end their threat. Then he took a minute to hot-wire the vehicle and drove them from the structure as if in no hurry, even stopping to extend the parking stub to the bored elderly man in the exit booth along with the required amount due.

Susanna was buckling on her seat belt.

"Don't get comfortable," he told her as he made a

quick U-turn on the street to cut in front of an incoming ambulance, forcing it up over the curb. "Get out."

He joined her on her side of the van and took her arm, hauling her toward the rear ambulance doors. The sight of his weapon quelled any resistance from the medic and youthful beat cop inside. They quickly locked their hands behind their heads.

Jacques boosted Susanna up inside with instructions to get whatever supplies she might need while he waited and watched for pursuit.

The young man strapped on the gurney, his forehead and shirtfront bloody and his breath stinking of alcohol, gushed, "Hey, can you help a brother out?" He lifted his hand to the limit of the cuff locking him in place.

"Sorry. I don't think we're related." Jacques reached up to help Susanna hop down with her armload of supplies, then he shut the doors.

They drove north in a big looping circle, Susanna sitting quietly while Jacques kept his eye on the rearview. He stopped the van under a busy overpass where a black SUV with Indiana plates was pulled off to the side. Giles St. Clair got out, asking no questions as he moved Max onto the rear bench seat and tucked a pale and somber Charlotte into one of the middle captain's chairs. He blinked at Susanna but had no comment when she climbed in next to Charlotte.

Jacques got into the front and as Giles slid behind the wheel, said simply, "Drive."

They'd gone several miles down the interstate with

Giles glancing worriedly in the mirror at the detective before he asked, "She get hurt?"

"No."

"The doc decide to come along?"

"No."

"All righty then. I'll just be driving."

Susanna leaned up between the seats, the scent of her hair enough to make Jacques dizzy.

"We need to stop someplace. I can't assess their situation in the back of a moving vehicle."

"Once we're in Indiana we'll get a motel."

She turned toward him, face so close he sucked in a quick breath. "Indiana?"

"Over, then down. Figure they'd be looking for us on the straight shot. It's out of our way but a helluva lot safer. Unless you think there's any immediate danger to either of them. Is there?"

"I don't think so, but sooner rather than later, okay?"

"You're the doctor."

She continued to stare into his eyes, then nodded. As she backed away, she glanced curiously toward their driver. "Did you kidnap him, too?"

Giles grinned at her. "Just along for the ride and minding my own business." He passed her an orange that was rolling about in the console. "Here. Didn't get the chance to finish my lunch. This'll give her some energy." Then he sobered. "Max okay?"

"I don't know yet." That was the best answer she had.

It was dark by the time they pulled into a past-its-prime motor lodge off the highway. Giles left the engine running while he went in to get two adjoining rooms in the back, paying cash. He backed the vehicle in close to the walk to hide a plate number that wouldn't match the one he gave to the desk clerk.

While Susanna checked on Charlotte, Giles stood outside the room in the bracing cold smoking a cigarette as Jacques walked across the parking lot to the fast-food place next door to buy them something quick and filling. The wind cut through the leather coat he wore over the security uniform. He'd forgotten how damned cold it was in the North, then was surprised by that recollection. He wondered if he'd lived in the changeable clime all his life or just the part of it he'd spent with Susanna. Did she know that little detail of his history? Would she tell him if he asked?

What else wasn't she telling him?

His mood was as frigid as the air by the time he got back to the rooms. Giles met him at the door, letting him know that Charlotte was resting easy and that Max had been sedated. He offered to keep watch from their room and disappeared inside with half the food and coffee.

Warily, Jacques entered the second unit.

The bathroom door was shut and the shower was running. After setting down the food, he went back to the vehicle to bring in the bag he'd hurriedly packed for the trip. Carefully, he opened the bathroom door and hung a clean T-shirt on the knob inside before shutting it again.

There were two double beds. She'd put her large shoulder bag on one so he took the other, stretching out on top of the bedspread without removing coat or boots. He closed his eyes and the next thing he knew the sound of her rummaging through the takeout bags woke him.

"Chicken or burger?" she asked without looking up.

"Burger, unless you want it."

She set the carton on the edge of the nightstand. "Fries or onion rings?"

"Onion rings."

"What if I want them?"

"Too bad." He sat up, enjoying the sight of her slight smile. Enjoying the sight of her in his T-shirt with her legs bare and her hair towel-dried and fluffy. She smelled delicious. And she had yet to make eye contact with him.

They ate in silence, each sitting on the edge of their own bed, knees nearly touching, making quick work of the food. After she'd sucked up the last of her drink, Susanna asked, "Can I make a call?"

"No. Sorry. Not while we're on the road."

She nodded but didn't look up.

"How's Charlotte?" he asked.

"She shouldn't have any trouble making the trip. Probably just a hormonal thing."

"And Max?"

"I don't know." Her gaze flickered up and away. "It depends on how much they gave him. We won't know until he wakes up, and it might be best if that didn't happen until we get where we're going."

"Agreed." He was silent for a moment and then it just burst out like a crack of lightning and boom of thunder. "Dammit! How could you do that? How the *fuck* could you do that to me?"

When he surged to his feet, she flinched back, startled. He quickly put some distance between them, pacing the length of the room in fierce, stalking strides as long-smoldering anger caught flame.

"You stole my memories," he accused in a low rumble as she watched him through the fringe of her lashes. "You stole my *life*. How could you *do* that do me?"

"I had no choice," she whispered.

"No choice." He considered that, getting angrier because he believed her. "What about that mark you wear? No choice there, either? Did that mean anything to you? Ever?" She shrank beneath the force of his roar. "Tell me, because I sure as hell don't know."

There was a tap at the door. He jerked it open to see Giles standing there, stoic and formidable.

"Thin walls. Everything okay in here?" He glanced around Jacques to where Susanna was huddled on the bed, his eyes narrowing.

"Just clearing the air," she told him with a wan smile. "Rather loudly."

"Mind your own business," Jacques snarled at the other man.

"As long as you mind your manners," Giles countered. There was no mistaking the threat.

Jacques rubbed a restless hand over the top of his head and relaxed his stance. "I will."

"Okay. Good night then."

Susanna sat quietly, her eyes upon the rigid figure at the door. She'd expected that explosive fury ever since he'd stepped out of the elevator all geared up for battle. Now that the danger of their external situation had eased, all his pent-up aggression had turned toward her.

She was tired and beaten down with worry and not about to take any more of his temper no matter how well justified.

"You don't get to yell at me."

Jacques turned at that quiet statement of fact. His brows veed down in anger but she didn't let him speak.

"You lost your past, but I lost *my* future. I gave you the chance to have one without going through *every* day and night for seven years *knowing* what you were missing." Her voice thickened and faltered, but when he took a step toward her, she put up a hand. "Go take a shower and let that sink in. And don't come out of there until you're ready to have a civil discussion that doesn't involve a raised voice."

For a moment, Jacques didn't move. She could see the astonishment blanking his brain of all the blame he'd been about to heap upon her. Frustration and hesitation worked his jaw. Intensity banked in his eyes until they appeared as black as the cold night outside.

When she wouldn't look away, he pivoted to storm into the bathroom, shivering the thin walls with a powerful slam of the door. She didn't let out her breath until she heard the shower running.

He was in there for a long, long time.

Susanna waited, mentally sorting through her rational arguments, lining them up into an unbroken wall of circumstances that would absolve her guilt. So why did she feel so ashamed? Why did the thought of the anguish and uncertainty tormenting him for all the weeks, months, and years cut to the heart of her until the pain was a raw, bleeding ache of blame?

She was responsible for what had happened to him. She'd initiated their forbidden relationship. She'd wanted him beyond all reason and that desire had weakened her ability to see the truth. That what she'd done was wrong. That what they'd done was wrong.

And that left her with one sobering revelation. She wouldn't change a damned thing even if she could go back and do it over.

The water stopped running and suddenly courage failed her. The room was abruptly too bright, the setting too stark for the conversation they were about to have. She wasn't sure she could face his glowering stare again without breaking down completely.

Jacques paused in the open doorway, backlit by the harsh bulbs above the sink. All he wore were jeans that hung low off lean hips. Shadow and highlights delineated the sculpted muscles of arms, shoulders, and chest. She couldn't see his expression clearly from where she was tucked under the covers in the darkened room. As he reached for the bathroom switch, his features were etched in silhouette, fierce and strong, and her pulse trembled the same way it had that first time she'd seen him.

Instead of moving toward the beds, he went to the window, parting the drapes a scant inch so he could peer outside.

"Your Shifter bodyguard," he began, his manner subdued and cautious, "that was me?"

"Yes."

"The one you found exciting, the one you loved, the one who marked you, that was me?"

"Yes."

"My name was Jack Stone?"

"Yes."

"What else do you know about me? Did I have a family? Where was I from? Was there anyone I was close to, who cared about me, who missed me?"

His poignant questions made her throat burn. "I don't know. You didn't talk about your past."

"How interesting could a slave be? I probably didn't have time for a lot of hobbies."

She tried to ignore his bitterness by telling him softly, "You talked about the future you wanted, what we'd do, the life we'd have."

He gave a harsh laugh. "And what was it I wanted?"

"What you have now."

"Everything except you." He turned toward her and she was glad she couldn't see his face. "Right?"

"Yes."

"What the hell were we thinking?"

"That we deserved more than we were allowed to have."

He pondered that for a moment, his mood quiet yet still simmering. "You could have left with me."

"No. They'd made an investment in me that I hadn't paid back. The project I was on was very valuable. They would have killed you and dragged me back."

"I could have stayed."

"Under their control? With no chance of ever obtaining those dreams? I wanted more for you. I had to let you go. I had to. I loved you too much to keep you prisoner and watch you die." Her voice fractured painfully.

"Didn't you wonder what happened to me? You never tried to find out?"

She drew a hitching breath. "I didn't dare. If I'd known, I wouldn't have been able to stop myself. Any more than you could have stayed away if you'd remembered any of what we'd shared. The only thing I had to hold on to was the belief that somewhere you were living those dreams, that you were free." She smiled, a fulfilling sense of satisfaction making her voice husky. "You did well for yourself. I knew you would."

He stepped away from the window, rubbing his arms distractedly. "I remember how much I hated the cold up here."

"You used to say even wrapping up inside another

animal couldn't keep you warm." She paused as his fingertips brushed over the worn leather of the coat hanging on the back of a chair. "But that I could."

His eyes glowed in the darkness.

And she took a chance.

"It's warm over here."

Nineteen

Jacques slipped out of his jeans and under the covers, his weight upon the soft mattress threatening to bring her softer body to him. Even though she braced to keep from rolling up against him, the space they shared beneath the sheet was suddenly, gloriously warm.

He lay on his back, arms crossed upon his chest in a tense pose that didn't exactly invite intimacy. She approached him carefully, the way one would a dangerous wild thing that had had its trust abused and broken, with a gentle hand and a soft word.

He held his breath as her knuckles grazed his cheek where scars barely remained.

"When I saw you lying on the floor at the club, I thought they'd killed you."

His stare stayed focused on the ceiling as he started breathing again in slow, wary respirations.

"I was so afraid that you'd died thinking I'd betrayed all of you." She paused, giving him an opportunity to speak. When he didn't take it, she asked, "Is that what you believe?"

"No. I think you were deceived right along with the rest of us."

"Damien used my calls to find me. He traded Max

to get me back. I had no idea he was capable of such things."

"And you're going back to him, knowing what kind of man he is?" A quiet question without blame or derision.

"Everything I thought we had together was a lie. I could never trust him again, knowing that."

He turned toward her then, his eyes gleaming in the darkness. "And you've never told any lies?"

"Only when I told myself I could forget you."

As her words snagged on that admission, his head rolled away in a denying gesture. "You didn't answer my question. Are you going back to him?"

"I don't want to. I have to. He has things I need. My work. My daughter. You don't understand."

"I understand more than you think."

She was silent for a moment, studying his harsh profile. When she placed her hand atop his, his fingers spread to squeeze hers tightly for an instant, then released them as she was asking him to release her. "I know you do. And that's why you won't stop me."

"I want to," he growled low.

"I know."

"It's not fair," he said suddenly. "You know my dreams, but I don't know yours." His gaze was intense when he regarded her. "I have none of those memories of us together." He brushed the wide neck opening of the T-shirt she wore aside so his fingertips could trace the scars it covered.

"There's nothing we dream of more than finding

and claiming our mate. There's nothing that binds us like that connection. That claiming and the link from it are more sacred than a marriage vow. It can't be broken. It can't be denied." His tone grew wistful as he continued.

"I have none of those memories even though I know we're mated. I dream sometimes of what it must have been like between me and the one I'd hoped would be mine to protect and treasure for the rest of my life, but I'll never know."

Susanna fit her palm to the side of his face. "Let me show you what I dream about."

She kissed him, at first with a slow, sweet yearning, treating herself to the taste and yielding softness of his sinfully full lips, then treating him to the seductive swirl of her tongue. He responded but didn't pursue, eyes closing, breath quickening.

She'd dreamed of him constantly, vividly, but the reality far surpassed those pale interpretations. Dreams couldn't flood her with sensation, couldn't flush her with heat and hunger as she learned him again there in the darkness by texture, touch, and taste. Dreams didn't kiss back. Kisses so drugging and deep they sucked at her soul.

A tender devotion tangled with that hot blast of passion. She feasted on his mouth, her hands worshipping the hard contours of his body. Everything she knew of desire and all the pleasures that came with it, she'd learned from him. He'd taught her trust and temptation and the wild bliss of casting off restraint.

He'd been protector, teacher, lover but all those cherished moments she clutched close in her heart were lost to him.

In his loneliness, he couldn't find solace in reliving that first dangerous shiver of attraction, those purposeful accidents that brought them into skin-to-skin contact and sent lust and longing into an agony of denial. He couldn't replay the first touch of their lips, so unexpected, so sweet, so forbidden. Or the chain reaction of reckless stolen moments: secret gazes, hurried kisses, trembling touches that spiraled greedily out of control. He didn't have the memory of his own heroics, when he'd ripped her from the arms of terror to surround her with his own comforting and possessive embrace. She'd gone to him that night, overcoming his caution and the last shreds of his reluctance to hold him and have him and love him. She couldn't imagine giving up any one of those precious slivers of discovery.

Yet that was what she'd taken from him.

Perhaps she could give some of it back.

Susanna wore nothing beneath his T-shirt. When she slid her thigh across him, the contact of her moist sex with his ready hardness sparked instantaneous combustion. Without breaking from their urgent kisses, she began to move slowly, suggestively against him until his big hands clamped to her hips to direct the rhythm. She allowed him to guide the intensity toward its inevitable peak, yet when he tried to lift her slightly so he could sheath himself inside her, she hit Pause.

"Not yet."

He was panting hard, obviously way past the point of no return. "What? Anna?"

They were nose to nose, breathing in each other's urgent breaths. Her palms pushed up the slick of his chest to clasp the sides of his face, her fingertips pressing firmly against his temples to begin a slow massage. All the while her tongue teased against his parted lips until he groaned aloud.

"Anna."

"Close your eyes. Trust me, Jacques. Trust me and let go."

Not understanding, still he did as she asked, not questioning the request or the strangely disorienting pressure she was quickening inside his head the same way MacCreedy had. He closed his eyes and let the tension leave his body.

Letting her essence flood into him just as she took him into her.

Everything changed in that instant. Jacques's world expanded with shattering flashes of light and heat. And in him, around him, through him was Anna. Her lips on his, her hot, greedy sex clutching his, her thoughts, her emotions, her every sensation exploding until he couldn't find the separating line between them, because there was none.

Let go, Jack.

Her siren's whisper tongued his every nerve ending until desire followed with a need so raw, so violently pure it surpassed anything he'd ever experienced.

He let go. He couldn't help himself. He couldn't

hold back the beast inside him. Under the silken slide of her flesh over his, his muscles bulged with power as control dropped away, replaced by seething instinct. Coaxed by her lapping kisses, his teeth became fangs, his breath quick, aggressive growls.

She was kissing him, riding him, urging him with hoarse pleas.

Take all of me. Make me yours. Claim me, Jack. Don't ever let me go.

She hadn't said the words aloud, yet they streaked through him like lightning, sizzling hot, icy cold all at once, too exciting, too compelling. Too much to resist.

He groaned in mindless ecstasy at the feel of her soft skin against his mouth. Her neck, her shoulder, warm, throbbing with life and temptation. Urges, dark, fierce, on fire, raged inside him, forcing his intentions to escape acceptable boundaries as he bit down hard. Senses swirled at the taste of her. He could feel her pulse pounding through him, taking over the tempo of his own heartbeats. And then that harsh beautiful rhythm became the fierce waves of her climax as she cried out his name.

Jack!

And he lost himself, possessing her, claiming her, coming inside her. Endlessly.

Then all Jacques could hear were his own ragged breaths.

Susanna lay on her stomach beside him, her eyes shut, her hand curving about his jaw, her thumb languidly rubbing over his lower lip.

What had just happened?

They'd had vigorous sex. His body was depleted by it. The scent of their mutual satisfaction lay heavy on the air. Had that been all?

He scrubbed his tongue about the inside of his mouth. No sign of elongated teeth or the metallic sweetness of blood. He looked to Susanna in confusion. She was resting easy, no scratches marring her skin, the T-shirt mussed but not torn. Nor was there any indication that he'd just savaged her neck in the throes of mating madness.

He caught her hand in his, drawing it away from contact with him. Her eyes opened on a tender smile.

"What was that?" he asked shakily.

"Memories for you to keep," she whispered, her eyes already drifting shut again. "I love you, Jack."

He lay in the darkness for a long while as her soft breaths punctuated his escalating panic.

Memories?

Almost afraid to check, he reached back into his mind, cautiously searching. And there they were: the images, the sensations, the sounds of them together, consummating that intensely personal moment that bound one to the other. Not a dream, but a memory, the only one he had of his life before New Orleans. Solid, rich with delicate detail, ripe with emotions. Real. A slice from that great emptiness when he was Jack Stone and she was the female he had to possess even if it meant his life.

And in a way, it had.

Only now Jacques knew it had been worth it. Completely and totally worth the sacrifice of everything that had come before to have her.

But how to hold on to her?

Jacques awoke to faint slivers of daylight seeping through a slight part in the curtains. Though the sheets tangled about him still held her scent, he could tell Susanna had left the bed they'd shared some time ago. He relaxed when he saw her bag on the dresser top. She hadn't gone far.

Even before getting out of bed, he checked to see if it was still there, that precious nugget of his past. Smiling to find the memory nestled safely amongst his years as Jacques LaRoche, he grabbed a quick shower and clean clothes, and went out to find his mate.

Giles St. Clair stood out in the blustery wind, a dusting of early snow dotting his jacket, melting at first contact with the steam from his coffee. He passed Jacques a second cup and they stood for several minutes sipping in silence. Finally, Jacques glanced at the closed door.

"How are they?"

"Charlotte's scared out of her mind, but she'd never let on. Max hasn't come around yet. What did you bastards do to him?" His tone was deceptively mild.

"I didn't do anything to him. They aren't *my* kind."

"But they're *her* kind."

Jacques didn't answer.

"Are they going to want him back?" All manner of bad intentions rumbled through Giles's question.

"If they do, they'll be disappointed."

"That was my thought, too."

Both turned when the door opened behind them. Susanna hesitated, her gaze touching almost shyly upon Jacques's as she stepped outside and shut the door behind her.

"We should be ready to leave in about ten minutes," she told Giles.

He swallowed down the last of his coffee. "I'll go gas up."

Left alone on the frigid walkway, Jacques and Susanna tested the relationship waters. He managed a smile that was both nervously awed and fiercely possessing.

"You have questions." She could see them banked and uncertain behind his eyes.

"I do. They can wait until we're safe at home."

At home. His apartment. His bed. The two of them together. Susanna trembled. Instantly, he whisked off his coat, intending to engulf her in its warm folds, even though it meant shivering in his shirtsleeves. She put up her hands in protest.

"No you don't. That's not necessary. I'm used to the cold."

"And I've got a bit more bulk to protect me from it," he argued.

Seeing he wasn't going to relent, Susanna dropped her arms and let him swaddle her with the coat. Its weight pulled on her shoulders but the heat and his scent had her drawing it close about her.

"Besides," he rumbled, "it's the least I can do after you warmed me so sweetly last night."

"Good morning."

Charlotte's greeting startled them. They hadn't heard her open the door. She looked between them, dark eyes filled with speculation and amusement until Susanna flushed red and muttered something about gathering her things before disappearing into the other room. The detective then turned an interrogative eye to Jacques.

"So?"

"She's my mate." A strange exhilaration came over him as he voiced that aloud.

"Ahhh. That would explain the strange noises last night. Thin walls. I thought maybe you were watching something on Animal Planet."

He grinned wide and shook his head. "Not from last night. From seven years ago."

Charlotte blinked. "Wow. What are the odds?"

"Was wondering that myself."

"Wow," Charlotte repeated as her quick cop brain began processing the sudden change in her friend's status. "So she's the one you nailed and bailed on back in the day."

"It wasn't my choice," he growled, insulted by her word choice.

But Charlotte's thoughts had already jumped ahead to something more intriguing.

"Then her daughter . . . is yours?"

Twenty

The question stunned like the sharp crack of a bat to his head.

"Easy, now." Charlotte gripped his forearms as he listed sharply on suddenly weak knees. "Take a breath."

He sank down onto his heels, palms pushing into his temples as if trying to shove the square peg of that incredible notion into the round hole of his limited knowledge.

Could it be true?

The timing, the circumstances all fit, but one thing didn't. He looked up at Charlotte, who'd crouched down with him, his voice low and unsteady. "Wouldn't she tell me if that was true?"

But then, Susanna hadn't come right out and said up front, "Hey, I'm the mate you can't remember from seven years ago! Good to see you again!"

Charlotte's advice was brusque and to the point. "Ask her."

They straightened as Giles backed the SUV up behind them and got out to open the rear hatch. He bumped past Jacques with a casual, "Help me load up, Wolfman."

Scrubbing away his stupor, Jacques went inside the

second room to assist in wrapping Max's slack form in
the hotel bedspread. After Giles left a handful of cash
on the nightstand to cover the loss, the two of them
carried the heavy bundle out and tucked it into the
back end of their vehicle.

"Get your lady," Giles told him. "Time to saddle up
and get the hell outta Dodge."

Something was very wrong.

Susanna sat quietly in the back, watching Jacques
fidget restlessly where he rode shotgun next to Giles.

After talking to Charlotte, he'd burst into the room
they'd shared to snatch up his things and declare
gruffly, "We're leaving." She'd been standing right in
front of him yet he'd never made eye contact.

And as they approached Indianapolis, he still hadn't.

Had the gift she'd given him last night been a mistake? Perhaps the very idea of her tinkering with his
mind, implanting information, reminded him all too
chillingly of how different she was, that she was of the
Chosen, the caste that had subjugated him, that she
was the one who'd stripped him of those memories in
the first place. Perhaps he doubted they were real, that
she'd pushed a falsehood upon him to gain his cooperation so she could escape.

She'd told him she loved him. Had that made no
difference at all? Or maybe fatigue was stirring up anx-
ieties where none were warranted.

She'd lain awake beside him for most of the night
just listening to him breathe, attuned to his slightest

movement, drawn to his body heat. She'd selfishly thought about waking him with a kiss and lusty caress but remembered all too clearly how only days ago he'd been lying in his own blood. He needed the rest to complete his healing and she needed to decide what she was going to do.

She didn't want to go back to Damien, but realized her companions were safe only as long as he believed she was with them involuntarily. How much time did that give her?

Jacques was edgy, his gaze flickering from window to window, everywhere but behind him where she sat. She'd never seen him so agitated, so distracted. Finally, he turned on the radio, fiddling with the buttons until he found a classical station.

Susanna smiled to herself, remembering his reaction the first time he'd heard a symphony orchestra. She'd convinced Damien to let her go to a holiday concert provided her stoic bodyguard remained at her side. She'd worn a sophisticated beige sheath but found herself enviously admiring gowns in jeweled seasonal hues of red, green, and gold. And she was more than appreciative of her somber companion's appearance in a tux. A gorilla in evening wear, Damien had commented with an unkindness that had surprised her.

Soon she'd been distracted from a simple enjoyment of the chorale selections as her usually silent escort murmured questions about the instruments, about the arrangements, about his reaction to the swelling emotional sounds. And she found herself hugging to his arm as they whispered back and forth, earning stern glances from the patrons surrounding them.

In the darkness of the auditorium, lost to the heart-tugging sound of the string section, as he'd leaned down to catch something she was saying, she'd impulsively stolen her first kiss from him. And nothing had ever been the same for her again.

Giles reached for the channel selector, stating, "Driver picks tunes. Another minute of that stuff and my brain'll be bleeding."

Another classic type of music filled the air. The Allman Brothers. Classic rock.

By the time they reached the Kentucky border, snow had become a miserable icy sleet and Giles declared he needed to pull off into a truck stop for a break and a cigarette. He parked some distance from the entrance, and as they gave Charlotte lunch orders to pick up at the attached neon-lit diner, Max woke up.

His feet slammed against the rear-door glass, knocking it off its track. And he was up and out before the rest of them could blink.

Giles, Charlotte, and Jacques leapt from the vehicle but Max had disappeared between the rows of trucks parked to wait out the storm. Charlotte gestured them into separate directions to make their search more efficient.

With the visibility reduced by the frigid spray and rising fog, Jacques jogged between the eighteen-wheelers, ducking low to check beneath them, pulling open any unlocked tractor cabs to do a quick search.

His teeth chattered with cold as his hurried breaths plumed on the air. Even his tough-soled work boots slipped and slid on the glazed surface of the lot, but that didn't slow him.

A brief rattle of sound from overhead caught his attention, sending his gaze upward in time to catch a glimpse of movement.

"Go high," he shouted to the others.

Max was jumping from truck to truck off the tops of the trailers.

Face upturned, catching the slashing brunt of the sleet, Jacques raced behind the vehicles, always a step too slow to see more than just a fleeting trace of the figure he pursued. Then he skidded around the last truck to find Giles there and Max teetering on the edge of the trailer's metal roof, his hospital garb plastered to his lean form, his eyes wild with a confused desperation, and no place to go but back the way he'd come.

As Max turned to retrace his escape route, Giles planted a well-aimed slush ball between his shoulder blades with enough force to knock his feet out from under him. He scrambled for purchase, bare hands and feet clawing at the ice-coated top and sides and, finding none, fell hard to the ground between his two friends.

"Easy, boss man. Easy now. Don't want to hurt you."

Giles had him clamped in a headlock, subduing him long enough for Charlotte to join them, snapping on cuffs, securing his wrists behind his back. As he was hauled to his feet, he made another lunging attempt at freedom only to have Jacques grip him by the ears to knock him out cold with a head butt.

A hurried look around showed no witnesses to their chase and capture. Each grabbing an arm, Giles and Jacques dragged him back to the SUV, where Susanna waited with a sedative prepared. Then, as a stony-featured Charlotte bundled his limp form up in the bedding to dry and warm him, Giles puffed out a breath and announced he was going to pick up their lunch while Jacques struggled to restore the glass to its track.

"Let me look at your head," Susanna called to Jacques as he opened the passenger door to return to the front seat.

He touched fingertips to his brow, surprised when they came back bloodied. "I'm fine," he murmured.

"Sit and let me see."

Wordlessly, he climbed into the back and dropped into the seat Charlotte had occupied, staring unblinkingly out the windshield as Susanna dabbed and wiped and bandaged. Her scent bit into him like those icy pellets outside, tingling, burning until he could barely sit still. His awareness of her increased until each inhalation was near torture.

"I'm fine," he insisted testily, pushing her hands away in his hurry to put some space between them so he could breathe. So he could think about anything other than how much he wanted to kiss her, tear off her clothes, and take her right then and there.

What the hell was wrong with him? He ducked down and reached a long leg over the center console so he could ease back into the front seat and sit there ramrod stiff in all interpretations of the word. His breath hissed noisily between clenched teeth as Susanna was no doubt gaping at him in alarm.

Was he the father of her child? Why hadn't she told him, especially after what she'd shared with him last night? How could he expect the truth from her when she'd hidden all the facts from him for so long?

His child. His *daughter*. Heart beating so violently he feared it might refracture those yet tender ribs, Jacques closed his eyes and concentrated on recovering his composure.

His daughter.

A smile trembled over his lips.

It was close to daybreak when they entered Orleans Parish. Max had been stirring for some time, but Susanna advised against drugging him again so soon unless absolutely necessary.

As they drove beneath an overpass, lights swept through the interior of the vehicle from above, startling a semi-lucid Max into a panicked crouch behind Susanna's seat. When Charlotte reached for him, he cringed away, knotting up even smaller, face averted, eyes tightly closed, knees tucked up to his shoulders. His breathing came loud and fast.

"Max. Baby, it's me. It's Charlotte." She touched his hair, making the gesture light and gentle, but still he squirmed out from under it with a low anxious whine.

"Charlotte, he doesn't know you," Susanna explained.

"What? What do you mean?"

"What they did to him scrambled his thought process. It'll take some time for him to put things back together, to sort them out."

"What do you mean he doesn't know me? How could he not know me?"

"His mind's like a jigsaw puzzle with all the pieces dumped into a pile. They don't make any sense to him yet. They don't make a picture he recognizes."

"And what if some of those pieces are missing?" Though she bit down hard on it, some of the fear shivered through Charlotte's tight words.

"Don't worry. They wouldn't be that careless with him. They wouldn't have kept him alive if they'd damaged him."

"Damaged him," she echoed numbly, her worried gaze on the feral creature huddled just out of arm's reach.

"Stop at the club," Jacques instructed Giles as they slipped unnoticed into the quiet Quarter. After Giles pulled in behind Charlotte's screamingly orange muscle car, Jacques got out and opened the slider, putting up his hand to Susanna. Hers fit into it trustingly. He nodded back toward the pregnant detective. "Make sure she's okay."

Instantly alert, Charlotte regarded him suspiciously. "What are you trying to pull, LaRoche? Take us home."

"This is as far as you're going, Charlotte. Get down."

She knocked his hand aside with a snarl of, "Like hell. Where he goes, I go."

"Where he's going, you can't go."

"Fuck that."

He gripped her arm, pulling her steadily toward the door as he explained, "I'll take good care of him. I'll make sure he's okay."

She dug in her heels mulishly. "*I'll* make sure he's okay."

He curled his arm about her waist and lifted her out of the vehicle. Then he held her close against him so she couldn't dish out any damage. As she struggled furiously, he said softly into her hair, "For the next few days, he needs to be among his own kind. He'll be watched and protected until we're sure."

She shoved away, taking a few stumbling steps back. Her eyes were bright with fury and fear. "Sure of what?"

"That he hasn't been compromised by what they did to him." He held up his hand to halt further questions. "Trust me. Charlotte, just trust me. Please."

She hesitated and he took that as a positive sign to continue.

"Go with Dr. Duchamps. Let her examine you and make sure the baby is all right. That's the best thing you can do for Max right now. Get some rest and I'll call you as soon as I can."

She searched his expression rather desperately but relented when he leaned forward to kiss her brow. Then he strode around to the driver's side and opened the door, motioning Giles out.

"Take care of them," he told the reluctant-to-leave bodyguard.

Giles climbed down and thrust his forefinger into Jacques's chest. "Anything happens to him, it's on you."

Jacques nodded. "Understood."

As a major contributor, Max's name opened doors at the hospital. Charlotte identified Susanna as her private physician and once her credentials were checked, they were provided with an exam room. By the time Charlotte was gowned up and fidgeting on the table, Nica arrived, having responded to Susanna's call.

"If you're concerned at all about your baby's health," Susanna told her, "put one of those on and I'll check you next."

Without comment, Nica picked up one of the hospital gowns and disappeared into the bathroom.

It was morning by the time she'd taken genetic samples from both expectant mothers.

They filled Nica in on the adventures in Chicago and though she expressed concern over Max's situation, she encouraged Charlotte to trust Jacques.

After leaving the samples with Dev Dovion to have them worked up into usable data, and stopping at an electronics store to buy a small computer on a credit card Damien had yet to cancel, Susanna had Charlotte drop her off at the Towers. Despite her suggestion that she take it easy, Charlotte planned to go to work, saying she had to check in with her partners at the NOPD. Susanna promised they would make a visit to Mary Kate the following day. By then, she hoped to have made some headway.

The apartment was quiet and dark with its drapes closed against the dull morning light, inviting with its memories and traces of Jacques's scent. More than anything Susanna wished she could fall into the big bed and sleep off her fatigue until Jacques joined her, but her own work beckoned. While the laptop booted up and installed her programs, she made coffee and changed her clothes, hoping she'd hear from Jacques. No call, no messages, so she sat down at the computer and began to work, letting the hours of the morning, then afternoon, slip away.

She was dozing at the table, head gently bobbing as she wandered uneasily through her subconscious. In the dream, she walked down an overly bright corridor with observation windows on both sides. The first rooms were filled with newborns. All looked identical except for the tags at the ends of their bassinets, which separated them as Human, Shifter, Chosen. The next set of rooms held toddlers, again all identical yet divided into groups by color, each with a different teacher reading from a book of fairy tales. She slowed her step to check the titles. *Humantales*, *Shiftertales*, *Chosentales*. All the stories sounded the same as they were repeated to each group in unison.

Puzzled, Susanna moved on as the walls fell away and she was outside on a playground in a middle-class Chicago suburb. On the other side of a fence, two girls were spinning jump ropes in a fast double Dutch while another skipped to the rhythm they chanted. All looked exactly like her daughter, Pearl. Susanna paused, her eyes misting up as they fixed upon the girls. *Pearl.* Though she wanted to call to them, she was unable to move, unable to do anything but cling to chain link, listening to their ditty.

"Human, Shifter, Chosen, Ancient. One and one and one we fall. Human, Shifter, Chosen, Ancient. One plus two plus three saves all."

Susanna straightened with a gasp, cold hands fluttering over her face to brush away the remnants of sleep. She stared at her screen, at the combinations and divisions she'd been working on and realized what had been missing from her equations and why they had never added up.

She'd been missing one of the components.

Twenty-one

Are you sure he can't get out of there?" Jacques turned from the thick plexiglass window to Philo, who stood beside him.

"No way," his friend assured him. "No internal hinges, catches, locks, or bolts. Solid three-inch steel." He tapped the glass. "Bulletproof, shatterproof. He's not going anywhere."

Jacques frowned as he observed the six-by-eight room, which held only a basic sink and stool and a cot that was bolted to floor and wall. Max had tucked himself into the shadows beneath the cot like an animal backed into a hole.

Philo placed a hand on Jacques's shoulder. "He'll be fine. One of the shipping companies used it as a temporary brig. Everything's reinforced and he'll be watched 24/7. Any changes, any surprises, we'll call you. Now, go home and get some sleep before you drop. Let me take care of this for you."

With a tremendous exhalation, Jacques let the tension drop from him. "Okay. Just make sure you tell them not to trust him. He's smart and he's fast and right now, he could be very, very dangerous."

"I know what to tell them. Go home, Jackie."

As he moved away from the glass, Philo added, "I hear she came back with you." His tone was carefully guarded.

"Temporary situation. Nothing for you to get excited about. We used her to get to him, and we're still using her for what she knows."

"Are you sure it's not more personal than that?"

"Nothing's changed on that score, Tib."

No, nothing had changed. She still belonged to him, and the only temporary part of the situation was her belief that he'd let her go.

After LaRoche had gone, Philo called in a group of his most trusted men and explained the situation tersely.

"Savoie may or may not have been compromised by whatever those bastards did to him. Until we know the degree of contamination, he stays put in that room. No one goes in there for any reason. Understood? There's no telling whether he's their eyes and ears now, so be careful what you say or do anywhere near him."

"Won't they be coming back for him?" Morris asked from the back of the group, eager to recover his standing amongst his peers now that LaRoche had shunned him. "Should we set up a perimeter?"

"Not a bad idea. Put together a rotation. They kicked our asses to the curb last time. They won't find it so easy to do it again." Bold words Philo wasn't sure he could live up to, but his brother's spirit still roamed restlessly, looking for retribution.

"Is he worth it?" asked another, voicing what they all were feeling. "Can he actually do any of the things he promised to? Why should we trust him? Do you?"

"I don't trust Savoie," Philo admitted. "I think all he'll bring is trouble and the last thing I want are those monsters who killed Tito and our friends to come back to our city. But I do trust Jacques, and he believes in him. For him, there's nothing I wouldn't do."

After a lengthy stop at the club, Jacques opened the door to his apartment, so weary he could barely stand. He drew a breath, tasting Susanna upon it, but the scent was old. She wasn't here.

"Anna?"

He moved swiftly through the rooms. The bed was untouched. The clothes she'd worn were folded on a chair. There was cold coffee in the brewer and a recently purchased laptop sat in hibernation on the table. His panic quieted at that sight, but wasn't totally erased.

He tried her cell but got voice mail. While he fretted over what to try next, his phone rang.

"Anna?"

"She's with me," Nica said.

Relief, then annoyance. "Where are you? What are you up to?"

"Girl stuff," was her chipper response. "Don't worry. She's in good hands. You sound terrible. Get some sleep, then call my man. You two have lots to talk about."

He stared at the silent phone, aggravation growling through him. He didn't want to talk to MacCreedy. He wanted Susanna here with him. But if she was with Nica, at least she wasn't escaping back to the North. So he might as well try to get a few minutes' rest, if possible.

He took off his coat and lay back on the bed, kicking off his unlaced boots as he closed his eyes. He never heard them hit the floor.

"Now, we're of one mind, one heart, one soul. Nothing will ever separate us again."

Susanna's words whispered through his dream, now as real as the soft mouth caressing his. He opened his eyes to find the room in darkness.

"Time's it?" he mumbled, catching Susanna at the waist when she began to straighten.

"Eight o'clock. I didn't mean to wake you."

"Then you shoulda stayed in the other room." He gave a slight tug that brought her sprawling across him. He lifted his head to plant a deep, thrusting kiss, then murmured, "You mean you didn't want to wake me for that?" A quick roll and she was beneath him, the flex of his hips pressing his shaft into the grove between her thighs. "Or for that?"

Susanna reached between them for his zipper, purring, "Since you're up . . ."

A bit of hurried tussling got them both naked below the waist, then he eased one of her legs up over the jut of his hipbone and settled in deep and sure. As she tightened around him in welcome, he groaned, "You have absolutely no idea how good this feels," easing back and sliding home again for emphasis.

She took his face between her palms. "No. But I know how good *you* feel." She pulled him down for another kiss as he began a slow, pleasing rhythm, in no hurry to get to the satisfying release that finally left them replete in each other's arms.

If only time could stop and let them linger.

Questions and worries seeped in, pushing for resolution.

What can I do to make her stay?

His restlessness returning, Jacques rolled out of bed, restored his clothing, and went into the kitchen to heat up the coffee in his microwave.

Susanna followed, trying to gauge his mood as she sat down at her keyboard, torn between the work she couldn't wait to get to and the man who distracted her so easily from it.

"How's Max?"

He shrugged. "I haven't heard anything, so I guess there's been no change." He carried the heated cup to his balcony doors, sipping as he stared into the night. "You know more about those things than I do. Will he recover?"

"It depends on how far into the process he was. They empty the mind first, then imprint whatever they choose upon it. If they didn't have time to repattern him—"

"I'm familiar with that outcome."

She winced. These were the things she'd allowed to be done to him, the man she'd taken to be her mate.

"If they were blanking his mind," Jacques speculated uneasily, "does that mean they already got what they wanted from him?"

She had no answer.

"I'm going to meet MacCreedy at the club. We need to get a plan together. Have you eaten yet? Do you want me to make something before we go?"

"I had a late lunch. I'll just stay here and work."

Susanna almost told him then about the fantastic discoveries she'd made that afternoon, about what they'd mean if her test results were even half as positive as she hoped they'd be. But she wasn't sure yet, and she couldn't give him false encouragement.

But soon everything would be different.

"Are you worried about your daughter?" Jacques's sudden question surprised her. "He wouldn't mistreat her, would he?"

"Damien? Not as long as he believes I'm here involuntarily. He knows as long as he has Pearl, I'll come back."

"Would it be so bad," Jacques asked without turning toward her, "living here with me?"

She was too startled to respond, then a huge knot of emotion thickened in her throat. Bad? It would be *wonderful*.

He hurried on. "You could work here in New Orleans, set up a clinic, do your research. I was going to use the extra room for an office, but your daughter could have it for her bedroom. There are other kids for her to play with. Max's brother, Oscar. Amber's little girl. She'd like it here." A slight pause. "I'd like to have her here."

When Susanna remained silent, Jacques took a breath. *Just ask her. Is she our daughter?*

"You'd take in another man's child as if she were your own?" she asked softly.

Another man's child, not his.

Jacques's eyes squeezed shut against the awful disappointment. But his voice was steady. "Did you think I wouldn't? She's a part of you. It would be a privilege to help raise her, to be a part of her life. Unless . . . unless you think it would be better for her to stay with her own kind. I don't have the sophistication or education that her father has. She might not want to be around a laborer, an inferior."

Susanna crossed to him and hugged her arms about his middle. "You're exactly what she needs," she told him. "And she'd love you. But let's not get ahead of ourselves."

His hands caught hers, his so rough and strong, hers so soft and small. The contrast said everything about the different worlds they lived in. He released her and went to get his coat, slipping his arms into the sleeves as he came back into the room.

"You'll be safe here. Charlotte's on the next floor up if you need anything. I'll have my phone on. Stay put. You're not going to run away, are you?"

She smiled. "If I'd wanted to, I'd be long gone by now."

His features were drawn with worry and a fatalistic sadness that broke her heart. *Have patience. Have faith in me, in us. Just a little more time and I can tell you everything you need to hear.* She went to him, reaching up to pull him down for a kiss.

"You be careful," she told him. "I'll miss you. No getting sidetracked for beer or gumbo."

He smiled then, a broad flash of knee-weakening charm. "Why would I do that when I have everything I could possibly want right here?" And he was gone, engaging the complex locks behind him.

Susanna rubbed at her arms, missing his heat already. Then she turned to her laptop with determination.

Human, Shifter, Chosen. Ancient.

She'd uncovered the secret. The Shifters and Chosen weren't two parts of one whole. They were two-thirds of it.

The other third was human.

The club was full of the curious. Rumors had quickly spread that Jacques LaRoche and Max's tough human lover had gone North and snatched him out of Chosen hands. The ballsy act had the clan flushed with both exhilaration and fear. What a coup to claim against such a fierce enemy! What disastrous consequences would such an act carry? "A Gathering," whispered between tables like the dread of a coming plague.

So when Jacques strode amongst them, they weren't sure if he should be viewed as hero or bringer of their own destruction.

In fact, Jacques didn't care how they saw him as he looked right past them in his search for Nica's coolheaded mate. MacCreedy was leaning on the bar watching Nica work. When he saw Jacques he picked up a couple of bottles and carried them to an isolated table.

"You've had a busy few days," he remarked. "You've become quite the folk legend. Nica and Amber want to start up a fan club. They think it would be good for business."

Jacques snorted. "What would be good for business is getting back to business. What do you want me to do for you?"

"I don't want you to do anything for me."

Before Jacques could bristle up in insult, Mac-Creedy hoisted his beer.

"I need you to work with me. I know books and ledgers and laws. I don't know people. I'm not a leader. These men will never look to me the way they already do you, especially now that you've gone into hell and not only come back unsinged but with a rescued soul."

Jacques smiled ruefully. "They may applaud me and buy me drinks, but that doesn't mean they'll follow me. I couldn't even get them to cross a room to save my ass. You did that for me. Thanks again, by the way."

"Will they come after him, do you think?"

"Depends on if they got what they wanted. Or if we pissed them off bad enough for them to want to prove something."

"Nica said something about a Gathering. What's that?"

"Last time we pissed them off, they came down here, killed every man and child they could find, and took all the women. That was almost three generations ago but it's remembered like it was yesterday."

"They're afraid," MacCreedy said.

"Who? The Chosen? Of us? That's a laugh."

"Rulers always fear the masses if there's someone who can pull them together and make them into a threatening force."

"And they think that someone is Savoie?"

"Don't you?" MacCreedy took a drink, his shrewd eyes narrowing. "It's not just this little pocket of outcasts here in New Orleans. It's all of the clans, together. They're afraid if the least of us can successfully strike out at them, the others will be encouraged to follow. Bad business for them. Possibly fatal business for us if we can't get someone to stand with us."

"So we should just crawl underground again on our bellies?"

"Or pretend to, while we gather our ranks. A few of us spat in their eye, but they believe the majority are cowards."

"They could be right about that."

MacCreedy ignored Jacques's sour claim. "We have

to show them that we're not a threat, that we're not defying them. We do that by returning what we've taken from them, along with their arrogant pride."

"You want to give them Max?" Jacques was stupefied.

"No. Susanna."

Jacques came out of his chair so violently it crashed to the floor, startling the room into silence. "No way that's gonna happen," he growled menacingly.

"Sit down."

"I'm not gonna listen to this."

"Sit. Down. Now. Listen to me."

Impressed by MacCreedy's fierceness, Jacques righted the chair, noting Nica poised to intercede. On whose behalf, he had to wonder as she came from around the bar to place her hands upon his shoulders.

She leaned down. "Listen to him, boss. This is a time for cool heads, not angry hearts."

He shrugged off her calming touch. "I'm listening."

Nica gave his shoulders a squeeze, then went to stand behind MacCreedy.

"We need time to reach out to the others," Silas began. "We're not strong enough to repel an attack on our own, but if we had even a couple of the clans standing with us, they'd hesitate. We're vulnerable because of our lack of affiliations. That's why Max came to me; because of my connections. Give me time to use them. Nica knows this Damien Frost. He'll move hell and earth to get Susanna back. Not because it's personal. He's nothing without her and he knows it. If he doesn't rattle their cages, things may quiet down on their own."

"By sacrificing Susanna. I guess that would be a pretty easy choice for *you* to make."

"We're not going to take her from you," Mac-Creedy said. "It would have to be your decision. Yours and hers."

Everything inside Jacques rebelled against placing his mate in danger, against letting her out of his sight. He didn't even want to think about the odds of seeing her again if he let her go back to them. So much could go wrong. The possibilities had him sick with dread.

"If our roles were reversed, and it was you who had to surrender your mate, would you be able to do it?"

The recoil of MacCreedy's body, the instant objection in his eyes said as much as the way he possessively gripped the hand Nica had resting on his shoulder. And he considered his words carefully before answering.

"Yes. I would. I wouldn't like it, but if our positions were reversed, I would. Because that's what I promised Max I'd be willing to do, and because Nica knows nothing would ever keep me from coming for her."

Nica leaned down to whisper something in Silas's ear. Without a word, he rose and went to the bar for another couple of bottles. Nica settled into his seat.

"Ahh," Jacques drawled, "the more attractive half of the double-team."

"He's right and you know it. Are you afraid for her safety or afraid she won't come back to you?"

Right to the heart. The daring assassin didn't know any other way to strike.

"Both," he admitted quietly.

"She loves you. You know that."

"I know she loves who I was, but I don't know who that is."

"Maybe Silas can help you with that. He's a Reader, the strongest one I've ever seen. He might be able to go into your mind and find those memories for you."

"If I agree to let Susanna go? Is that the price I have to pay?"

"No," Nica stated frigidly, "because I thought you were my friend." She surged up out of the chair, shoving past MacCreedy.

He arched a brow as he looked after her, then placed the beers on the table. "Rub her the wrong way, did you?"

"No. Just being a dickhead." Jacques picked up his bottle and drained half of it. "I can have Susanna ready to go tomorrow, but there's something I want you to do for me."

"Name it."

"Try to read Savoie. I need to know if he can come back to lead us before I risk everything I have for nothing."

MacCreedy regarded him for a moment, then stood. "Let's do it."

Seeing them readying to leave together, Nica hurried over. MacCreedy told her brusquely what they planned.

"Amber," she called to the other waitress. "Fill in behind the bar for me."

"Did you promote her without telling me?" Jacques asked.

"No. I promoted me to manager, and I'm making her my assistant." She stared at him impatiently. "Do you have a problem with that?"

"I guess not. Are you sure I even need to come to work anymore?"

"Only if you want to, boss. And to sign the paychecks." She linked her arms through theirs. "I'm going with you in case my man needs a little psychic backup."

But when they got to the docks, they found Max Savoie gone.

Twenty-two

Charlotte opened the door to her apartment to find a breathless Susanna in the hall.

"I found it." She was laughing and crying all at once.

"Found what?" Charlotte took her arm and pulled her inside.

"The key. It works. It opens everything." After collapsing onto the sofa, she tried to explain. "The key to our species. I had Nica take me back to Dovion's lab this afternoon so I could double check the data. There's no mistake. We're all one. Shifter, Chosen, Human, all derived from Ancient DNA. We've always believed that it was just Shifters and the Chosen. That's why all attempts to recombine were futile. We were missing the human element. Balance is the key: a triangle. The Alpha for Ancient with its three corners."

Charlotte stared at her. "Then you can heal Mary Kate."

Susanna nodded. "And our children." Her voice broke. "Our children will survive."

"My son and your daughter. Your daughter who's Chosen and Shifter."

Susanna blinked damp eyes. "Yes."

"Then you'll be staying here in New Orleans," Charlotte said as if it were a fact.

"It's not that simple. Jacques's made a life for himself here. I don't know how I'd fit into it or how he'd blend into mine. The work I'm doing is important in the North. Not for the Chosen and their politics, but for *all* of us. I don't know how to bring our two worlds together without one of us having to make a terrible sacrifice."

"Maybe there's more of a place for you here than you realize. Let me work on that while you get that serum ready to go."

"It'll only take me a few hours. I've collected all that I need: human DNA from your friend Dev, Ancient from Nica, Shifter from Jacques, and my own Chosen. I've determined the percentages. I just need some more time in the lab."

"Let's go."

Susanna hesitated, and Charlotte intuited the problem.

"Leave him a note. I'll take responsibility."

Preparing the serum using her computations was as easy as mixing a protein drink. When they went to the hospital and she stood at Mary Kate Malone's bedside, Susanna looked at Charlotte. "Are you *sure* this is what she'd want?"

A slight hesitation, then a firm, "Yes. Do it."

After the injection was given, Charlotte's tension drained away on a sigh. Her hand stroked over the invalid's blonde hair as she leaned down to murmur, "We'll talk again soon."

"I'll leave instructions with the staff," Susanna said. "I'll receive updates online any time there's a change."

She suddenly noticed a priest standing in the doorway.

Charlotte made stiff introductions. "Dr. Susanna Duchamps, Father Michael Furness. I think each of you has something the other wants."

"How did this happen?" Jacques raged at Philo Tibideaux. "He was secured, sedated, and now he's just *gone*?"

Philo glanced to where MacCreedy and Nica stood out of earshot. "He didn't just walk away."

"What did he do? Fly?"

"Near as I can figure," Philo continued uncomfortably, "Morris and some of the others took him."

"What do you mean, took him? Where? Why?"

"It's my fault. I was going on about keeping the monsters who kilt Tito outta our city, and how they'd be coming sure as shit for Savoie."

Jacques's hand fisted in Philo's shirt, yanking him to his toes. "You gave me your word!"

"And I meant to keep it, Jackie—I did. But some a them got to thinkin' that I was letting my friendship with you get in the way a takin' care a business. So they decided to take matters outta my hands."

Jacques shoved him away. "So what do the bastards plan to do?"

Philo's expression grew grim. "They mean to make whatever sacrifice is necessary to protect our own."

"They're going to *kill* him?" The notion was too incredible to grasp at first. "Is that what they plan to do?"

Philo didn't answer.

Jacques sank into a crouch, clasping his head in his hands. Then he snapped, "These were your men. You vouched for them."

"They're our friends, Jackie, yours and mine. We work with 'em, drink with 'em, bury our dead with 'em. They were doing what they thought was right."

Jacques exploded up and began to pace furiously. "Where did they go? Where did the sonsabitches take him?"

Philo set his jaw. "I don't know."

Jacques rounded on him, eyes blazing. "Don't know or won't say?"

"What are you meaning to do? Go after 'em? Maybe let your new friends there tear 'em into little pieces? I ain't gonna let that happen. I'm surely sorry about Savoie, but I'm not turning on our friends, our *brothers*. I won't give you any names."

"Morris will give them up."

Philo gripped his friend's arm. "And then what? Jackie, think this through. After all we been to each other, you planning to turn on your own for an outsider?"

Jacques threw off his hand. "They weren't treating me as one of their own when I was bleeding on my floor right in front of them. Maybe to them I'm just an outsider, too. And maybe deep down, you're thinking the same thing."

He stormed away in fury and frustration, turning his back on seven years of friendship in favor of the calm and deadly pair that so recently had become a part of his life.

"They took Max. They're gonna kill him."

"Do we know where?" MacCreedy asked.

Jacques shook his head, ready to howl in aggravation and from a deep-seated fear that whatever they did, it would be too late.

"Silas can find him," Nica insisted. At her mate's perplexed look, she explained, "You linked psyches with him to free me. You know the pattern of his thoughts."

"What if that pattern's gone?"

The three of them sat in Jacques's trailer in near darkness.

Jacques wouldn't have believed such things were possible. He knew the Chosen had strong mental abilities, but discovering them in those he'd thought were like him was unsettling. He'd always known Nica was somehow different. Discovering she was part of the early race generally thought to be pure myth was startling, but he'd go with it because it explained that uncanny insight she displayed. But finding out Silas MacCreedy was of that same ancient blood was even more disturbing.

It was some consolation that MacCreedy seemed as uneasy as he was with these mysterious powers. Nica had to work to get the usually level Silas relaxed and receptive. With his coat and tie off, shirt collar open, and sleeves pushed up, the Shifter cop took a deep breath and let his mate coax him into closing his eyes.

"I'm right here, lover," Nica soothed, beginning a gentle massage of his temples. "Just let your thoughts empty. Breathe. That's it. Now concentrate on Max. Breathe in his scent." When Silas's breathing altered encouragingly, she urged, "Look through his eyes. What do you see?"

"Nothing. Darkness."

"What do you feel?"

"Motion. Vibration. A vehicle. He's in a vehicle. A big one. Lot's of open space. A van, maybe."

"Good. What do you smell?"

"The river, but it's faint. The city. He's still in the city. Stop and go." MacCreedy began a slight rocking as if he were a passenger, too. "Sirens. Ambulance. Hospital? Circle?"

"He's at Lee Circle," Jacques interjected, excitement beginning to build.

"What is he thinking? Is he awake?"

MacCreedy's head moved from side to side. "Confusion. Can't think clearly. Danger. Darkness." His breathing quickened.

"How many are with you?"

"Hear voices. Familiar but don't know them. Five, maybe six. Crossing tracks. Going to . . . the park?"

"Audubon? Riverside? Armstrong?"

"Audubon," Jacques declared.

MacCreedy's rocking grew more manic. His voice took on an almost childlike singsong. "Jimmy, help me. Jimmy, save me."

Nica looked to Jacques in question.

"Legere. Max's mentor. He's dead. Why would he—?"

MacCreedy gave a sudden lurch forward, dropping to his knees, his palms flat on the floor. He took several huge gulping breaths, then lifted his gaze to Nica's. "He's out. He's loose. I lost him."

"Where? Where would he be going?"

A revelation struck Jacques. "I know. We need to hurry."

MacCreedy remained slumped on his knees and forearms, trembling from the telepathic effort. When Nica's hand touched his head in concern, he panted, "Go. I'll be fine. Go!"

Nica's little sports car ripped out of the Quarter toward St. Charles in the Garden District.

"Where to?" she asked without looking at her passenger.

"Lafayette Cemetery. Turn on Washington."

"I thought Legere was interred in St. Louis Number One?"

"He is. But Max is confused. He'd go for the familiar, for protection. Dammit, this is my fault."

"They're your friends. You trusted them."

"But I knew how they felt about Savoie. I just never thought—"

"That they'd betray you?" She did a quick downshift, then reached over to press his hand. "It wasn't personal, Jacques. It was business. Remember that."

It was cold comfort.

An old white panel van sat parked on the wrong side of Washington near the locked gates of Lafayette No. 1. Nica parked behind it.

"Looks like this is the place," she said with a soft purr that had the hair standing on Jacques's arms. "Hand me that bag under the seat, would you?"

He passed her the roadside emergency kit and watched as she flipped it open and plucked out the jumper cables, flare, and lug wrench. When she caught his look, she showed her teeth in a feral smile.

"A girl's got to be prepared."

At that moment, Jacques was very glad he was with her and not against her.

They got out of the car and, quickly shifting into the deadly predators they were, went over the eight-foot stone wall and landed without a sound.

The old cemetery was a lush, tranquil spot during daylight hours. In the deep midnight shadows, it whispered with long-dead ghosts. Row after row of vaults created a maze of gleaming marble, ancient brick, and crumbling stone, many of the family tombs neatly fenced in like the elegant homes in the surrounding district. Nica gestured for him to head down a long row of wall ovens, then she trotted, low and sleek, down the wide main drive.

Unlike St. Louis No. 1, with its narrow, hard-packed paths, Lafayette Cemetery was parklike, with old spreading oaks reaching across wide avenues with late fall branches twisted and gnarled like arthritic bones. Paved aisles were edged by grass slick with gathering fog as cool, night air met warm, resting earth.

Jacques moved swiftly, gaze darting through breaks between the mausoleums, senses keen as he searched for any sign of Max and the van's occupants. If he could find them before Nica, he'd have a chance to talk them down from unnecessary violence. These were friends he was chasing, not enemies. But he couldn't allow them to harm the potential savior of their race.

The night was still with no breeze to carry the sound of hurried breaths, scuffling footfalls, or the scent of nonresidents roaming the city of the dead. Darkness was relieved by the pale, eerie glow of silent figures staring down at him in spectral disapproval, monuments honoring the departed shaped like angels, lambs, saints, and children at prayer.

Jacques didn't hear Nica. She moved as quiet as a cloud across the fingernail moon above. But now he could detect the presence of intruders who weren't worried about stealth. Because they didn't know they were being hunted.

A crunching of gravel brought Jacques sharply about. He peered through the narrow opening between two centuries-old mausoleums and saw furtive figures skimming down the next row, searching hurriedly just as he was. He ran parallel to them back toward the central drive, catching fleeting glimpses every now and again. Then he heard a trickle of loose stone from above.

As Jacques lifted his head, he saw eyes flaming red and a jaw stretched wide baring lethal fangs. There was no time for talk or reasoning before he was struck to the ground by the plummeting assailant.

With one hand, Jacques gripped a thickly corded neck, pushing snapping teeth away as his other groped wildly about, finally closing around a weighty cement urn. He swung hard, hearing bone crack as contact was made. Suddenly freed, he scrambled up, getting a brief look at the crushed features of Rohm Bentley. They'd spent many a late night together over cards and stories, stories they'd never share again. Jacques forced himself to look away and moved on.

He'd barely gone three running strides before another figure slammed into his back, knocking him facefirst into a marble wall etched with a list of the generations housed behind it. Blood spilled from a split in his brow, staining both stone and shirtfront as he was dragged back and up onto his knees by the huge hand crumpling his windpipe.

Just as his vision began to fade and spark, he saw an image glide out of the shadows, long weighted whips whirling overhead before spinning in a deadly arc. The pressure abruptly disappeared from his throat, allowing him to suck a sharp, sweet breath of air as his attacker fell back, broken neck tangled in jumper cables.

Jessie Vaughn, who'd taught him to spear fish from his flat-bottomed pirogue, would never return home to his mate and three children.

Jacques wobbled to his feet and focused on stealthy shadows moving rapidly up on Nica. Using all his strength, he wrenched one of the metal pickets from the grillwork fence surrounding the Bartlet family and hurled it like a spear straight through the jugular of Bobby Tibble, whose head he'd held over a planter box outside Pat O'Brien's after one too many Mardi Gras hurricanes. In the darkness, his lifeblood flew like ropes of Krewe beads.

Jacques dropped down onto all fours, stomach roiling, blood and tears blinding his eyes. And then he saw a flash of movement, a sinewy figure springing up to the top of one of the tombs, leaping with the fluidity of spilled mercury from one to the next and the next.

"Max!"

Jacques staggered to his feet, rushing in pursuit.

He heard just a whisper. Like a fierce bird of prey, Nica swooped down from the concrete cross atop one of the crypts, leaping over his head and onto the man lunging at him from behind. He heard them both fall but didn't look back as the sound of Nica's snarls overtook brief panicked cries.

Finally, Jacques paused, breathing hard, gaze flying the length of two shadowed paths, seeing nothing. Then a ripple like dark smoke from a chimney.

"Max!"

He took a running step and the stone beneath his feet cracked, splitting open for a jarring drop into a buried vault hidden beneath tangled ropes of ivy. His feet broke through aged and weakened wood, landing atop he didn't want to consider what . . . or who. It took him a dazed moment to take stock of his situation, wedged midchest between two slabs of stone caving downward, arms pinned to his sides.

And then he heard a soft rumbling growl.

Jacques couldn't turn toward the sound, but he could sense Savoie somewhere close behind him.

"This is your doing, LaRoche."

As his gaze came up, a pipe slammed against his jaw. Pain burst through his brain like fireworks, bright and explosive, settling into dizzying pindots of color.

Morris came into view. "You think you're something, don't you, with your fancy new friends and that manipulative little whore, stripping me of my job and my pride right in front of everybody. You're not much now, are you? You should have minded your bar and your own business. Now I'm gonna have to finish it because Tib didn't have the heart to."

As Morris raised the pipe to deliver a skull-cracking blow, a hiss sounded behind him, followed by the blinding phosphorescent flash of the road flare. It struck Morris in the back, igniting his shirt, sending him in tight circles, arms flailing. Nica knocked him to the ground and crouched down, knee on his sternum, her smile coldly vicious, her mouth wet and red.

"I got to wondering on the drive out here," she began. "Why keep Savoie alive? Why didn't you just kill him and take him out to dump in the swamps? He was worth more alive than dead, wasn't he?"

"I don't know what you're talking about," Morris moaned.

"Frost said he had someone on the inside, and that someone was you, wasn't it? How much did it take for you to betray your own kind?"

"It wasn't like that. They caught me on my Patrol, told me no one had to die if I'd let them have Savoie. They gave me a card with a number on it. I was gonna throw it away, until he brought them back." He screamed wildly to Jacques, "Why did you bring them back? You're gonna kill us all!"

"Oh, yeah, right. You were just doing your duty to your clan, removing a dangerous threat," Nica sneered. "For a tidy profit. That's what this was about. You were turning Savoie in for cash."

Morris surged up suddenly, fear lending him the strength to topple her. He'd scrambled a few yards when the lethal shape of Max Savoie sprang and flattened him to the ground, separating head from shoulders in one swift killing blow.

Nica gripped Jacques under the arms, twisting his torso, pounding on the stones with her heels until they gave way, increasing the opening far enough for her to pull him out. He crawled onto the grass, weaving up to his feet only to be taken down on his back again with Max crouched over him drooling blood, eyes flaming gold and red.

Instead of struggling, Jacques caught his face between his hands, holding him away, keeping him still. "Max, you know me. Look at me. I'm your friend. I'm here to help you. I'm here to take you home."

Panting, snarling with each breath, Max hesitated. And that gave Nica enough time to come up behind him, seizing the side of his neck in a fierce compression that had him dropping across Jacques in a motionless heap.

"Vulcan neck pinch," she confided as she lifted Savoie's slack weight off Jacques, then hoisted Max up over her shoulder. "I'll put him in the car while you call for a cleanup crew. We make a pretty kick-ass team, boss."

Jacques was silent. The asses they'd kicked had belonged to friends whose faces would haunt his dreams.

Twenty-three

Dawn pinked over the river as Susanna let herself into the apartment. She hummed with an excitement she couldn't wait to share with Jacques, news that would change their future.

Even cut short by the terse message Charlotte received from MacCreedy, the meeting with Father Furness proved one of startling hope and opportunity. Imagine, the burly priest, a leader of the Naturalist movement in New Orleans with a network and contacts even more sophisticated than the ones she'd tapped in the North.

Furness was surprisingly knowledgeable, and after several enthusiastic hours of discussion, he'd made her a dream offer: a place within their network to conduct her research, unmolested by fear or ignorance. Her own lab, funded by a cause she believed in, to further the health and safety of those she cared for. Unrestricted avenues to explore with a database and technical support equal to what she was used to.

And best of all, the chance to make New Orleans her home. To have a real family, a rich life to experience with all her senses.

Her first thought was to get to Jacques. Her heart

quivered expectantly. To begin a true relationship with him, to confess her secrets, her soul. Picturing Pearl's reaction to decorating her own room with color and texture and art flooded her with tender joy. Her mate, their daughter, days and nights entwined. Her vision grew starry with tears of something she'd never expected to find—happiness.

The apartment was dark, drapes drawn tight against the lightening sky. She felt Jacques's presence before actually seeing him seated at the table, an empty plate pooled with fresh meat juices before him, an unopened bottle in his hand. The stillness of his mood checked her, making her cautious and concerned.

"I left you a note," she began. Was he angry with her for breaking her promise? There was something unsettling about him. He didn't look her way.

"I saw it."

A flat statement of fact with no hint of what lay in wait behind it.

"I've had a breakthrough in my research. It was right there in front of me the whole time." Her euphoria surged again as the words burbled up and with it, her need to share everything with him.

"Then you'll be glad to return to your own lab."

His words stopped her cold.

As Susanna's eyes adjusted to the dimness, she could see something else on the table—printouts of an airline confirmation and a boarding pass.

He continued in that low, level tone that had her trembling. "Your flight leaves at 10:30. You'll want to call and let him know your arrival time so he can pick you up."

She held herself up by sheer force of will. "Why?"

"I promised you'd be returned. It's best you go now."

"But things have changed. We need to talk—"

"Things have changed," he agreed gruffly. "Everything's changed."

A horrible sense of dread settled in her belly. "Jacques, what's happened?"

He was so still, so terrifyingly calm.

"To keep you here any longer would invite retaliation we can't afford. Maybe once they get you back they won't feel inclined to punish us."

His words were a harsh slap. "You only came for Max."

His fingers followed the shape of the bottle as if memorizing its cool contours. "He's our leader, our future. Sacrifices need to be made to protect both. I didn't really understand that until tonight."

"Jack, what's happened?"

He looked up at her then, his eyes a flash of silver. "That's not my name. That's not who I am."

Why was he pushing her away? What had she done?

Then she saw the black sheen of blood on his shirt-front, on his face, and gasped.

Jacques blinked painfully as Susanna turned on the overhead light. He angled away as she came to crouch down beside his chair, shying from the touch of her hand.

"You're hurt. Let me see."

"I'll live." His glum tone said that wasn't necessarily a good thing. He resisted as she cupped his cheek, then finally allowed her to turn his face toward her.

The damage was fading, the split in his brow almost healed. But the way he avoided her gaze hinted at things unmended. Terrible, hurtful things.

Without a word or a sound, he leaned against her, resting his head upon her breast, eyes closing, pose vulnerable despite the tension strung tightly through him.

What had happened? What hadn't he told her?

She held him close, one hand stroking over the coarse bristle of his hair, the other riding the seismic tremors that shook briefly through massive shoulders. Then he pulled away.

"Get your things together," he told her with a savage finality. "I'm going to clean up, then we'll send you home to your family."

Her wide gaze followed him down the hall until he was out of sight. Before panic could control her twisting emotions, Susanna reached for a steadying numbness to get her to her feet, to get body and mind to comply as her expectations fell away in ruin. It was somehow simpler to remove herself from those awful, wrenching feelings of loss and crushing sorrow, to find comfort in the cloaking blankness she'd practiced since birth.

She went into the bedroom to gather what she needed to take with her, ignoring the things that linked her to this colorful world. She shut down all her sensory receptors, refusing to process the scents and sounds of Jacques in the shower, the way the water heated his skin, the crisp, clean smell of lather. She packed with an automatic efficiency, then returned to the living room to wait, refusing to feel anything.

If he wanted her gone, she'd go. Why make it complex with questions, arguments, or pleading? The obvious fact was he'd risk his life for the future Savoie represented but not for a chance for them to live in it together. That chance had died when she'd had his past stripped from him, when she hadn't trusted him with that truth upon her return.

Susanna burned the sight of him into her mind as he came into the living room. He'd pulled on loose jeans, work boots, and a crisp, barely buttoned white shirt. Moisture from the shower still dotted the expanse of chest left uncovered. The shadow of a beard darkened the line of his strong jaw and arched up to circle the swell of his upper lip. Under the heavy ridge of his brows, his deep-set eyes appeared black and impenetrable as he took in her attire, the soft ivory blouse and crisply creased beige slacks, and the carry-on sitting next to her sensible shoes.

"You're traveling light."

"I won't be allowed to keep anything from here where I'm going." Nothing except her memories. "I'm ready."

No reason to prolong the inevitable. She picked up her bag and started for the door. When her hand closed over the knob, his surrounded it.

Jacques's body pressed up behind her, flattening her against the door. Her eyes squeezed shut as he nuzzled her throat, the heat of his mouth sending tremors along her nervous system. His strong tongue stroked up from her delicate collarbone to circle her ear, eliciting more powerful quivers, weakening her knees, altering the tempo of her heartbeat. As his other big hand dragged up her thigh, she rocked back, grinding her hips into him, provoking an ever-hardening response.

The quick pants of his breath became low and raspy, deepening into growls. His nails lengthened and curved, snagging on the fabric of her pants. His already massive body thickened, increasing until he overwhelmed her with his preternatural size and primitive, unstoppable power. Yet he hesitated.

Susanna's hand slid over his, fingers threading, lifting his rough palm to her lips. "Yes," she whispered.

He snatched her against him with an abruptness that struck the breath from her lungs, carrying her to the couch, not to lay her upon it but to drape her over its arm. She heard fabric tear as he shed his shirt. Then he caught the collar of her blouse to rip it from her. His bare skin brushed over hers, hot, smooth, glorious.

Emotions roiled through her in a wild, urgent tangle; desire, need, demanding to be satisfied. She heard a vibration rumble in her throat, an answering growl as he tore down her pants and kneed her legs apart.

Yes. Please. Take me. Keep me. Don't send me away.

As his hand clutched at the back of her neck to still her movements, she was sure his claim would be swift and aggressive. And she'd welcome it, not afraid of him even in this fierce, primal state, because she knew what awaited. Pleasures unimaginable. A connection of body, mind, and soul she craved with an unquenchable thirst, an ungovernable hunger.

She tried to press back against him, swaying, inviting, frustrated when his other hand steadied her hips before slowly rubbing up her bare back until he reached her shoulder. Gripping there.

He took her in one slow stroke, covering already ceded territory with a conquering force until he was sure his claim was complete. Her tiny body tensed and trembled. Then she welcomed him home with a gusty sigh of relief that turned quickly into an impatient groan for more. Each purposeful thrust brought them closer, sparking need into higher flame, expanding sensations until they couldn't be contained within separate hearts, separate bodies, separate minds. Until they were one.

Jacques's rough breaths scorched against her neck. His voice was unrecognizable, gravelly, rough.

"Need to taste you."

Yes. Claim me. Make yours again. Don't let me go.

Susanna reached back, guiding his head to her shoulder. His lips burned upon vulnerable, faintly scarred flesh, parting until she felt the sharpness of his teeth. The shock of his bite.

Ecstasy surged like a racing tide, filling her, rushing over her senses to drown them in a quick seething undertow. Swelling again to sweep her into a sensory bliss. She couldn't breathe, could find nothing solid to cling to, panicking for a brief moment until she felt the warm beat of water upon her skin.

Was it raining?

Susanna blinked her eyes opened, weak and disoriented, to find herself in the shower. She was perched on the marble seat. Jacques knelt with his back to the spray, gently washing the already healing scratches scored into her hips and thighs. His head was bowed, his brows lowered, as he concentrated on his task. And her heart stuttered.

Her palm cupped beneath his chin, raising it until their eyes met, his so intensely blue.

Never looking away from her gaze, he took her hand, moving it up to fit his cheek. Then slowly he bent until his head rested in her lap, his eyes closing.

Emotion clogged her throat as she stroked her other hand over the powerful swell of his shoulder and arm, marveling at this moment of purposeful submission. Wondering at its meaning.

Please tell me you love me, Jacques. Please say you don't want me to leave.

Then he straightened and stood, cranking off the water and opening the glass door to reach for towels. One he wrapped about his hips and the other he handed to her with the soft words, "We don't have much time. Get dressed."

Susanna's dreams plummeted.

He was still sending her away.

By the time she'd dried off, he'd left the bedroom. She could smell coffee brewing. Because all her clothes were already packed, Susanna picked from amongst those she'd purchased with Nica, finding a snug pair of leggings that would feel good against the cold Chicago air and a long tunic decorated with black Celtic designs upon bright scarlet. Its low V-neck edged with fluttery ruffles made her look as though she had more of what Nica called boobage. She admired the fit, knowing she'd never be able to wear anything like it again.

"There's time for coffee, if you'd like a cup," Jacques called from the other room.

Coffee wasn't what she needed to warm the cold sensation seeping through her.

"No, thank you. I have a couple of phone calls to make."

She sat on the edge of the bed they'd shared and placed the first brief call to Nica, then a second, with no little trepidation, to Damien.

"My plane lands at O'Hare at 12:50," she began without preamble. "It's Flight 407."

"I'll have someone there to meet you." His tone gave nothing away. No inquires as to whether she was all right, if she'd been harmed. Nothing that displayed any concern at all.

"How's Pearl?" She fought to keep her voice from quavering.

"She's adjusting to her new accommodations."

He'd moved her to the Community in her absence. Panic leapt, but she suppressed it. "I'd like to see her when I get home."

Damien's reply was dark and smooth. "That's not going to be possible."

"Why not?"

Instead of answering, he stated, "You've been very busy. Did you think we weren't aware that you were remoting into our computers? When you arrive, we need to go over what you're going to say to your program supervisors. I might have been able to cover for you, but I couldn't break through your firewall to modify your material into something, shall we say, less traitorous. It will look much better for you if you present it voluntarily."

Numbly, she asked, "Am I going to be arrested?"

"That depends upon you, my dear, and your willingness to cooperate with the terms I propose for both our futures."

He ended the call with that silken threat.

She sat for long minutes, not thinking, not feeling, just struggling for the courage to stand.

"Susanna, it's time to go."

They stepped into the elevator and Jacques pushed for the garage level. Susanna stood still and seemingly relaxed, but hadn't managed the strength to look up at the big male beside her. Then the car began to move and he spoke her name quietly.

"Anna."

Her gaze lifted, revealing nothing.

"Thank you."

Her brow creased slightly. "For what?"

"Leaving me with memories this time."

He might not have meant to hurt her with those

words, but they wounded deeply. She knew he couldn't tell from her expression so she forced a small smile. "You'll forget them soon enough. This is the Big Easy, after all. Beer, gumbo, good times rolling." She sucked a quick breath as his fingertips touched her cheek. Her composure shuddered, then held firm.

"You have friends who care about you here in this city."

"I know," she managed with a slight catch. "But they'll forget in time, too."

His hand combed back into her hair, bunching a handful in a fist so she couldn't turn away as his mouth lowered to hers.

Susanna stood motionless, eyes closed, breathing even as his kisses took and tempted with a greedy urgency. His arms banded about her tightly, pulling her close, refusing to allow her any dignity until she melted against him with a soft little cry. Her tongue mated with his as furiously as their bodies had earlier, leaving her gasping and dizzy when the elevator pinged and the door opened. She stepped away, placing a staying palm against his chest as she took her bag from him with the other.

"Nica's going to drive me to the airport."

Jacques blinked, not making any sense of that statement until he saw the slender dark-haired female lounging by the door. He nodded at the wisdom of a quick, clean parting.

"If you need me," he told her, his words rumbling

with heart-shredding sincerity, "you know where I'll be."

"Yes, I do." She stepped out of the elevator and concluded, "A world away from where I'll be."

She turned away, letting the door close between them.

And tears were falling before Nica's sports car cruised past the Superdome on its way to I-10.

"With all that sniveling over there, one would think you're not anxious to leave."

Susanna scrubbed at her eyes, braced by her driver's cool comment. "It wasn't my idea. I was blindsided with an airline ticket this morning."

"Isn't it just like a man to have such great timing with his gift giving." Nica zipped around a cluster of slow-moving tour buses. "And you, of course, told him you wanted to stay with him in that nice plush apartment."

"He didn't give me the chance." She swallowed down her pride to admit, "I would have stayed with him in that crappy little trailer." She squeezed her eyes shut to prevent fresh leakage, then blinked fiercely as she demanded, "What happened last night? Do you know?"

"I was there."

Susanna listened, horrified, as Nica laid out the events of the prior evening in unvarnished detail: Silas's shrewd plan, the grisly killings of Jacques's friends, the uncertainty over the fate of their clan.

"Why didn't he tell me?"

Nica snorted. "He's a man."

A man who would silently accept the burden of his own worries and woes without looking for comfort or asking for support. Why hadn't he trusted her with his pain? Was sex the only thing he thought she could have offered? She could have . . . what? Comforted him? Taken the terrible burden and consequence of his deeds away? Offered to stay with him? Apparently not an option. She was his mate. He should have turned to her.

But then, what had she done to inspire that kind of confidence? Erased his memories of her. Pushed all serious discussion of their future together away every time he'd broached them. He hadn't believed their bond was strong enough for the test. Why would he think differently when she'd never had the chance to tell him of her plans?

But Nica wasn't going to let Jacques take all the blame. "You might say my man is behind your quick exodus. And I'm beginning to feel a little annoyed with him about that."

Susanna shook her head. "No. If Jacques had loved me enough to want me to stay, he would have shared all this with me."

Nica laughed. "Yeah, right. What part of *man* don't you understand?"

"Apparently nothing but the good parts."

Nica downshifted for their exit. "He loves you enough to cut out his own heart. He's trying to protect you and your daughter from being caught in the middle. If anything had happened to her while you weren't there with her, he knows you'd never forgive yourself. Or him. Of course, if he knew it was his own daughter . . ." She let that marinate for a moment before throwing it on the fire. "If you loved *him* enough to trust him with that, he might have surprised you."

Susanna shifted in her seat to appeal to her friend. "What would you do in my place?"

Nica smiled. "I wouldn't wait for someone to hand me what I wanted. I'd go after it, no holds barred."

"And just take it?"

The dark daring eyes fixed on hers. "And just take it."

At Susanna's insistence, Nica dropped her off at her terminal without going inside with her. She exacted her promise to watch over Jacques and to let Charlotte know that she'd find a way to monitor Mary Kate's progress.

And as she waited at her gate at Louis Armstrong International through what seemed endless delays due to weather at O'Hare, she pondered Nica's words.

Just take it.

Her entire life, she'd been on the receiving end of another's control. She'd had no direction over choices. She'd been forbidden to do the work that supported her convictions, prevented from sharing a future with the man she loved, forced to hide the pedigree of the child she adored, made to bend to the will of a man she despised.

What of all the dreams she'd had? Would she let

them all go and conform to the demands and needs of others? Is that the legacy she wanted to leave for her daughter? Put away your feelings, your dreams, your desires and live an unfulfilling life devoid of love, of passion or control?

Pearl deserved better.

And so did she.

Jacques LaRoche had started out in an emptied shell with nothing, not even a name. He'd built a new life for himself with pride and determination. Because he'd seen what he wanted and he'd taken the risks and the hardships and the heartbreaks.

And now, so would she.

Susanna began by dialing her companion.

"I've been thinking," she began in a cool, firm voice. "Our arrangement isn't working anymore. You don't need to pretend that you care about me or my daughter. It's always been the prestige, the accolades."

"What are you suggesting?"

"A trade. My research for my freedom."

Damien Frost was cautious. And then he listened.

Susanna booted up her laptop the instant the stewardess okayed electronic devices. She worked for the duration of the flight, moving, adapting, saving data onto her flash drive, finally shutting down when the Fasten Seat Belts light came on.

When she deplaned and entered her arrival gate, a man said, "Dr. Duchamps? Mr. Frost sent me. I'll take those for you."

She released her bags into the care of the coldly efficient bodyguard and followed him into the main wheel of the terminal. There, she gestured to a gift store.

"Can you wait just a moment? I'd like to pick up something for my daughter. She's been ill."

A quick search and Susanna found what she was looking for, a rather drab-colored drawing tablet with a large thick plastic ring binding. She paid and carried it from the store, then followed the driver to the parking structure.

She napped on the ride from the busy airport to their cloistered subdivision. Then, with renewed determination, she entered the house that had never been her home, eager to put it behind her as quickly as possible.

Damien was waiting for her, elegant and inscrutable.

"How was your flight?" he asked as he took her computer bag from the bodyguard, then dismissed him.

"Uneventful." She glanced toward the stairs in anticipation. "Where's Pearl? I told you I wanted her here."

"She's where she belongs." As Susanna turned back toward him in question, he knocked her to the floor. "And now, so are you."

Twenty-four

Nica paused at the entrance to the main floor of *Cheveux du Chien*. Axl Rose was screaming through "Welcome to the Jungle." Amber and Jen were chatting in the servers' galley. Jacques was behind the bar, where he always was on a payday Friday happy hour. And there was just one customer instead of the usual packed house.

As she walked past the occupied table, the customer called out, "What's a guy gotta do to get service around here?"

"Call someone who cares," she snapped, not slowing.

A quick grab of her wrist, a short jerk, and she was on his lap, and definitely not happy to be there. Hanging on to her was like trying to restrain a greased cat.

"Whoa, whoa, whoa there." Silas's arms wrapped tightly about her, pinning hers to her sides in self-defense. "What did I do?"

She quieted but he didn't release his hold. "It's not you. It's your gender."

"Then I apologize on behalf of all of us for whatever offense we may have incurred, either on purpose or by nature of our inferior sex."

She glared at him, then stated primly, "Apology accepted." She nodded toward the bar. "How's he doing?"

"Do you mean has he come over here to pour out his soul to me, mano a mano? Not hardly." When she sighed unhappily and leaned against his shoulder, he relaxed his embrace. "How's Max?"

"No change. The priest has him someplace secure. Charlotte's with him."

Reading her agitation, he kissed her brow. "You don't trust Furness?"

"I have little reason to trust the man or his motives. But maybe he can help us. Or maybe we've just turned over our entire future into the hands of someone intent on destroying us. And the only one who really could help is gone."

Then he understood her mood. "It was necessary."

She pushed away from him. "For the many, not the one. Isn't that what *they* believe? Since when do we feel the same way?" She got off his knee, expression growing fierce. "And I don't think I like how damned quick you were to say you'd toss me away for the sake of the many. So I guess it *is* you I'm pissed at."

When she tried to take a step back, his arms encircled her hips, drawing her up so he could rest his head against her midriff. She began to struggle but his quiet voice stilled her.

"I said that because it's how I *should* feel, because it was the smart thing to do, the *right* thing to do. I thought it was what you'd want to hear, you being such a strong, tough, independent creature, not reliant upon any male. But if it came down to it, I wouldn't let you go. Not for anything or anyone." His palm rubbed over her still-flat belly and his tone deepened. "Especially not now."

Her hand rumpled his hair. "That's probably why I love you."

He glanced up, smiling slightly. "Is that the only reason?"

"That and the fact that you're a bright guy and I'm counting on you to come up with some way to make this right, seeing as how Jacques is her little girl's father."

"What?"

"Think of something fast."

Nica ignored Silas's dumbfounded look and walked to the bar, settling on a stool. "Hey, boss. Doesn't look like you'll be needing me tonight."

"No. I think we've got it handled."

There was nothing in his words or tone that was out of the ordinary. His actions were easy and natural. But the way he wouldn't meet her eyes had Nica worried. The way he seemed to be staring at nothing at all.

She reached out, closing her hand over his. He stopped polishing the beer stein he held, but he didn't look up.

"We had no choice," she said firmly.

"I know."

"We did what we had to do."

"I know." Softer, less sure.

"No one is going to blame you."

A short laugh. "The jury's out on that one from the looks of it." His shoulders slumped. "Were they the right choices, Nica? I just don't know anymore."

Her fingers squeezed tight. "Go home. Get some sleep."

"I'm not tired."

"You're ready to drop."

"I've got nothing to go home to."

Instead of commiserating, she rounded on him with a curt, "And whose fault is that?"

He blinked up at her, expression blank. "I didn't want her to go."

"Did you tell her that?"

"Not in so many words."

"In *any* words?" She shook her head, exasperated. "You don't tell her what's wrong. You don't tell her to stay. You don't tell her you love her. You don't tell her you'd fight any odds to keep her. And then you mope around here with your tail between your legs, wondering what the hell happened. Did you *talk* to her? Did you *tell* her what was bothering you? Of course not. And then you're crushed because she hasn't read your mind? You are *such* a guy."

"There was nothing to say. I couldn't protect her here," he blurted in his own defense.

"And who's protecting her now? You think she's better off? Her and that little girl up there in the hands of those cold, heartless monsters? You know what they are. You know what they do."

"MacCreedy said—"

"Don't listen to him, she's not *his* woman. I thought she was yours. And so did she. Stop thinking about what's best for everyone else. What does she want? What do *you* want?"

His jaw worked fiercely, then he spoke in a low rumble. "It's not just about what we want. There's her daughter to consider."

"And if she were *your* daughter? What then?"

"I'd be on my way north right now to get them," he roared in frustration, "and no one, not your smartass mate, not Max, not the ghosts of the friends I just killed, would get in my way. Dammit. *Goddammit.* What the hell have I been doing, just standing here?" He smashed the heavy glass to the floor, shocking them both.

His fingertips dug into his temples. "None of this matters if she's not here. She needed me to say the words and I couldn't find them."

"Tell her now."

Jacques's startlingly clear gaze fixed on hers then. "You don't think it's too late? Why should she believe me?"

"Because she wants to. Because she loves you—or she wouldn't have gone to such lengths to protect your daughter."

He stared at her, expression frozen.

"Why do you think I called in that favor?" she chided him gently. "You think it was just a coincidence that the two of you would bump into each other after all these years? The first time I met you, the first time I looked into your eyes, I saw Pearl. But I wasn't sure until I got you and Susanna together."

It took Jacques an inordinate amount of time to swallow.

Nica smiled at him. "Go get your family. I'll handle things here."

He leaned across the bar and kissed her hard. No tongue. "Thank you."

"Be careful. And be happy. Be fruitful and multiply, so our little pup will have a best friend to grow up with."

His grin flashed wide. "I'll do my best on all counts."

Everything became razor sharp, falling into slots of priority and purpose as Jacques circled around the bar. The last thing he expected was for MacCreedy to fall into step beside him as he strode toward his office.

"Do you know where you're going?"

"I'll find my way," Jacques growled.

"How will you get there?"

"Drive. Walk. Snowshoe if I have to."

"I was thinking private jet."

Jacques shot him a quick look.

"If I'm going to travel, I like to do it in comfort."

"Who asked you to go along?"

"Do you have a connection in Chicago who can put you right at her front door?"

"No."

"Then ask me along."

"This is my business," Jacques snarled, unwilling to allow interference.

"Oh-kay. Does that mean you have to take care of it by yourself?"

"Why would my business matter to you?"

"Because I'd just as soon you not get yourself dead since I can count my friends on one hand, and one of them doesn't even remember my name. And because I'm kind of a smart guy and pretty helpful in a pinch. And because when I get back, I know I'm going to have the most fantastic sex on the planet for as long as I can stay conscious."

Jacques glanced at MacCreedy. "You ride shotgun."

"Yes, boss."

"When did we get to be friends?"

"Damned if I know."

"A private jet, huh? How you gonna manage that?"

"Did I mention that the female I'm going to have all that sex with is almost richer than Savoie?"

"No." And neither had she. What was she doing working behind his bar? Or anywhere for that matter?

"Don't tell her I told you. She likes to keep things like that under the wire."

"Afraid she'll cut you off from all that great sex?"

MacCreedy grinned and winked companionably. "I don't think there's any danger of that."

Jacques chuckled and turned toward his office when a hand closed about his throat, propelling him across the hall to slam into the opposite wall. The cold circle of a gun barrel pressed into his ear as a haggard Philo Tibideaux leaned in to get nose-to-nose.

Jacques held up a hand to halt MacCreedy's aggressive move as his gaze locked onto the bloodshot eyes of his best friend.

"You sonuvabitch," Philo hissed. "How could you cut down those boys we worked with, drank with, shared our meals and our homes with, like they was dogs? How could you do that?"

"I'm sorry. I can't change what happened. I wish I could."

The pistol barrel shoved harder as Philo panted in fury and frustration. "Is that what you wish, you bastard? That it'd been you instead a them? That you could have given your miserable life to save theirs?"

"Yes. Under different circumstances you know I would have, without a thought." His voice broke slightly, then firmed. "They didn't give me a choice."

"They were our *brothers*. Our *family*."

"Then what were they doing there, Tib? Why did they turn on me instead of talking it out like brothers are supposed to? Then I wouldn't be burying them in Savoie's backyard tomorrow night."

Philo's breaths seethed from him. "It shouldn't a mattered. They shouldn't be dead."

"No," Jacques agreed quietly, "they shouldn't be. It never should have happened."

Philo pulled a ragged breath, rage vibrating through him. "This is my fault? You saying this is my fault?

"That's not what I'm—"

The pistol butt smashed into Jacques's temple, dropping him to one knee. Still, he stayed a tense Mac-Creedy with a shaky hand while his ears rang and vision doubled. When he could see straight, he found himself staring up that deadly barrel while Philo raged on.

"Me and Tito, we took you in when you was a nobody, no better than garbage on the streets. We shared everything we had with you. We trusted you to stand with us, for us, and now Tito's dead, and them boys is dead. And you're *sorry*?"

In a deep, strong voice, Jacques told him, "I've spent the last seven years of my life trying to repay you for what you did for me. If it's not enough by now, it's not ever gonna be. If you're gonna shoot me, shoot me. Otherwise, back the hell outta my face."

For a long moment, neither blinked nor moved. Then Philo lowered the gun. His lips curled with a bitter contempt.

"We're square now, Jackie. And we're done."

With that, Philo whirled and slammed out the back exit door.

Jacques let himself slide down to sit on the floor. His head was bleeding, and so was his heart, but his focus was undeterred.

"Why didn't you tell him it was your other friend Morris who betrayed you all?" Silas wanted to know.

"Morris is dead. That's punishment enough for his family."

MacCreedy frowned, trying to puzzle out that logic. "Philo will think whatever he's gonna think anyway. I can't afford to spend any more time looking behind me, second-guessing what I coulda or shoulda done." He held up his hand for MacCreedy's firm grasp to haul him to his feet. "We got a plane to catch."

They had the charter to themselves. Jacques had never been in a plane before, but after the turbines whined up to full capacity, the vibration knocked him out faster than a sedative. The next thing he knew, MacCreedy was shaking his shoulder.

"We're here."

As Silas drove their rental out of the parking garage, Jacques noticed a pattern of scarring on his left wrist.

"The brand of the Terriot clan," MacCreedy told him simply. "It reminds me that nothing is more important than my family's freedom."

Asked and answered. All Jacques needed to know. For the same reason, Jacques didn't question where they were going or why. MacCreedy was all calm competence and if he wasn't worried, Jacques wasn't about to be.

MacCreedy pulled up in front of a stately apartment building. Jacques silently hung back out of the way, staying close enough to step in if asked but otherwise willing to let Silas take care of business, knowing whatever it was would bring him that much closer to Susanna and his child.

His child.

He suppressed the sharp shiver of longing so it wouldn't distract him. Yet still it whispered to him.

His daughter. Their child.

MacCreedy climbed the steps to the second floor and knocked on the first door, his manner relaxed.

The door was opened by a plumply average man with a receding hairline and some alarming scars cutting across his face. At MacCreedy's pleasant, "Hello again," he shrieked and fled back into the tastefully decorated room. In a few long strides, MacCreedy caught him by the back of the neck and tiptoe-walked him into the kitchen to drop his quivering form into a chair.

Jacques blinked, regarding his friend with a new respect for whatever he'd done to inspire such unabashed terror.

"W-w-what are you doing here? I haven't done anything," the little man blubbered.

"Not yet. But you're going to."

Furtive eyes darted over to check him out as a potential threat. "Who's he? What does he want?"

"A friend. He wants what I want. Friend, meet Hawthorne, the greedy piece of Controller trash who tortured the woman I love into obeying his instructions."

Jacque's eyes narrowed, dangerously.

"What kind of information can I get for you?" Hawthorne squeaked.

"Damien Frost. He hired Nica to find a kidnapped child. What do you remember about that?"

"He paid up front. Twice. A lot."

"For you to do what?"

"To have two men snatch the kid, then have Nica rescue her, leaving no witnesses."

"Did Nica know about the first hire?"

"No. It would have been difficult to get her to do the job if she knew she was killing her fellow operatives."

"And, of course, you didn't let them in on it either."

He didn't answer.

Jacques spoke up, his voice deceptively matter-of-fact. "So Frost hired you to kidnap a child in his care, then hired you again to return that same child? Why would he do that?"

"I didn't ask."

But Jacques knew. To terrorize and control Susanna. To make her feel vulnerable and needy. To threaten the well-being of her child, then provide a blanket of protection to earn her gratitude. He swallowed down the growl rumbling for release.

"I need an address for Frost," MacCreedy said.

"Work or home?"

"Home," Jacques interjected. "I already know where he works. And where we can find the child, Pearl. She's six years old." He choked up unexpectedly and had to clear his throat. "She's in some kind of community school dormitory." *Prison* would have been a more accurate description.

Don't worry, baby. Daddy's coming to get you.

"I'll have to look it up on my computer. It's in my den."

Hawthorne might have been a nasty little weasel

but he was a weasel who knew how to wiggle his way around security red tape. In minutes, he had locations, blueprints, security passwords, and a picture of Pearl Frost.

She had Jacques's blue eyes and the shape of his mouth, all pouty and full and ripe with rebellion. It took only an instant for him to fall deeply and devastatingly in love. He had to turn away to blink his vision clear, hearing MacCreedy order the pages to be printed.

"The photo, too," Silas added. "And we'll need security passes. You also owe me that list of Nica's friends. Their names, aliases, where they've been, where they are—the works. Then you won't have to worry about me ever popping up ever again. Unless you share any of what's happened here today, of course." His smile was cold.

Twenty-five

Susanna pressed a cold cloth to her cheekbone, wincing as the ache spread through her face. After three hours of isolation in her bedroom, the ugly red held the promise of blooming into blue, black, and yellow.

She'd seriously underestimated Damien. She knew him as an arrogant, erudite preener who liked to give orders, who prided himself on the creases in his trousers and the softness of his skin. She'd never guessed those manicured hands could turn so violent.

He'd stood over her as she lay sprawled on the floor, his face a florid stain of fury. "You thought to bargain with me? Fool. Go wash your face and take off those garish clothes. You're embarrassing both of us. Once you've had a chance to adjust your attitude, we'll discuss how things are going to be from now on."

He'd left her lying on the expensive floor while he carried her laptop into his office.

She'd retreated to her bedroom, picking a loose, flowing beige knit top. Defiantly, she kept on the leggings and black flats with their perky red bows.

The bag from the airport bookstore was on her bed. She took out the drawing pad and made room for it in her purse. Inside the back cover, she placed the picture Pearl had made for her, the one of their future family of four.

"Soon," she whispered, tucking it safely away.

And then she waited.

"Susanna, come down here." Damien's terse voice rang up through the open stairwell.

She straightened her shoulders and took a deep breath. There was nothing he could do to her. He needed her. Pearl was her weak spot, but as long as the little girl was safe in her restricted dormitory, he had nothing to threaten her with.

He could no longer fool her with that benevolent smile, with the words of a generous spirit. Now she saw the cold, grasping villain that he truly was. A master manipulator, living off the blood of others.

She was counting on that greed to negotiate her freedom.

Damien was waiting at the bottom of the stairs. When his gaze touched on the mark he'd left on her face, sharp satisfaction glittered in his eyes. Self-righteousness, cruelty, even a glint of arousal.

"I seem to have come to an impasse with your program security."

Her expression serene, Susanna replied, "You've always been adamant that I protect my work from those who might try to steal it for unsavory purposes."

"Unlock it. Now."

"Why? You wouldn't understand any of it. You're just a layman."

That brought a tic to his finely shaped lips. His ego couldn't stand hearing that he wasn't intelligent enough to comprehend or that his education was lacking.

"Then you will explain it to me in layman's terms. Or do you need more convincing?"

She'd stopped on the last step so her position was elevated, then said, "You wouldn't dare put another mark on me. One could be explained by a careless fall, but not several. You wouldn't be so foolish as to think no one would notice and wonder."

"They would only wonder if you were seen. Your very busy computer log suggests you no longer need to leave this house in order to be productive, so you will remain here, under my supervision." His fingers curled about her wrist as he jerked her off that last step, then gave her a push toward his office.

Susanna walked calmly ahead of him, glad he couldn't hear her heart pounding. She would not be trapped under this roof with him, singing profitably within his cage.

Her laptop was open and running on his austere desk. Instead of sitting down in front of it, she chose a chair on the opposite side of the thick glass block that was more aesthetic than utilitarian. There was a plate on one corner holding pieces of fruit, cheese, and prosciutto rolls. Her belly rumbled, reminding her she'd eaten nothing but the small bag of pretzels on the plane, but she refused to reveal any weakness by reaching for food unless it was offered.

Damien settled into his desk chair, his displeasure now apparent. "What are you trying to hide?" he demanded.

"I've unlocked the genetic code that binds and divides our species."

He blinked at that cool admission and after he absorbed the financial ramifications, she could almost see the greed pooling in his mouth. Then his gaze narrowed. "Then why aren't you more excited?"

"I was searching for a cure for Pearl's malady, and it wasn't there. The work has no value to me." But it would have spectacular value to others. She watched that knowledge brighten his eyes.

"If it means nothing to you, why do you protect it?"

"Because it's the only way to purchase my release. I'll provide you with the passcodes. You can peddle the information to the highest bidder. And you will let Pearl and me go."

He tented his elegant hands beneath his chin, appearing to consider her offer before saying, "I think not."

Frustration rumbled alongside her hunger. "That's illogical. You have no affection for me and you see Pearl as an aberration. My only value has been my work and I'm giving that to you."

"But, my dear, why would I release my goose with her golden eggs back into the wild? That's where you'd be going, isn't it? Back to that inferior beast? Do you honestly think I would allow you to shame me again with something like that? You are so mistaken."

She hadn't taken his pride into account. A pride she'd abused by mating with her Shifter bodyguard. A pride she'd affronted by bearing a half-breed child. A pride she'd spat upon by traveling to the heart of his enemies to resume her illicit passion. It was more than ego; it was a personal insult born of his elitist prejudice. In his mind, she belonged to him. She was his shining accomplishment, a testament to his careful grooming, a reflection of him. And she'd betrayed both in a way he found beyond offensive. He simply could not tolerate her preference for a lower species.

So he'd ordered her lover killed. He'd pretended to offer salvation when, in fact, it was enslavement.

She owed him nothing.

And Susanna told him frigidly, "You will never see another dime at my expense. I will not work on another project. I will not use my knowledge to feed your hunger for attention and praise. I am finished here. Take what you have and be grateful. A generous parting gift considering all your lies." Her voice quavered. "You ordered him killed after your promise that he'd be unharmed."

"It's so hard to find good help," he sneered. "Apparently they weren't very good at their job."

"To think I admired you. You disgust me."

That brought a quiver of response to his tightly clenched jaw. "Well, then let's be completely honest, shall we? Why do you *think* I took you in? Why do you *think* I spent all that time and effort to direct your talents, to secure you positions, to placate your delicate sensibilities, and pretend to care about your traitorous causes? You were my discovery. *Mine*."

He drew a seething breath and continued. "I made you what you are. I pampered and spoiled you because you were my protégé and oh, how others envied me. I let you harbor your illusions. I allowed you unnecessary freedoms and you repaid me by rutting with that stupid, sweaty animal. You polluted yourself with his dull seed. You brought that abomination into this perfect world I created for you. You tried to ruin everything with your impulsiveness and your unnatural desires, and yet you expect me to be grateful? You have no idea what I'm capable of doing to protect what I created."

Damien leaned across his desk and Susanna knew a crippling fear. She wasn't going to escape him. He would destroy her first. She saw her fate in the vicious intent gleaming in his agate-hard eyes.

"You think to threaten me? Let me promise you something, and this time you can be assured I'll keep my word. You will continue to repay me with your finest efforts or I will have your monstrous progeny destroyed, as it should have been before it was allowed to take its first breath."

Susanna came up out of her chair in an unholy fury, palms slapping on the glass surface, shaking with violent intensity. "Harm my child and it will be your *last* breath."

Surprise, shock, then an instant of caution flickered in Damien's eyes before his stare chilled into black ice. "It's time you realized something, Susanna," he said with a malicious quiet. "You have no power here."

As he picked up the phone, the taste in Susanna's mouth was the metallic bite of terror. "Damien, I spoke rashly. I take back my words."

His lip curled. "Too late for that, my dear." He dismissed her to turn his attention to his purpose. "This is Damien Frost. You have a child there, Pearl Duchamps Frost. A change in her plan of treatment needs to be made immediately."

"Damien, no!" Susanna grabbed for his arm but he swiveled away, out of her reach. "Please!"

"I'm making arrangements to move her to the research section. I'd like a complete study to begin in the morning. Yes. I understand and I insist on the full battery. Yes, I'm aware of the possible outcome. Of course. I'll stop in tomorrow morning to sign the required papers."

Susanna sat frozen in her chair. A full battery for research purposes culminated in dissection while the subject was still living.

Damien ended the call. "Your security password. Now."

The metal door swung open to reveal a small, eight-by-eight square room with one high gridded window to allow light in but no view of the outside. A cot, a metal study desk, and a chair were the only furnishings. The young girl with head bent over a notebook looked up, stealthily tucking whatever she'd been working on out of sight. Her inquisitive blue eyes darted past the school administrator to the large motionless figure behind him in the shadows of the hall.

"I was almost finished with my lesson, Mr. Chapman. Could I have a few more minutes before lights-out?" There was no defiance or pleading in her quiet tone, just a hopefulness quickly crushed.

"Gather your belongings, Miss Frost. This gentleman is here for you. Don't keep him waiting."

Without question or hesitation, she got up to retrieve a small bag from under the bed and placed the books from the desk inside it atop already neatly folded clothes. The paper she'd secreted away went into the pocket of her hastily donned jacket. There was no looking back with regret as she left the room to stand beside the stranger the school official fawned over.

"If you'd just sign here and here to acknowledge receipt. It's not exactly protocol to request a transfer at this time of night." He glanced at the name. "Is there anything else, Mr. Stone?"

"No. We're done here."

"Just go back the way you came in. Be sure to check out and pick up your credentials at the desk."

"I will. Thank you. You've been very helpful. I'll be sure to let Mr. Frost know."

The pallid fellow almost smiled. "That would be most kind. We're happy to be of service to such a well-respected family." Without a word of farewell or even a glance at the child, he bustled off with his clipboard.

Small fingers curled inside the big, rough hand of the man beside her and were quickly engulfed. With the other, Pearl passed him the picture she'd just completed.

"I made this for you."

"For me?" Jacques took the single sheet, surprise edging his deep voice.

"We need to leave. Another hall monitor will be coming by in a few minutes. I don't want to stay here anymore. I want to see my mommy."

"Do you know who I am?"

Those crystal clear eyes lifted and with an angelic smile, she said, "Of course. I've been waiting for you."

It was all Jacques could do not to drop to his knees right there in the hall to hug her tight. But they weren't out of danger yet so he had to hold to his role for just a bit longer for the benefit of the security cameras. Very softly, he murmured, "I'm here to take you and your mama home with me."

Her hand clutched his. "We should hurry."

Shortening his strides so Pearl could keep up with him, Jacques headed not for the elevators by the floor monitor's desk but for a stairwell, slipping the badge he'd lifted from the stuffy administrator through the security lock to gain entry.

Once out of view of those watching, Jacques surrendered to impulse and sank to one knee beside his child. Pearl flung her arms about his neck and squeezed tight. He turned his face into her pale, soft hair and breathed deep.

"I knew you'd come to get us. I knew it," she whispered.

"And I'm never letting you go," was his gruff promise. He swept her into his arms and stood, carrying her and her meager belongings quickly down two flights of steps to the main floor where MacCreedy waited similarly dressed in black. He smiled at the girl.

"Hi. I'm Silas. I have a nephew just a few years older than you. His name is Oscar."

A return smile. "I'm Pearl. I can't wait to play in his big yard."

Silas glanced up at Jacques, who simply raised his brows, equally mystified. He placed a hand on the blonde head and told her confidently, "We'll be there soon."

MacCreedy cracked the stairwell door to peer down the long hall. "The guard should be leaving the desk right . . . about . . . now." He pushed the door open. "Go."

Jacques briskly headed toward the exit with MacCreedy just behind him. He set his features into a formidable scowl and didn't look anywhere but straight ahead through a dedicated tunnel vision. With their black leather, strong, loping strides, glowing eyes, and single-minded ferocity, Jacques knew what others would see: serious muscle-for-hire, and no one on the facility's meager salary would step in their way with any questions.

Thirty feet from freedom. Pearl was relaxed in his arms, her head trustingly on his shoulder.

There was activity at the desk ahead. The night clerk returned to answer the phone and immediately, his posture straightened.

Jacques increased the length of stride, Silas doing the same.

The clerk's animated conversation ended and he was quickly making calls. His agitated movements telegraphed his fear.

Twenty feet.

"What do you mean she's not there?" the clerk was sputtering. "I was just talking to him. To *him*, Frost. She's supposed to be moved to Research in the morning. Who the hell took her? You still have the paperwork?" His frantic eyes lifted, fixing on the two rapidly approaching figures and growing wide.

They rounded the corner, ignoring the desk to continue purposefully toward the exit.

"Alert security," the clerk whispered before calling out, "Excuse me. I need to see some identification."

They stopped as one, both looking back over their shoulders with an expressionless menace.

The clerk swallowed hard and managed to sound authoritative. "I need your IDs."

Another motionless moment passed as sweat gathered on the clerk's brow.

"Of course," MacCreedy intoned flatly. He glanced at Jacques. "You go ahead and get the subject secured. I'll take care of this inconvenience."

Without a blink of response, Jacques continued for the door, letting Silas head back toward the desk to cover their escape.

"You there, stop," the clerk called after him. "I need to see your paperwork, too. Stop!"

A soft blat of sound, then hurried footsteps. Silas reached past him to shove open the first of two outer doors, saying, "Go. Fast."

Alarms screamed behind them. The doors automatically locked down, trapping them between the two sets. Without breaking stride, Jacques pulled his pistol, firing three rounds into the heavy glass. Pearl buried her face against his neck, hugging tight.

Arm raised to protect his head, MacCreedy lunged through the weakened outer door without breaking his stride, making a opening for Jacques to follow. They hit the cold slap of evening air and started running. Fast.

Their car was parked in the circle drive. Lights flashed as MacCreedy keyed the locks.

Jacques couldn't hear the shots over the wail of the alarms but saw puffs of cement flying up around their feet. A sudden sharp punch in the back just below his ribs made him stumble, dropping him down on one knee. Silas snatched Pearl from his arms and grabbed his elbow, hauling him back up, dragging him toward the car, yanking the door open, shoving him into the passenger seat with Pearl on his lap. Jacques wrapped himself about her small form, becoming a protective shield as bullets thudded into metal and shattered the door glass. All the while, Pearl never made a sound.

The engine roared to life.

"Hang on," MacCreedy shouted as he put foot to floor, speeding away from the curb in a shriek of burning rubber.

Then all Jacques could hear was the ragged catch of his own breathing and a soft whisper in his ear.

"I love you, Daddy."

Twenty-six

Explain 'gone.'"

Susanna watched as a vein pulsed to life on Damien's forehead, contrasting with his level tone.

"You're telling me they just walked into a facility where I have paid a fortune for the best possible security and out again? I don't care about your employee." His voice spiked in fury. "He's going to wish he *had* died."

Jacques had Pearl.

Relief made her giddy.

He was here. He'd come for them.

"I want them found. I don't care what it takes. Alive! Do you hear me? Get something right."

Damien ended the call, his hands shaking. His narrowed stare met Susanna's. Her features remained carefully neutral. "He won't get far," he assured her. "And he won't come for you. We'll be blanketed with security in a matter of minutes. If he's smart, which I highly doubt, he'd just take his bastard brat and run."

Susanna allowed a chill smile. "I hope he does. Then they'll both be out of your reach and you'll have nothing to threaten me with."

He seethed over that for a moment, then reminded her with a silky venom, "I'll still have you, my dear."

She laughed, making that vein beat all the harder. "Do you think that matters to me? Do you think I care what you do to me as long as they're safe?"

"I care."

The low rumbling voice brought her head snapping about.

In his black leathers, he looked very much like he had that first time she'd seen him: big, fierce, brutally powerful. Only what burned in his eyes wasn't defiance, it was determination. Though his pistol was trained on Frost, his stare was for her.

"Pack whatever you need for the two of you," he told her.

She rose up, her heart fluttering in her breast. "I'll get my bag. I have everything else." Her welling eyes entreated. "Don't I?"

"She's in the car with MacCreedy. Hurry."

She bolted from the chair, but instead of rushing by him for the stairs, she paused to place her palm on his firm middle, rubbing over the hard ridge of his abs to assure herself that he was solid and real. And hers.

He spoke to her softly without taking his eyes off Frost. "I apologize for letting you leave New Orleans without telling you I didn't want you to go."

She stretched up for a quick taste of his lips, whispering against them, "I love you. I always have."

Jacques's brows lowered dangerously as he touched the colorful mark on her face. "Did he do this?" His hot, laser-blue gaze shifted to Damien Frost, glinting as red as the blood about to be shed.

Reading his own death in that glittering stare, Damien sneered, "Kill me and you'll never know one second of freedom. You'll be hunted down relentlessly like the animal you are."

Jacques's facial bones sharpened, growing more prominent, more bestial as fierce instinct rose, feeding the violent need to rip apart this fool who *dared* harm his mate. He smiled, displaying sharp teeth. "It would be worth it."

Susanna stroked his tense jaw to distract him from potential carnage. "No. Leave him. Jacques!"

His fiery glare touched hers.

"Promise you won't harm him."

"You don't owe him anything," he spat out.

"But to you, I owe everything. Trust me. Jack?"

"All right."

She raced for the stairs.

The two men stared at each other.

"What could you possibly offer her?" Damien sneered. "Look at you, you bulky, graceless, square-headed beast. What interests could you share with her, you with your IQ on the same level as that chair? Look at all I've given her. Yet instead of being grateful for having more than she deserves, she throws everything away for a brute like you. Why?"

"I used to ask myself that. Apparently I'm everything she wants and needs." He shrugged. "You're the smart one. Go figure."

"What kind of man would demand a woman like that leave all this for a life as a fugitive? All that potential, wasted. All that promising work she could have been doing, thrown away, for what?"

"Freedom." Then stronger, "Love."

Frost stared at him blankly.

"Concepts you would never understand," Susanna told him as she reentered the room with her bag over her shoulder and medical satchel in hand. "I'm ready to go." Then she paused, gaze riveted to the floor at Jacques's feet. "Are you hurt?"

Damien wrinkled his nose in distaste as he viewed the bright splotches of crimson. "You're staining my carpet. Dare I hope it's something fatal?"

"Merely inconvenient," Jacques assured him.

But Susanna was staring at the hole in the back of his coat, her eyes going wide and glassy. She slipped her arm about his waist beneath the heavy drape of leather and found a huge, spreading patch of dampness at his belt line. And for the first time, his steady stance faltered.

"Let's go." Her tone was low and urgent.

"You won't get out of this subdivision," Damien warned. "They'll bring you back in chains."

Susanna observed him coldly. "At what cost to your reputation? What will this fine, upstanding community think when they discover how you've made fools of them all these years with your pretended mate, knowingly harboring a hybrid child?"

Damien blinked at a logic he'd never considered.

"Better you take the information I've left you with your precious public opinion intact, and say good riddance to us."

He glanced from the computer, so brimming with promise and potential wealth, to the troublesome female clutching at her paling bestial lover. "Good riddance."

"Nothing fatal," Susanna pronounced, studying the metal slug held in the prongs of her probe.

Jacques released the breath he'd been holding to groan, "Feels like it should be." He took another tentative breath after Susanna completed her packing and binding. Not too bad. Not nearly as painful as the thought of living without them.

He let her button him into a clean white shirt, breathing in the fragrance of her hair.

"She's so beautiful, Anna," he murmured, still unused to the way his chest seized up at the thought of his daughter. It was a wonderful distress.

The same kind of distress that shimmered in his mate's dark eyes. "I'm sorry I didn't tell you. I couldn't risk either of your lives. I'm sorry for so many things."

He cupped the back of her head in one hand so he could kiss her brow. "None of that matters now. None of it." He reached behind him, wincing slightly as he pulled a folded piece of paper from his coat. "She drew this for me. Before I met her."

Susanna studied the drawing of a man behind a

high counter, and a table where a girl and a woman holding a baby sat.

"I'd guess that's my bar and the big, square-headed fella is me." He chuckled, then asked quietly, "Did you tell her anything about me?"

"No. She just knows things." She searched his face for signs of repulsion or dismay. Would he reject those Chosen qualities?

He smiled. "Good. She can help me find my keys when I'm late for work."

"Can I come in now?" a small voice asked from the other side of the curtain.

Susanna pointed sternly to the mattress and helped Jacques lie back. Then she opened the fabric divider.

Pearl bounded in, hopping up on the bed with an exuberance that had Jacques grimacing happily.

"Hey, baby girl. Don't worry. I'm going to be fine."

"I know." Not the least bit of doubt showed in her expression.

Susanna placed a calming hand on her head. "Your daddy needs his rest, so don't pester him too much."

Jacques patted the space beside him. "Why don't we both get some rest. You can keep me company. There's room for two."

Pearl kicked off her shoes and curled up against his side.

Susanna tucked a thin blanket about them, saying softly, "I've got something I need to do but I'll be back in a minute."

As she left, she heard Jacques ask, "What color should we paint your room?"

"Red."

A chuckle. "We'll see. Is that a baby brother or baby sister in your picture?"

"Brother."

"Yeah? What's his name?"

"Tito."

A pause, a hitch of breath, then a quiet, "Nice name."

It had taken all Giles St. Clair's powers of persuasion to coax Charlotte to join him for a crack-of-dawn breakfast. She sat restlessly across the table, picking at her eggs, her eyes darkly shadowed, her color wan with worry. He didn't ask any questions. He could see the answers in her tense, denying posture. So he poured her coffee, put a thick smear of jelly on her toast, and constantly prodded her to take another bite.

Giles had spread the cover-up that Max had been seriously injured in a motorcycle accident, that he and lawyer Antoine D'Marco would be acting as temporary liaisons as Max ran his business from a secluded hospital room. So far, no one was questioning the story.

Awkwardly thrust into a position of authority, Giles almost wished the wily and deceitful Francis Petitjohn was still among them. But it was the least he could do for Max, mumbling a few words here and there to keep his company going. As for his other, less than human interests, Silas MacCreedy would act as proxy.

And that left Charlotte alone, adrift, and unattended.

All he could offer was silence and support. And breakfast.

"I just talked to Mac a bit ago," Charlotte spoke up. "He said they should be landing soon with Jacques and his family."

"Good to know. Be good to have them back."

He liked the bulky Shifter with his booming voice and his surprisingly feisty doctor girlfriend. It would be good for Ozzy to have a new friend out at the house to distract him from his loneliness. And MacCreedy had proved to be a stabilizing presence and rock solid ally. All of them would form a strong circle of community about his boss. And maybe that would be enough to bring him back.

Charlotte's cell rang. She was grateful for the chance to escape Giles's insistent mothering, hoping for some sensational news, like a grisly murder, to drag her from her sorrow.

"Lottie?" came a faint voice she hadn't heard for far too long. "It's Mary Kate."

Susanna placed her hand upon Silas's shoulder. He opened his eyes, and removed one of his earbuds to look up in question.

"Hi. Everything okay?"

"Yes. Thank you. For everything."

He smiled as she took the seat across the aisle. "That's what friends are for." Then his expression grew more serious. "You know Frost isn't going to let you go, don't you? He'll eventually blow through whatever he gets from trading the information you left behind, and want you back to earn him more."

"It doesn't matter what he wants. He's not going to get it."

Her hard tone piqued Silas's interest. "Yeah? And how are you going to stop him?"

She opened the onboard portable computer and brought up a document from the flash drive she'd secreted in the hard binding coil of a notebook from her purse. She passed the netbook to him.

"A little something I composed on my flight up to Chicago. I was about to send it."

He started to read, a slow appreciative smile curving his lips.

It was an e-mail addressed to the governing board of the project she worked for.

It's with sincere regret that I write this message but I cannot in good conscience allow you to be betrayed as easily as I have been by our enemy, Damien Frost. He has deceived me regarding his intentions, pretending to be a respected member of our Community and supporter of our Purist Movement. Only recently have I discovered his true allegiance to a rebel faction that would bastardize our race with their tainted heritage.

Damien forced me to be his envoy in New Orleans by threatening our daughter's life. When I was unable to make contact with an organization suspected of plotting an uprising or to find any evidence of unrest, he devised another plan to gain your trust and through it, bring about your collapse. It is only upon being freed of his vile domination by a faithful bodyguard who gave his life for mine that I'm able to come to you with this truth.

Damien Frost will bring information he claims to be my work and he will try to sell it to you as the solution to our problem of ethnic impurity. This is a lie. The files he plans to sell are infected with an undetectable virus that, once in our operating system, will breach our security and destroy all the data we've collected in an act of unconceivable terrorism. I urge you to use caution in your dealings with him.

Please do not attempt to find me. My failure to support his plans and now my betrayal of them has placed my safety and that of my daughter at unacceptable

risk. By the time you read this, I will be
out of the country and forever out of his
reach.
      I remain faithfully,
      Dr. Susanna Duchamps.

"Brilliant," Silas mused. "If they believe you, they
arrest Frost and destroy your data. If they don't believe
you and access your data—a big surprise?"

"A mild surprise, but unpleasant enough to do the
job, discrediting Damien either way. The information I
left on my computer was useless. His influence will be
destroyed. He won't have the means to come after me.
He'll be lucky if he gets out alive, which will be better
than he deserves." Her gaze flashed up to Silas's. "He
was turning Pearl over to Research."

Silas flinched. "Far better than *he* deserves." He
pressed Send on her e-mail and shut down the computer.

Susanna exhaled, all the tension draining from her
with a shudder.

"We've got another hour or so," Silas told her. "Go
get some sleep."

As Silas plugged in his earphones and settled back
in his seat, Susanna returned to the rear cabin, where
the soft light brushed over the two slumbering figures.
Her emotions took a tender twist at the sight of a small
hand resting upon the hard, massive chest. Her mate.
Their child. Both safe.

She sat on the edge of the bed, brushing her hand

over Jacques's head, then over their daughter's silky hair. Jacques's eyes blinked open. He smiled and murmured, "I love you." Then he drifted off again.

What more could she ever want?

With a tender sigh, she joined her family on the bed, where they'd left room for three.